UNFORESEEN

ERICA ROSEN MD TRILOGY: BOOK 3

DEVEN GREENE

Black Rose Writing | Texas

The author grants the final approval for this literary material.

First printing

ISBN: 978-1-68513-012-1
PUBLISHED BY BLACK ROSE WRITING
www.blackrosewriting.com

Printed in the United States of America
Suggested Retail Price (SRP) $21.95

Unforeseen is printed in Georgia Pro

*As a planet-friendly publisher, Black Rose Writing does its best to eliminate unnecessary waste to reduce paper usage and energy costs, while never compromising the reading experience. As a result, the final word count vs. page count may not meet common expectations.

To my amazing son, Eric, for making me proud to be your mom every day.

CHAPTER 1

"Help! Call the doctor! Don't let my daughter die! She's only eight years old."

"Please, ma'am, step back. You need to give us some space. The doctor will be here shortly."

I wasn't on duty in the emergency room but had been walking through it before the start of my evening shift in the Pediatric ICU to get a heads up on imminent admissions. Looking around in search of the charge nurse while dodging the usual aides and nursing staff rushing through the hallway, I overheard the screams coming from behind one of the curtains separating patients from the corridor.

Seeing no other physicians in the hallway and unable to ignore the pleading of a mother worried about her sick child, I pulled back the curtain and rushed into the room. One nurse held the hysterical mother at bay as another held onto a girl whose arms and legs were rigid, bent strangely. The child's limbs shook, her eyes turned upward, and she groaned, her face frozen. I recognized her as one of my patients. She was having a grand mal seizure.

A passing medical student wearing the obligatory short white jacket stopped and looked at me expectantly, unsure what to do.

Ignoring the student, I said, "Let me help," as I assisted the nurse holding onto the child, preventing the contorted girl from falling off the exam table onto the floor. "I know her. She has epilepsy which has been well-controlled for several years. I saw her in the clinic recently."

"Dr. Rosen, I'm so glad you're here," said the mother, tears streaming down her face. She relaxed enough to allow the nurse holding her to step back.

"What happened, Mrs. Mendoza? The last time I saw Rosa, she was doing well on her medication. She hadn't had a seizure in three years, as I remember."

"That's right, Doctor. I don't know what happened. I've been giving her the medicine, just like before. Then this morning, she had a seizure. A full seizure, like the ones she used to have. The pills aren't working anymore, so I brought her here. We had to sit for two hours in the waiting room. We just got in here, and now this happened—another seizure. She needs better medicine. Something stronger."

"Are you sure you remembered to give her the medicine?"

"Oh, yes, Doctor. I would never forget. I'd forget to breathe before I would forget to give my Rosa her medicine. I gave her a pill this morning as usual."

As I held Rosa's legs, the tension in her muscles began to relax. A lessening of her movements followed.

"She's coming out of it," I said.

"Thank you, Mary and Jesus," Mrs. Mendoza said as she crossed herself, her tears now reduced to a trickle.

I released my grip on the girl, as did the nurse standing opposite me, and we all gathered around Rosa while she settled down and fell asleep. I wondered if perhaps Rosa's mom had been mistaken about giving her daughter medicine that morning or had given her the wrong pill. I doubted the pharmacy had made a mistake with her prescription, but I needed to check that out.

"Do you by any chance have the bottle of carbamazepine pills with you?"

"Yes, Doctor. I always bring them with me when I take Rosa to see a doctor."

She handed me a pill bottle, over half-filled with oblong blue pills I didn't recognize. "These look different than what I'm used to.

"I know, Doctor. The pharmacist told me they changed to a cheaper generic. He said it works exactly the same."

I looked at the bottle. The manufacturer's name was printed in the lower right corner. I'd never heard of the company, but with so many generic drug manufacturers, that wasn't surprising. I opened the Epocrates app on my phone. Epocrates contains all sorts of information useful for physicians, including color pictures of all manufactured pills. I found an image of the appropriate generic carbamazepine pill I prescribed for Rosa. It was an exact match to those in the bottle.

"Looks like everything's in order," I said, handing the container back to Mrs. Mendoza. I turned to one of the nurses and said, "Draw a STAT carbamazepine level and have her admitted to the Pediatric ICU. Better order a STAT MRI too. While you're at it, request a neuro consult."

"MRI? Why does she need another MRI?" Rosa's mother asked. "She had one when she started having seizures, and it was normal."

"We have to make sure nothing has changed. We need to look for a new abnormality that may have caused her seizures since she hasn't had any for several years."

"I know what you're thinking. You think Rosa may have a brain tumor, don't you?" The distraught mother began to cry again.

"Let's not get ahead of ourselves now. We just need to rule out the possibility."

Mrs. Mendoza was pleading with God, Mary, and Jesus between loud wails, praying that her daughter would be okay, attracting curious looks from those walking by. She leaned heavily on one of the aides in the room for support as if she were too weak to stand.

I've seen parents in difficult situations before, and I know they each react in their own way. Rosa's mom had always struck me as overly emotional, but now she seemed over the top as if she was grasping for attention. For several minutes, I tried to comfort her but was unsuccessful. I checked my watch and noted my shift would start in five minutes.

"Don't worry," I said, patting Mrs. Mendoza on the arm. "I'll be starting my shift in the Pediatric ICU soon, and I'll take good care of Rosa. Meanwhile, these wonderful nurses will look after her. They'll call me immediately if I'm needed." After extracting myself from the room, I quickly checked with the head nurse and learned there were no other patients currently in the ER that would be sent to the Pediatric ICU.

Upon reaching the unit, I greeted the clerks seated at the nursing station and was briefed on the patients by one of the other physicians on duty. The census was low, so there were plenty of empty beds. I looked forward to a fairly easy shift as I checked the computer for lab results.

An hour after I arrived, Rosa, having completed her MRI, was brought in on a gurney accompanied by her mother, still loudly praying to Jesus and Mary. Mrs. Mendoza showed no signs of letting up as her daughter was transferred to a bed and hooked up to monitors. I didn't know how long this woman would be able to keep up with the histrionics. Stares from the staff didn't seem to bother her, and it was wearing on me. Lab results on other patients were becoming available, and some were abnormal.

Mrs. Mendoza clearly had some problems, but I needed to concentrate and wanted her to shut up.

Rosa, who appeared lethargic when first brought in, perked up after a while. Her vital signs remained stable, and she was awake and alert. Although she tried to assure her mother she was okay, the woman's dramatic display remained unrelenting.

I tended to the other patients, including a diabetic girl who came in with ketoacidosis, a young boy with sickle cell disease in crisis, and a teenage girl with a cardiomyopathy. When I was examining the latter, a nurse interrupted me.

"I think you'll want to see this right away, Doctor," she said as she handed me a slip of paper. On it was written: *Rosa's carbamazepine level: 0.5.*

I looked up at the nurse, who nodded her head knowingly. Leaving the patient I had been evaluating, I rushed to a computer terminal nearby to confirm the result myself. Sure enough, the level of anti-seizure medicine in Rosa's system was 0.5 micrograms per milliliter, well below the therapeutic level of four to twelve. I immediately jumped to the only conclusion that seemed reasonable—Rosa's mother had not given her daughter any medication that morning and probably had skipped several previous doses.

Was she mentally deficient, incapable of keeping track of her daughter's medicine? I didn't think so. I'd met with her several times, and she seemed intelligent and aware of all the issues with her daughter's health. I was left to conclude she had intentionally denied her child the medication she needed. Although she had always appeared conscientious and willing to do anything for Rosa, her actions now led me to suspect something had changed. Mrs. Mendoza seemed to be seeking attention and sympathy from others, wanting recognition for the difficulty she faced taking care of a sick child. She might even plan to ask for financial assistance from compassionate people in the future. I didn't know what had caused this change in her, but despite whatever hardships she'd come across, I couldn't condone putting a child in danger.

I had recently been involved in a case of Munchausen's Syndrome by proxy, a situation where a parent poisons or harms a child in some way, hoping to get attention for themselves. This typically involves multiple hospitalizations and painful procedures for the child who is the victim, usually unaware of their parent's involvement.

This was on my mind when I discovered Rosa's blood carbamazepine level was dangerously low. Instead of the usual type of Munchausen's Syndrome by proxy, where a toxin or infectious agent is given to a child, Mrs. Mendoza appeared to have withheld needed medication from her daughter.

I pulled Rosa's mother aside. "Your daughter's carbamazepine level is much lower than it should be. That's why she's having a seizure."

"I don't understand," Mrs. Mendoza said. "She took her medicine this morning. I gave it to her myself."

"Are you sure? Could you have forgotten?" I asked, giving Rosa's mother every opportunity to admit she'd been remiss but hadn't intentionally deprived Rosa of her medication. To my surprise, she insisted she had given her daughter the pill.

After Rosa received a loading dose of carbamazepine, I needed to report my observations, as was my duty when I suspected child abuse. I opted to call the police rather than Child Protective Services, knowing the police would respond much quicker. An hour later, a female police officer was in the Pediatric ICU questioning Mrs. Mendoza.

At first, their conversation was quiet but quickly escalated to a shouting match. Before I could direct the women to continue their discussion outside the ICU, Mrs. Mendoza pushed the officer hard. I thought she would slug her before the cop quickly took control of the distraught mother and snapped handcuffs around her wrists, behind her back. Whether Mrs. Mendoza heard her Miranda rights is questionable, as her wails drowned out the officer's voice.

Rosa appeared confused and started to cry. I sat next to the bed and tried to comfort her, explaining that her mother hadn't given her the medication she needed, and the law required an investigation. An aunt had been notified and would visit her soon.

Rosa dried her eyes and looked at me. "But she did give me my medicine," she said.

"That can't be. We checked. I'll bet she hasn't given it to you for days."

"You're wrong. Mom always remembers to give it to me, even when I forget. She makes me take it on time when I tell her I'm busy and want to take it later."

"Maybe she gave you something else, something she pretended was your medicine."

"No, she gave me the same pills we picked up from the pharmacy. I opened the new bottle myself and looked at the pills when we got them last week. She only gave me pills from that bottle. I know it."

Smart kid—only eight years old, and she's saying all the right things to protect her mother. If I didn't know better, I'd believe her. I momentarily thought about counting the pills in the bottle but decided against it, not knowing the exact day she started using that bottle. Additionally, Mrs. Mendoza could have thrown some pills away, making it appear she had given Rosa more of them.

"The lab results prove you didn't get the medicine you need. Although I'm sure your mother loves you very much, what she did was dangerous. She could have hurt you very badly."

"You're lying. Now my mom got arrested. I don't understand why you want her to go to jail." Rosa started crying.

"I don't want your mom to go to jail," I said. "She wouldn't have been arrested if she hadn't fought with the policewoman." I put my hand on Rosa's.

"It's all your fault," she said, pushing my hand away.

"You're my patient, and I'll do whatever I can to help and protect you. I don't think your mother should be taking care of you right now."

"I used to like you, but now I hate you."

I understood Rosa's perspective. Nonetheless, her words hurt. From that moment on, Rosa never looked at me with anything other than mistrust and animosity. Being on such bad terms with a patient was something I wasn't used to. A short time later, the radiology report on Rosa's MRI came back: *No abnormalities found.*

The next day, after Rosa's carbamazepine level had been stabilized in the therapeutic range, she had an EEG. The consulting neurologist deemed her stable, and she was discharged into her aunt's care. For the time being, Rosa would live with her aunt and three cousins. I hoped Mrs. Mendoza would get whatever psychiatric help she needed so she'd be able to take care of her daughter in the future. Although Rosa's prognosis was good, this case left me with a bad feeling, and for some time, I wondered how I could have handled it better.

CHAPTER 2

The following Monday, I had a fairly uneventful day in the pediatrics clinic, where I usually worked. Walking home after finishing all my chart entries and paperwork on that cool spring evening, I looked forward to picking up Maya, my three-year-old daughter. She was with my in-laws, Enlai and Fung, who lived one floor below us in our condominium building. I always delighted in finding out what new skills Maya had learned and what her most adorable moments were. She enjoyed spending weekdays with her grandparents, as well as her four-year-old cousin, Mingyu, who lived with his mother, Ting, and siblings in the unit adjacent to my in-laws. Mingyu's sister and brother, Wang Shu and Kang, were nine and seven, respectively. They were in school a good part of the day and had after-school activities lasting until late afternoon. Often when I returned from work, all the children were playing together, with Wang Shu often taking on the role of a teacher.

Although Enlai, Fung, and my sister-in-law, Ting, still felt more comfortable speaking their native Mandarin, their English had improved significantly in the four years they'd been here. Typical of many Chinese, they still said "he" for both "he" and "she." Wang Shu, Kang, and Mingyu were fluent in both English and Mandarin. Maya was learning both languages equally and was able to help me communicate with my in-laws.

Upon entering Fung and Enlai's unit, Maya showed me a picture of a bird she had drawn with crayons earlier. She was growing by leaps and bounds, and her brain was soaking up so much information, it was a joy to behold. She was a beauty, with straight black hair, brown eyes, and delicate features with an Asian influence. When Maya was next to Lim, my husband, she looked remarkably like him. When next to me, she was obviously my daughter. She brought me more joy than I had thought possible.

A doctor had implanted her in my uterus when she was a microscopic-size embryo. The miraculous embryo destined to become my daughter had been formed by in vitro fertilization using my egg and Lim's sperm. It had undergone testing to ensure she didn't inherit Huntington's Disease, a genetic disease that had claimed the life of my mother, and I had a small risk for developing. We planned to repeat the process soon to make a brother for Maya but hadn't told her yet.

Maya and I took the stairs up one flight to our condo on the third floor. Lim and I had bought the unit next door to us and combined it with our own into one large residence, with two studies and four bedrooms. Completing the major remodeling job to our liking, although challenging, was worth all the hassle in the end. Since Lim had sold his previous company to Google, money was no object.

I first met Ting's brother, Lim, several years earlier when I went to China with my best friend, Daisy Wong. There, we investigated Fengshou, a secret Chinese government facility involved in embryonic stem cell gene editing to produce super athletes for Olympic competition. Ting, who had escaped China and was living in San Francisco with her two oldest children, had informed me about the program in which all of her three children had undergone gene editing without her consent. Wang Shu's eye color had been changed from brown to blue. Kang and Mingyu had DNA alterations giving them unusual stamina and strength. Although we didn't know it at the time, an additional change in one of Mingyu's genes had unfortunately caused his liver to enlarge from accumulating abnormally high levels of glycogen. Ting hadn't been able to bring Mingyu with her when she escaped, so he was still living at the Chinese facility at the time. Daisy and I exposed the gene-editing program, forcing the Chinese government to shut it down, and rescued Mingyu.

Lim, who I had become romantically involved with in China, was able to escape his native country. We grew close after he came to San Francisco and later arranged for his parents to be released from a Chinese prison and immigrate to the US. Aside from being strikingly handsome and athletic, Lim was brilliant and kind with a strong moral compass and a good sense of humor. Other than leaving the toilet seat up, he was a perfect husband.

Lim was making dinner when Maya and I walked in. "Smells good, Amazing Husband," I said as Maya ran to Lim and grabbed him around the legs. Lim picked her up and held her as he continued to stir the contents of the wok with his free hand. Our lives were so perfect now, I worried that there was no room for improvement. I didn't want anything to change. "How were things at the company today?" I was asking Lim about Cyber Dash, the new start-up he founded barely one year earlier.

"Great. I signed a contract to help the FBI access information on cell phones. Remember me telling you about my program for that?"

"Something about going through the back door, right?"

"You must have been listening for a change. Yes, we disable the kill switch, the feature that erases the phone's information when the wrong password is entered ten times. Then we try every combination password possible. This could be very big. We're such a new company, we can really use the name recognition we'll get from this. I decided to celebrate by coming home early."

"I'm glad you did." I walked over to Lim and kissed him. My moment in paradise was interrupted by my cell phone. "Good. It's Daisy," I said, looking at the caller ID. I always enjoyed talking to my best friend.

"Dinner will be ready in seven minutes," Lim said.

"Okay, I'll make this quick." I pressed the answer icon.

"What are you doing in exactly seventy-five days?" Daisy asked, not waiting for me to say hello.

"Damned if I know. I don't have a calendar in front of me. What day of the week is it?"

"Saturday."

"I'll have to check. I may be working in the peds ICU."

"If you are, get someone to cover for you. I want you to be my matron of honor."

I paused for a moment to let her words sink in, then shrieked into the phone, "You're getting married! My god, I can't believe it. It's about time you became respectable."

"I may be getting married, but I have no intention of becoming respectable."

"We are talking about Arvid, aren't we? The handsome guy from Denmark?"

"Yep."

"Just checking. I never know with you. Why seventy-five days?"

"According to my parents, who still believe in all those Chinese superstitions they were raised with, that's a very lucky date. I don't want to argue with them since I don't really care about what day it is. You agree to be my maid—I mean matron—of honor, don't you?"

"Of course. I'd love to."

"Great. I can check that off. Gotta go, now. Lots of people to call."

I checked my wall calendar as soon as we disconnected. I wasn't scheduled to work that day and had nothing planned. I circled the date and wrote "DW" in big letters, then entered it on my phone calendar. I felt even happier than I had a few moments earlier. My best friend was getting married to a wonderful guy. I was glad she was finally settling down, so I would no longer have to listen to her going on and on about her latest fling. Her parents would be so happy. Every time I saw them, they asked me to find someone for Daisy to marry. As if I could make her settle down.

I thought about my appointment to be implanted with Maya's brother soon. The embryo was safely frozen in the lab of a friend of mine, ready to go. If this pregnancy were anything like my last one, I wouldn't begin to show until after the wedding. I looked forward to spending the next seventy-five days working at the job I loved, coming home and relaxing with my wonderful family, helping with wedding plans, and shopping with Daisy for her wedding dress and my matron of honor getup. What a great way to enjoy myself as the little ball of cells in my uterus grew into a life-size baby boy.

Something gnawed at me ever so slightly. I had checked on the most recent labs I'd drawn on Ting's children. I continued to monitor them, looking for early signs of trouble from the gene editing they'd undergone. I wanted to quickly catch any unexpected abnormalities that might show up and hopefully prevent irreversible health problems.

On the last set of labs, one of Mingyu's liver enzymes was slightly elevated. I needed to repeat the test. Hopefully, it was a spurious result, and the next test would be in the normal range. I would tend to disregard such a result on pretty much any other kid. But Mingyu was anything but normal. For over three years, I'd worried it was only a matter of time—how much time I didn't know—until his enlarged liver was damaged. I felt that time was fast approaching.

CHAPTER 3

The next two days were a blur. The clinic was busy, with sore throats, diarrhea, pink eye, rashes, lacerations, and two broken arms from skateboard injuries. Fortunately, none of the staff had called in sick.

Thursday morning, I was fast asleep when Lim brought me coffee. As usual, he was already dressed and prepared for the day. I wish I could jump out of bed every morning and be geared up for the day like him, but wake-up time is always a struggle for me. In Maya, he had someone happy to jump out of bed and keep him company as soon as he was up.

"I'll take her to my parents on my way out," he said. "It'll give you a little more time to get ready for work. I've got to leave now for an early meeting."

"Thanks," I said, following Lim to the kitchen with my coffee. He turned to give me a quick peck on the cheek and lifted Maya so I could kiss her without bending over. It didn't take much time for me to drop Maya off at her grandparents' as I usually did, but I enjoyed the few extra minutes of solitude as I prepared for another day in the clinic.

I arrived at work a few minutes early and found Martha having what appeared to be a private conversation with Dr. Jeremy Nilsen outside one of the exam rooms. Martha had been my assistant since I began working at the clinic. She never failed me when I wanted her to get something done. Dependable and resourceful, we'd developed a great working rapport—she seemed to anticipate what I needed without being told. Martha was a fabulous assistant, and I often wondered how I'd be able to function without her.

Jeremy, a pediatrician, had joined our department a few months prior. A tall, handsome, single man with blond hair and blue eyes, I had noticed several female members of our staff giving him special attention. Upon seeing me approach, Martha's face turned red, and she appeared nervous. "You're a bit early this morning," she said, as Jeremy turned and walked away.

"Only about ten minutes. Lim left early with Maya. I didn't realize how much quicker I could get ready for work without Maya to sidetrack me. I can't resist playing with her, even if I'm in a hurry. I'll catch up on a little paperwork before I see my first patient."

Martha smiled as she walked toward me. "Want me to get you a cup of coffee? Your first patient isn't scheduled for another fifteen minutes."

"Thanks, Martha, but I had an extra cup at home," I said as I turned to walk to my office.

I used to worry about Martha. Until recently, she seemed to take no interest in her appearance. Not one to dress stylishly, wear makeup, or spend time fixing her hair, she appeared plain and stodgy. She was a sweet, intelligent woman, and I wanted her to find happiness outside of the satisfaction she got from her job. Though we weren't close like Daisy and me, we often shared stories about what was happening in our lives.

Martha had been to dinner at my place at least a dozen times. Lim found her to be a good conversationalist, and Maya was fond of her. I would occasionally ask if she was dating anyone, but the answer was always the same—negative. I'd helped her fill out forms for several online dating sites and even counseled her on where to meet the few respondents. None of the dates had panned out. Sometimes at the end of the day, she enjoyed showing me images of her cats, which now numbered three. I had feared she was on her way to becoming a cat lady.

I stopped worrying about Martha a month earlier when I noticed a change in her. She'd always been pleasant but lately had taken on an extra layer of cheerfulness. Previously introverted, I began to see an extroverted side of her, as she smiled while sharing pleasantries with other staff members. At the same time, she took much more pride in her appearance. Her long, straggly brown hair had been cut mid-length and styled. Instead of her usual loose, grandmotherly skirts, she wore fashionable, form-fitting clothes and makeup. I couldn't help but notice how much more attractive she looked. I was able to think of only one reason for this dramatic transformation: Martha had her sights on a man. Although she never spoke of it to me, all evidence pointed to that conclusion. Seeing the way Martha was talking with Jeremy, I wondered if he was that man.

"Your first patient is Ethan Wells. I'll put him in Room Seven. Remember, fifteen minutes."

"Thanks, Martha." I'd seen eight-year-old Ethan two days earlier for an infected laceration on his arm. A routine case, I'd cleaned the area, sutured it, and given him an antibiotic prescription. I hadn't expected to see him again until it was time to remove the stitches.

Fifteen minutes flew by, and I'd barely made a dent in my backlog of paperwork. Not wanting to get behind, I headed to Room Seven. Before referring to the computer monitor to look up the reason for Ethan's visit, I had all the information I needed immediately upon seeing him. His arm was swollen and reddish-purple, as if the antibiotic had no effect.

"Goodness," I said. "That looks terrible. I'll bet it hurts."

"Sure does," said Ethan.

I turned to his mom, a woman who'd been bringing her children to me ever since I'd begun working in the clinic. She was a responsible, concerned parent who always followed my instructions to the letter. "What happened? Weren't you able to get the antibiotic I ordered?"

"I got it, all right, for all the good it did."

"Did he miss any doses?"

"Not once. It's just gotten a lot worse, as you can see."

"I'm really sorry. He must have a very unusual infection. I'll take a culture."

"How long till you get the results?"

"I'm afraid it will take a few days, but I'll change to another antibiotic right now, something more powerful."

"I had a funny feeling about those pills you prescribed."

"Oh? What do you mean?"

"I have a pretty good memory, and I know he had a prescription for the same antibiotic, Keflex, when he'd gotten an infection last year. These capsules weren't the same, so I called the pharmacy. The person I spoke to told me they'd switched to a generic. Although the capsules looked different, she assured me the antibiotic was the same. I was still worried, though, because some of them looked a bit discolored. It didn't seem right."

"Did you bring them with you, by any chance?"

"Sure did." She rummaged through her purse, pulled out a prescription bottle, and handed it to me.

I opened the container and counted the number of capsules left. It was the appropriate number, so I checked the label. Cephalexin, 250 mg, take one every eight hours, #21. Exactly what I had prescribed, cephalexin being the generic name for Keflex. I poured a few of the yellow capsules into my hand and noticed two of them had a slight brownish discoloration focally. I opened the Epocrates app on my cell phone and brought up pictures of cephalexin capsules. It checked out—one of the pictures was an exact match with the capsules.

After excusing myself, I found Martha in the hallway and asked her to get me a culture tube and dressing change kit. Back in the exam room, I explained to Ethan's mom I would be doing a culture and sensitivity test on Ethan's wound to determine the best antibiotic for him if the infection evaded the one I'd be prescribing. I entered a prescription for Bactrim in the computer, finishing as Martha entered with everything I had requested.

She handed me a sterile culture tube. I removed the swab, dabbed it around Ethan's wound, returned it to the tube, and handed it back to Martha. She placed the wound dressing tray on the counter and left with the culture tube. As usual, she knew what to do without my needing to say a word.

"We should have all the results we need after the weekend," I said to Ethan's mom. "In the meantime, Ethan should take the new antibiotic I just prescribed twice a day." I looked again at the pill bottle in my hand and noticed the manufacturer's name in the lower right corner. Umbroz. I'd never heard of that company and wondered why some of the capsules were discolored. A disquieting thought flashed through my mind. *Could there be something wrong with the medications this company was making?*

I told myself that was impossible. The FDA would never approve pills made by a sub-par manufacturer. For a moment, I wondered if our pharmacy might have received inferior, counterfeit drugs but rejected that idea. Improvements in packaging and barcoding of pharmaceuticals had essentially eliminated that possibility. I remained uneasy and made a mental note to look into the company. "Do you mind if I take one of your capsules?" I asked Ethan's mom.

"Keep the whole bottle, Doctor. That medicine hasn't helped Ethan at all. I'll pick up the new prescription right after we're done here."

Ethan winced as I cleaned his wound, spread antibiotic ointment over it, and taped a sterile gauze pad on top. "I'll be calling with the culture results when I have them," I said as I left the room.

"New patient, a boy, Room Five," Martha said once I was in the hallway.

"I'm on it," I replied. "While I'm seeing that patient, could you find out for me where I can have a pill analyzed to be sure it has the right amount of the active ingredient?"

"I don't understand," Martha said.

"I know it's unusual, but I have a funny feeling about this medication. It was made by a company I've never heard of, and I want to have it analyzed by an independent laboratory. Can you find me a place where I can send it?"

Martha seemed to be forcing herself to smile. "Sure, Doc. I'll give it a try while you're in with your new patient."

"I know. Room Five."

After introducing myself to my new six-year-old patient and his mother, I checked the computer and learned the boy had a mild sore throat and runny nose in addition to a rash. I examined the pink splotches on his face and diagnosed him with the viral infection erythema infectiosum, or fifth disease. Usually a mild illness, I assured the boy and his mother he would be fine. The visit took about ten minutes.

When I had finished, I glanced down the hall and saw Martha speaking to Jeremy's assistant.

"Did you get a chance to find out where I can send this capsule for analysis?"

Her face turned red as she explained, "Sorry, but I couldn't locate a place that will test medications."

Martha's response surprised me. She was usually very adept at figuring out how to get non-routine things done.

"I just got off the phone with Dr. Pressley in internal medicine," she continued. "I thought if anyone could help, he could since he's been here forever. Even he didn't know of any place that could do the analysis. He couldn't think of a situation where it would be needed, and the lab committee would never approve the cost of the test. Instead of sending the pill for analysis, he suggested thinking about mistakes that may have been made in prescribing the medication."

I didn't know Dr. Pressley. I'd never spoken to him directly but knew who he was and that he'd been working in the clinics here for over thirty years. Despite his vast experience, I was offended by his insinuation that I was misguided. I made a mental note to address that if I ever spoke to him directly.

The rest of my day was hectic as usual. After I finished my chart entries, I wondered if Martha had exhausted all avenues available to find a lab that could analyze the medicine. I had no reason to doubt her abilities or dedication to her job. Yet, I couldn't believe there were no labs anywhere that could test these capsules.

I did my own internet search, which didn't take long. California Analytics, located a mere forty miles away, analyzed all sorts of specimens, including medications.

CHAPTER 4

At eight o'clock sharp the next morning, I called California Analytics. I was pleasantly surprised when a real person answered. After explaining what I needed, I was transferred to the technical department, where I spoke to a man who told me the company received several requests to analyze prescription medications each year. There wasn't much backlog, and if I got my specimen to them soon, they would probably have the results in a few days. The cost was reasonable, and I opted to pay for the analysis myself to save time. I was directed to complete the test request form, which was available on the website. If possible, I should send a non-generic capsule of the medication for them to compare.

Between combing Maya's hair and kissing Lim goodbye as he left for another one of his important work meetings, I printed the form, filled it out, and found an old bottle of Keflex in the medicine cabinet. I took one of the two capsules left and placed it in a Ziploc sandwich bag labeled "Keflex, 250 mg (control)." In another Ziploc bag labeled "Cephalexin, 250 mg (test samples)," I placed three of the generic capsules.

I dropped Maya off at my in-laws early so I'd have time to stop by the post office, buy a small box, and mail everything to California Analytics. I arrived in the clinic five minutes late, tired from rushing around and feeling stressed about the time. Martha found me and stated, "Raymond Murray, Room Two. Six-month well-baby checkup. Already weighed and measured."

Good, an easy one. I barely looked at Martha before heading to Room Two. Raymond, a cute, slobbering little mass of warmth, cooing, and kicking legs, was in his young mother's arms as I walked in. His father was standing close by. Mom and Dad watched intently as I went through my usual routine of physical exam and testing for milestones. Raymond's weight and length were both above average, and everything in my assessment indicated Raymond was a healthy baby. After answering his parent's questions, I glanced at my watch. I had managed to finish on time.

Still worried about Ethan from the day before, I called his mother. "How's he doing?" I asked.

"Better already, Doc. It's less red this morning, and there's no pus. Thank you for prescribing the new medicine."

"I don't have the culture results back yet, but since Ethan seems to be responding well, let's keep him on the Bactrim. Be sure to call if there's a change for the worse. Otherwise, plan to bring him back Monday to have his stitches removed."

"I won't forget."

I was relieved Ethan was doing better. I had a full ten seconds to bask in my feel-good moment before Martha approached me. "Missy Kraft, Room Seven."

I dispatched Missy's earache quickly, and the rest of my day was unremarkable—no catastrophic cases, emergencies, or staffing problems. I managed to leave work on the early side, leaving some routine paperwork undone. When I picked up Maya from my in-laws, I noticed Mingyu lying on the couch, looking listless.

"Why isn't he playing with you?" I asked Kang.

"He doesn't feel well. He was like that last night and all day today."

"His tummy hurts," said Maya.

"Mom's worried about him," Kang said. "Could you look at him?"

"Sure," I said, walking over to Mingyu. The children and grandparents hovered as I kneeled, looked in Mingyu's eyes, and felt his abdomen. I tried my best to hide what I was thinking. The whites of his eyes had yellowed, and his liver was more enlarged. Now I was sure. The time had come. I quickly wiped the tears from my eyes, hoping no one had seen them.

"Let him rest for now," I said. "I'll draw some blood for testing in the morning." I left with Maya for my condo upstairs, knowing I would need to have a difficult conversation with Ting soon.

Once we were home, I fed Maya, then started heating leftovers in the oven for Lim and me. It wasn't long before Lim walked in, and we embraced. Maya joined in, grabbing each of us around our legs. Then she played hide and seek with Lim as I put dinner on the table. As we ate, I told Lim I was worried about Mingyu. I would test his blood but was pretty sure he would need a liver transplant soon to survive.

"Ting's been expecting that," Lim said.

"I know she's been aware he would probably need a new liver in the future. Unfortunately, the future is here now. It's no longer theoretical."

"Take your samples tomorrow. If you're right, which you probably are, we'll need to tell her right away. I can tell her if you like."

"She'll figure out something's up when I come to draw Mingyu's blood. I think you'd better talk to her tonight."

I'd forgotten Maya was still well within earshot. "Is Mingyu going to die?" she asked, her voice shaking and her eyes wide.

I'd missed the Parenting 101 class where parents learn how to talk to their kids about death and dying. I'd had plenty of uncomfortable discussions with my patients' parents and with my patients themselves after they'd already heard bad news from their own families. But now the shoe was on my foot.

Ever since Maya began asking questions, with almost every other word being "Why," I'd been learning in countless short, unplanned lessons how little we're prepared to talk to our children about certain things. We may have envisioned speaking to them about difficult topics under the appropriate circumstance at just the right age, but life doesn't work that way. Kids have a way of listening and putting things together when you least expect it and are unprepared. Neither Lim nor I were the heaven and hell types, so I wasn't planning to go there.

"Mingyu is probably sick and may need an operation," I said. "Daddy needs to talk to Auntie Ting about that, so don't tell her before Daddy talks to her."

"If he has the operation, will he die?"

"He may need surgery so he won't die."

"What if he dies, anyway?"

I wished she'd stop with these questions. "I don't think that will happen, so let's not talk about it."

Maya looked at me with an expression of disappointment, like she knew I was speaking to her as if she were a child. But she was a child. I had a feeling of déjà vu. In the situation I was recalling, I was the child, and my mother was speaking to me the same way I was speaking to Maya. My mother's sister had recently taken ill and was hospitalized. I loved my aunt dearly and was frightened. I wished I could remember exactly what my mom said to me after my aunt died.

Lim went downstairs to speak to Ting after dinner. When he returned, he told me she'd agreed I should test Mingyu's blood. Lim and I didn't talk much for the remainder of the evening. I put Maya to bed, and Lim went into the study and shut the door.

I would have tried to cheer him up, but I was as worried as he and knew there were no words that could lift the veil of gloom enveloping us all.

The next morning, being Saturday, Lim let me sleep an extra hour. By the time he brought me my morning coffee, he and Maya were dressed and had eaten breakfast. I forced down a small bowl of cereal, then retrieved the box on the top shelf of my bedroom closet, where I kept my stash of tubes and blood-drawing equipment. I was sorting through the contents, lost in thought, when I was startled by a high-pitched voice coming from behind me.

"Is that for Mingyu?"

"Yes, Maya. I guess nothing gets past you. I need to get some of his blood to see how sick he is."

"I hope he doesn't die. I would miss him. Even though sometimes I get mad at him when he takes my toys, I would let him have all my toys if it would mean he won't die."

I couldn't find appropriate words, so I held Maya tight and kissed her. "We're all hoping for the same thing, sweetheart."

"When I grow up, I want to be like you. I want to help everybody who is sick."

"I'm proud of you, Maya. You don't have to decide what you want to do when you grow up yet, but I can tell you have a good heart." I hugged her before I stood up. I felt closer and more attached to Maya every day. There wasn't one thing I would change about her. It was hard for me to believe I could feel this close to a second child, and wondered if I should go ahead with another embryo implantation as planned.

On the other hand, I never expected to adore Maya as much as I did. Perhaps I would feel that close to another child. Would that be possible? Did I have that much love to give? I didn't know. I did know many other couples who had more than one child and seemed to love all of them. Equally? I wasn't sure, but my parents at least acted like they loved me and my late brother the same. I also thought about what would happen when Lim and I were gone. I imagined Maya would be glad to have a sibling then. For her sake, another child seemed like the right thing.

I went downstairs to Ting's unit. "Mingyu is still in bed," Ting said, teary-eyed. "You can get his blood now." As I walked through the living room, Kang and Wang Shu were sitting in silence, forlorn looks on both their faces. I went straight to the bedroom Mingyu shared with Kang, where Ting's youngest was in bed, propped up on pillows. His eyes were at least as yellow as they'd been the day before. I found little resistance from him as I drew a tube of his blood.

After saying my goodbyes, I went straight to the lab to drop off the specimen. I wanted to walk alone so I'd have time to think. The darkness that had recently blanketed our lives was stifling. Assuming the test results confirmed my suspicion, I would contact the UCSF doctor Mingyu had been seeing biannually regarding his liver disease. Ting had already made it clear that if Mingyu needed a new liver, she wanted to donate part of hers. Since they were the same blood type, and Ting was in good health, waiting for a donor probably wouldn't be necessary. My in-laws could take care of the older children, Kang and Wang Shu, while Ting and Mingyu were in the hospital. They required little supervision, and Fung loved having them around and cooking for them. I felt marginally better, knowing at least childcare wouldn't be a problem.

On the way home, I called Daisy to tell her about Mingyu's decline. She'd been going over wedding plans with Arvid and invited me over, hoping a change in scenery might cheer me up. I agreed that talking about the wedding and getting to know Arvid better might lift my spirits. I got the okay from Lim and set out for Daisy's.

After Daisy buzzed me into her condominium complex, I took the stairs to the unit she now shared with Arvid on the third floor. Arvid was standing by the open door and welcomed me in. Tall, muscular, and good-looking, with blue eyes and long, dark blond hair, he wore jeans and a red T-shirt. Daisy, her straight, long black hair hanging loose, was seated at the kitchen table and invited me to join her. As soon as I sat, she shoved fabric swatches in front of me. "Which one do you like best?" she asked.

"What's this for?" I asked.

"The wedding, Doctor Clueless. Whatever color you pick, that's the color you're going to wear as my matron of honor. I'm going to be wearing white."

"Of course you are. I would expect nothing else from a blushing bride like you." I took a moment to look at the samples. "I like them all, but I suppose this is the best," I said, tapping on one of them.

"Great. Write this down, Arvid. Teal Mist."

"Got it," he said. "Are we done now?"

"That's enough for today. Now, let's turn our attention to Erica and Mingyu. Remember, Arvid, Mingyu is the child I smuggled out of the Chinese gene-editing facility when he was an infant. I hid him under a fake pregnancy belly, so he's pretty special to me. Not that Ting's other kids aren't."

"I know," Arvid said, putting an arm around Daisy. "You've mentioned it more than once."

"Sorry," Daisy said. Then she turned to me. "How are you holding up with your stressful job, Lim's startup, taking care of Maya, getting ready for another kid, and now Mingyu's health problems?"

"I'm pretty stressed out, to be honest. I'm trying to spare Lim from my anxiety. He's so busy with his company, but sometimes I feel like the person in that famous Danish painting—I think it's called *The Scream*."

"I'm deeply offended," Arvid said with a hint of a smile. "That picture is by a Norwegian. Even though you Americans think all Scandinavians are alike, you should never confuse Danes and

Norwegians. We Danes are much friendlier. And not nearly as lazy as the Norwegians."

"My apologies. I'll try to remember that the next time I see one of those slothful Norwegians."

Daisy turned to Arvid and gave him a knowing nod as she said, "Now I'd like to cheer Erica up." I figured she was signaling her fiancé he was now free to leave.

Arvid excused himself and disappeared into one of the back bedrooms. I figured he would rather read a book or pull off his fingernails than talk about my problems. I started to explain my concerns about Mingyu when I looked up and momentarily forgot my troubles.

Daisy was laughing almost uncontrollably, and I caught a serious case of the giggles from her. There stood Arvid in a pink karate gi, his hair in a man bun. As he waved around a plastic sword, he yelled words in what sounded like Japanese. He reminded me of the late John Belushi playing a samurai in old videos I'd seen from *Saturday Night Live*. He proceeded to jump and twirl around the living room with the grace of an ox as he knocked over a side table and spread decorative pillows all over the floor. When he had finished, I had to admit to feeling better.

"I forgot to tell you," Daisy said, "although Arvid is an engineer by day, he is an expert in martial arts by night. You'd never know it from that performance, though. He's planning on opening a martial arts school for kids."

"And the pink gi?" I asked.

"Kids really like it," Arvid said. "I like to make the training fun. Disciplined, but fun. Also, I'm going to offer classes to teach women self-defense. I've taught Daisy a few things already. I'd be happy to teach you too. I could teach the two of you together."

"Good idea," Daisy said. "It's actually pretty fun. You might like it, Rosen."

"Thanks, but I don't have time."

"You're just worried I'll be better than you."

"Don't flatter yourself. It's just that I haven't ever needed anything like that and don't plan to. It's not like I'm going to take a walk in Golden Gate Park at two in the morning."

"That's the thing," Daisy said. "You can suddenly find yourself in a dangerous situation with no warning. Even if you're playing it safe like you always do."

I could tell Daisy wasn't going to let up, so I turned to Arvid. "I look forward to seeing your new school when it's all set up." I was being polite, having no interest in martial arts.

"I'm going to change back to my regular clothes," Arvid said, making an exit.

"Now, let's talk about what's really on your mind," Daisy said, leading me to the couch. Once we were seated, she asked me more questions about Mingyu. "I know you'll make sure he has the best treatment," she said. "We all knew this day would come. At least Kang and Wang Shu are healthy, so your glass is more than half full."

I knew she was right, although it was good to hear it from her. We commiserated for another half hour and made plans to have dinner with our significant others the following Saturday. I left feeling better than when I arrived. On the short walk home, I noticed a homeless person in a doorway talking to himself. For a moment, I thought about taking Arvid up on his offer to teach me self-defense moves, but as soon as the man was out of earshot, I dismissed the idea.

CHAPTER 5

After I returned home, Lim, Maya, and I went to my in-laws, where Fung had made dinner for all of us. Mingyu lay on the couch, sleeping most of the time, unable to eat. Our dinners were usually noisy affairs, but that night was different. I tried to liven up the conversation by mentioning my visit with Daisy and Arvid. The children laughed a bit when I described Arvid's martial arts performance, and they expressed interest in attending his school when it opened.

Kang mentioned a photographer showing up at school and taking pictures. Wang Shu talked about being in a school play involving robots and space aliens. While both revelations would have normally drawn a lot of discussion, neither gained much traction that night, our enthusiasm tamped down by the heavy veil of melancholy we all felt.

After dinner Lim, Maya, and I returned to our condominium for two rounds of Fish and a game of Candyland. We didn't allow Maya to win all the time, but she legitimately won all three games that evening. I got her ready for bed and read *Goodnight Moon* to her as Lim worked in the study. We both tucked her in and kissed her goodnight. Needing a distraction, Lim and I watched two old episodes of *Ozark* on Netflix. It was comforting to see another family with big problems. Nonetheless, I didn't sleep well that night.

The following morning, dressed in sweatpants and a baggy sweater, I sipped coffee on the balcony. The skies were gloomy and didn't do anything to lift my spirits. Maya was playing with her dolls in the living room as Lim straightened up the kitchen. A loud banging at our door interrupted the tranquility. Lim looked through the peephole, then opened the door. Ting rushed in holding a newspaper and started yelling at him in Mandarin.

I rushed in to find out what was going on as Lim grabbed the newspaper from her and put it on the kitchen table.

"See? See?" Ting screamed, using English for my benefit, I assumed. She was pointing to the front of the San Francisco Chronicle Sports section.

Lim and I both looked, then Lim picked up the paper to read the article above the fold as I tried to read with him.

"Sensation" was the headline in large lettering, above the picture of a young Asian boy. Kang. He was running in a grassy field, his clothing and hair pulled back by the wind, giving the impression of incredible speed. I finally understood the significance of Kang's mention of a photographer at his school. The Chronicle was doing a story on the second-grade phenom Kang Chen who could run faster and farther than any of his fellow students, even the fifth graders. He could kick and throw a ball farther than any of the other kids. Reading the article, I learned that local professional sports teams were already tracking him.

"This is quite a story," Lim said when he'd finished reading. "I know he's quite athletic, but I didn't realize others had noticed him."

"Yes, yes," Ting said. "I get letters. Giants, 49ers, Warriors, Earthquakes. I throw them out. I told the school not to give them my address. We are not interested. They must leave Kang alone."

"You never told me about that," Lim said.

"I thought maybe you would want him to play on these teams, so I kept it a secret. I didn't tell anyone. But now everybody knows." She started crying uncontrollably.

I put my arm around her. "Ting, I don't know why you're so upset. Kang is a smart young man. He won't lose sight of what's important and run off with one of these sports teams. He'll finish school and decide what he wants to do with his life when he gets older. I'm sure he'll make you proud. You have nothing to worry about."

"You do not understand. Now Kang is famous. The Chinese government will find us."

"You don't need to worry about that anymore. The embryonic gene editing program was exposed and shut down, as far as we know. There's no longer any reason for them to harm you or your children," I said.

"That's right. You haven't caused them any trouble since then," Lim added. "There'd be no reason for them to look for you now."

"I still worry. I worry about revenge."

"Would you like us to hire security for you?" Lim asked.

"No, no. I don't want to upset the children. Do not tell them about my concern. Do not tell Kang. I do not want him to feel guilty. I have to spend all my time worrying about Mingyu now. But I will be very careful. More careful than usual."

Despite our assurances, Ting remained anxious when she left. I hoped that with time, she would relax.

Maya had come into the kitchen to see what the fuss was about. She saw Kang's picture in the newspaper but was unimpressed. "The photographer didn't do a good job," she said. "His hair is messy." Lim and I laughed.

*

The next morning, Monday, I left for work early so I could review the lab results that had come in over the weekend before I started seeing patients. I planned to clear time later in the day to talk to Mingyu's hepatologist at UCSF and set up future appointments for him and Ting.

When I entered the clinic, I noticed Martha speaking quietly with Jeremy near the coffee maker as I walked past the staff room. Upon noticing me, although she forced a smile, her face turned red. She took a few steps in my direction and asked, "Want me to pour you a cup?" Meanwhile, Jeremy turned to straighten the stack of napkins on the counter—a stack that wasn't in need of straightening.

"No thanks, Martha." Coming up with no other explanation, I concluded Martha most definitely did have a crush on the new doctor and didn't want me to know. Jeremy, on the other hand, seemed to be embarrassed by her attention. I hoped it wouldn't end badly for her but was afraid it would. If nothing else, though, the experience might get her into the dating world.

I continued walking past, into my office, and started going through the notes and lab results that had accumulated on my desk. Ethan's wound had grown out Streptococcus pyogenes. Although the antibiotic sensitivities weren't yet reported, I suspected the bacteria would be susceptible to cephalexin unless this were an unusual, unrecognized strain. I expected the results to be out later that day. Martha came into my office to announce my first patient, a five-year-old girl with a headache, Room Nine. My schedule was jam-packed for the day.

"Martha, could you check the sensitivities on Ethan's culture in an hour or so and let me know the result? If they're not ready, call every hour till you get the result, please."

"Why are you so interested? I thought you changed the antibiotic, and he's doing fine now."

"That's true. I'm just checking up on a hunch. I got the culture results back, and I think the first antibiotic should have worked, so I'm wondering if it was defective. It was a generic by a company I'd never heard of called Umbroz."

"You never heard of Umbroz? Why, Dr. Rosen, they're a very large company with an excellent reputation." As Martha spoke, I noticed her looking away, avoiding eye contact. "I can't believe there's anything wrong with their medication. Maybe the lab made an error."

"I suppose that's possible, but please check for me."

"Sure."

When I left my office to see my first patient, I noticed Martha reach for her cell phone. By noon I'd seen seven patients, two complicated. Martha brought me a falafel wrap from a food truck, which I grabbed and began eating.

"Ethan's culture sensitivities are in," she said, rubbing sweat from her hands onto her black pants. "The bacteria that grew out of his wound appears to be sensitive to cephalexin. I'll bet Ethan's mom forgot to give her son his medicine and was too embarrassed to admit it."

"Maybe, but I'll keep an eye on that brand. It wouldn't be the first time a drug manufacturer cut some corners."

"I'm sure if the medication was bad, it was only a one-time thing."

"Why?" I realized I was channeling Maya with my "why" question but legitimately wondered why Martha thought that.

"I'm just, well, it's just that the company has such a good reputation. Hard to believe there's a problem with their manufacturing process. Your next patient is Sly Dabrowski, Room Five. Annual checkup."

Martha left me to wolf down the rest of my lunch. I didn't share her belief that Ethan's mom had neglected to give him his medicine and thought it odd she had come to that conclusion. The boy's mother had accompanied Ethan to clinic visits many times in the past and always appeared to be conscientious. The concern she showed at their last visit was entirely appropriate.

I looked up the results of Ethan's culture on the computer as I ate and confirmed he had a garden variety Strep infection that should have responded to the original antibiotic I'd prescribed. I wondered how often a pharmaceutical manufacturer made a bad batch. Although I'd read about that happening occasionally, this was the first time I had personally encountered such a possibility.

Next, I checked to see if Mingyu's lab results were back. They were, and they were more abnormal than previously. I called his doctor at UCSF to discuss my findings, and he scheduled Mingyu to be admitted to the hospital for evaluation the following day. If appropriate, he would talk to the transplant surgeon about scheduling Mingyu for a living donor transplant, assuming Ting passed all the criteria for donation.

Already late, I went to see my next patient in Room Five. The remainder of the day was hectic but unremarkable. I left around 6:00 p.m., satisfied I was caught up with my paperwork. When I reached my condominium building, I first went to pick up Maya from my in-laws. Ting was sitting on the couch, holding Mingyu. I thought this would be a good time to talk to her about bringing Mingyu to the hospital the next day and go over what to expect. The following weeks would be stressful at best.

Maya was playing quietly with Wang Shu, and Kang was crawling on top of the kitchen cabinets, just under the ceiling. I wasn't sure how he'd gotten up there, but as soon as he saw me, he held onto the top of the cabinet with his hands and lowered himself to the countertop below in one quick, smooth motion. *Exceptional strength for a kid his age. Or any age.* From there, he jumped down to the floor and stood at attention. I looked at Ting, expecting some sort of explanation.

"He thinks you don't like him to climb on things," Ting said. "He does it all the time when you are not around."

"I must have a reputation as a killjoy."

"No, nobody thinks you killed anyone," Ting answered.

"I said killjoy. It means someone who is very strict and doesn't like other people to have fun."

"I see. Well, he thinks you worry a lot about safety because you are a doctor."

"I think exercise is good, but it should be safe. It would be better for him to climb on bars in the playground. If he falls there, he'll land on something soft. If you can't stop him from climbing on your furniture and cabinets here, he should at least wear a helmet. Of course, he shouldn't do it at all."

"I tell him that, but he will not listen to me. Maybe he will listen to you."

I told Kang I wasn't mad at him, just concerned about his safety. He listened politely, but I'd been dealing with children for a long time and knew when they were going to ignore my advice. He was going to ignore my advice.

I asked Ting if she'd take a walk with me. I wanted to be away from everyone else when I discussed what was in store for her and Mingyu. The sun was low in the sky, and it was cool and breezy outside when we left the building. There weren't many people on the sidewalk, so it would be easy to have a conversation. We started walking in the direction of the San Francisco Bay, and I told Ting I'd arranged for Mingyu to be admitted to the hospital the next day for testing. They would probably try a few medications, but I suspected they would recommend the transplant we had been talking about for the past three and a half years.

While we walked, Ting appeared distracted, looking around as beads of sweat collected on her forehead despite the cool temperature. We stopped at an intersection for a moment before the light turned green. As I stepped into the street, Ting suddenly grabbed my arm, turned sharply to her left, and said, "Go this way."

Strange behavior. I didn't want to question her at this stressful time, so I turned as she directed. We finished our discussion as she led the way directly back to our building, walking quickly. Once inside, with the entry door closed behind us, Ting stopped and took in a few deep breaths. Her arms were shaking, and she was sweating profusely.

"I know it's a lot to take in, Ting, but you and Mingyu will be in the best of hands. As we've been saying over the past few years, Mingyu should start feeling much better when this is over. Please try not to be so nervous."

Ting stared at me, an incredulous expression on her face. "Did you not see?"

"See what?"

"That woman!"

"What woman?"

"The woman following us."

"No, I don't know what you're talking about." I wasn't sure which one of us was crazy.

"A woman followed us. She was very bad at following. Very obvious. She stopped following when I made a sudden turn."

"How do you know she was following us?"

"I just know. She's Chinese. Probably an assassin. She found us because of that stupid newspaper article."

"But she didn't do anything. She didn't try to kill you."

"She will wait for the right time. Maybe she wants to kill my children too. I don't know the exact plan, but I know she followed me. Next time I go out, I will bring a gun."

CHAPTER 6

That evening, I spoke to Lim about my fear that if Ting carried a gun, someone might get hurt—probably her. Lim said he would talk to her about it the next day.

Changing the subject, Lim told me he'd called Kang's school to complain about the newspaper article. He didn't want to stress the already beleaguered school system with a lawsuit but was angry at the breach of confidentiality. The principal expressed surprise at Lim's ire, thinking the family would be proud to have Kang featured in the paper. Nonetheless, he promised not to allow that again without permission.

The following morning, Lim left to help Ting check Mingyu into the hospital for his scheduled admission. My workday was fairly typical, other than Martha's nervous behavior. That evening, Lim told me Mingyu was in a private room, receiving medication to control some of the effects of his failing liver. Ting insisted on staying with him, and a cot was brought in for her to sleep on. Lim left for work after his sister and nephew seemed comfortable in their new surroundings.

"I think the surgery will be next week," he said, "as long as everything checks out with Ting's blood tests." He was silent for a moment as he checked his mail, appearing to stall for time. "One more thing. I couldn't talk her out of bringing her gun. I tried to remove it from her purse a couple of times, but she became so upset, I left it with her. For what it's worth, I checked, and the safety is on."

"That's not good enough. She can't have a gun in there. She might become suspicious of an Asian nurse or phlebotomist and decide to shoot them. I didn't see anyone following us yesterday when she became practically hysterical. She may be getting unstable under all this pressure."

"I know, I know. So I removed all her bullets." He smiled as he held up an oblong black object I recognized as a gun magazine. "I got the bullet out of the chamber, too, when she wasn't looking. She's going to be very mad at me when she finds out."

I hugged Lim. My hero. "Are you at all worried about her? What if someone actually is out there, trying to kill her and her kids?"

"I hired a security service. The same one you used when you came back from China and hid from assassins. She wouldn't give me permission, but I did it anyway. They won't let her see them."

I hugged Lim again. "Thank you, Amazing Husband. Is there a guard at the hospital now?"

"Yes, and I have one outside our building too. Anyone who tries to follow someone in without the passcode will be stopped. In the morning, security guards will follow my parents when they walk Kang and Wang Shu to school. They'll stand watch outside until my parents pick them up, then follow them home. Only my parents know, so the kids won't be alarmed."

*

Work the next day was uneventful until I received a call on my cell phone from California Analytics, the laboratory I'd sent the cephalexin capsules to. Luckily, I was between patients, so I ducked into an empty room and answered. The caller identified himself as one of the company scientists.

"I wanted to call you myself to explain my results. I tested all three of the Umbroz capsules, as well as the proprietary Keflex capsule."

"And?" I felt myself getting impatient, a quality of mine I was constantly trying to rein in, with varying success.

"The Keflex capsule had the antibiotic cephalexin in the amount expected. Each of the three Umbroz capsules, however, was deficient. None had more than twenty percent of the expected dose. They also had a small amount of a contaminant, N-nitrosodimethylamine or NDMA. It's a breakdown product, and has been loosely associated with cancer."

"Damn," I said. "That's terrible. One of my patients was taking that, so in addition to not getting the medication he needed, he was exposed to something dangerous."

"Since this is an antibiotic, I suspect he didn't take the medication for long."

"Only a few days."

"I wouldn't worry about the cancer risk, but, of course, he will need a different prescription."

"I already switched him, and he's doing fine. What do you think happened? Do you think this was a one-time event when something happened during the manufacture, ruining this batch of medication?"

"Doubt it. The discrepancy is so large, I think this company has some big issues. They may be taking shortcuts, maybe even faking some of the quality control reports. It's happened before with a few generic manufacturing companies, especially foreign ones, although it's been several years now since I've heard of any such incidents."

I thanked the scientist for his help and disconnected, feeling self-satisfied that I'd already changed Ethan's medication. I called our pharmacy to warn them against using Umbroz products in the future. After being transferred several times, someone on the staff told me I'd get a call back from the pharmacy director to discuss the matter.

When I returned home after work, I saw a casually dressed man standing by our building, talking on his cell. I recognized him as one of the security guards we'd had previously. I nodded to him, and he nodded back, smiling as he ended his call and put his phone in a pants pocket.

"You remember me?" I asked.

"Sure do. You and the rest of your group."

"Did you see anything unusual today?"

"Ask your husband." His answer would have alarmed me if he hadn't been shaking his head side to side and smiling.

When I walked into our condominium, I heard Maya playing a toy piano in her bedroom. Lim was seated at the kitchen table across from Kang, a solemn look on his face.

I thought the worst and worried that Ting, Mingyu, or Wang Shu had been killed, despite having seen the unconcerned-appearing guard in front of our building minutes earlier. "What's going on?" I asked.

"Kang brought home a letter from his school today," Lim said, looking at Kang sternly, his nephew squirming in his seat. "My parents couldn't read it, so they gave it to me."

"What's it about?"

"Kang has been climbing on the school building despite being warned multiple times not to."

"What do you mean—climbing on the school building?"

"Seems he's figured out how to climb up walls by grabbing onto things, like windows, trim—anything that sticks out." I could see Lim was trying to maintain a serious demeanor as he suppressed a smile. "I talked to one of the guards, and he told me Kang's been climbing on our building too."

"Why would you do that?" I asked, turning to Kang.

"It's called free climbing. Lots of people do it. You can check it out on YouTube."

"That's something for crazy people. It's very dangerous. You could get seriously injured," I said. I wasn't making it up. Several of my patients had suffered broken bones while attempting to perform such shenanigans.

"But I'm really good at it, and it's fun. I don't like playing sports with my friends anymore. They're all bad at everything. This is something I can do by myself."

I turned to Lim. "You've got to say something to him to make him stop."

"I want you to stop," Lim said, looking at Kang sternly. "I don't want to get any more letters from your school and no more climbing on our building. When your mom gets back, you can take it up with her. Meanwhile, how about I take you to a rock-climbing wall this weekend? There's a place not too far from here."

Kang smiled and hugged his uncle. "Thanks, Uncle Lim. That'd be really cool. Someday, you'll see, I'll free climb Half Dome."

"Not if I can help it," I said.

After Kang went back to his grandparents' unit, I turned to Lim. "He's a good kid, though I can see he's going to need an outlet for all his energy. I have a feeling rock climbing in a gym won't be much of a challenge for long."

"I was thinking the same thing."

CHAPTER 7

The next day started as usual with a variety of patients in the clinic. Still no big reveal from Martha. After lunch, she directed me to Room Five, where Lucas McGarrett and his older sister were waiting. I'd met the sister, Cassie, once before when she brought Lucas in for a routine checkup because Mrs. McGarrett had to tend to her ill husband. Cassie was an intelligent young woman, in graduate school at UCLA. Her brother, Lucas, was a sweet eight-year-old boy who I saw for annual physicals and the occasional scrapes and viral illnesses that visited most children. I checked the computer screen and saw one word, "nausea," written in the space allocated to Reason for Visit. *Should be easy. Check for dehydration. Tell his sister to feed him broth and other liquids until he improves, yadda yadda yadda.*

I entered the exam room with a smile. "Hello, Lucas," I said. Lucas was lying motionless in a fetal position on the exam table, dressed only in his underwear. Nothing like the talkative, rambunctious boy I was familiar with. "I understand you're not feeling well." I looked at his sister. "Cassie, how long has Lucas been feeling sick?"

"My mom says he's been sick about a week. Last night I came home for a few days to give her a hand with Dad. She didn't want to leave him, so she asked me to bring Lucas in."

"Why do you suppose your mom waited so long before having him seen?"

"He's so healthy, I'm sure she thought he'd get better. She's also been pretty preoccupied with my dad."

I approached Lucas and asked him to lie on his back. He flopped to a supine position, eyes closed. "When's the last time he ate?" I asked Cassie.

"Probably yesterday morning. Very unusual for him. He usually has a big appetite."

I asked Lucas to describe his symptoms but couldn't get more than a few words from him. "I feel sick," is all he would say.

I pried Lucas's lids open to look at his eyes, listened to his heart and lungs, and felt his abdomen. He winced when I pressed his upper right quadrant. It was becoming clear this wouldn't be a quick routine visit.

I sat in front of the computer and turned to Cassie as I typed. "I'm going to order some blood tests. While we're waiting for the results, I think it would be best to admit him to the hospital. There may be something wrong with his liver. His eyes look yellow, and his liver is slightly enlarged and tender. I see that he's had his hepatitis vaccines, so he probably doesn't have viral hepatitis."

"Then why would there be something wrong with his liver?"

"It's too early to tell. I should know more after we run some tests."

Cassie teared up.

"I wish I could tell you more right now. I'm afraid we'll have to wait for the test results. Meanwhile, we have reason to be optimistic. I'll call ahead to the hospital. Do you have a car here?"

"Yes, I drove."

"Great. You can drive him there yourself. They'll be expecting you. Do you think you can handle checking him in?"

"Not a problem. I had to check my dad into a hospital once."

"Call me if you have a problem. If I don't hear from you, I'll come by after I'm done in the clinic today to see him. We should have some information by then."

"Thank you, Doctor. I know both my parents would like to be there with him, but Dad's having such a hard time getting around these days. He's on oxygen now."

"I'm sorry to hear that. The hospital's probably not a good place for him anyway. He could catch pneumonia there, and he certainly doesn't need that to add to his troubles."

I left the room to arrange for Lucas's hospital admission.

"Is Lucas okay?" Martha asked.

Strange question. I had no reason to believe Martha was particularly fond of Lucas, as he wasn't what I would call one of our regulars. "I don't know. Right now, he needs to go to the hospital."

Martha started to ask me a follow-up question, but as I was behind, I simply said, "No time now." I headed off to see my next patient, a swollen ankle in Room Two.

When it was finally time for me to leave for the day, I noticed Martha deep in conversation with Jeremy. Neither was smiling—it looked like they were discussing something serious.

I walked to the hospital and found Lucas in the Pediatric ICU. I spoke to one of the doctors on duty, who explained that Lucas's tests indicated liver failure of unknown cause. A CT scan would be performed in the morning to rule out a tumor. He had already discussed this with Lucas's mom, who had arrived a half hour earlier.

Melinda McGarrity was at her son's bedside, in tears. "Cassie's home taking care of Roger," she said. "If I didn't have her, I couldn't go on. I don't know how much more I can take.

I've taken Ambien the past two nights so I could get some sleep. I can't seem to think straight because of the medication."

I put my arm around her shoulder to try to comfort her, but she was understandably inconsolable.

"We'll let you know as soon as we learn more." I checked Lucas's lab results on the computer, confirming that his liver was failing. Without more information, it was impossible to know what the cause was.

Before I left, I glanced around at the other beds. I noticed Rosa Mendoza was back, her aunt sitting at her bedside. Surprised to see her in the ICU again, I approached Rosa to find out why she'd been readmitted. Her aunt jumped up as soon as she saw me and started yelling.

"You stay away, Dr. Rosen. You cause nothing but trouble for my sister and our whole family. My sister was always a good mother for Rosa. Now she can't even see her daughter and must go to court. We have no money for a good lawyer. Now I have to take care of Rosa. I love my niece, but my house is small, and one of my girls has to share a bed with her. I know I gave Rosa the pills. Still, she had seizures. You don't believe my sister. Now what? Are you going to have me arrested too?"

"Are you saying Rosa is back in the hospital because she had more seizures?"

"That's right, Doctor. Now leave us alone."

All eyes in the ICU were on me as I reflected on Rosa's health, her family's predicament, and my role in it. A thought crossed my mind, one that hadn't occurred to me before.

"I know you're very mad at me, and I don't blame you," I said. "But I have an idea. Do you by any chance have Rosa's pills with you?"

"They're in my purse. Why?" Rosa's aunt stood, hands on hips, head tilted. She glared at me out of the corner of her eye.

"Can I see them?" I asked.

Rosa's aunt continued to stare at me. Without speaking, she conveyed a feeling of deep distrust.

"I have a hunch. It's only a hunch, but I would like to have your pills tested. They may be no good."

"No good? Whoever heard of such a thing?"

"I know they passed all the usual testing mandated by the government, but they could still be ineffective. I'm sorry I didn't believe your sister before. Now I believe both of you did give Rosa the pills. I would like to send them for analysis. If the test shows the pills don't have the right amount of medication, I will do all I can to make sure all charges are dropped against your sister, and she can take care of Rosa."

Rosa spoke up for the first time. "Give her the pills, Auntie. It could help Mom."

Rosa's aunt relaxed her posture and appeared to be mulling over her options. "Okay, what have I got to lose?" She reached into her purse and produced the carbamazepine pills.

With the bottle in my hand, my pulse quickened as I scanned the label for the manufacturer's name. I took in a deep breath as I read, "Umbroz." Although I had ignored that name the first time I'd seen it on Rosa's prescription bottle, this time it caught my attention. "I'll keep this bottle because you shouldn't give Rosa any more of these pills. When Rosa is discharged, insist on Tegretol pills, no generics. Let me know what they cost, and I'll pay you back."

"Do it Auntie," Rosa begged.

Rosa's aunt looked at me skeptically, but she agreed.

I stopped by the clinic that night to see if I could scrounge up a Tegretol pill, a known brand of carbamazepine. I looked through the stash of free samples we kept but didn't find any, so I called in a Tegretol prescription for myself at a neighborhood pharmacy near my house. On the way out, I checked Martha's desk to look at my patient list for the next day. Knowing who I'd be seeing would help me prepare mentally. I found the list and picked it up to read the names, noting my schedule was packed as usual.

Glancing at the desktop underneath, I spotted another patient list, different from the one I held in my hand. Included on that list was Lucas McGarrity, the boy I'd sent to the hospital earlier. An asterisk had been placed next to his name. The other names were patients I hadn't seen for a while. I found the list of names curious and wondered if their parents had called recently with a question or requested their records to be sent elsewhere. That explanation didn't make sense for Lucas unless the hospital had called in a request for information. I had a lot on my mind and filed that puzzling information in the dark recesses of my brain.

The following morning, before I started work, I picked up my Tegretol prescription and mailed two of the pills along with several Umbroz carbamazepine pills to my go-to chemical analysis company.

I took time away from my busy clinic schedule to check on Lucas's results. His liver tests remained abnormal, but fortunately his imaging study showed no evidence of a tumor. Viral hepatitis labs were pending, but I doubted they would be positive. He'd been vaccinated against hepatitis A and B and hadn't been exposed to a blood transfusion, a source of hepatitis C. He was scheduled for a liver biopsy the following morning.

I checked with Ting and learned she'd been cleared for surgery. The partial liver transplant, when a portion of her liver would be removed and transplanted into Mingyu, was scheduled for the following Tuesday. That evening I walked with my in-laws, Wang Shu, Kang, Maya, and Lim, to visit Ting and Mingyu in the hospital. Ting, finished with all her testing, was in Mingyu's room, dressed in street clothes. I noticed the bulge of a gun under her waistband, in the back. Not very conspicuous, I didn't think anyone would notice if they weren't looking for it.

Mingyu looked comfortable and more alert than the last time I'd seen him. I was glad the medication was helping, although that was a temporary fix, surgery being the only permanent solution. Ting was happy to have visitors. She congratulated Wang Shu on her excellent grades and being the fastest in her class in the fifty-yard dash. Not a stupendous sprinter, she was still better than her peers by a small margin. Her athletic abilities were heartening—she'd gotten them the old-fashioned way, by direct inheritance from her parents, both Olympic athletes.

After Ting finished congratulating Wang Shu, she commended Kang for his good grades. Then, speaking in Chinese, which Lim translated to me later, she ordered Kang to obey all the school rules and never climb on any buildings. "She also told him to stop climbing on the cabinets in their kitchen," Lim said, "but I don't think he's going to obey her. That kid needs more discipline."

"Let's hope taking him rock climbing helps," I said.

After our visit, Lim stopped to talk to a muscular man seated near the nursing station, with a clear view of Mingyu's room. On the walk back home, Lim explained the man was one of the bodyguards he'd hired. The guard had seen no suspicious activity. I suspected Ting's paranoia was unfounded. If only I could be sure.

CHAPTER 8

The subsequent morning, Saturday, Lim and I were enjoying our morning coffee while reading the paper. When I looked out our window facing the bay bridge, I screamed. Lim turned around to see what had alarmed me. There was Kang, smiling at us through our third-floor window.

Lim carefully opened the window and pulled his nephew inside. Such yelling in Chinese I'd never heard before. I figured there was a lot of cursing. He marched Kang down to my in-laws' condo and came back fuming.

"I think he needs attention, especially now that his mother isn't around. Maybe I can find a good psychologist for him," I said.

"No psychologist. He needs to learn he can't go around peeking in people's windows. And he needs a good place to burn up some of his energy. Probably a good thrashing too. I know, I know—you don't believe in such things in this country." Lim thought for a moment, then added, "I'm going to talk to our security people. They need to stop Kang from climbing on our building."

"I thought you were going to take him rock climbing. I know this isn't a good time, with everything else that's going on, but Kang needs to be reined in before he's hurt."

"Let me think about it," Lim said before ensconcing himself in his office to make phone calls and prepare financial spreadsheets for investors in his company. For me, the hours went by slowly. I was impatient, waiting for the results of Rosa's medication analysis. There was also the question of Lucas's mysterious liver disease. He would have his liver biopsy soon, but I wouldn't learn anything about it until Monday at the earliest.

Shortly before noon, Lim emerged to tell me he was going downstairs to get Kang and take him to a nearby rock climbing gym.

"I hope this cures him of his need to climb on buildings," he said as he left, grabbing the backpack containing water bottles we kept by the front door for emergencies.

"Fingers crossed."

I hoped rock climbing would be a good experience for Kang. Just seven years old, I didn't want his pride damaged if he wasn't able to perform as well as others. I figured most of the climbers would be repeat customers, and much better than him. If Lim brought him there regularly, Kang would surpass many of them in no time.

While I was mulling that over, Daisy called to let me know she'd made reservations for dinner at Kokkari Estiatorio. I'd almost forgotten we'd made plans to have dinner together that evening but was glad we had. With Ting and Mingyu in the hospital, having a fun evening out would be a good diversion. The restaurant was a good choice as Arvid, even with his strange Danish palate, enjoyed the well-prepared Greek food there, and Lim found it tolerable, usually ordering fish.

Three hours after he left, Lim was back from the rock-climbing gym. I was full of questions.

"How'd it go?" I asked. "I hope Kang didn't feel embarrassed."

"Kang? Embarrassed? Hardly."

"Did he enjoy it?"

"At first he wanted to leave. He said it looked like someone had hurled chunks of barf onto the concrete rocks." Lim chuckled. "I told him to keep his voice down, it didn't look like vomit at all, but to be honest, I thought it did."

I couldn't help but laugh, knowing how uncomfortable Lim must have felt trying to convince his nephew the rocks looked legitimate. "You got him to climb, though, didn't you?"

"Eventually, after he almost got us thrown out."

"Damn. What happened?"

"They required him to wear a harness. Kang, of course, thought that was beneath him and refused."

"And?"

"I finally convinced him he'd better do it their way, or he'd have to help his grandma cook dinner every night for a month."

"Did that work?"

"He hates to cook, so he swallowed his pride, put on a harness, and climbed to the top of the tallest peak. It took him almost no time. People noticed, and a crowd formed around him. He loved it, but after he'd practically run up the hill three times, he was bored. Then I had the brilliant idea to make it more difficult by having him wear the backpack I brought. Even that was no problem for him."

"Not exactly what I expected. Do you think he'll want to go back?"

"Let me finish."

"Don't tell me he got hurt!" I instinctively raised my hands to the sides of my face.

"No, he didn't. After he climbed up carrying the water bottles, someone brought over a stack of books he was going to return to the library. Must have weighed at least 15 kilograms—that's about thirty-five pounds. He put those in the backpack."

My eyes were probably wide open when I asked, "Was he able to climb with those on board?"

"Not only did he climb to the top almost as quickly as he did with no weight on his back, but he had managed to slip the harness off before he did it."

"Oh, no! How could you let him?"

"He's pretty sneaky—caught me off guard. He got up and down the mountain without a problem. Only thing is—"

"What?"

Lim couldn't help but smile. "Only thing is, they told him he could never come back."

We both started laughing. I could tell Lim wasn't mad. Deep down, he was proud of Kang. Still, we hadn't come up with a plan to control his behavior. He needed more discipline than his uncle could occasionally mete out.

I told Lim we were having dinner with Daisy and Arvid that evening, and I sensed he was eager to tell them about his nephew's latest escapade.

At 7:00 p.m., Lim and I brought Maya to my in-laws' unit. Our daughter looked forward to spending an evening with Kang, Wang Shu, and her grandparents. Lim and I met Daisy and Arvid outside our building, and we walked to the restaurant, about twenty minutes away. I noticed homeless people settling in for the night against buildings, often in the doorways of closed businesses. It was a sight I didn't usually see in my immediate neighborhood. However, in many areas of my beloved city, as rents skyrocketed, the number of people living on the street had multiplied. This was a major thorn in the side of our mayor and the city council and was an important issue in local elections. Lim always carried five-dollar bills for these people, as did Arvid. They took turns dropping money into the collection cups and cans these unfortunate souls had set out, but only donated to about a quarter of those we saw, not wanting to make that the focus of our walk.

We discussed some of Daisy and Arvid's challenges in planning the wedding to Daisy's parents' satisfaction. When we were a few minutes from our destination, Arvid started us off on what had become a tradition of ours. We'd observed waitstaff making annoying assumptions about us almost every time the four of us dined together and had taken to betting on when it would occur. "Who wants to take the first fifteen minutes?" he asked.

"I do," I said without hesitation.

"Damn you, Rosen," Daisy said. "I wanted that one."

"You can have the second fifteen," Arvid said.

"Okay, then I'll bet on everything after a half hour," Lim said.

"And, as usual, I'll bet it never happens," Arvid said.

"You're such an optimist," Lim said. "Don't you ever get tired of losing?"

We reached the restaurant and were seated at a rectangular table, Lim and I sitting next to each other on one side, Daisy and Arvid on the other, with me facing Arvid. After a short discussion, we ordered wine. As we waited for our bottle of Santorini, I looked around the room, appreciating its tastefully understated elegance. I enjoyed peeking at the dishes others were eating, trying to figure out which menu items they corresponded to.

Soon, the wine was poured at our table, and my attention turned to the dinner menu. Lim and I decided to share the fish entrée. Our waiter arrived to take our orders, starting with me.

"I'll be sharing the fish entre with my husband, but I want to start with the dolmathes appetizer," I said. "I don't know what my husband wants to begin with."

As I handed my menu to our server, he turned to Arvid and asked, "And what appetizer would you like before the fish, sir?"

Arvid looked up from the menu and said, "I'm not having the fish."

"Excuse me, sir. The lady said you'd be sharing the fish—"

"I'm not her husband," Arvid said. "He is." Arvid nodded toward Lim.

Our server's face turned red as Lim said, "I can understand your confusion. You obviously thought my wife was much too beautiful to be married to someone like me." Lim squeezed my hand under the table as he spoke. "I'll be having the small Horiatiki salad before the fish."

"Very good, sir," the waiter said before blustering his way through taking the other orders. When he had finished and was out of earshot, we all burst out laughing.

"You're the clear winner, Rosen," Daisy said. "Barely over ten minutes. Now you get to pick the restaurant next time."

"Damn," Arvid said. "I'd like to win just once."

I think each of us secretly enjoyed watching people's reactions when finding out who was with whom when the four of us went out together. People assumed the two Caucasians, Arvid and I, were a couple, as were the two Asians, Daisy and Lim. I couldn't think of one time anyone thought I was with Lim and Daisy was with Arvid.

Our dinner was delicious as usual, and the conversation lively, filled with talk of Kang's rock-climbing adventure and, of course, wedding planning horror stories. Fortunately, neither Daisy nor Arvid was overly concerned about the wedding details. I had the feeling that if the caterer were to back out at the last minute, Daisy and Arvid would be happy to order from McDonald's. My best friend's parents, however, were a different story. All of Daisy and Arvid's preparations were aimed at pleasing them. I looked forward to the date in two weeks when Daisy and I planned to try on dresses in the bridal department at Nordstrom.

As we were settling the bill, I saw a foursome I hadn't noticed before leaving the restaurant. I recognized one of the men as Dr. Jeremy Nilsen. When he put his arm affectionately around the smartly-dressed woman next to him, I nearly gasped. *Should I tell Martha? She'll be so disappointed. Maybe I should hold off. After all, she hasn't confided anything to me. On the other hand, I'd like to spare her any heartache . . .* Moments later, the object of Jeremy's affection, whose back had been toward me, turned her head. I was stunned to see it was none other than Martha. I smiled to myself. Martha didn't need my help at all. In a flash, I realized it all made sense. She and Jeremy needed to keep their relationship secret as there are rules against intradepartmental romances.

When we exited the restaurant, I noticed Martha and Jeremy on foot about a block down the street. The other couple they'd been with, an attractive blonde woman and a tall, sandy-haired man, were waiting at the valet stand. Moments later, the valet drove up in an expensive-looking, road-hugging yellow sports car. The man who had been with Martha and Jeremey tipped the valet, and I watched out of the corner of my eye as he and the woman got in and drove off.

Sunday, I invited Ting to take a walk with me so I could answer questions she might have about the upcoming surgeries, namely the removal of a portion of her liver and the subsequent transplantation of it into Mingyu. Although I didn't have expertise in that area, I could answer general questions. At first, she refused to leave Mingyu's side for a walk but agreed when Lim offered to sit with him while she left the hospital for the first time in days.

We'd gone two blocks when I heard footsteps running toward us from behind, then a struggle. I turned to see the bodyguard who had been stationed at the hospital holding a diminutive Asian woman fighting to break herself free. She looked sickly and weak, hardly a threat, as she yelled words in Chinese.

Ting yelled back at her angrily in Chinese, the woman responding in a quieter tone, while our protector maintained a tight grip on her. Ting didn't draw her gun, as the bodyguard had the situation controlled. After several more exchanges, Ting became teary-eyed, walked to the woman, and hugged her.

"He is okay," she said to the guard. "Let her go."

Confused, I said, "Ting, this must be the person who was following you before. She could be dangerous. Why do you want to let her go?"

"This is Mei. He is not dangerous. He wants to talk to me about Mingyu. Mei found me after he heard about the newspaper article with Kang's picture. He followed me before but was afraid to talk until today. Mei has a son like Mingyu, with a failing liver, but he is in China. Mei was forced to have genetically engineered children like me. Her son is six months older than Mingyu, and now he is dying, but the Chinese government is no help. Mei heard rumors about me in China. She heard my children are okay, living in San Francisco. He came here to look for me and see if I can help. I told her Mingyu will get a new liver. It is the only hope."

The guard released his grasp on Mei, who spoke to Ting some more. After Mei nodded her head in agreement, Ting turned to me. "I told her to go with you. Give her some food. Now he understands what he must do. He will go back to China and try to get a liver transplant for her son."

I wondered how many other children there were like Mingyu still in China, doomed to die from liver failure as the government turned a blind eye. We returned to the hospital, where Ting said goodbye to Mei.

"Take this," Ting said to me quietly. In her hand was a gun. "I almost made a mistake and shot Mei. I don't need this anymore. Not with a bodyguard."

"That was a good decision," I said. "You need training to be safe." I grabbed the weapon and shoved it into my purse. I was relieved Ting would never have to learn Lim had removed the magazine. Even knowing the gun had no ammunition, I felt uneasy having it in my possession.

Accompanied by the security detail, Ting entered the building to resume her place by Mingyu and sent Lim downstairs to meet me. She did not object to the presence of the bodyguard.

Once I saw Lim exit the hospital, I handed him Ting's gun. He walked with Mei and me to our condominium. There we gave her food, and she spoke to Lim for several hours. We invited her to spend the night, but she insisted on leaving, wanting to return to China as soon as possible.

Monday morning started like any other beginning of a week. I went through a backlog of lab results and checked my schedule. Another busy day. Martha directed me to Room Eleven for my first patient.

"How was your weekend?" I asked.

"It was fine," was all the information forthcoming.

"I'm pretty sure I saw you with a handsome hunk last Saturday at Kokkari's," I said.

Martha's face turned red. "Am I in trouble?"

"Don't be silly," I said, smiling. "I'm happy for you and don't plan to tell anyone. As long as you don't tell me Dr. Nilsen has used his position as a superior in the workplace to pressure you to go out with him."

"Hardly," Martha said, smiling, her face still red.

In the middle of examining the first patient after lunch, my cell phone rang. I excused myself to take the call from California Analytics. I walked to my office as I spoke to the same chemist I'd talked to before.

"Looks like another bad batch of pills. There's very little carbamazepine detectable in the Umbroz pills, less than a third of what there should be. The Tegretol you sent as a control came in on target."

The news wasn't unexpected, but I felt overwhelmed. I realized the histrionics displayed by Rosa's mother were genuine, not intended to bring attention. I had been dead wrong about her. She just happened to be more emotional than most. "Looks like this company has a problem," I said.

"No question about it."

"I'm not sure what my next step should be."

"I've been doing this a while. About ten years ago, I came across something similar. I evaluated samples made by an Indian generic manufacturer, and they tested well below the advertised levels. A physician, like you, had become suspicious about the medication's potency and notified the FDA after we analyzed the pills. I don't know what happened after that. I never heard from the FDA myself, so I suspect the whole thing got buried."

"Once I get your report, I'll notify the FDA. I won't let them ignore me. This company is too dangerous to continue unabated."

"I'll have my report emailed to you by the end of the day."

I rushed back to my patient and finished up. I was behind as usual but took time before the next appointment to phone Rosa Mendoza's home.

I spoke to Mrs. Mendoza, who had recently raised the money for bail. Upon hearing my voice, she yelled and threatened to hang up. I didn't blame her but was able to interrupt her tirade and explain my findings. After apologizing profusely, I assured her I believed she was an extraordinary mother and had taken excellent care of her daughter.

Rosa's mom gave me the name and phone number of her court-appointed attorney. After I explained everything to the public defender, she assured me she'd request having all the charges against her client dropped, including assault of the police officer. I offered my help should the district attorney's office contact me. Satisfied Mrs. Mendoza would be vindicated, I wondered about Umbroz. *Was anyone else aware they were making substandard drugs?* Not having time to think about it more, I saw my next patient.

CHAPTER 9

After a series of sore throats, vomiting, and pink eye, I was hurrying to see my next patient when I noticed Cassandra Roberts and her father heading to an exam room. Cassandra, a delightful nine-year-old girl, had been a regular patient of mine for at least three years. Usually energetic and bubbly, she appeared sluggish in the few seconds I observed her walking. She was holding onto her dad's arm, seemingly in need of support. I didn't recall seeing her name on my patient list for the day. I took a detour and swung by the front desk area to determine which doctor was scheduled to see her.

"Why that would be Dr. Nilsen," the receptionist said.

I was hurt and surprised as I mulled over the reasons Cassandra's parents might have requested to change doctors. "Do you know why Cassandra is seeing Dr. Nilsen instead of me?" I asked.

The receptionist seemed flustered. "I thought you requested it," she said. "That's what Dr. Nilsen said. He said you were so busy you wanted him to help you out by taking some of your load."

I thanked her and walked away calmly while seething under my skin. *What does he think he's doing? We're all salaried, so it's not as if he'll get paid extra by seeing more patients. Is he trying to undermine me? Does he want to take my place as head of the clinic?*

I thought about what I might say to Jeremy as I went from patient to patient, and ultimately decided to hold off. Maybe he thought he was doing me a favor, not that I ever complained to him about being overworked. I would tell him diplomatically that I didn't need to offload any of my patients.

Before entering the room for my last appointment of the day, Martha grabbed me and said the pharmacy director was on the phone. She followed me to a nearby extension and instructed me how to pick it up, as if I didn't know. All she had to do was tell me which line he was on. Martha remained in close proximity, seeming to keep busy shuffling papers. I noticed her talking quietly on her cell phone briefly, then holding her phone up, facing me. I had the feeling she wanted to record my call or hold the phone so someone else could listen to my end of the conversation. I wondered if I was becoming paranoid as I turned my back to her.

"I wanted you to know I have discovered severe deficiencies in two medications made by the generic drug manufacturer, Umbroz," I said to the pharmacy director.

"That company has a sterling reputation, and their prices are significantly lower than the competition."

"The drugs may be less expensive, but that doesn't help our patients if they don't work. I sent samples of their cephalexin and carbamazepine to a chemical analysis company, and they found the active ingredients to be much lower than they should be. One also had a contaminant which is a possible carcinogen."

"I'm sure the company you used isn't authorized by our system, so I have no reason to trust those results. I don't think you understand what a hardship it is for our patient population to pay for expensive drugs, and for our health system to subsidize costs for those who cannot afford them."

I felt my face turn red as I tried to control my urge to shout at this jerk. "Of course, I'm aware of all that, but I also want my patients to get the best treatment possible. Using substandard medications doesn't square with that."

"I'm finding your attitude quite inappropriate, Doctor. All the companies we use are properly vetted."

"I'm sure the chemist who analyzed the pills would be happy to explain his findings. He's a very smart Ph.D. chemist."

"We're not going to change our pharmacy list because of the opinion of one chemist not in our employ."

As pissed off as I was, it was clear I wasn't going to get anywhere with this fool. I couldn't wait to get a letter off to the FDA.

I planned to miss work the following day, so after the clinic closed, I caught up on my emails and went over all the lab results that had come in. When finished, I rushed home to join Maya, Lim, and the rest of the family to visit Mingyu and Ting in the hospital. The surgery to remove part of Ting's liver was scheduled for the following morning, with Mingyu's transplant to follow. Our visit lasted over an hour, Mingyu sleeping most of the time.

Ting was looking forward to the whole process being over so she could get home and return to what had become her normal life of work and taking care of her children. We didn't speak about Kang's recent obsession with climbing on buildings or his experience at the rock-climbing gym. Instead, we focused on how well both Kang and Wang Shu were doing in school, Daisy and Arvid's upcoming wedding, and Lim's company. As we were leaving the hospital room, a man wearing surgical scrubs entered, nodded to us politely, and began talking to Ting. I reasoned Ting must have met him previously, as he wasn't met with her usual suspicion and nametag inspection. On the way out, Lim checked with the bodyguard on duty, who assured him he hadn't seen anything unusual.

The next morning, Maya and I walked Kang and Wang Shu to school, while Lim went to the hospital with his parents to wait for progress reports during the surgery.

When we got home, Maya wanted to play. After a few games of Candyland and Go Fish, I took out our basket filled with Play-Doh, stencils, and plastic tools. As Maya entertained herself making animals, I composed a letter to the FDA describing in detail my experience with two Umbroz products, cephalexin and carbamazepine. I demanded they be removed from circulation and insisted on an immediate investigation. I addressed the letter to the director of their Center for Drug Evaluation and Research, whose name I found on the FDA website.

As if he'd been watching me, Lim called as soon as I finished printing the letter. Ting was out of surgery and was doing well. A portion of the left lobe of her liver had been successfully removed, and the transplant to Mingyu had begun. It would be at least four hours until they were done. I breathed a sigh of relief. At least Ting's surgery was over. I needed to keep my mind occupied until Mingyu was out of the operating room.

Curious about Cassandra Roberts, I logged into the UCSF VPN to see if there were any notes or lab results of significance in her electronic health record. To my surprise, not only did she have lab results, but they were alarming. She tested positive for infectious mononucleosis, but this was no ordinary case. Cassandra's liver studies were markedly abnormal, and her blood counts were low.

Although proper protocol would dictate otherwise, I wasn't going to let that stand in my way. I needed to call Cassandra's parents and tell them to take their daughter to the hospital. I found their home phone number in the chart and dialed. I got a "this number is no longer in service" message. *Damn.*

I called Martha and asked if she had an updated number for Cassandra. "Sorry, they moved and got a new landline, but I didn't enter it into the chart yet. I'll take care of that as soon as we hang up. Why do you need it? I don't remember her coming in to see you recently."

"Her mom asked me about something a while back, and I didn't have time to answer her until now." That was the best lie I could come up with on such short notice. It was unusual for Martha to ask why I was calling a patient's parents, and I found her statement worded peculiarly. "I don't remember her coming in *to see you* recently." As if she knew Cassandra had been to the clinic but had seen another doctor. I disconnected the call as soon as I got the phone number.

I called Cassandra's home and wasted no time in telling her father to bring Cassandra to the hospital so she could be taken care of by the doctors there. Then I arranged for her to be admitted and ordered infectious disease and hematology consultants. By the time I'd finished, my muscles were tense, and my heart was pounding. If Dr. Nilsen was miffed because I insinuated myself into his case, tough.

Seemingly right on cue, Maya brought me a blue Play-Doh cat. "You look sad, Mommy. I made this kitty to make you feel better."

I took the cat and placed it on the desk, then grabbed Maya and hugged her. "Thank you, sweetheart. You're such a tonic."

"Is that good?"

"It's very good. It means you make me feel better."

"I'll make Mingyu a cat, so he feels better too."

"Can't hurt."

I fixed us a light dinner, then played a game of Lotto with Maya. I'd been checking the clock every five minutes when Lim finally called. Mingyu was out of surgery. It had taken longer than anticipated due to excess bleeding, but the transplant was a success. I told Maya the wonderful news and played music from her favorite artist, Raffi, to celebrate. When the excitement wore off, I tucked her in bed and waited for Lim to come home. I barely noticed, hours later, being picked up off the couch and carried to bed.

For the first time in quite a while, I woke up before Lim. I let him sleep as I made coffee and tied Maya's shoes. She was old enough to pick out her clothes and get dressed independently, except for the shoe tying. When I placed a cup of black coffee next to Lim's bed, he opened his eyes.

"How is everything?" I asked.

"Couldn't be better. I stayed until Ting and Mingyu were awake. The doctors assured me both were recovering as expected. I'll take Maya, my parents, Wang Shu, and Kang to the hospital later after they sleep in. No school for them today. You can go ahead and leave for work. I'll call you if anything changes."

I left for work despite feeling a tinge of guilt for not visiting with the rest. The clinic needed me, and I knew my presence at the hospital wouldn't help either Ting or Mingyu recover. The family would probably feel more comfortable without me—they'd be free to let the Mandarin fly without Lim feeling the need to translate for me.

On my way to the clinic, I mailed the letter for next-day delivery to the FDA, hoping for a quick reply. Once at my desk, I checked my schedule. My first patient, a four-year-old, was in for a routine physical. The remainder of patients that day were simple, with no serious illnesses. Lim called me a few times to tell me both Ting and Mingyu were doing well. I planned to visit them that evening but had a few loose ends to tie up before leaving. The clinic was empty when I got around to looking up the labs and hospital notes on my inpatients, Cassandra and Lucas, before I left.

Checking on Lucas first, I learned his doctors, including a liver consultant, had no exact diagnosis for him. Miraculously, his most recent liver tests showed some improvement despite no specific treatment. The liver biopsy had revealed non-specific inflammation and tissue damage. All viral studies were negative, leading the liver specialist to suspect a toxin.

Despite detailed questioning, she hadn't discovered a potential source of exposure to harmful chemicals. In an effort to find the cause of Lucas's illness, she ordered blood samples sent to various labs to test for unusual toxins. So far, all results had been negative, but a few were still pending. Lucas was feeling better, and if he continued to improve, the doctor planned to discharge him in a few days. The news was so good, I wished there was someone else still in the clinic I could high five.

Cassandra wasn't so lucky. She was deteriorating, her lab results becoming more abnormal with time. A hematology consultant suspected a rare disease called severe chronic active Epstein-Barr virus, or EBV, infection of T-and NK-cell type, systemic form. This is a serious, sometimes lethal, condition. A bone marrow biopsy was scheduled for the following day.

I decided to call the parents of both patients before leaving. I was sure they had spoken to the doctors taking care of their children in the hospital, yet I always found parents appreciated speaking to a doctor they'd had a longer relationship with, someone they trusted and felt was less intimidating when it came to asking questions. I called Lucas's mom first and discussed the good progress of her son. She had quite a few questions which I answered, explaining that as long as Lucas was never exposed to the putative toxin again, he would likely recover and do well. If the offending chemical weren't identified, she should be alert to the early signs of liver damage. If the toxin was in her home, she and her husband were also at risk of becoming ill, so they should be on the lookout for early symptoms. She thanked me and left me feeling satisfied.

I looked up Cassandra's home number in her chart and called. When I reached another "this number is no longer in service" message, I checked the number in the electronic chart again and confirmed I had dialed correctly. *Damn. Martha's been so preoccupied with her new boyfriend, she forgot to update her chart.* Unfortunately, although I had spoken to Cassandra's dad on my cell phone the day before, I had erased the number I'd gotten directly from Martha.

I went to Martha's desk to search for what I needed. I didn't find Cassandra's home phone number, but my conversation with her parents could wait since she was being well cared for in the hospital. While rummaging through the papers on Martha's desk, however, I found the strange patient list again, the list I'd seen the week before with the asterisk next to Lucas's name. Now there were asterisks next to additional names: Cassandra Roberts and Ryan Farooqi. I knew Cassandra was seriously ill. Was Ryan Farooqui also ill?

CHAPTER 10

Ryan was a twelve-year-old boy who had been my patient since he and his family moved to San Francisco four years earlier. Tall for his age, he was active and fearless. For him, that wasn't a good thing—he seemed to be accident-prone, and over the last few years, I'd seen him for numerous cuts and sprains, as well as a broken tibia. The latter was the result of a friend daring him to ride his skateboard down one of San Francisco's super steep streets, the kind of street the city is famous for. I wondered if Martha had forgotten to give me a message that he had been treated in the emergency room for another injury.

I logged into the electronic medical record and discovered Ryan had been seen in the clinic earlier that day by Jeremy. I hadn't seen Ryan, but that wasn't surprising—many patients come to see other doctors and leave without my seeing them. I wondered if his parents had wanted a new doctor for him or if Jeremy had again routed one of my patients to himself. Ryan had come to the clinic with a chief complaint of malaise and abdominal pain. I considered the possibility that one of his buddies had challenged him to eat Tide pods. Reading further, a brief note read: Abdominal mass. Admitted to UCSF Pediatric ICU.

I immediately called Ryan's home, where Mrs. Farooqi answered. A tall, dignified woman, Ryan's mother didn't speak English well, and I often relied on Ryan or a Farsi translator to communicate with her. She was clearly distraught and managed to tell me the staff had changed her appointment with me to a new doctor, Dr. Nilsen. Ryan had been feeling ill for a week, lying in bed, and refusing to eat. The doctor had told her Ryan had a "little lump" in his belly and would probably be okay. To be sure, he wanted Ryan to go to the hospital.

"Do you still want me to be his doctor, or do you want Dr. Nilsen to remain in charge? It's okay if you want Dr. Nilsen."

After a long pause, Mrs. Farooqui said, "I want you to be his doctor, yes. I don't trust Dr. Nilsen. I thought maybe you didn't want Ryan to be your patient."

"No, that's not the case at all. I will be checking on him while he's in the hospital. Do you understand?"

I knew Mrs. Farooqui had a lot on her mind. Her husband had brittle type I diabetes and had suffered just about every complication associated with it. He was now on dialysis, awaiting a kidney transplant. After another long pause, Mrs. Farooqui answered, "Yes, I understand. I use Google translate."

I checked Ryan's hospital chart and noted the ICU doctors had ordered labs and an MRI for the morning. I was left wondering if Dr. Nilsen was incompetent. I'd never thought that before, but what Ryan had seemed like a lot more than a trivial "little lump."

After I hung up, I couldn't help but wonder what was going on. I now had more enigmatic, seriously ill patients at one time than I remembered ever having. *Was it a coincidence the names of all three of these patients, Lucas, Cassandra, and Ryan, had asterisks by their names on a list Martha was keeping?* The timing for this mystery couldn't have been worse. I was already dealing with the stress of Ting's and Mingyu's surgeries, Kang seemingly on his way to becoming a juvenile delinquent, my husband starting a new company, and me planning to undergo IVF again. Still, I couldn't let my patients down. They needed the best care I could give them. I had to focus separately on my patients and my personal issues.

That evening I visited Ting and Mingyu in the hospital, joining the rest of the family members. Both patients were doing well. Ting was seated in a wheelchair in Mingyu's room when I arrived. I could already detect Mingyu's improvement. Despite the pain medication being delivered intravenously, he said more words in fifteen minutes than I remembered him saying in all of the previous month.

Mingyu's transplant surgeon came by to check on him and went over the latest labs with me, which were much improved. He assured me Mingyu was tolerating the immune suppressant drugs he was taking and reiterated that he would need to take them for the rest of his life to avoid rejection of the transplant. The surgeon hoped a lot could be learned from Mingyu's misfortune. UCSF being a noted center for research, there were at least five groups of scientists dividing up the damaged liver removed from him. Such a liver had never been available for study and probably never would be again, as the mutation causing Mingyu's condition had never been described before.

Shortly after the surgeon left, the man in scrubs I'd seen enter Mingyu's hospital room before the surgery came by. Ting introduced us to Dr. Ron Yee, Mingyu's anesthesiologist. He asked Mingyu how he was feeling, then kneeled next to Ting and spoke quietly to her for a few moments, presumably asking how she was doing. Upon standing up to leave, he grabbed Ting's shoulder in a familiar way. I thought it strange but not entirely inappropriate. After all, he wasn't Ting's doctor. He seemed awkward as he waved to us, bowing slightly as he left. Ting was smiling.

I left the hospital with the other visitors. My in-laws took Kang and Wang Shu to their condominium, while Lim, Maya, and I had a quiet late dinner together in our unit. Maya was filled with questions about Mingyu, which I answered as well as I could. I was relieved I didn't need to have a serious death talk with her. Ting and Mingyu were expected to be discharged from the hospital in about a week if all went well. Wang Shu and Kang were planning to go back to school the next day, Lim was ready to return to his usual work schedule, and Maya was scheduled to stay with grandma and grandpa. Life for us would return to normal as much as possible while we awaited the return of Ting and Mingyu.

The next day, after the usual morning routine at home, I found the semblance of normalcy comforting. I breezed through my first five patients at the clinic, an assortment of injuries and gastrointestinal disorders, noting with increasing irritation Martha's quiet discussions with Dr. Nilsen.

I usually ignored the goings-on at the front desk, where parents check their children in. Typically, the two receptionists check patients in quickly and quietly. Occasionally I might hear voices raised when a disgruntled parent was asked to bring the child's insurance information next time or was told the doctor was behind, and they would have to wait longer than usual. As I was on my way to see my next patient, I couldn't avoid overhearing a loud argument between a mother I was familiar with, Mrs. Reinhold, and one of the receptionists.

"My appointment is with Dr. Rosen, and I want to see her."

"I understand, but it's been changed in the system. Perhaps Dr. Rosen is too busy to see you. I don't know the reason, ma'am. Now you are scheduled to see Dr. Nilsen. He's an excellent doctor, so I can assure you, your daughter will get the best care."

"I don't care about your damn schedule. I want to see her regular doctor, Dr. Rosen. I will wait here until she's available."

I'd always known Mrs. Reinhold to be a caring, intelligent woman. A single mother who suffered from rheumatoid arthritis, she was savvy when it came to maneuvering through the various obstacles in the health care system that had been thrown her way. Despite being on the newest biologics for her condition, she suffered daily from the damage to her joints, walking with difficulty, even while aided by a cane.

Her daughter, Skylar, was an adorable ten-year-old who had a proclivity for picking up random gastrointestinal disorders from her classmates, seeming to alternately affect one of the two ends of the food tube. Her office visits usually didn't take long. I was unaware an appointment with her had been changed to Dr. Nilsen. I'd made no indication about being too busy to see her. Whatever the reason for this inexplicable rescheduling of Skylar, I needed to set things straight. Jeremy was seeing a patient, so I decided to question Martha instead. I suspected she was behind my patients being siphoned off to him. Perhaps she thought that by doing so, her beloved might advance to clinic director.

Mrs. Reinhold was banging the floor loudly with her cane when I found Martha. I interrupted Martha's conversation with Jeremy's assistant and asked about the change in Skylar Reinhold's appointment. I'd never seen Martha's face turn such a bright color of red.

"I . . . I don't know how that happened," she said.

"Things like that don't just happen," I answered. I was trying not to show my anger but was losing my patience with her slinking around with Jeremy and his assistant and the occasional job performance lapses of late. More importantly, I was starting to lose my trust in her,

"Well, you are busy today. Maybe it would be best if you just let Dr. Nilsen see Skylar."

"Not a chance in hell," I said. "I want to see her after I finish in Room Twelve."

"But the next—"

"I don't care. Skylar Reinhold after Room Twelve." I walked off to see my next patient before Martha could say another word. Sadly, my relationship with her had just taken a substantial downward turn.

I was able to take care of the patient in Room Twelve quickly. When I finished, I found Martha. She looked tense as she directed me to Room Ten, her voice shaking.

I entered the room to see Skylar sitting in a chair with her head in her hands, her mother in the adjacent chair. Checking the computer, I learned that Skylar had a temperature of 102, an elevated heart rate, and low blood pressure.

"Look at her, Doctor. I wanted you to see this. My daughter is very sick." I detected anger in Mrs. Reinhold's voice.

"She looks very uncomfortable," I said. "Headache?"

"Headache, fever, and cough. She's been sick for over a week and seems to be getting worse. I knew something was wrong when she was too exhausted to tend to her garden. She loves gardening. For the last week, she's been too tired to go to school. And now, look at her arm. I saw this for the first time this morning." Mrs. Reinhold held up one of Skylar's arms, revealing several skin nodules and areas of ulceration.

Skylar coughed several times, then moaned.

I turned to Mrs. Reinhold. "I understand why you're so upset. Skylar seems to be quite ill. Can you tell me when this all started?"

"Hard to say, exactly. It came on so slowly. I can't help but think it's all because of those pills you started her on."

My mind drew a blank. I didn't remember prescribing any medication for Skylar. Maybe the stress I was under was causing me to forget things. That hadn't happened to me before, and I'd soldiered on through plenty of difficult times in the past. I hoped it wasn't an early sign of Huntington's disease I may have inherited.

Not wanting to appear incompetent in front of my patient and her mother, I scrolled through Skylar's medical record on the computer. I was relieved when I found no prescription listed. Then I wondered if perhaps a child psychiatrist had prescribed something. Psychiatric visits are excluded from medical charts to protect mental health patients, although their medications should be listed. I'd never seen a psychiatric medicine result in such severe side effects, and I never had an inkling Skylar suffered from a mental condition.

"I think you may be mistaken about who prescribed the medication Skylar is taking. I don't remember prescribing anything for her, and I don't see anything in her medical record. Did you take her to a psychiatrist or a doctor outside our system? Maybe that's where she got her prescription."

Mrs. Reinhold rolled her eyes. "Of course it's not in her medical record. The pills are part of your study, the clinical trial. Don't you remember?" Mrs. Reinhold looked mad as she banged her cane into the floor for emphasis.

I didn't want to get too close to her for fear of being beaten. To say I was confused would be an understatement. "Clinical trial? What clinical trial?"

"I know when your research assistant visited us at home, he instructed me never to mix Skylar's clinic visits with the study follow-ups, but right now, I don't give a flying fuck about your rules. My daughter is very sick, and your research staff hasn't done shit, as far as I'm concerned. Your assistant hasn't even returned my calls. I'm not leaving until you do something for Skylar. Find out what's wrong with her. I want to know if it's related to those pills, and you should, too, as clinical trial director. You may be dealing with something very dangerous."

My befuddlement was only getting more intense. I didn't know anything about a study I or any of the other clinic doctors was involved in. If there were such a study, I would know, as I was the clinic director. Mrs. Reinhold seemed terribly confused. For a moment, I thought she might be suffering from steroid psychosis which can result from taking steroid medications. These can be given for a variety of conditions, including rheumatoid arthritis. I needed to be gentle yet firm with this woman. I also needed to tend to her child, who appeared to be quite ill.

"If Skylar is taking a dangerous medicine, of course I want to find out what it is. But I'm not the one who gave it to her. You must have me confused with another doctor, one that isn't in our clinic. It's easy to get different doctors and clinics mixed up. Can you remember where else you've taken her?"

"Don't talk to me like I'm some sort of psychotic or demented old lady. And in case you're wondering, I'm not taking steroids, so I don't have steroid psychosis. I suffered through that nightmare over ten years ago and have sworn off steroids if I can possibly avoid them. I don't know what kind of game you're playing here. I used to trust you, but now I see I've been wrong about you all along."

As mistaken as Mrs. Reinhold was, her words stung. I was at a loss what to do. "What is the name of the medication?" I asked.

"How should I know? It just has a number because it's experimental. I shouldn't have to explain that to you."

"Do you have the pills with you by any chance?"

"Sure do." I watched as Mrs. Reinhold slowly reached into her purse with her right hand, every movement of her gnarled fingers obviously causing pain.

"I'd be happy to look for the pills in your purse if you'll let me," I offered.

"Not a chance." Mrs. Reinhold grimaced as she wrapped her fingers around a pill bottle and handed it to me.

By now, I was more than a little curious about the nature of the pills and what doctor's name was listed as the prescribing physician. The first thing I saw when I looked at the label was the name of the medication: RA23567. The second was the prescribing physician's name: Dr. Erica Rosen. My heart skipped a beat.

CHAPTER 11

"I don't know what's going on here," I said, "but I didn't prescribe these pills."

"Then why is your name on them?"

"Good question. Do you remember me sending the prescription to the pharmacy and talking to you about it?"

"You know that's not how it happened."

"That's always how it happens when I prescribe a medicine for the first time. Even if I need to make a change in medication, I'd talk to you over the phone."

"Except for this study. That's what your research assistant told me."

"Research assistant? You mentioned him before. I don't have a research assistant. There's something awfully fishy going on here."

Mrs. Reinhold's expression turned from anger to concern. "Are you saying that young man lied when he told me you authorized this study?"

"Absolutely. I don't even know what young man you're talking about."

"Then when I called here to the clinic about it, why did Martha tell me you were fully in charge of it?"

I was aghast. If what Mrs. Reinhold said was true, Martha was deeply involved in something nefarious. "I have no idea, but I'll be sure to find out. What was the assistant's name?"

"Name was Karl Kanestrom. Norwegian fellow, I believe, who works for the pharmaceutical company. He's visited us at home several times to check on Skylar and take blood samples, but he hasn't returned in weeks. The first time he came, he had me sign some papers. It all looked very up-and-up."

"Did he give you an address or phone number? Any way to contact him if you have questions or Skylar has a bad reaction to the medicine?"

"Now that you mention it, no. I always assumed I could contact you in an emergency."

"I've never heard of this Karl Kanestrom fellow, but believe me, I'm going to find out about him. Meanwhile, let's see what's going on with Skylar. I need to get her taken care of before I look into the source of these pills. Mind if I keep them?"

"Be my guest. It's not like I'm going to give them to her now that I know you didn't prescribe them."

"What were you told the pills were for?"

"They were supposed to prevent her from getting rheumatoid arthritis when she gets older. They said you ordered her to be screened, and she was found to have the same genetic variation as me—HLA something—so she was probably destined to get this awful disease. I'd do anything to stop that from happening. Looks like I was duped." Mrs. Reinhold, who up until a few minutes before looked intimidating, ready to fight anyone who stood in her way, broke down in tears. I rushed over to comfort her, putting my arm around her gently. I didn't want to apply too much pressure and add to her physical pain.

"I'm going to get to the bottom of this. Whatever you do, don't blame yourself. This seems like a well-organized scam. I don't know who exactly is behind it or what the goal is, but there's something strange going on there."

Once Skylar's mother regained her composure, I turned to examine my patient. She had skin lesions on her arms and legs, probable pneumonia, and possible meningitis.

"It looks like a disseminated infection," I said. "She's going to need more tests, but I'll get things started right now by culturing one of her oozing skin lesions. To be safe, I want her admitted to the hospital this afternoon. Excuse me for a moment. I need to get tubes for culture."

I found Martha and asked her to bring what I needed to culture Skylar's wounds. "Also, could you put these pills on my desk?" I started to hand Martha the bottle of RA23567 pills, then thought better of it. "Second thought, I'll hold onto these myself."

"You sure? It would be no problem for me to drop them at your desk."

Maybe it was my imagination, but Martha seemed strangely eager to get her hands on the pill bottle. "Thanks, but I want to keep them with me for now." I placed the pills in the breast pocket of my white coat and returned to the exam room, where I examined Skylar's arms, looking for the best lesion to culture.

Several minutes later, one of the other physician assistants, Roy, brought me the culture tubes I needed. He offered to help me out for the rest of the day, explaining Martha had become ill and left.

"I saw her just a few minutes ago," I said. "She seemed fine."

Roy shrugged and looked at me apologetically. "She just went home. I guess she got sick pretty suddenly."

Strange. After I obtained samples for aerobic, anaerobic, and fungal cultures, Roy took the tubes to the lab send-out area. I busied myself arranging for Skylar's hospital admission. Given her mother's condition, I had Skylar transported by ambulance and requested Mrs. Reinhold be allowed to accompany her. If Martha had been there, I might have strangled her.

Once I had finished, I wanted to collapse from exhaustion. Since I had two more patients to see, that wasn't an option. Roy directed me to Room Six, as I made a mental note to call the police department when I had a few extra minutes. I had to think about exactly what I would report. I wasn't sure what criminal laws Mr. Kanestrom had broken, but he needed to be stopped from harming more people. Before I reached the next patient, my cell phone rang. The caller was a pediatric oncologist I was friendly with, having had over a dozen patients in common with him in the past. He told me he was calling about Ryan Farooqi.

"Should I be talking to you or Dr. Nilsen?" he asked. "Dr. Nilsen had him admitted and called radiology for the results, but the parents are here in the hospital and want you involved, not Dr. Nilsen."

"Dr. Nilsen is no longer on the case."

"Clear enough. I'll give you the results. They found a large abdominal mass on MRI."

"Since you're the one calling me, it must be suspicious for malignancy."

"Actually, it was biopsied yesterday. Today the pathology was out. Burkitt's lymphoma."

"Damn. I was afraid it was something bad." Burkitt's lymphoma is a highly aggressive form of lymphoma usually seen in children and is sometimes associated with Epstein-Barr virus, the same virus that causes mononucleosis and chronic active EBV infection of T- and NK-cell type.

"I already spoke to his parents using a translator. They're both here at the hospital with him. The boy needs to start his chemotherapy as soon as possible. I don't think the parents understand what I told them. They want to talk to you, so I said you'd give them a call. It would be best if you could call his mother's cell phone. I'll text you the number."

"Will do." That was a conversation I wasn't looking forward to, but I made the call, and Ryan's mother put the phone on speaker. Between the Farsi translator, the mother's sobs, and the father's questions, I believed I had explained the situation to their satisfaction. They agreed to the oncologist's treatment plan.

I took advantage of the break from seeing patients and checked on the status of Lucas. I was happy to receive a bit of good news. He had been discharged from the hospital that morning, much improved from his mysterious liver disease.

Then I called the local police department. I had to explain several times to the woman on the other end of the phone that nothing was stolen, nobody was killed, and no drug abuse was involved, but I suspected a child had been harmed by a person named Karl Kanestrom, posing to be a researcher distributing pills. I didn't have his address or phone number but requested it be treated as an emergency, as he was possibly a psychopath, and other children may have received harmful medications. "Someone will call you back," the woman told me. "It may take a while. This sounds complicated and will probably be kicked upstairs." I left my number, wondering how long, exactly, "a while" was.

I saw my last two patients, leaving me mentally and physically drained. Something very strange was happening, but I couldn't put the pieces together. I wondered about Karl Kanestrom. *Who was he, and why did he pretend to be in a research project with me and give pills to Skylar? Were the pills behind Skylar's illness? Had he given pills to anyone else? Did Martha and Jeremy know about this? Was this related to my patients being siphoned off to Jeremy?* I hoped Martha could clear some of this up the following day when she returned to work. Before I left, I noticed an email in my in-box from the FDA.

I clicked on the email attachment, a copy of a letter printed on official stationery from the Office of Pharmaceutical Quality. The letter assured me a senior scientist had reviewed my concerns, and records of testing performed at Umbroz had been examined. The documents confirmed that the company's cephalexin and carbamazepine had passed the scrutiny of the FDA. While they had no clear explanation for the findings at California Analytics, they gave no indication anyone at the FDA would be following up on that. The letter ended with "Thank you for your concern." Frustrated doesn't begin to describe how I felt. Before I left the clinic, I stopped by Martha's desk and moved her papers around until I found the mystery list I had become familiar with. The name Skylar Reinhold now had an asterisk by it.

CHAPTER 12

I didn't know the exact significance of the list but doubted it was a coincidence that the names of patients who had recently developed serious medical conditions were specially marked. The list was important evidence of something. I snapped a picture of it with my phone.

I considered leaving the pills from Mrs. Reinhold in my desk but thought the better of it. I removed them from my white coat and placed the amber container in my purse. After leaving work, I went straight to my condominium. Lim wasn't home yet, and Maya was with her grandparents. I sat at the kitchen table with a pad of paper and a pen. The only noise was the refrigerator. I had time to think, although I kept glancing at my phone, hoping to get a call back from the police.

I looked at the image of the list of patients on my phone. What did these patients have in common? The children attended at least ten different schools, were in grades ranging from kindergarten to middle school, and had different interests and backgrounds. Other than the four names denoted by asterisks, none had suffered anything consequential recently to my recollection. I decided to focus on my ill patients next. What did these four have in common, and why had Martha placed an asterisk next to each of their names? I wrote down their names and stared at the list. Lucas McGarrett, Cassandra Roberts, Ryan Farooqi, and Skylar Reinhold. Again, I could think of nothing they had in common. I doubted they knew one another, or their parents were acquainted. *What did Skylar Reinhold, a ten-year-old second-generation San Franciscan who enjoyed gardening, have in common with Ryan Farooqui, a twelve-year-old skateboarder who had moved to San Francisco four years earlier with his immigrant parents?*

Then I thought about the big question. *What was RA23567? What was the study Mrs. Reinhold said her daughter was enrolled in, and why did Martha assure Mrs. Reinhold I was in charge of it? Who was Karl Kanestrom, and how did my name wind up appearing as the prescribing physician of those pills?*

I went through my purse and found the vial of pills Skylar's mom had given me and stared at it, hoping it would give me an idea. It didn't. An instant message notification diverted my attention. Another annoying text from a political candidate, which I deleted. I picked up the pill bottle again, this time noticing a QR code on the label. Nothing to lose, I scanned the image with my cell phone app. I wished I could have seen my expression when I read the translation: "RA23567," with smaller letters underneath reading "Umbroz." *WTF*?

I returned the pills to my purse, turned on my laptop, and went to the Umbroz website. The home page displayed a photo of a sizeable building bearing the name Umbroz. There were tabs for information typically found on the websites of pharmaceutical companies, including descriptions of the company, the board of directors, news, products, research, and jobs.

I was already convinced Umbroz was making substandard medications. *What else were they doing?* I read everything I could find on the site. Umbroz was a privately held company, started about fifteen years earlier in Norway by its founder, Haakon Rakvag. I felt a slight jolt, like my heart skipping a beat, when I read "Norway." The same country Mrs. Reinhold thought Karl Kanestrom was from.

I continued reading, learning Mr. Rakvag, a Norwegian national, had moved Umbroz seven years earlier to Raintree, Montana. The company specialized in making generic drugs as economically as possible, providing "the best medicine for the least cost." The list of generic drugs they made was long, the list of medications in the pipeline getting ready for production even longer.

Under the heading "Personalized Medicine" was a vague description of the company's research into medicines aimed at preventing people who inherited faulty genes from developing diseases they would otherwise get. This is a relatively new research field of great interest to pharmaceutical companies. The payoff for success in this area would be huge. I wondered if Umbroz was trying to push its way to the front of the line in preventing genetic diseases by taking risky and illegal shortcuts.

Many job openings were listed, indicating Umbroz was a successful, growing company. Pages describing Umbroz's dedication to community support, social responsibility, the environment, employee well-being, and rigorous quality assurance were similar to those of other large companies. The Umbroz officers all had names that sounded like they might be Norwegian, with two besides the founder himself having the last name of Rakvag.

No smoking gun, but then, I wasn't expecting one. The website looked respectable enough, but if the late Bernie Madoff had a website, I suspect it would have looked respectable too. I searched for Raintree, Montana, on Google Maps and found it in the northern part of the state, a distance from any sizeable cities. I wondered why Mr. Rakvag had chosen such a remote place for his company.

Once again, I read over the names of my seriously ill patients, then looked through the website a second time. *Was there a connection? What was I missing?* My mind drifted to Mrs. Reinhold and her cane. Thinking about that brought my attention to her severe rheumatoid arthritis. My mind skipped from that to my discussion with Lucas's mom about her husband and his need to avoid exposure to pneumonia. He now required oxygen because of his advanced emphysema, which I had known about from previous discussions. My stream of consciousness meandered to Ryan's father, ill with complications of type I diabetes. Although it hadn't come up at the recent office visit, I knew Cassandra's mother had diabetes too. All these kids had a parent with a significant, heritable disease. While that connection was intriguing, I didn't know what to make of it, but I had a hunch.

I looked at the list on my phone again and noticed that a few names were cut off at the bottom. Nevertheless, I concentrated on the names I could see without asterisks. I pictured a light bulb shining brightly over my head as I realized that many, if not all of these patients, had a seriously ill parent. Rheumatoid arthritis, type I diabetes, emphysema. I doubted that was a coincidence.

I didn't know what Martha's involvement was, but she could at least explain her list. If some of these patients had secretly been given pills from Umbroz, pills that might be harmful, I would notify their parents tomorrow. I called Martha at home, but she didn't answer. I needed someone from the police department to call back soon, so an investigation could be started.

My train of thought was interrupted by the sound of a key in the door. Lim and Maya entered, and the usual pandemonium began. I hadn't solved the mystery, but as I hugged the two most important people in my life, I resolved to confront Martha in the morning. Between now and then, however, I would try to focus my attention on enjoying my family.

*

I carried Skylar's pills in my purse when I left for work the next morning, wanting to show them to the police should they finally get back to me. As I walked, I thought about what I would say to Martha when I faced her. Once I arrived in the clinic, however, I was disappointed. I should have known Martha would call in sick. She had notified a receptionist she'd be out for several days. The only other time she'd missed work due to illness had been three years earlier when she had appendicitis.

I knew she was afraid to show up, and for good reason. I tried to call her several times, but she didn't answer. The clinic was busy, my workday made even more difficult by Martha's absence. In the meantime, I again worked with Roy, who volunteered to do double-duty, helping me as well as the doctor he usually assisted.

I looked on Martha's desk for the hidden list of patients I'd seen the day before. I wanted to retake a picture of it to include the names at the bottom, but the list was gone. Frantically searching for that sheet of paper, I moved everything from the desk surface to the floor. Coming up empty-handed, I concluded Martha had come in late the night before and taken it.

Rushing to see my first patient in Room Nine at the same time I checked my phone for messages, I tripped. It was more than a stumble. I landed spread eagle on the floor with a thud, my phone making a racket as it bounced several times. Under me was a toy fire engine. I'm sure I looked a sight as two physician assistants and a receptionist rushed over to help me up.

"What happened?" one of them asked. "Are you okay?"

"I seem to be fine," I said, making sure my arms and legs were in working order. "I didn't see that firetruck. I suppose I was too absorbed in looking at my phone." After assuring the group around me I was okay, albeit a bit shaken up, I continued towards Room Nine.

Following three more patient visits, I checked Skylar's lab results. The microbiology laboratory had identified bacteria consistent with Nocardia on a gram stain. Nocardia typically causes clinically significant infections only in immunocompromised people. It can be picked up in soil, so Skylar was likely exposed when working in her prized garden. However, she was a healthy girl, with a fully intact immune system as far as I knew. I saw that one of the doctors at the hospital had ordered an HIV test on her, searching to find a reason for Skylar's immune system to malfunction.

Without Martha, I had to fend for myself during the lunch hour. I found a food truck with the shortest line and ordered a Thai chicken dish. After returning to my desk and taking the first bite, I understood why the line was short—but being ravenously hungry, I ate it anyway. By the time I finished, my first patient had been waiting ten minutes for me. I plowed through the next three cases—diarrhea, an ear infection, and ringworm. Walking behind the reception area, I heard a mother raising her voice to the receptionist, demanding to see me, and not Dr. Nilsen. She understood this was a last-minute appointment and appreciated them fitting her in, but she wasn't willing to see anyone other than me. I went to investigate and discovered Lucas's mom, Melinda, uncharacteristically red in the face, yelling at the receptionist in frustration.

"What seems to be the problem here?" I asked, trying to sound surprised, although I was sure someone was trying to manipulate the inner workings of the office. Since Martha wasn't there, I knew somebody else was responsible.

"Lucas is ill again, like he was before he went to the hospital. I want you to see him. I don't want another doctor trying to figure this out. I made that clear when I called earlier, but now that I'm here with Lucas," she said, pointing to her son slouching in a waiting room chair, "they're telling me I need to see this Dr. Nilsen."

The receptionist turned to me and said, "I'm sorry, Doctor. Dr. Nilsen's assistant told me you were too busy to see Lucas and wanted me to switch his appointment to Dr. Nilsen."

I didn't want to air our dirty laundry in front of Lucas's mom, so I took several deep breaths to calm myself and said to Roy, who happened to be nearby, "Show Lucas and his mother to one of the exam rooms. I'll see them as soon as I finish with my next patient."

After assessing the two-year-old with pink eye waiting for me, I met with Lucas and his mom. I was surprised Lucas had suffered a downturn so soon after being discharged from the hospital.

"He's sick with the same thing," Melinda McGarrett said. "My daughter Cassie is home with my husband. She's a smart girl, but I thought this was too important to leave to her, so I brought Lucas in myself."

"You did the right thing," I said. "I'm sorry Lucas didn't continue to improve. He seems to be getting jaundiced again—his eyes look yellow."

"Exactly. They were perfectly white when I brought him home, and now look at him."

"They never did find out exactly what made him sick in the first place. Isn't that right?"

"Yes. His doctors said they thought it was a toxin, something he was exposed to at home. He got better in the hospital because there was no toxin there. I can't figure out what it could be. Neither Cassie, my husband, nor I am affected by it."

"Maybe it's not in your house. It could be at school or a friend's house."

"I've kept him home, in his room. I've been afraid he'll be re-exposed to whatever was causing the problem."

"What about food? Does he eat anything you and your husband don't eat?"

"Quite the opposite. He's such a picky eater. Doesn't like his vegetables or eggs. But everything he eats, we eat too."

"Is he exposed to any detergents or cleaning products you don't use?"

Melinda made a chuckling sound, the closest she'd come to laughing. "That'll be the day he starts using cleaning products. I can assure you he hasn't been near any such things."

"He isn't taking any over-the-counter medications or supplements, is he?"

"Not a thing. Only, of course, those pills for your study."

I froze. I'm always amazed at how sometimes crucial information comes out at the strangest times, almost as an aside.

"What pills?"

"You know, the ones you ordered. Didn't Cassie ask you about them when she brought him in?"

"Maybe she forgot. Tell me which pills. I want to be sure we're talking about the same thing." I silently chided myself for not suspecting Lucas's illness was caused by unapproved pills from Umbroz. Maybe all the patients on the list had been receiving potentially dangerous medication.

"Those pills that are part of your clinical trial. I know I was told not to mention them in the clinic because it would interfere with the double-blind nature of the research, but I told Cassie to mention them. Since Lucas has been sick, I thought it would be okay to ask about them. I assumed you were sure they weren't the problem."

"There has been a misunderstanding. More than a misunderstanding, actually. I did not authorize any research study involving Lucas. Furthermore, I want you to know I'd never tell a patient's parents there was anything off-limits for discussion in the clinic."

Melinda gasped as her mouth fell open. "What about that nice young man, Karl?"

"I didn't send him."

"Then how did he find us? What are those pills he gave me? Are they dangerous?"

"I'm sorry. I can't answer your questions with any certainty, but I suspect those pills are causing your son's illness. You're the second case I know of where it appears someone has impersonated being my research assistant and recruited patients to be in a clinical trial I've never heard of."

"Well, I'll be damned." Melinda paused before asking, "What should I do now?"

"First of all, don't give Lucas any more of those pills. Do you have them with you?"

"No, I left them home."

"What were they called?"

"I don't remember. Some letters and numbers. Not like a real name."

"Do you know who the manufacturer is?"

"I don't remember seeing a company name."

"When you get a chance, can you bring them to me?"

"Sure. I don't want them in my house after what you just told me."

"I want you to take Lucas to the lab today to have some blood drawn. I suspect he will get better on his own from here on out, now that he won't be taking those pills. I know he won't like it, but I need you to take him back to the lab tomorrow and the next day for more blood tests. I need to be sure he is improving steadily."

"Thank you, doctor. I'll do exactly as you say. Anything else I can do?"

"Promise me that in the future, you won't give him any medicine you think I've prescribed without talking to me directly. Not Martha or anyone else here. Only me."

"You got it."

I left the room feeling unsettled, yet buoyed, knowing I'd probably saved Lucas from an unknown toxin. Unfortunately, I was no closer to understanding what was going on. Now that it was clear two of my patients had been given pills under the pretense of being enrolled in an experimental trial I had authorized, I suspected my two other hospitalized patients were victims of the same scam. I no longer wondered if Dr. Nilsen was merely trying to replace me as medical director. Something much more sinister was going on.

CHAPTER 13

I was convinced Dr. Nilsen had involved Martha in the clinical trial scam, and they were trying to prevent me from seeing the patients that had been recruited. So far, the police hadn't responded. I needed to act.

I knew where Martha lived and decided to confront her after work. I would demand she tell me what patients were involved. Most likely, all those on her now-missing list were receiving potentially harmful medication, but there might be more. I'd call their parents that evening and tell them to stop giving the medicine. The people involved in this scheme would need to be prosecuted once everything was sorted out, but first I needed to inform the parents of their children's involvement as soon as possible to prevent more from being sickened.

On the way to see my next patient, another toy, this time a dump truck, turned up in my path, and I fell forward, again landing ungracefully on the floor. Aside from the pain in my back and right elbow, I was unharmed. Several people gathered around and helped me up. I told everyone I was uninjured and wanted them to stop asking me if I was okay. In the back of my mind, I wondered if, just before I fell, I'd noticed the door to my left, Room Seven, open a few inches, then close. I couldn't shake the feeling someone was rolling toys in front of me, so I'd trip. Was the Umbroz enigma making me paranoid? I was about to see if anyone was in Room Seven when Dr. Nilsen rushed into the room as if he were about to see his next patient. I heard him say loudly, "Hello, Mrs. Blair," before he shut the door behind him. I continued to Room Five.

After seeing my last patient of the day, I checked the roster of patients Dr. Nilsen had seen that day. No one named Blair was on the list. Jeremy had entered the room pretending to see a patient so I wouldn't see who had been inside and rolled the dump truck causing me to fall.

I decided to visit my hospitalized patients before dealing with Martha. As I walked to the hospital, I noticed more people living on the street than usual. I remembered a news story about a planned protest by homeless people. It would likely last for days, and I wondered if some of the people I was seeing had come to San Francisco specifically to participate in the demonstration.

Upon reaching my destination, the first patient I saw was Ryan Farooqi. He was stable, but feeling the ill effects of his chemotherapy treatment. His mother was with him, trying to cheer him up.

"Did anyone give you some pills for Ryan as part of an experimental protocol?" I asked her through an interpreter.

She looked surprised by my question. The interpreter answered for her, "Of course. I got the pills from your assistant, Mr. Kanestrom. I followed all your instructions exactly. I told all of that to Dr. Nilsen when I saw him in the clinic."

"Actually, I didn't authorize that investigation. I have recently learned that a few other patients were given medication by Mr. Kanestrom and told I wanted them to participate in a drug trial. In truth, I'm not involved in any clinical trial."

As I waited for the translator to tell Mrs. Farooqui what I had said, I was sure she understood when her eyes widened. "Are you saying those pills we gave him aren't from you?"

"That is correct."

"Who are they from? Mr. Kanestrom told us they're from you."

"He wasn't telling you the truth. I don't know who is behind this, what is in the pills, or the purpose of this ruse, but I think the pills may be responsible for Ryan's illness."

Mrs. Farooqi looked like all the blood had been drained from her face.

"If you have the pills with you, please give them to me. I want to have them tested."

"I don't have them with me, but I'll bring them by the clinic."

Next, I went to the Pediatric ICU. First, I visited Skylar Reinhold. Her mother was seated by her bed and appeared very worried, for good reason. Skylar was receiving IV antibiotics and had unstable, low blood pressure. The reason for her immunosuppression was still a mystery. She was HIV-negative and had the normal number of immune cells. So far, she didn't appear to be improving. I tried to comfort her mother, but there wasn't much I could do short of lying to her, which I wasn't willing to do.

Cassandra Roberts was a few beds away. Her eyes were half-closed, although she was awake enough to say hello, and tell me her mother had just left to get something to eat. I stayed with her a few minutes and checked to see that all appeared in order. The staff had ordered many labs on Cassandra, searching for the reason she was deteriorating. She had almost a complete lack of one type of lymphocyte, a type that predominated in patients with HIV. The reason for this was mystifying. Whatever the cause, the deficiency appeared to have opened the door for a latent EBV infection to take hold and overwhelm her.

She had recently been started on antiviral medication which would hopefully stabilize her but was far from being in any condition to go home. If one of her parents had been there, I would have asked if she'd been on an experimental medication. She wouldn't be given any in the hospital, so I planned to ask about that another time, before she was discharged. As I was preparing to leave, a male nurse I didn't recognize clumsily bumped into me, apologized, then began to check Cassandra's IV pump. I didn't want to waste time introducing myself and exchanging pleasantries, so I bid him a good evening and left.

Outside the hospital, I ordered an Uber to take me to Martha's apartment, about thirty minutes away at that time of day. It would be a seven-minute wait for my ride, so I took the opportunity to rehearse what I would say to her. When the car arrived, I still hadn't decided on my opening words. *Should I come on strong and berate her immediately, or start slowly and let her try to explain her actions?* Five minutes from Martha's apartment, my cell phone rang. The caller was one of my colleagues on duty in the Pediatric ICU that evening.

"Erica, I wanted to call you about Cassandra Roberts. I know she was your patient."

"Yes, I visited her recently." I stopped myself, realizing the doctor had referred to Cassandra in the past tense. "Did something happen?"

"She coded a little while ago. We couldn't bring her back. I'm sorry."

Unable to stop the tears from flowing, I needed to know exactly what had happened to take Cassandra's life so suddenly. "I was just there, and she seemed—"

"I know, we were all surprised. Her blood pressure and heart rate had been stable, but she seemed to have an allergic reaction. We hadn't given her any new medication, though. Maybe it was an unusual, delayed reaction. Her mother recently returned from getting dinner and is, of course, beside herself."

"This is a very odd case."

"Tell me about it."

"I mean really odd. I think there was some foul play. See if the Medical Examiner will take the case. I suspect her illness was caused by a toxin."

"Can you give me more information? You know the ME doesn't usually take cases when someone has died in a hospital."

"I have pills that were given to another patient. Some sort of experimental medication. I don't know what's in them, but I suspect Cassandra may have gotten another experimental medication from the same source, and that's what made her sick."

"You have the pills?"

"Yes, the mother of one of the children involved gave them to me. It's called . . . hold on a sec, and I'll look for them." I rifled through my purse but couldn't find the pills.

"We're here," my driver said.

"Just a minute," I said as I dumped the contents of my purse on the seat next to me in frustration. I searched through everything, but the pills were gone. Someone had removed them from my purse.

CHAPTER 14

I left the Uber ride, reeling from the realization that Skylar's pills, my only proof of the bogus drug trial, had been stolen. Thinking back on my visit to the hospital, I remembered the nurse I didn't recognize bumping into me, in retrospect seeming to go out of his way to do so. Now I understood why—he'd reached into my purse and taken the pills, making it difficult to prove anything. Sure, Mrs. Reinhold could testify she'd been given these pills, but there would be no way to prove they were anything other than sugar pills. I'd have to get the pills from Lucas's or Ryan's parents. I suspected Cassandra had also received a toxic medication but hadn't verified that with either of her parents.

I tried to put that out of my mind as I walked to Martha's apartment and knocked loudly. I hoped she would open the door when she looked through her peephole and saw me. No matter, I was prepared to bang on the door until she let me in.

I heard footsteps approaching. There was a moment of silence, then the door opened slowly. Before me stood Martha stroking a grey cat in her arms. She was dressed in pajamas and sniffling, her eyes red. I felt sympathy. She looked like she'd been crying for quite some time, was expecting me, and felt defeated.

All the words I had prepared left me. She remained silent as she turned and walked back into her darkened apartment. I followed her to the sofa where she sat, still holding her cat. She began speaking, looking at the carpeted floor as an orange tabby sat at her feet.

I sat in a nearby armchair, where a white cat quickly occupied my lap.

"I knew you'd come," Martha said. "I know I've made a mess of things. You'll never know how ashamed I am. I don't expect you to forgive me." She broke down in tears.

She had done some terrible things, I was sure of that. I didn't know what her role in all of this was, or even what all of this was, but she had played a part. She'd probably been played, too—coerced into doing what she did—although that wasn't a good excuse in my eyes.

I wasn't sure how I should react. *Should I yell at her and have her arrested on the spot—for what, exactly, I didn't know—or should I try to comfort her?* She looked nothing short of pathetic. I fought my inclination to hug and console her. Instead, I sat motionless for a few moments, waiting for Martha to pull herself together. When her crying quieted down, I spoke.

"You owe me an explanation." An understatement, I know. Unsure how to proceed, I reasoned that probing the situation gently would be best. Once I knew what she would tell me freely, I would judge how much I could trust her.

Sniffling and dabbing her eyes with a tissue, Martha said, "I don't know what you already know, but I'll tell you everything. The secrets. I'm not comfortable with things like that. I've known for over a week I couldn't keep this up. Ever since Lucas came in, I was worried the medication had something to do with it." Martha started crying uncontrollably again.

"It's okay. Take your time. Tell me what happened."

"Shortly after he started here, Dr. Nilsen started talking to me a lot, telling me what an asset to the clinic I was, and how he could tell how much I cared about my patients. He told me he was new in town and didn't know many women. Then he said I had beautiful eyes and asked if he could take me to dinner. He was aware it was against department policy, so he said if I felt uncomfortable, I needed to tell him. I knew it was wrong, but I said yes."

"I understand," I said. "He's a good-looking man."

"I should have known. I've never had any luck with men. Here was this handsome, successful guy who was immediately attracted to me—or so I thought. We seemed to have so much in common too. I see now I was manipulated. I'm sure he wouldn't have had trouble meeting tons of women if he'd wanted to. He doesn't care about me, never did. He only wanted to gain access to you and your patients."

"Why? Why would someone want to harm my patients?"

"That wasn't it at all. They didn't want to harm your patients."

"Who is this 'they' you're talking about?"

"There's Jeremey, Johan—"

"Who is Johan?"

"That's the man who was with Jeremy at the Greek restaurant, Kokkari. Johan Rakvag. He and Jeremy are cousins."

The name Rakvag sounded familiar. I racked my brain for several seconds until the inner workings of my mind retrieved the pertinent file. "Rakvag is the last name of the founder of Umbroz Pharmaceutical."

"That's Haakon Rakvag. Johan is his younger brother. He's a vice president."

"Is Umbroz behind all of this?"

"Yes. They set up this whole complicated scheme to develop new, groundbreaking drugs that could completely change the way some diseases are treated. They started off wanting to do good. Then things got out of hand."

"They sure did. I just received word that Cassandra Roberts died."

Martha gasped. I believed she was genuinely surprised and upset.

"Yes, she died. Do you understand?" I continued, my voice raised. "I'm not sure what's going on, but I strongly suspect she's dead because of some toxic medicine she got from your boyfriend and his pals."

"That wasn't their intention. You have to believe me."

"Well, the patient is exactly dead, and I have good reason to believe she died from something you and your accomplices tricked her parents into giving her."

Martha started crying again before she could continue. "They probably made her sick, but they wanted to save her. This morning they told me about their experimental antidotes—antibodies—to neutralize the medications they'd given."

"How were they going to give antibodies to a patient in the hospital? They have to be given IV."

"They have a nurse working there now. He was going to do it—add it to the IV when no one was around. They wanted to treat Cassandra first because she was the sickest."

"From what you're telling me, it's likely Cassandra was given the antibody treatment earlier this evening. If that's the case, there's a good chance that's what killed her."

"That's not what they wanted, believe me. The antibodies were still being developed and hadn't been tested on humans yet, but they were pretty sure they would work. They desperately wanted to prevent anyone from dying from their medication because they feared they'd be found out."

I sat in stunned silence for a moment, then recalled the nurse I saw tending to Cassandra before I left, a nurse I hadn't seen before. I felt sick. He must have put the antibody preparation in her IV. If only I'd known, I could have stopped him.

"What's the name of the nurse?"

"I don't know his name. I'd tell you if I did."

I wished I had checked his nametag while I had the chance.

"I had no idea how dangerous all of this was," Martha said. "Until recently, all the kids in the studies were doing fine."

"I doubt they would have told you of other children they made sick."

"Whether or not there were others, Lucas was the first I knew about."

"Why didn't they stop him from taking their pills after he was released from the hospital? The pills made him sick again."

"They weren't sure about the pills. They thought it might be something else. Jeremy would have stopped him from getting any more if he'd seen him in the clinic that day."

"Is that why he kept trying to steal my patients? To stop me from finding out about the phony clinical trials?"

"Yes, he recently began diverting your patients in the trials to prevent you from finding anything out. He wanted to discover any problems before you did and make sure the children were okay."

"To be clear, these children are victims, and there may be more out there we don't know about who are very sick. Some are probably beyond the point where they can be helped. Sounds more like he just wanted to cover everything up."

"That's not what they told me."

"Right. And now there's a dead child, and maybe more on the way. It's pretty clear to me they were willing to risk the life of a child to spare them from the consequences of being discovered. You're just making excuses for them."

Martha started crying again. "I see that now." Through tears, Martha continued. "I don't want anything to do with Jeremy or anyone else from the company anymore. Is there anything I can do to help?"

"Do you think they're dangerous? Should I be afraid of them? What about you?"

"They're not going to go around killing people, if that's what you mean. I think they're betting on covering up so well, no one will believe you if you blow the whistle. It will be hard to prove anything because they're tight with people in high places—Jeremy told me they bribe people and donate to political campaigns. I think it would be best if I try to help from the inside."

"Who is Karl Kanestrom?"

"He's another one of them. A second cousin, I believe. They all came over here together."

"Came from where?"

"Norway. They're all Norwegians. Johan's family makes a lot of money from the North Sea oil. He, and all his close relatives, get a very generous allowance from that. They're super-rich, from what I can tell. Even so, Johan's brother, Haakon, resents the government's high tax on oil drilling. There's a fifty percent tax on top of the normal corporate tax. Everyone in Norway benefits from the country's oil, and Haakon thinks that's made Norwegians lazy. He disapproves of the way the country is run, so he decided to come here with the company he started there. He wants to prove himself by making a fortune with Umbroz and is very happy he doesn't have to pay Norwegian taxes with his profits. He brought Johan, several cousins, and a lot of extended family members with him."

"He thought he could prove himself by making crappy medicine and killing people?"

"That wasn't his intent. I believe Haakon came here thinking he was smarter than everyone else and could make a fortune by manufacturing medicine much less expensively than any other company. He took some classes in Norway to become a pharmacist but never finished. He knows something about the field, but not enough. His problem is he's arrogant and self-confident, so when he learned it's not so easy to make inexpensive medicines here, especially if you follow all the rules of the FDA, he decided to cut corners to keep his profits high. He thought he knew just what corners could be cut and still make a good product. I think his heart was in the right place when he started. The terrible things that have happened were unexpected."

"That's no excuse. Medical research needs to be approached very carefully because there are so many unpredictable, unforeseen outcomes. Breaking rules the competition is following to make more money is inexcusable. I can believe he didn't start out wanting to kill people." I paused before sarcastically adding, "It just happened."

"I get your point. I'm not making any excuses. I'm only trying to explain how things got out of control."

"I still don't understand. They made substandard generic medications. I don't know how they got around FDA regulations, but I can at least understand why they did that. But these other pills? The ones Karl Kanestrom is pushing. What do you know about that?"

"That's Haakon's obsession. Jeremy and Johan had me convinced Haakon is some sort of genius. That's why I went along with it—that, and Jeremy's constant encouragement. Haakon sees himself as some sort of visionary, someone whose name will be revered for decades or centuries to come."

"People may remember his name, but I doubt he'll be revered."

"He thought he could make the most money by manufacturing medications to prevent people from developing diseases they were destined to get at a later time because of their genetics. I met Haakon once, and along with his brother and Jeremy, he convinced me that although what I was doing wasn't technically legal, it was the right thing to do since we would be helping countless people in the future. All I had to do was get our lab to send blood from your patients to a shell lab set up to receive the samples. The blood was left over from routine blood tests you ordered. It would be discarded anyway, so I didn't see anything wrong with what I was doing. They paid me and other physician assistants in the clinic pretty well for each sample. Several of us were doing it. We liked the money and, I suppose, we justified it by thinking we were helping people. Jeremy showed us how to order the samples to be sent to the fake lab."

"Did you order tests on everyone who was seen in the clinic?"

"No. They hired a company with access to a lot of medical information. That company scanned the files of lots of people—millions, I was told—in San Francisco, Sacramento, Los Angeles, and San Diego."

"Only California?"

"That's all I know about. That way, Karl didn't have to travel far to enroll the children, and it was easy for him to meet with the kids and their parents regularly. The company might have recruited patients in other places, but Karl worked solely in California."

"What about the company that was looking into people's files? What were they looking for?"

"Severe cases of rheumatoid arthritis, diabetes, and emphysema. That's what they're starting with. Once they identified these patients, and there were lots of them, they found out which ones had children younger than fifteen years old and gave them their names and addresses."

"That's illegal. Patient data is protected. It needs to be de-identified to be used in research like that."

"They bribed two people at the company to give them the information they needed. Then they got blood specimens from the affected adults and tested their DNA for genetic changes they thought would respond to early treatment. When they identified someone with one of those changes, they found out who their children's doctor was and arranged to have their kid's blood sent to their fake lab. That's where I came in. From the fake lab, the children's specimens were sent to Umbroz, where they were tested for the same genetic change. The children positive for the change were then targeted for enrollment in one of their clinical trials."

"You mean fake clinical trials."

"Yes, fake clinical trials."

The sophistication and enormity of this operation were mind-boggling.

CHAPTER 15

"How could this have been going on without someone knowing about it? What was the name of the company doing the data mining?"

"It's called Health Discoveries. They're located in San Jose. They've gotten a lot of angel investor money from people in Silicon Valley, I was told. These investors think they're supporting something cutting edge that's going to revolutionize healthcare. Other pharmaceutical companies are using Health Discoveries and similar companies to look through patient files for all sorts of things that can be used in research."

"What about these other pharmaceutical companies? Are they killing people too?"

Martha paused uncomfortably before she answered. "I don't think any of them are nearly as far along as Umbroz, so they're probably a lot more careful. If I can find it, I'll show you a brochure I got describing Health Discoveries. It seems very legit. When I was told Umbroz was working closely with them to develop life-saving treatments, I was convinced Umbroz was a great, trail-blazing company. It turns out, finding patients for studies is very expensive. Umbroz was paying so much for each child identified as a potential participant, the company was strapped for cash. As Johan explained to me, both he and his brother used some of their share of the family money to fund the research. After they'd spent a large amount and still needed a lot more, Haakon decided to cut additional corners in the manufacture of their mainstream drugs. They became more compromised than they were before."

"You tried to stop me from analyzing the cephalexin that didn't work."

"I know, and I'm sorry. When you asked me to find a lab to analyze the pills, I didn't know what to do. I still trusted all the Umbroz people, so I panicked. I wanted to protect them and the company. You got the pills analyzed anyway, so you can see my plan to prevent that wasn't very good."

"What about the secrecy? Keeping me in the dark? Ordering blood sent to an outside lab without going through the proper channels—didn't that make a few bells go off in your head?"

"It should have. God, I can't tell you how many times in the past week I've wanted to turn back the clock and do things differently. Before I got involved, Johan and Jeremy set up a video conference for me with Haakon. It made me feel so, well—"

"Special?"

"Yes, special. Haakon convinced me they were only getting around government red tape, red tape that would slow down this important research for years. So many people would be helped. He had graphs and DNA sequences I didn't understand, but I was very impressed."

"Didn't it occur to you I would want to help these children too? If the studies were legitimate, I would have been happy to participate?"

"They said you wouldn't go along because they were expediting things so precious time wouldn't be lost. Then Jeremy showed me how easy it would be for me to help."

"Did you ever have second thoughts along the way?"

"I asked some questions, but for each patient, Jeremy and Johan showed me pictures of the kid smiling, then the sickly parent in the worst light, looking sad, disheveled, bent over, sometimes in a wheelchair. They played on my sympathies. Of course, I didn't want the kids to wind up like that. I wanted to help them. Really, I did. I would have helped them for no money at all, I felt so good about it. Now I see I was an idiot."

"If it makes you feel better, it sounds like these people are professional slimeballs who are very adept at lying to people and getting them to do their bidding."

"You got that right. I have a private Facebook page. Only a few people even know about it. They must have hacked into it because Jeremy knew all the right things to say. He liked all my favorite movies and had read all the books I recommended. He even liked cats. He was always considerate. We were planning to go on an African safari to see big cats. Needless to say, I never got him to commit to a date. Now I know why. He was never planning on going. Stupid me, I didn't see through him. I guess I didn't want to."

"You're not the first smart woman to fall for a con artist, and you won't be the last. I'll bet he slowly gained your confidence."

"You're right. After we'd gone out a few times, Jeremy mentioned some important clinical trials he was involved in. He told me about it only after I asked a lot of questions. Here's another really embarrassing part. I asked him if I could participate. I had to convince him it was something I could do. That's when they set up the video conference with Haakon."

"How exactly were my patients enrolled?"

"I don't know how they got the parents' blood to test. They probably had someone like me collecting their blood when they went to see their doctor. After all the testing was done, and they identified candidates for their treatment, Karl made appointments with the parents. He explained that their children had the same genetic variants they had and were doomed to get the same debilitating disease unless they received early intervention. He had all sorts of information about the children and the affected parent, so it seemed he had legitimate access to the medical information. Then he offered them a spot in a clinical trial to keep their children healthy."

"A chance to save your child from a terrible disease? What parent wouldn't fall for something like that?"

"From what I know, they all went for it. Almost everything they told the parents was true, but they didn't say the research wasn't approved by a university or the FDA. They implied UCSF was sponsoring this and, for patients in your clinic, that you were the principal investigator."

"They must have told the parents not to mention the study to me during office visits."

"Right. They told all the participants that since this was a double-blind study, it was crucial you didn't know who was participating. If they spoke to you about it, the results wouldn't be reliable, so their child would be kicked out of the trial and wouldn't receive this life-changing therapy."

"But that's not the way double-blind studies work. The doctor knows who is in the study, just not who gets the experimental drug, and who gets the placebo."

"I know, but Karl is very good at confusing people, especially people who aren't very familiar with how these things work."

"I saw your list—the one you kept at work. Is that a list of all my patients who were enrolled?"

"I didn't know you'd seen it. Yes, those are all your patients. Fortunately, most of them don't seem to have had any bad effects from the medication."

"Not yet, anyway."

"Right. I brought it home. I didn't know what to do with it."

"First, I think, all the parents need to be notified immediately and told to stop giving the experimental medication to their kids. After that, I'm not sure what the next step needs to be. That's up to law enforcement." I didn't reveal that I'd tried contacting the police but hadn't heard back. Perhaps they were too busy or thought I was deranged. I needed to use the ace up my sleeve. I'd call April Wells, the officer I'd worked with previously on the suicide bomber case. She'd help me.

"I can give you the names of all your patients who have gotten one of these medications. There's about twenty-five in all. I wouldn't be surprised if you were followed here, and they suspect you know everything now."

"You said they aren't dangerous."

"Still, I'd be careful if I were you. They'll do everything they can to discredit you if they think you'll endanger their company."

A thought flashed through my head. "I had pills in my purse from one of my patients. On the way here, I couldn't find them. Do you think the nurse could have taken them?"

"I'm sorry, but when I saw you had the pills from Skylar Reinhold, I told them. I know I shouldn't have, but, again, I panicked. They said they would look for them in your office. When they didn't find them, they probably told someone to look in your purse. That's exactly the kind of thing they might do. Cover up by removing all evidence."

"When I call the parents to tell them not to give any more of the experimental medication to their kids, I'll ask them to hold onto their pills so I can collect them. I want them as evidence."

"If you want, I'll help you call everyone on the list. I have their names here, but we'd have to go back to the clinic to get their phone numbers."

"Calling them is something I need to do myself."

"I understand if you don't trust me. Please know I've learned my lesson. I won't be moving or trying to get out of whatever punishment I deserve. I'll hand in my resignation in the morning. Better yet, you should fire me."

I thought a moment about the best course of action. "I think it would make sense if, for the time being, you pretend you told me nothing. I'll take a photograph of your list. That way, you'll still have it. You can tell them I asked you what's going on, but you didn't tell me anything important. You're not sure I believed you, but I have no proof of anything. Come to work as usual Monday. Meanwhile, I'll go back to the clinic and try to reach the parents of everyone on the list tonight. At least that will stop any more harm from being done."

"There are a lot more patients out there getting the same meds, the patients of other doctors in other clinics."

"I figured as much. There's no way to know how many of them are ill from the medicine. That's why I need to put a stop to this ASAP. I'll call the DA's office first thing in the morning."

Martha showed me the list, and I took another picture of it, making sure all the names were included. "Call me if you need me. I don't plan to go anyplace this weekend," she said. "I'll see you Monday morning."

"Right. Remember, we'll have to pretend nothing between us has changed."

I ordered an Uber and left her apartment to wait for my ride. I didn't know what hit me before I blacked out.

CHAPTER 16

I woke up in a hospital bed, feeling groggy. The first thing I saw was Lim sitting in a bedside chair.

"You're awake," he said, jumping up. He came over and kissed me on the cheek.

"What happened?" I asked.

"You were hit by a bike messenger. It was a hit and run. A witness across the street saw the whole thing and chased after the messenger but couldn't catch him. You're in Zuckerberg San Francisco General Hospital. You were out for a long time. Over twelve hours."

"What? I've got to get out of here." I remembered my meeting with Martha and all the people I needed to call. I tried moving my lower extremity and was glad to see my knees bend and my feet flex, proving my spinal cord was intact.

"You're not going anywhere. I think they want to do more tests."

A doctor came in and introduced herself. Her nametag indicated she was an intern.

"What's going on?" I asked. "When will I be discharged?"

"It's not up to me," the intern said. "I was just speaking to my attending."

"Well, what did your attending say?"

"Um, do you want me to tell you now? Maybe you'd like some privacy."

"This is my husband," I said. "You can say anything in front of him."

"You sure?"

"Yes, of course." I probably sounded testy, but I was getting impatient with this intern who didn't seem to know how to interact with patients appropriately.

"Well, it doesn't appear you have any serious injuries. No broken bones. Your MRI didn't show any evidence of brain trauma. But, uh, your labs came back with, uh, a high level of morphine."

"What are you talking about?" I yelled. "There's been a mistake."

"I'm afraid it showed up in two out of two tests."

I felt my face turn red as I tried to grapple with this information. "Somebody must have given it to me when I was unconscious."

"There's no record of that. The paramedics who picked you up said you were already unconscious, so there would have been no reason for them to give you morphine."

"I think we'd better speak to the attending. We need to get to the bottom of this," Lim said. He looked visibly upset, like he wanted to punch his fist through a wall.

"Where's Maya?" I asked, not only because I wanted to know, but also because I wanted to take Lim's mind off the conversation.

The intern raised her shoulders as if to make herself inconspicuous and left quietly.

"Maya is with my parents," Lim responded. "Now, what's going on with this morphine?"

"I don't know. I certainly didn't take any, if that's what you're thinking." I was wondering at that moment whether Lim suspected me of being a closet drug addict.

"I don't know what to believe. The lab can't be that wrong, can it?"

As if on cue, a man with a white coat, a stethoscope around his neck, walked in. He held out his hand. "Hello, I'm the attending, Dr. Steven Phillips." He shook my hand, then Lim's, and said, "Hello again, Mr. Chen."

I realized Lim had already met him.

"I believe my intern already told you we found high levels of morphine in your blood."

"I don't understand how that could be the case. Someone must have given it to me after the accident. Unfortunately, I don't remember anything, not even the accident."

"What about the vials of morphine found in your purse?"

"I didn't have morphine in my purse. There must be some sort of mistake."

"When the paramedics looked for identification in your purse, they found five vials of morphine, apparently stolen from the Pediatric ICU at UCSF."

I was startled. "This isn't making any sense," I said.

"Unfortunately, this has already been reported to the medical board and the head of the pediatrics department at UCSF. He put me in touch with one of your colleagues in the clinic who told me you had fallen at work several times for no apparent reason. He was sure others would corroborate that if there's an investigation."

He was right about that. Many had seen me fall. Now I understood why someone had mysteriously pushed those toy trucks in front of me. They wanted me to trip so it would appear in retrospect that I was under the influence. Something to have in their back pocket in case they needed to discredit me to get me out of the way.

"I hope you get the help you need, I really do," Dr. Phillips said, "but your privileges at the hospital and your position at the clinic have been suspended. Someone from UCSF will be calling you soon to officially inform you. There's a good chance you'll lose your medical license after a thorough investigation. The good news is you suffered little damage from the accident and will be discharged today if your next neuro check is normal."

I sat in shocked silence as the attending left. Lim looked lost, like he didn't know what to believe.

"You don't believe I took that morphine, do you? Or put those vials in my purse?"

"I don't know what to believe. I've been waiting for you to wake up so you could give me some sort of explanation."

"You haven't been around much lately, not enough for me to tell you about the strange things going on at work. Everything points to one thing—I was set up."

"Set up? What for?"

"Someone is trying to make me look like a junkie, to smear me. I think the collision with the bike messenger was no accident. He must have purposefully run into me, then injected me with morphine and put the vials in my purse. It makes perfect sense. Somebody wants me out of the way."

"I knew you'd have an explanation for all of this. Sorry I've been so busy lately, between all my projects at Cyber Dash and visiting Ting and Mingyu in the hospital. It's Saturday, and even if you still had a job, you're not scheduled to work in the Pediatric ICU today, so let's have a long, leisurely lunch after you're discharged. You can tell me all about what's going on."

"Deal."

A few minutes later, the intern returned to do a neuro check. In fewer than two minutes, she checked my cranial nerves, arms, and legs, and pronounced I had passed. While waiting for my discharge, I wanted to go over the list of patients in the clinical trial I had photographed at Martha's. I reached into my purse and realized my phone wasn't in the side pocket I usually kept it in. *Must have gotten misplaced when they went through my purse at the hospital.* I dumped the contents onto the table. Still no phone.

"They stole my phone!" I felt panicky. Like many others, I was so attached to my cellphone, being without it felt almost like being without air.

It was gone. *Of course. These guys are thorough.*

Lim used his phone to call Cyber Dash and have one of the programmers find the phone numbers for Lucas's, Ryan's, and Cassandra's homes, taking advantage of their proprietary software. Then he handed the phone to me. I called Lucas's and Ryan's residences first and spoke to their mothers. I told them I didn't want to wait until their son's next clinic visit but needed to pick up the research pills soon. Lucas's mom told me she'd be happy to oblige. My conversation with Ryan's mom was difficult due to the language barrier, but I thought she said she'd cooperate. Then I bit the bullet and called Cassandra's house. When her mother answered, I offered my condolences. After confirming her daughter had been enrolled in a clinical trial, I asked if I could collect her pills too. Cassandra's mother agreed. I wanted to collect all of them before word got out that I had lost my medical privileges.

I was wearing my street clothes when a female volunteer came by to transport me out of the hospital via wheelchair. The woman was pleasant, though more talkative than I would have liked at the moment. She asked Lim if he was my neighbor and seemed confused when he told her he was my husband. "Well, looks like you're going to need to buy your wife some new clothes when you get home," she said. "Look at the blood on her pants. That stain's gonna be hard to get out." The woman went on about where she liked to buy her clothes, and how much she missed her dog when she was volunteering at the hospital.

Once we were free of her, I examined the stain on my pants, over my right lower leg. I lifted the fabric to look at my skin underneath. A small hole surrounded by a bruise and a few specks of crusted blood stared back at me. I wondered why it hadn't been noted by the hospital staff, although I suppose it didn't stand out from the other bruises on my arms and legs resulting from the bike assault. I asked Lim to take a picture with his cell phone. I was sure that was where I'd been injected with morphine.

*

Lim drove me to Lucas's condominium, where his mother greeted me. She ushered me in to wait in her modest living room, then disappeared down a hallway. I heard drawers being opened and slammed shut. A few minutes later, Mrs. McGarrett emerged.

"I can't understand it, Doctor," she said. "I was certain the pills were in the medicine cabinet, lower right corner, where I keep them. They seem to have disappeared. I looked all over but still can't find them. Please accept my sincere apology."

"I understand," I said. "It's not your fault. These things happen."

No, these things don't happen. Not unless someone makes them happen.

My visit to the home of Cassandra's parents was similar. Mrs. Roberts met me at the door, invited me in, disappeared for several minutes, then reappeared and apologized, explaining that she had looked for the medicine, but it had mysteriously disappeared.

At Ryan's apartment, Mrs. Farooqi waved me in, then motioned she was going to get the pills. Shortly after she disappeared down a hallway, I heard her yell to her husband in Farsi. After what seemed like ten minutes, she reappeared. Using vigorous hand gesturing and sparse English, she indicated she had been unable to find the pills. "Sorry," she said, shrugging her shoulders. I thanked her for trying and again left empty-handed.

Lim and I had lunch at an old-fashioned French restaurant where the service was slow, the food unhealthy, and we could take our time. Seated at a quiet table in the corner, we discussed the current situation in private. A lot had happened in a short time, starting with Martha dating one of the clinic doctors, and the reports from California Analytics confirming my suspicions that the Umbroz medications were inadequate.

"I can understand why someone from Umbroz would be upset you were gathering information about their shoddy manufacturing," Lim said. "It makes sense they would want to discredit you. But what does that have to do with Martha and her new boyfriend?"

"Her boyfriend works for Umbroz and recruited her to help the company. Not only has she been keeping an eye on me, but she's been supplying their company with my patients to participate in their dangerous experiments."

"Experiments?"

"It seems unbelievable, but, yes, experiments." I told him about my meeting with Martha and everything she had confessed to. I explained how Umbroz had access to a database listing people with certain diseases, then identified which of their children had genetic variations they suspected were linked to the underlying conditions. The parents were then offered the opportunity to treat their kids and hopefully prevent them from developing the same disease.

"It sounds like a noble quest," Lim said.

"If done correctly, I agree. However, the way they're doing it is both illegal and reckless."

"Why are they going to all this trouble to run fake clinical trials? They could still make a lot of money by sticking with the generic medicines they're already approved to sell."

"From what I can tell, the owner is exceedingly greedy. Pharmaceutical companies nowadays want to make medications to treat chronic conditions, so people will need to take them for their entire lives. There is no longer much interest in making new antibiotics, for instance. People take them for a short time, then stop. That's why we may be in trouble in the near future, when bacteria are resistant to everything we have now, and there are no new antibiotics to save the day."

"I had no idea," Lim said. "I always thought the pharmaceutical industry was working for the good of mankind."

"They are when it can bring in a lot of money. Drug companies are constantly looking for new blockbuster medications to bring in record profits. A big area of interest is preventative medicine. With today's technology, tests will be able to predict who is at risk for certain diseases. Medications to prevent those diseases will open an enormous market. Pharmaceutical companies have a lot of interest in that, but not much headway has been made yet. There are legitimate companies, like Health Discoveries, with databases that can help pharmaceutical manufacturers identify patients who might benefit from preventative medications."

"I understand why there is so much interest in this field. Why haven't any of the major companies made much progress?" Lim asked.

"It's very costly. Just identifying people who might benefit is very expensive, requiring a lot of data mining. Then running a clinical trial takes a lot of money and time. Umbroz wants to get a head start over companies that are following the rules. That's why they're running these risky clinical trials that haven't gone through the proper channels. I don't know how many children have been taking these medications, but three kids in my care have become seriously ill from them, and another has died." I described how Cassandra had died unexpectedly after I'd visited her.

"These people are outlaws," Lim said. "No wonder they want you out of the way."

"By discrediting me, they know I won't be able to go after them in any meaningful way. I had a list on my phone with names of all the kids in my practice who were getting these experimental pills from Umbroz, but they took it. If I write back to the FDA, like I was planning to, I'm sure they'll believe the people at Umbroz over me, with their fancy website and all. They've removed the experimental pills from my purse, as well as from the homes of the patients I know about, so even if I get someone to listen to me, I'll have no proof. No pills to show them."

"Is there anything Martha can do to help you now?"

"I can contact her to get the names of the children on the list again. I might be able to get some pills from the ones who aren't sick."

"It's worth a try. Can you trust her?"

"I think I can at this point, but then what? What am I going to do if I get some of the pills?"

"We'll go to the district attorney together. We need to put a stop to this right away."

"What if they don't believe me? I'm going up against a big company. For all I know, Umbroz has donated to the DA's election campaign."

"One step at a time. Don't jump to conclusions. They can't have undue influence on everyone. Call Martha. Call her now." Lim handed me his phone.

"Good idea. She told me she'd be home."

Fortunately, I remembered her number even though I usually speed-dialed it. All I got was her phone mail. *Where is she?*

CHAPTER 17

Lim drove me to a local store to buy a new phone, then took me to Martha's apartment. We both walked up to her door and knocked. Many times. The door was locked. With no signs of life, we tried looking through the three windows we could access, but curtains blocked our view. I knocked on the doors of several neighboring apartments, but only two residents answered. They hadn't seen Martha that day, although that wasn't unusual as she was quiet and mostly kept to herself.

"I think we should file a missing person's report," Lim said.

I called the SFPD number for missing persons and was politely informed that since Martha was an adult, they would not take a report before she was missing three days. I asked for a welfare check, and they agreed.

"I'm worried about Martha. Despite what she did, I don't want her to get hurt."

"You've done what you can. Whatever happens to her, she's at least partly responsible. Let me drop you off at home. I need to get some work done at the office. Before I come home, I'll stop by the hospital to see Ting and Mingyu. Then we can brainstorm. I shouldn't be late."

I was glad to have Lim's help. I couldn't do this alone. Despite his already overflowing schedule, the time had come when I had to involve him in my troubles. He didn't know much about medicine, but he recognized evil, and I was sure he'd want to put an end to Umbroz and the activities they were involved in as much as I did.

I needed time to think—quality time, without interruption—so I didn't stop by my in-laws to pick up Maya. I went straight to our condominium and sat at the kitchen table, my favorite place to mull things over. I was powerless now—Umbroz had taken care of that. Pretty clever, making sure I would have no credibility with my patients' parents, the clinic, the FDA, and probably law enforcement. I didn't have a lot of time to waste. Children were in danger. Not only my patients, but the patients of other doctors. I didn't know how many, but I imagined there were hundreds of unsuspecting parents giving these potentially lethal medications to their kids. I had no way to find all of them and stop them from using the pills.

Being Saturday, I felt stymied. I'd have to wait until Monday to call the San Francisco District Attorney's office. Since my phone had been stolen, I didn't have the cell number of April Wells, my one friend on the San Francisco police force. Though not a close friend, April and I met for coffee every few months. She always asked about Zaron, the young autistic man we had worked with to solve the suicide bombing case and rescue some of his classmates.

Our last meeting had been several weeks earlier. As I had visited Zaron recently in the Kentucky residential facility where he resided, I was able to tell her he was doing well and had taken up word jumbles. I'd given her a sketch done by Derek, the talented autistic artist who was rescued on account of Zaron and lived in the facility with him. Derek drew buildings from memory with surprising accuracy. I had noticed a particular picture among many of his on display that I thought April would like. It was a perfect rendering of the third avenue San Francisco police station where she worked.

Although Derek's work could fetch a good price, the director gave me permission to give it to April in thanks for her help. When presented with the picture, the tears brimming in April's eyes told me she was deeply touched. I felt good at the time because I had done that. Looking forward to calling April for a favor, I felt even better—she would have a harder time telling me no.

I called the police station, and as expected, April wasn't at work. The receptionist refused to give me her cell phone number but told me she was scheduled to work the next day, Sunday. She promised to leave her a message I had called.

Meanwhile, time was wasting. With no call yet from the local police department and unable to contact April that day, I called the crime hotline for the SFPD. A nice woman took my complaint about Umbroz using false pretenses to give children harmful pills and told me they'd send an officer by in several days, maybe more, to speak with me. I didn't have several days to wait for an interview which would likely result in nothing. Not while Umbroz continued to distribute pills, some of which were ineffective, others potentially deadly.

I checked the email on my computer and noticed a message from the Medical Staff office. It was the letter I was expecting, although I thought it wouldn't come until Monday. An administrator informed me I was suspended from the hospital and clinic until further notice. Although I felt like screaming at the computer I would sue them for millions of dollars for this great injustice, I knew I'd be wasting my breath.

I went through my email contact list and sent my new cell phone number to the people I wanted to have it, including Martha and the parents of my hospitalized patients.

I needed cheering up, so I picked up Maya from my in-laws and took her for a walk. Maya was always an effective tonic for me when I felt like a tightly coiled spring. I was lost in thought as I held her hand, and we walked towards the water.

"Mommy, why are there so many people camping out?" she asked.

I noticed for the first time there were more people than usual lying and sitting on blankets and cardboard along the sidewalk. Many were in small tents. In some places, the walking space was significantly narrowed by the sprawl of humanity on the pavement. I saw several police officers ahead shooing people back. I felt like I was walking through one of the tent cities I sometimes saw when driving through certain neighborhoods.

"These people don't have homes. They live on the street."

"Is that what they want?"

"Most of them want to live in houses like us, but they don't have enough money."

Then came the dreaded word: "Why?"

I didn't think it would make sense to discuss gentrification of the city fueled by Silicon Valley or the increasing wealth gap in this country. "I'm sure they all have different stories. In general, they haven't been lucky like us and aren't able to make enough money to pay for a place to live in." I reached into my purse, retrieved my wallet, and pulled out two five dollar bills. I gave one to each of the next two panhandlers we walked by. "But we can try to help."

"Now can those people buy a condominium?"

"They'll need a few more people to give them money before they can afford it."

I bought Maya an ice cream cone at the Ferry Building and picked up a cup of Peet's dark roast coffee for myself. On the way back home, I told Maya the story of Goldilocks, one of her favorites.

Lim came home shortly after we arrived, and we enjoyed a quiet evening. Rather, Lim and Maya enjoyed the evening. I only pretended to, being preoccupied with saving my patients and my career.

Sunday, I awoke to the sound of bullhorns in the distance. I grabbed the coffee Lim had set by my bed and looked out all the nearby windows. There was nothing out of the ordinary in sight. Lim was focused on the TV, showing large protests going on in many areas of the city. The demonstrations against homelessness had started and were expected to last at least a week. The mayor was set to speak in a few hours.

Undeterred, I called April. I was happy she took my call and explained everything that had transpired regarding Umbroz and their bad medicine.

"This sounds like quite a case," she said, lifting my spirits. "If I didn't know you, I'd probably think you were a nutcase. However, knowing you, I'm sure you're onto something important." Then it came—the hammer. "But as you are aware, we're in a crisis situation here. There are rallies and marches all over the city. The entire police force, including myself, will be tied up for probably an entire week, managing the large crowds. I'll mention this to my boss, but honestly, I don't think anything will happen until this is over. Unless there is a murder in progress, police activity will be focusing on these demonstrations. Any other time I could try to help."

Disappointed, I realized I couldn't rely on the local police to investigate. If only they had responded earlier, the criminals might have been apprehended already. But they hadn't, and I couldn't dwell on what-ifs.

I called one of my colleagues in the Pediatric ICU, hopeful she hadn't yet heard about my recent fall from grace. The coldness in her voice conveyed she had. I told her I was concerned for Skylar's safety and was suspicious a new nurse had caused the death of Cassandra. It quickly became apparent she interpreted my words as nothing more than the rantings of a drugged-out conspiracy theorist. I asked her to speak to Skylar's mother, who could corroborate the existence of pills given to her under the pretense of a clinical trial. I wasn't sure she had even heard me before stating she had to attend to a seizing patient immediately.

For the rest of the day, I periodically watched the demonstrations on TV. Once, I saw April forming a line with other officers. The mayor spoke about solving the problem of homelessness, but I heard nothing new and didn't expect anything to change.

Monday morning came, and I lay in bed wondering what the parents of my patients would think when they arrived at the clinic and were told I was no longer on staff. I felt embarrassed and imagined Dr. Nilsen had managed to kiss enough ass to be appointed the interim clinic director until he could manage a permanent appointment. He'd be in a great position to oversee recruitment of more patients into Umbroz's risky experiments. Thinking about that, and what I imagined he was saying behind my back, made me tense. I imagined my blood pressure being way out of normal range.

Lim brought me back to the present with a cup of coffee. After a leisurely breakfast, he left for work, and I told Maya I was staying home because I was on vacation. She wasted no time in bringing out the Candyland game.

At 10:00 a.m., I called the District Attorney's office. I didn't have high hopes, but it was worth a try. I was told I could file a complaint if I came to one of their offices. I'd have to wait several weeks before my allegations were considered.

Not giving up, I called the Medical Examiner's office and spoke to one of their pathologists. I told him about the unapproved medications patients had received, and my belief that Cassandra Roberts had died from an antibody cocktail administered in an attempt to cover it up.

I warned that other deaths might ensue, either as a direct result of the illicit pharmaceuticals or due to the antibody treatments given in attempts to conceal them. The pathologist told me he would discuss this with his boss and get back to me if he had any questions. I left my number but didn't hold out much hope he'd be contacting me.

Lim was going to meet with some of his FBI contacts regarding the phone-hacking system he was working on. I called him to ask if he would request their help. Three hours later, he told me that since there had been no crime reported for which the FBI could be brought in, they couldn't be of assistance.

Between games of Go Fish, Candyland, hide and seek, and Hungry Hippos, I concluded I didn't have time for the wheels of justice to turn. I needed to take things into my own hands.

I had an idea I was pretty sure Lim wouldn't like but felt I had no other option. I'd go to the Umbroz manufacturing facility and collect whatever data I could there. Lim was too busy, between his company and checking on his sister and nephew in the hospital, to help even if he wanted to. I called Daisy.

"How's the wedding planning going?" I asked.

"Done. I don't know why people make such a big deal out of it. I could see it for maybe a coronation, but for a wedding? I don't think so. I'm basically copying what you did. Invite guests, order a few flowers, get a dress, and find a caterer."

"How are things at work?"

"I'm at a bit of a lull now. Our company is doing some reorganizing. I think that's their code word for 'lost a big government contract.' My department's on solid ground, but the bottom line has suffered. Why'd you ask? You're never interested in my work."

"Only because you're not allowed to tell me about it, and I wouldn't understand it anyway. When's the last time you asked me how things were going at the clinic?"

"Hmm. I don't remember ever asking. But then you always unload when you're upset about something big there. Did you have difficulty getting to the clinic with all the demonstrations going on?"

"I didn't because I didn't go to work today."

"Why's that?"

"That makes for an excellent segue into what I'm calling you about. I'm upset about something big there."

"Ouch. Sorry to hear that."

"I discovered something far from okay going on, and now some people from Umbroz Pharmaceuticals are trying to ruin my career. It may even hit the news at some point. It's that bad."

"I had no idea. I've never heard of Umbroz, but it sounds awful. Do you want to just up and quit? It's not like Lim doesn't make enough money to support both of you, and his whole family, for that matter, in style."

"I don't want to quit. I want to stop these people. They're making ineffective and dangerous medicines."

"Just the type of thing you'd want to put an end to, do-gooder that you are. So what are you planning to do? Did you file a police report?"

"They won't even return my calls. Even if they did, as you know, the wheels of justice move slowly. I don't have any tangible proof right now. I did have some of their dangerous medicine in my hands, but they stole it. Now they're trying to discredit me by making it look like I'm a drug addict."

"Nobody would believe that."

"Well, they do." I described what had happened to my patients, the bike accident, the vials of morphine that had been planted on me, and the falling episodes I'd had at work, in hindsight laying the groundwork for the assassination of my character.

"Is that why you're not at work?"

"Yes. Things moved pretty quickly, and I was suspended from my job. Right now, I'm at my kitchen table, mulling over my options and playing with Maya."

"I can't believe this. You want me to come over and try to cheer you up?"

“No need for that. But I would like you to consider helping me out.”

“Of course, what can I do?”

“I want you to think about going with me on my next vacation, which I’m planning to take rather soon. Haven’t even told Lim about it.”

“Sure, things are slow at work, and I don’t want to think about the wedding anymore. I’d love to get away. We’ll be back in time, won’t we?”

“Sure. We’ll only be gone a few days.”

“So, where are we going? Vegas? Napa Valley? Hawaii?”

“I was thinking of Raintree, Montana.”

Daisy was silent for a moment. “Montana? I’ve never heard of Raintree. Is there something special there, like a dude ranch? Not sure I’d like to spend a lot of time on a horse.” Daisy’s voice had become decidedly less enthusiastic.

“There’s something special there, alright. Umbroz Pharmaceuticals.”

Another moment of silence preceded Daisy’s next words. “Now I get it. Frankly, you’re making me wonder if you really are on drugs. You want to go there to collect information about the company. Something the government can’t ignore. Like you didn’t get enough of that need for danger out of your system when we went to China and spied on the embryonic gene engineering facility. I still have nightmares now and then about being captured by the Chinese police.”

“You see right through me. Before you tell me ‘No, I won’t go under any circumstances,’ hear me out. This place is in Montana. That’s still part of the US. The worst thing that will happen is they’ll figure out what we’re doing and kick us out. No danger of becoming political prisoners in a work camp for the rest of our lives.”

“What exactly are you planning? What sort of evidence are you after?”

"I'm still thinking about it, but I want to know if there's a chance you'll come with me."

"I'm not promising anything, but okay, there's a chance. About one in a million."

"Aren't you willing to risk just a little bit to save the lives of many innocent people? A pesky lawsuit, attorney's fees, or a night in jail is the worst that could happen."

"Come up with a plan. Then we'll talk. It needs to sound safe before the chances I go increase."

I detected a softening in Daisy's voice. She was starting to lean in my direction.

"Okay, just be sure to answer the next time I call."

I ran through different scenarios in my mind. Whatever I decided, I needed to act quickly. The longer I waited, the more people would be harmed or would die. I was deep in thought when my phone rang. I didn't recognize the number but answered anyway.

"Dr. Rosen?"

I took in a deep breath of relief. "Martha. I was so worried about you."

CHAPTER 18

"You're probably wondering what happened to me." Martha sounded nervous, but given the circumstances, that wasn't surprising. "I'm sorry I left so suddenly. I'm calling because I didn't want you to worry. Karl Kanestrom kept calling me. He wanted me to do so many things for him, like get more tests ordered on patients and look into patient charts. I decided it would be best to turn off my phone and leave."

"Where are you?"

"Nebraska. My mom's pretty much bedridden, so I'm taking care of her. I should have come earlier. I'm glad I've made time for her now."

"Sorry to hear about your mom. Is it serious?"

"No. She was in a car accident, so she should be okay. But for now, she needs a lot of help. She can hardly walk and can't drive."

"What about your cats?"

Martha sniffled. "Jeremy's taking care of them." Martha sniffled again.

"You okay?"

"Just a little cold I caught. I think I heard my mother fall. Have to go."

"Thanks for calling." I barely got those words out before Martha disconnected the call. I was ruminating about what Martha said, glad she had made up with her mother from whom she had been estranged, when Lim came home carrying take-out from a local Thai restaurant.

"Smells good," I said.

"My parents will keep Maya tonight. I told them we had a lot to talk about. I'll bring her to their place now. She'll have dinner with them."

"Thank you, Amazing Husband," I said as Lim bent over to kiss me. He took Maya downstairs to be with her grandparents, and I got two plates and four chopsticks from the kitchen. Lim was back in less than five minutes, and we started eating. I hadn't realized how hungry I was.

"Any ideas?" Lim asked as he shoved a clump of pad thai into his mouth.

"Now that you ask, yes. I think I need to go there. To Umbroz."

Lim put his chopsticks down and looked at me. "You've got to be kidding. It could be dangerous. For all we know, they've already murdered Martha."

"I knew you wouldn't like the idea, but hear me out. They're not murderers. In fact, Martha just called to let me know she's okay. She decided to get away from them because they kept asking her to do more things she didn't want to do. Now she's helping her mom out in Nebraska."

"Just because they haven't killed Martha doesn't mean you'd be safe snooping around their company."

"Daisy will go with me."

"You already got Daisy to agree?"

"Not exactly. But she agreed to consider it."

Lim folded his arms and looked down at his plate. I could tell he was thinking about my idea.

"Where is this place?"

"A small town in Montana. Looks very close to an Indian reservation on the map."

"I'll bet there are no direct flights."

"We'll rent a car from the nearest airport."

"How are you going to get in? I don't think they'll let anyone from the public wander around."

"I got into Fengshou. I'm sure I can figure out a way to get into Umbroz," I said, feeling a bit more confident than I had a right to.

"You had a lot of help from others with Fengshou."

"This isn't a secret government operation. Should be much easier. Maybe I can get a job there."

"Doing what?"

"I'll check out their website. They had a lot of job vacancies last time I looked. They're in the middle of nowhere, so jobs are probably hard to fill. Since I'm not working, I don't have to arrange time off. Your parents will be happy to look after Maya, I'm sure. I won't be gone for long, anyway."

"I think this is a bad idea."

"I don't see any other way given the lack of help by the FDA or law enforcement. I need to do this. I may wind up doing more damage to my reputation, but I feel perfectly safe going there."

"I wish I had your confidence. I know I can't stop you from going, so I'll help you in any way I can so you can finish your visit to Umbroz quickly. Still, I'd like you to reconsider."

I smiled, already anticipating going to Raintree and gathering dirt on Umbroz. "Please understand. I have to stop this."

"I understand all your concerns, but I still don't want you to go. As you Americans say, I don't have a good feeling about this."

After dinner, Lim left to visit Ting and Mingyu in the hospital, while I started thinking about how I would carry out my investigation.

I looked over the list of job vacancies on the Umbroz website and decided to apply for a job in the quality control, or QC, department. Although I was utterly unqualified, my last memory of mixing chemicals coming from my undergraduate organic chemistry course, I figured I could fake it for a few days while being trained. Daisy would be best suited for an opening they had in Information Technology, or IT. The closest airport was Glacier Park, but the area around it looked mountainous, and probably difficult to drive over. Great Falls International Airport seemed the best bet. It was serviced by several airlines and was about two hours away by car. We could catch an Alaska Airlines flight from San Francisco to Seattle, change planes, and continue to Great Falls. The whole trip would take eight hours, counting drive time.

To my surprise, finding a place to stay was a bit more problematic. According to Google Maps, there weren't many residences near the company outside of the Indian reservation. It struck me that a lot of the workers might live on the reservation itself. The closest hotel, The Palms, was ten miles away. With two stars, I was sure Daisy and I wouldn't want to stay there any longer than necessary.

I was going to need Lim's help landing a job there. I'd ask him to hack into an American drug manufacturer and find the name of an employee in the QC department. Using that name, I'd apply for a job at Umbroz. If the Umbroz Human Resources, or HR department, asked for references, Lim could handle that by sending fake letters from spoofed email addresses. He could do the same to help Daisy get a job in the IT department. I expected Lim to complain but knew it would be easy for him to do everything I needed.

I called Daisy. After I explained the details, she was in. "As soon as that man of yours gets the names of the people we're supposed to be, I'll write up a resume that will be hard to pass on," she said.

"Are you going to check with Arvid? He might not want you to go." Daisy was nothing if not independent. Still, I didn't think it was a good idea for her to start their life together without discussing the trip with her future husband.

Daisy laughed. "I already told him I was going. I said you were sure it's perfectly safe, and he's fine with it. You know those Danes—always concerned with making sure everyone's happy and healthy. He was pretty pissed off about what Umbroz is doing and wants me to help put a stop to it. To tell you the truth, I think the fact that it's a Norwegian company helped. Asked if there was anything he could do."

"It doesn't look like we'll need him, but it's nice to know we have his support. The most pressing thing right now is getting hired quickly. For most jobs, it usually takes at least a month. We need to cut that to a few days."

"I see on the website they have a lot of jobs open," Daisy said. "They might be able to rush things if we tell them we're desperate to move to the area right away."

"Check out Raintree on Google Maps—I'm sure nobody's desperate to move there. That's why there are so many job vacancies."

"I've got it!" Daisy said. "Lim can route the emails from us to appear as if they were sent a month ago. We'll both call to find out about the status of our applications. We'll tell them we've had other offers, but we're waiting to hear from them."

"Why would we wait? Why wouldn't we just take the first job offer?"

"There's a reason we want to work there like—shit, I don't know. Why would anyone want to work there?"

"We've both got to have good reasons, and they've got to be different. Think!" I said.

"I know, I broke up with my boyfriend and need to get away from him. I want to go someplace remote, where he can't easily get to me. This place sure fits the bill for that."

"Okay. One down."

"Now you think of something."

"Hmm," I said while I tried to come up with an idea. "I could have allergies. All the other jobs are in warmer places, with too many things I'm allergic to growing."

"Sounds convincing to me."

"Okay, we've got our reasons for wanting to work there nailed. Let's work on our resumes tonight. I'll ask Lim about making it look like we emailed them a month ago. Do you think you can have yours ready tomorrow?"

"Not a problem. I'll just brush up my old one. Shouldn't take more than ten minutes. I'll still have time to beat Arvid's ass in Grand Theft Auto."

"I knew you two lovebirds were meant for each other."

Lim came home a half hour after we hung up. He agreed to route our email applications to the Umbroz HR department and make them appear to have been sent a month earlier.

"You sure these people aren't dangerous?" he asked.

"They're civilized. Norwegians. Nothing to worry about. Martha should know, and she's not afraid of them."

"Correct me if I'm wrong, but I recall learning the Vikings weren't the nicest, most civilized people."

"That was a long time ago. Really, you have nothing to worry about. I'm not worried."

"That's what I'm worried about."

CHAPTER 19

By 10:00 a.m. the following day, both Daisy and I had our resumes ready. Lim had spent the time we were working on them finding several suitable candidates for each of us to impersonate. I chose Mandy Winston from Celgene in San Diego, while Daisy decided on Donna Liang from Eli Lilly in Indianapolis. Before 11:00 a.m., Lim had created accounts for both Mandy and Donna in the Umbroz job application portal, backdated a month for Mandy and six weeks for Donna. He uploaded both of our resumes and cover letters, dated appropriately, and left for work. I called Daisy to let her know step one had been completed.

Maya was spending the day with me again, so I played Candyland and a few games of Go Fish before setting her loose with building blocks to see what she would create. I sent another letter to the FDA, this time alerting them to the unauthorized testing Umbroz was performing. If I got a positive response this time, I would bail on the trip to Montana. I wasn't optimistic.

Maya was building a castle, quite elaborate for a child her age, in my opinion, when I called the Umbroz HR department, inquiring about my application. After several transfers, I spoke to a woman with a friendly demeanor named Janice Williams.

"Ms. Winston, I'm terribly sorry, but we just located your application. Let me be the first to apologize on behalf of our company. I don't recall this happening before, but your application somehow got passed over by our system."

She sounded so upset, I felt guilty putting her through this unpleasantness. "It's okay. I understand how these things happen. I'm so glad I decided to call today. I was excited by your job posting and applied as soon as I saw it. I don't mean to sound boastful, but I know I'm qualified and was hoping to hear soon."

"Thanks for reaching out. Unfortunately, we've lost a month. It usually takes at least that long before we can hire someone."

"Is there a way to speed that up? To be honest, I have a couple of other job offers, but I'd rather work at your company. I'm not trying to pressure you into rushing my application if it's against your company policy, but I'm going to have to get back to these other places soon. In a few days, they're going to rescind their offers."

"Oh, gee. We do have a problem. Let's see. Can I ask you—what is the reason you'd prefer to work here?"

"I've researched your company, and it seems you have a good management style and are working on some interesting projects. Aside from that, I have bad hay fever. In San Diego, where I'm living now, my allergies are terrible. That's why I need to leave. I love my job, but it's become too difficult for me to live here. The other places I applied to are better, but Montana's got to be the best. My allergies shouldn't be a problem there at all."

"You're right. I haven't heard even one of our employees complain about hay fever. That's one advantage of living up here in the cold climate."

"What's the soonest you could make a decision? I'm sure I can get people to write letters of recommendation for me pretty quickly."

"I'll check with our head of QC and get back to you. Please don't take another job until you hear from me."

I called Daisy as soon as I disconnected. "I think I may get a job offer," I said. "Spoke to a very nice lady at Umbroz named Janice Williams. She couldn't understand what had happened to my application but showed no suspicion. I suggest you wait a few hours before calling."

"Will do. I think I'll mention the malware I'd heard about developed in Estonia. It was made by someone who was mad about being turned down for a job, and randomly hides ten percent of job applications."

"Sounds believable. Should keep their cybersecurity department busy for months, looking for all those lost applications."

"I'll ring you after I make the call."

I can't say I fully enjoyed the rest of my day off, but I appreciated the extra time I had to spend with Maya. We walked to a neighborhood toy store, where she picked out a baby doll and a toy army tank.

Daisy called to tell me she had also reached Janice Williams in HR at Umbroz, who said she was familiar with the problem of lost applications. She promised to rush Daisy's along.

When Lim came home, I had finished giving Maya her dinner and was heating leftovers for Lim and me. I told him about the progress I'd made that day, and he offered to check out The Palms, the nearest hotel to Umbroz, while I got our meal ready.

"Funny thing about the hotel," he said when we sat down to eat. "They don't take online reservations. You have to call. While I was digging around, I discovered that the hotel is owned by Umbroz. They didn't bury that connection too well. Probably didn't think anyone would look into it."

"I doubt if it's illegal. Still, it does seem odd."

"I think you need to be careful. There's a reason these people own the only hotel in the area. They probably want to keep an eye on all outsiders who come and go."

"Good point. FDA relies on surprise inspections to approve drug manufacturers. They show up unannounced and start inspecting. If a company is located in a remote area that can't be reached from a large city early in the morning, the inspection team will stay in a local hotel the night before. People at the hotel could alert Umbroz if a group of people arrives at the hotel for a short stay. It would be easy to find out if they work for the FDA."

"Do you think that would help them pass an inspection?" Lim asked.

"Absolutely. The Umbroz people could spend the whole evening the day before a supposedly surprise inspection, preparing. They'd have plenty of time to hide things, print up fake documentation, and clean up unsanitary areas," I said. "I've heard of that happening in foreign countries, where the FDA often notifies companies before they show up. In this country, pharmaceutical companies are never notified ahead of time. But Umbroz could have a heads up because there's a direct line between them and The Palms."

"Clever. Like I said, you need to be careful. Despite what Martha told you, these people could be dangerous."

We were silent while we finished dinner. Even Maya was quiet as she played with her new doll. I believe Lim was as lost in thought as I was. After dinner, we put Maya to bed. When I began to read a medical journal, my cell phone rang. It was a local number I didn't recognize. Hoping for some good news from somewhere in the universe, I answered.

"Dr. Rosen, this is Skylar's mom. I'm so sorry to bother you. I didn't know who else to call. It's about Skylar."

"You probably heard I'm no longer working at the clinic or the hospital. But of course, I'm still very much concerned about Skylar. What's happened?"

"I was with her, and she seemed to be getting better. There was a new nurse, a man. For some reason, I had a bad feeling about him. Then, out of nowhere, Skylar's face turned red, she couldn't breathe, and her blood pressure fell."

My mind was racing, as was my heart, thinking Skylar had died, and I had been unable to prevent it. I wasn't sure what my first question should be. "When did this happen?"

"About fifteen minutes ago. Fortunately, the doctors were able to save her. Said she had an allergic reaction but couldn't figure out what caused it since they hadn't changed any of her medicines lately."

I exhaled audibly as my body relaxed. "So she's okay now?"

"Well, she's alive. They expect her to recover, although right now, she's worse than before. I think the new nurse gave her something."

"It sounds like your daughter may have suffered from anaphylaxis—a severe allergic reaction. Did you get the nurse's name?"

"No, but I'm going to. I don't want him getting near Skylar again."

"You should make sure of that. There was a new male nurse the last time I was at the hospital, and although I don't have proof, I believe he's responsible for the death of another patient."

Mrs. Reinhold gasped. "So my intuition was correct. They've got to fire him. Better yet, arrest him. Now tell me, Doctor, what's going on? Why did you suddenly quit? Your patients need you. Now more than ever, I'd say."

"I didn't quit. I was suspended while they arrange to fire me. I'm only telling you this because it has something to do with the unauthorized clinical trial your daughter was involved in. There seems to be a well-orchestrated conspiracy at play here. They didn't want me to expose anything, so they planted drugs on me to get rid of me."

"How can that be? Couldn't you take a drug test?"

"Unfortunately, it's not that simple. Needless to say, I don't take drugs and never did. I expect to prove that in due time, but for now I can't work there. I haven't stopped looking into what's going on, though. Please call me if you see anything else suspicious. As long as Skylar doesn't take the medication Karl Kanestrom gave you, which I think suppressed her immune system, she should improve as her body recovers. If she has another setback, I would be suspicious of foul play. I suggest you take her home as soon as her doctors think she's well enough. Until then, keep an eye on her. Be wary of any nurses you're unfamiliar with."

"I will. Thank you, Doctor. Good luck with everything."

I slept restlessly that night. The following morning, Lim brought me coffee in bed before he left to take Maya to his parents and meet with investors at his company. I had nothing to do besides prepare for my trip to Montana.

I got busy searching the internet to learn what I could about pharmaceutical production and QC in particular. I wanted to know enough so I wouldn't show my incompetence in the realm of QC and get fired on the first day. I also needed to be able to understand everything I saw in terms of production infractions. I figured if we were lucky, Daisy and I would be able to get the proof we needed in three days or less. Thinking about evidence, I regretted having to dump all our spy cameras when we left China. Of course, I'd have my cell phone, but I needed a way to record things less obviously, and in places where cell phones weren't allowed.

I located two local stores that sold spyware—mostly nanny cams and outdoor cameras—but also hidden cameras in pens and watches. I took an Uber to one where I picked out two watches, twelve pens, and extra SD cards.

At the second store, I bought two pairs of spy glasses, one black with square lenses, the other brown with oval lenses. Both were highly unattractive, with unusually thick frames and temples to hide the camera and electronics, but I reasoned they might come in handy if we were prohibited from bringing our phones or other devices into the work areas. I spent a lot of money for someone without a job, but I needed all of it. As an extra precaution, I purchased two prepaid phones and had them activated.

I dropped off all the electronics at Daisy's, she being more able than me to figure out how everything worked in detail. While I was there, I received a call from Janice Williams, the Umbroz HR woman I'd spoken to the previous day. She sounded excited, again apologized for the oversight, and asked if I could get three letters of recommendation to her quickly. If my letters were good, I could interview via phone on Friday and start as early as Tuesday.

"That would be fantastic," I said. "I already have some of my things packed, and my husband can finish up after I leave. We'll need to look for a place to live, but I found a hotel in Raintree, The Palms, and I can stay there for a short while."

"Perfect. I was going to suggest you stay there. Once you're here, you can find a more permanent living situation. We have three nice apartment complexes, and there are usually a few houses on the market. I don't know what—"

"We're going to rent. An apartment would be fine."

"Fantastic. Get those letters to me, and I'll call you back as soon as we've had a chance to look them over. The head of QC was very impressed by your resume, so unless there's a big surprise from one of your references or the interview, the job offer will be coming."

I turned to Daisy and smiled as I disconnected.

"It sounded like you got the job," Daisy said.

"Pretty much. I just need to write up my recommendation letters and have Lim take care of making them look like they're coming from Celgene. If all goes as planned, I'll be starting there on Tuesday."

"Way to go, girl," Daisy said. "I haven't heard yet. What if I don't get hired?"

“You’ll have to give me a crash course in what to look for in their data system.”

“Let’s hope it doesn’t come to that.”

I left Daisy’s place feeling optimistic. I got busy writing letters of recommendation for Mandy Winston, piling on the accolades. Although the letters were for me, the fact that they were written for someone with a different name removed whatever awkwardness I would have felt writing such flattering things about myself. I emailed the letters to Lim and asked him to send them to Umbroz about an hour apart, spoofing the return email addresses as we’d discussed.

I was studying the FDA’s regulations regarding drug manufacturing current Good Manufacturing Practices, the rules pharmaceutical companies are required to follow to get FDA clearance, when Daisy phoned. She’d gotten a call from Janice Williams and was told she could probably start early the following week. I asked her to write up her reference letters and email them to Lim.

“Be sure to lie in your letters and make it seem like you’re the best of the best.”

“Don’t worry. I’ll brag like a Jewish mother.”

“Perfect. They’ll have no choice but to hire you.”

The next few days were a blur. Lim bought two portable external drives to store all the information we gathered at the end of each day. We would then connect the drives to our phones and transfer the data to Lim over the 3G network that serviced the area. I promptly dropped one of the drives off at Daisy’s condominium.

After my letters of recommendation were received at Umbroz, Janice called to set up a phone interview for the next morning. I crammed that evening, but the interview was harder than I thought it would be, and I was unsure about some of my answers. Luckily the interviewer, Petter Gustavson, didn’t see me sweat. I was hired Friday afternoon, and Daisy received her congratulatory call later the same day. I would start the following Tuesday, Daisy the next day.

When I told Lim, he looked crestfallen. "To be honest, I never thought you'd get hired so quickly. I was hoping your enthusiasm would fade, and you wouldn't go."

"I wish you didn't worry so much, but I have every reason to believe Daisy and I will be fine. I'll still need you to do a few more things so my trip will be a success, but I'm going."

Daisy and I made separate plane reservations, and each of us reserved a room at The Palms. I spent several hours brushing up on the subjects I realized I was deficient in during my interview. Saturday afternoon, I visited a local beauty salon to have hair extensions taped on, making my hair look a good seven inches longer. Although I didn't expect to run into anyone I knew up there, I didn't want to risk being recognized by a description Martha or Dr. Nilsen may have given them.

Lim, through connections I didn't want to know about, got each of us a fake driver's license in our new names. Daisy's was a little more challenging to get, as she was supposed to be coming from another state, Indiana, but he managed.

After Daisy went over the recording devices with me, I packed. My fact-finding mission would take longer than Daisy's. I would need to explore the physical plant to look for areas where secret research might be taking place, and parallel manufacturing and quality testing performed. I suspected they used one set of high-quality, expensive ingredients to show inspectors from the FDA, and another set with lower quality and cost for mass production. I also planned to look for two separate areas of quality control—a fake one to show FDA inspectors, where all the rules were followed to a T, and the one they typically used, where corners were cut. The plant was large, so exploring the entire campus would take some time.

Daisy's mission, checking out the computer system, was more circumscribed than mine, so she probably wouldn't need more than a day. If all went well, we'd have enough information by the end of work on Wednesday or Thursday.

Lim was quieter than usual the days before I left. I knew he didn't want me to go, and would be worried until I returned home. Although he tried to hide it, he was already under stress from overseeing his company and concerned about the post-op recovery of his sister and nephew.

I learned that Ting and Mingyu would probably be released from the hospital on Monday, the day I was leaving.

"I'm sure they won't be doing much for a while," I said. "Just walking around the condominium, maybe going next door to your parents' place."

"That's what I was told," Lim said. "Wang Shu is excited about taking care of them."

"What about Kang?"

"I'd say he's less realistic. He wants to race with Ting, something they did before she had the surgery. I tried to explain to him that she won't be up to it for a while."

"He's young and full of energy. Remember, he's more energetic than most kids his age. He'll understand better when he sees them at home. I'm sure he'll be glad to have them back. I can't wait to see them when I return."

Sunday, I called Daisy to go over details one more time before leaving. That evening I packed, securing all my electronic devices in a false bottom Lim had installed in my small overnight suitcase. The next day, I got up early and kissed my daughter goodbye. Lim walked me to our front door and hugged me tighter and longer than usual before I left our home with my luggage in tow. I walked to BART and caught the train to SFO for my 8:00 a.m. flight, not knowing what I would find when I reached my destination.

CHAPTER 20

My trip was unremarkable. By the time I reached The Palms in my rental car, a white Hyundai Elantra, it was almost dark, and I was tired. I figured whoever named the hotel must have had a nasty streak of sarcasm. Nothing remotely resembling a palm tree was in the vicinity or probably within over a thousand miles. The land was flat and barren with scattered small run-down houses. Mountains in the distance arising from the desolation gave the land an eerie feeling. I parked my compact sedan in the asphalt lot, the cracks and faded white lines indicating years of neglect. The air was cool and crisp when I left my car, retrieved my suitcase, and walked past the two other vehicles in the lot. A faded sign directed me to the registration desk.

The building had the look of a Motel 6 that had fallen on bad times, almost as if someone had taken pains to make sure it was uninviting. I found the registration office but had difficulty opening the entry door, which was misaligned in the door frame. The small room smelled musty, despite a window being open a crack. Several pictures of buffalo decorated the gray walls, and a plastic lawn chair sat in a corner. I couldn't imagine anyone wanting to sit there. I walked up to the knotty pine counter covered in crumpled papers, used paper plates, and cups. An old-style metal hotel bell was prominently stationed in the middle. I thought for a moment. There was still time for me to turn around and leave. Nevertheless, I tapped on the bell, and a high-pitched ding filled the room.

A pleasant-looking middle-aged woman wearing jeans and a T-shirt appeared. She wore her jet-black hair in a long braid down her back, reminding me I was near an Indian reservation.

I registered with no problem, showing my counterfeit driver's license with a San Diego address for identification. I had to pause for a second when I signed the guest book, my fake name escaping me for a moment. I paid with a Visa gift card I'd purchased before my trip, as there hadn't been enough time to arrange a credit card under the name of my new identity. After I asked the desk clerk to recommend a nearby restaurant, she gave me directions to the closest diner and handed me a key to room sixteen—an old-style key rather than a key card.

My room on the first floor was adequate, with a bed and dresser, a cathode-ray TV on top. The adjoining bathroom had a shower/tub, toilet, and small pedestal sink, with almost no space to keep soap, toothpaste, or other items. There was one set of thin white towels. This hotel had been overrated at two stars.

I left my suitcase and headed off to the diner a mile down the road. I opted for a turkey sandwich, substituting a salad for the fries normally included. All the waitstaff appeared to be Native Americans, as did half the other customers. I had the feeling everyone knew everyone else. I figured only people having business with Umbroz, either employees, delivery people, or government officials, came through town. When I had finished eating, I paid in cash and went back to my hotel room. There I unpacked the few clothes and toiletries in my suitcase and plugged in all my electronic devices.

I called Lim, who filled me in on Ting and Mingyu. Both had been released from the hospital as planned and were doing well, resting at home. Fung and Enlai were hovering over them, with Kang and Wang Shu pitching in when their grandparents allowed it. I spoke to Maya, who was excited her cousin and aunt were back. After the call, I read a novel on my Kindle for a half hour, then went to bed. I remember repeating my new name, Mandy Winston, over and over in my head as I fell asleep. I needed to get used to it, so I'd respond as if it were my real name.

I was up and dressed before 8:00 a.m. the next day. After placing the recording devices I would use that day in my purse, I secured the remaining electronics in my suitcase's false bottom. I left the hotel feeling cold in the morning air, despite wearing a wool jacket. Looking around the parking lot, I saw cameras aimed at all areas outside the hotel. I couldn't tell if they were real or decoys placed there to prevent thefts. I suspected they were real. When I got in my car, I put on my spy glasses, then drove to the diner for a quick breakfast at the counter before heading off to start my new job at Umbroz. I was supposed to report there at 9:00 a.m.

Driving to the facility on the two-lane road, the only way to reach Umbroz, my stomach was in a knot. As I passed between the heavy growth of pine trees on both sides, I already regretted the small breakfast I'd eaten, hoping to keep it down. Every muscle I owned was tense, and when a four-point buck suddenly darted in front of me, I reflexively swerved. I breathed in and out slowly several times to calm myself after gaining control of the car and pulling to a stop on the shoulder. With my eyes closed, I reasoned that many people would be nervous their first day at a new job, so any anxiety I displayed would not be out of the ordinary. When I felt ready, I opened my eyes, pulled back onto the road, and continued toward my destination.

I passed over a bridge and noticed several cameras mounted above, aimed at the cars traversing. These probably served to give a last-minute warning that someone was coming to visit Umbroz. Five minutes later, I passed a sign informing me I had entered the White Mountain Indian Reservation. This was the first time I realized Umbroz was located on an Indian reservation, not just near one. I was sure this was no accident. Besides substantial tax breaks, this would afford the company certain freedoms from the local and state government.

After a few more turns in the road, I was looking at an imposing glass, steel, and concrete three-story building. It looked like the photo on the website but was much more impressive in person. The steel letters spelling Umbroz were at least three feet high and stood above the concrete overhang protecting the glass entry doors. Behind the building, detached and partially hidden by trees, was another structure. Less impressive, it had the look of an apartment building with regularly-spaced balconies, many with furniture and barbecues.

I drove through the well-maintained parking lot in front, predominantly populated by large buses, which I assumed had transported most of the workers to their jobs. A few dozen cars were parked, three of which were elite sports cars, leading me to speculate that some of the top brass were at work. I parked close to the building, locked my vehicle, and entered Umbroz through the front doors, which parted as I approached. A woman at the front desk greeted me, made a quick phone call, and escorted me to the HR department after I explained why I was there. It was obvious people weren't allowed to roam around freely.

Janice Williams, the woman I had spoken to on the phone, appeared at the HR entrance to greet me. As is typical, she didn't look anything like I had imagined, being ten years older, twenty pounds heavier, and three inches shorter, with short black hair, rather than the light brown I had envisioned. She appeared to be Native American, as did most of the other people I saw. She smiled broadly when she first saw me and had the same friendly demeanor in person as on the phone.

She led me past several co-workers busy typing and speaking on phones. She then took a seat behind a desk with a brass nameplate bearing her name, while offering me a chair opposite her.

"That must be your family," I said, noticing the framed picture on her desk.

"Yes," she beamed. "My sister, nephew, nieces, and that," she said, pointing to a sweet-looking boy around eight years old, "is my son, Paco."

"He looks adorable. And happy."

"Everything I do, I do for him. Do you have children?"

I caught myself before I told her I had a daughter. I was Mandy Winston, who had no children. "No, but maybe someday," I said.

Janice smiled, and I filled out some forms, one of which included my social security number. The real Mandy Winston would receive a few extra days of social security credit when she eventually retired. I doubted she would complain if she noticed.

"I almost forgot," Janice said. "You need to find a place to live."

"What about the building behind this one? I noticed it when I drove in. It looks like an apartment building."

"You are very perceptive. You're right, Umbroz built apartments there for employees. However, they're very desirable being so close to work here, so there's a long wait-list to get in. I don't have anything to do with rentals there, but after you've been here six months or so, I'll put you in touch with the person in charge. Meanwhile, let me get you a list of the apartments available. Could you come by around four? I'll have it ready then."

"Sure."

Janice looked a bit wistful. "I really like my job. I hope you like it here too. Some people don't stay long. I guess they find it hard living here, being so isolated. I'm sure they don't leave because of the job. The pay is good, and the company treats its workers well. Let's get you started now. I'll take you to see the head of our Quality Control. You might want to take your jacket off and carry it with you for now."

I was happy to follow her suggestion as it was warm in the building, and I was getting uncomfortably overheated. Janice walked with me up a flight of stairs, down a hallway past closed doors on either side, and knocked on a door similar to the others. Without waiting for a reply, she entered the small office with a reception desk fronting an inner office. I followed her in.

"Hey, Aponi," Janice said to the dark-haired woman at the desk. "I hope you like your new job."

"Still trying to figure everything out, but I'm sure I will. Thanks for helping me land this."

"My pleasure. Our chairman knows to call me when we have a new member who wants to work here. Now, I need to see your boss, so I can introduce our new employee here."

The receptionist pressed a button on an intercom next to the phone on her desk. "Janice Williams is here with a new employee."

"Send them in."

Janice opened the door to the inner office, and we both entered, Janice leading the way. Sitting behind a large desk was a tall, thin man around sixty years old with graying light brown hair and blue eyes.

After Janice introduced me to the head of Quality Control, the man stood and reached over his desk to shake hands with me. "Please have a seat." I detected an accent with the singsong intonation typical of many Scandinavians. *Probably Norwegian.*

Although he seemed to be going through the motions of someone welcoming, I sensed a coldness about him. I inconspicuously turned on my watch's camera and sat down. Janice left, taking all the warmth in the room with her.

The man had my resume on his desk and questioned me about a few of the items. Having prepared, I was able to respond with confidence.

"I'll have the QC supervisor, Petter Gustavson, orient you," he said.

"He interviewed me for this job," I said. "It will be nice to meet him in person."

Ignoring my comment, the Quality Control head pressed the button on his intercom and said, "Aponi, send up the QC supervisor to meet our new employee."

The reply came over the intercom loud and clear. "A or B?"

The man's demeanor changed to one of irritation. "You have to ask? She's new here. A, of course."

"Sorry, sir. I'll get on it immediately and send him right in when he arrives."

Shortly after, a man around forty years old with short, reddish hair, entered the office after knocking.

"Nice to meet you in person, Petter," I said after introductions were made.

"I am happy to meet you, too," he answered, shaking my hand. From his accent and his name, I assumed he was also Norwegian. Appearing rather formal, he didn't come off as overly friendly, but I didn't sense the same iciness from him that I detected from the man behind the desk—just more of the typical Scandinavian aloofness.

The older man asked Petter to show me around the facility, then take me to the QC area and orient me to my job of testing non-penicillin antibiotics. I'd read that production of antibiotics in the penicillin family needs to be done in a completely separate building from other antibiotics, so this separation of antibiotic types seemed appropriate.

"Ya, sure," Petter said before turning to me. "Let's get going." Janice was talking to Aponi as I followed Petter out of the office. As we went down a maze of hallways, he turned to me and spoke in a quiet tone. "I know you're not being honest."

His words caught me by surprise. Should I confess I was there to spy on them, or should I wait and see if I could salvage the situation? I chose the latter. Trying my best to sound above suspicion, I said, “I don’t understand,” as my heart beat wildly in my chest.

“You didn’t fool me. I know you lied about your work experience. I could tell from your interview. I suspect you got good letters of recommendation because your company wanted to get rid of you. The only reason I hired you is ve have a hard time recruiting people, and I needed someone right away. I didn’t tell anyone, so you can keep your job if you work hard. It will be our secret.”

“Thank you,” I said. “Thank you for giving me a chance. I really need this job.”

We reached a catwalk suspended above a cavernous room. The walkway was enclosed in glass or plexiglass on both sides, giving us a view of the activity below.

Technicians, many with clipboards, were dressed in white bunny suits, booties, and head coverings. Some were milling around, others were standing by machinery and conveyor belts, and a few were busy pressing icons on computer screens. The equipment was covered in clear plastic sleeves, something I’d read about to prevent cross-contamination between the different drugs being manufactured. Several large metal containers, two stories high, were mixing or granulating materials visible through glass windows along the sides. While I watched, one machined stopped mixing, and equal portions of the contents were dropped into smaller containers on a conveyor belt below as they successively passed underneath. These vessels were then moved via automated guided vehicles to another area, where the mixtures inside were processed further.

As we walked farther down the catwalk, some of the processed material was fed into tablet presses to produce pills. Those needing coating passed through rotating perforated drums where they were sprayed with coating, then dried. Encapsulation was performed by machines that filled the bottom half of capsules with the appropriate mixture, then affixed the top half. The final products, pills and capsules, came into view as we neared the end of the assembly line. I watched as they were loaded into small bottles and subsequently sealed. At the far end of the room, the bottles were labeled and packed into cartons. So far, the operation was impressive. From start to finish, there was no breach in the manufacturing process to allow for contamination. The seamless operation was constantly overseen by technicians who kept logs, probably recording temperature and other parameters. So far, I saw nothing out of place.

"Ve make over one hundred different medications," Petter said. "I know a lot of large companies make many more, but this is a pretty new company, and we're constantly adding more products."

"I only see four different production lines here," I said. "Do you have a lot of similar production areas where the other medications are made?"

"Ya, ve have three more just like this. Unlike some larger manufacturers, ve don't have dedicated areas for making each medication. Ve clean the machinery and switch the products being produced regularly."

"Of course." I knew it was perfectly legal to do that, provided the equipment was meticulously decontaminated to avoid cross-contamination. "How many pills do you make a year?"

"About fifteen billion," he answered, glancing at me from the corner of his eye. I suspected he wanted to see if I looked duly impressed.

His answer left an impression, in that this was my first indication something wasn't according to Hoyle. While preparing for my visit, I had watched videos of pharmaceutical production lines and knew roughly how many pills could be produced in that room over twenty-four hours. Estimating the number of pills being produced there and multiplying by four, the total number made in that room plus the three others like it,

I came up with a number far lower than fifteen billion. *There must be another production area, much larger than what I'm seeing, even multiplied by four.* I didn't want him to know I suspected something was awry. "Impressive," was all I said, while my watch was inconspicuously capturing everything in sight. Petter already knew I was capable of trying to pass myself off as someone I wasn't. I couldn't give him another reason to distrust me.

CHAPTER 21

"I'll take you to the QC area now," Petter said as we left the walkway. "That's where you'll be working."

I took one last glance at the large manufacturing room before following him down a series of hallways to an open area on the second floor, where a receptionist behind a desk greeted us. Three offices and a large laboratory with a window to the inside opened into the space.

After introducing me to the receptionist, a pleasant Native American woman, Petter walked me towards the lab. "You'll be spending most of your time in here. I'll show you where to store your things and get your lab coat. Ve don't have to change our clothes and wear those bunny suits here in QC. No cell phones are allowed in the lab, but since reception here is terrible, it doesn't really matter."

My plan to take pictures with my phone had just been dashed. I followed Petter through double doors which opened automatically into a small anteroom. Lockers were stacked against one wall, and clean white lab coats hung on a rack opposite, arranged by size.

Petter instructed me how to open and close the lockers with a combination of my choosing. He put on a lab coat and said, "Pick an empty locker for your personal items. Then put on a lab coat. I'll meet you inside." He stepped in front of the door to the main lab, triggering it to open. "You can shadow me for a day or so to learn the ropes." The door closed behind him after he entered the lab.

I breathed a sigh of relief, happy to be alone, if even for a short time. Now I would be put to the test, needing to fake my way around the laboratory convincingly. Fortunately, I wouldn't be asked to do much. Yet. I took a pen from my purse, locked my jacket and purse in a locker, and put on a medium lab coat. After activating the cameras on my pen and glasses, I placed the pen in the lab coat breast pocket, aiming the camera lens outward. I took in a deep breath, shook my arms to relax, and entered a world where I would be out of my comfort zone.

Petter introduced me to the other technicians, most of whom had Scandinavian-sounding names. I picked out a pattern; many native Americans filled clerical jobs, while the technical positions were held predominantly by Norwegians. I surmised that the only reason I was offered a job there was they were low on Norwegians at the time.

I struggled with some of the new names I'd learned and made small talk with my co-workers while Petter arranged for me to get a password. After a few minutes, he took me aside and showed me how to log into the computer system and use the basic features.

"Now, ve can begin to work," he said. "It's time to do the annual QC on some of our medications. I have a list of eight non-penicillin antibiotics to do in the next few days." Looking at a list on the computer, he read off the names: azithromycin, cephalexin, ciprofloxacin, clindamycin, doxycycline, erythromycin, gentamycin, and vancomycin. "Ve should be able to get three of them done today. Any preference?"

I was so eager to test their cephalexin, the antibiotic that had failed my patient Ethan Wells, I felt I would explode. I looked around to be sure no one was staring at me as I tried to control my breathing and appear calm. Nobody seemed to notice my excited state. In my most casual voice, I answered, "How about azithromycin, vancomycin, and, say, cephalexin?"

"Okay, that's what ve will do. The procedure for analyzing each drug is in our online manual. The steps for each drug vary a bit, but basically, ve take the drug, mash it up, dissolve it, and analyze it. Ve look for both contaminants and the amount of drug by comparing the graph from our analysis to the graph of the reference material in the manual. Ve do this with four samples for each product."

What he said sounded reasonable. I knew the analysis would be done by high-performance liquid chromatography-mass spectrometry or HPLC-MS. This is performed by complex machines that identify chemicals dissolved in liquids by measuring a variety of molecular characteristics. I was itching to see the analysis of cephalexin. I didn't know about the other medications on the list, but I expected the cephalexin to fall short of the target concentration. On the other hand, I wondered if cheating was built into the QC testing process, assuring all results came out normal. I eagerly awaited what I would find out.

"I'll get the first samples now, and ve can get started." Petter walked to the other side of the lab and picked up a test tube rack, then returned and placed the rack on the bench in front of us. It held four tubes containing a lightly colored blue liquid. "Here are the four cephalexin specimens."

"Are these the samples we're supposed to test?" I asked. "It looks like someone has already dissolved the pills."

"Ya, that's how ve do it here. They start the process in another department, then send the dissolved specimens to us to finish."

"That's strange," I said. "There's no way I can be sure what these dissolved pills are."

"I know it's odd. I asked about it, too, when I started working here. One of the techs who dissolves the pills for us signs the QC document attesting to what they've done, so it's all within the regulatory guidelines. I'm told it's much easier this way—otherwise, I'd have more paperwork, and ve would have to store the solvents in this department."

Although this part of the procedure appeared dicey, I figured it was technically acceptable. Given what I knew about Umbroz, however, I strongly suspected the person verifying the authenticity of the samples was flat-out lying. The dissolved pills were probably made by a reputable manufacturer, the original patent holder, so the results would always come out in the expected range. I wondered if Petter knew the truth or had any suspicions.

"Okay, what do we do now?"

"Ve follow the procedure here in the computer. I'll show you how to do everything." I tagged along as Petter went through the necessary steps to get all four cephalexin specimens ready for analysis, a process that took about an hour.

Finally, he transferred portions of each sample into wells on a square plastic plate and loaded the plate into the HPLC-MS machine. The apparatus was a modular contraption about the size of two microwave ovens standing on end. Syringes and a complex array of components were protected under the partially transparent machine covering. Petter programmed the device using the touch screen, and it began to hum.

"Should be ready in ten to fifteen minutes. Fifteen minutes to be safe," Petter said. "While ve are waiting, I can take you downstairs to show you where our ingredients are stored and kept in quarantine until they're ready for use. You'll be assigned to check that sometimes. Ve rotate that responsibility."

Petter and I took an elevator to the basement, where we walked down a hall to a large storage room. There he pointed out the areas for holding inert and active pharmaceutical ingredients purchased elsewhere. They were stored in large boxes, up to thirty cubic feet. These ingredients are highly regulated, the FDA requiring strict adherence to using the exact product during manufacture as was used in clinical trials. Buying less expensive formulations with reduced purity or potency is one way a dishonest drug company can significantly shave expenses. I used my watch to photograph labels from all the containers so they could be reviewed later.

We spent a good fifteen minutes walking around the storage area, during which time Petter pointed out the logs I would need to examine when it was my turn to check the area, explaining I'd have to verify that the box labels matched the log entries. I found no fault with the overall QC system in that section.

We exited the storage area through a different door and headed back to the elevator.

"What's that?" I asked, pointing to a long, dimly-lit hallway extending a distance, then disappearing around a bend. I saw no visible doors or passageways opening into it.

"Ve have tunnels here."

"Makes sense. I suppose it gets freezing and snowy here in the winter."

"Ya, sure. I've only spent one winter here. It reminds me of home."

"Where's that?"

"Kongsberg. It's a small town outside of Oslo. That's in Norway."

I laughed a little. "I know where Oslo is. We Americans aren't quite as ignorant about geography as the rest of the world thinks we are."

"I didn't mean to offend you."

I saw this as an opportunity to milk Petter for whatever information I could get. "No offense taken. I understand the owner of this company is from Norway."

"Ya, that's right."

"A lot of the employees here are also from Norway."

"Ya. The company hires a lot of Norwegians. Most are related in some way to the founder. He arranges for us to get work visas. Many want to stay and are in the process of becoming citizens. I happen to be a distant relative, a third cousin twice removed, I believe."

"Are you going to stay in the US?"

"I'm thinking about it. To be honest, I don't like living here in Montana so much. I'd rather live someplace like San Francisco or Seattle."

"Both are nice cities. I can tell you a lot about San Francisco. I lived there some years ago." I wanted to get on his good side but couldn't blow my cover by telling him I lived there currently. "I'd sure love to see where that tunnel goes."

"Sorry, but the area is restricted. Don't you see the sign?" He pointed to a sign reading "Apartments. Residents Only."

"That must be where the nice apartments I heard about are. Can't I see them? I might want to live there."

"There's important research going on there in addition to living quarters. That's why it's off-limits. They are very concerned about spies from other companies."

Now we were getting someplace. "I wouldn't have thought they do much R&D here. After all, they just make generics."

Petter's face turned red, a clear sign he was uncomfortable. "The company has things they're working on that aren't on the market yet. They have a paper that recently came out about a medication to prevent rheumatoid arthritis in people with a genetic tendency to inherit it."

To say that my interest was piqued would be an understatement. Was he talking about the same medication that had been given to Skylar Reinhold, whose mother has rheumatoid arthritis? The girl who became deathly ill from a Nocardia infection? I tried to act only mildly interested, but my muscles were tense, and my throat felt so tight it was hard to talk.

"That sounds interesting," I said, my voice scratchy. I hoped he didn't notice. "My aunt would be interested in it. She has rheumatoid arthritis and worries about her two children getting it. She'd do anything to help them. What journal is it published in? Maybe my aunt could find the article and read it."

"Better yet, I'll give you a copy later."

I suppressed the urge to run upstairs, dragging Petter, so I could get the article. "That would be nice. I could mail it to her."

"Ve should be getting back, now. The results of the cephalexin test must be ready."

I had two things to look forward to as the elevator climbed to the QC floor—getting my hands on that paper and seeing the cephalexin analysis results. I had a hard time standing still as we ascended.

CHAPTER 22

Upstairs in the lab, the HPLC-MS graphs were waiting. I was bursting with anticipation, mentally preparing what I would say if the tracings showed the medication to be grossly inadequate. I couldn't gloat outwardly, but there was no limit to how much I would wallow in triumph to myself. If the results came back normal, I would need to show no reaction, but I'd know the samples we analyzed weren't the same as the pills they sold commercially.

Petter took the graphs from the printer and waved me over to study them with him. The results from each of the samples were identical and indistinguishable from the expected result in the manual.

"As always, perfect," Petter said, looking at me with a smile. For a Norwegian, such an outward display of emotion could be considered equivalent to jumping up and clicking his heels.

I didn't respond for a few moments. Finally, I managed to say, "Impressive."

Petter continued to talk, going into detail about the analysis of the graphs and how each portion compared with the reference material in the manual. I'm sure he gave me more details than would be necessary for a competent, seasoned technician. He hoped to teach me enough so I could stay on the job and relieve some of the workload. Nevertheless, I wasn't listening. *Yeah, yeah. They're obviously the same. Don't need to look carefully to see that. Whoever verified that the samples were Umbroz generics lied. How do I prove that?*

We spent the next hour preparing azithromycin samples for analysis. Again, we started with pills that were already dissolved, rather than intact pills I could verify myself as Umbroz generics.

While we waited for the HPLC-MS results, I went to the cafeteria with Petter for lunch. Due to the late hour, few other people were there, and the selection was limited. I grabbed a turkey sandwich while Petter had Swedish meatballs, which he told me are popular throughout Scandinavia. Afterward, I went back to the lab while he fetched a reprint of the paper on the Umbroz clinical trial of their medication to suppress development of rheumatoid arthritis.

"Thanks," I said as he handed me the document. "I'm sure my aunt will be very interested." I glanced at the paper and noted it was published in *The Midwestern Journal of Preventive Medicine*, an obscure journal I'd never heard of. I ached to read the whole article then and there but forced myself to act blasé. I folded the paper and placed it in my lab coat pocket, looking forward to studying it carefully later.

We checked the graphs from the azithromycin we had analyzed. As expected, each one was flawless. Next, Petter retrieved the vancomycin specimens, and we prepared them for analysis over the next hour. Again, the resulting graphs were impeccable. I was far from having the evidence I needed to shut the place down.

My thoughts were interrupted by Petter. "It's early, but ve have finished everything I planned to show you today, so why don't you leave early? Maybe you could study some of the things you learned today."

"Great idea, thanks. I'll stop by to see Janice in HR. She's putting together a list of apartment rentals I can look into. I need to find a place to live."

I removed my lab coat, retrieved the journal article Petter had given me earlier, and collected my jacket and purse from the locker. I reached Janice's desk in the HR office at 4:05 p.m. "Did you get a list of apartments for me?" I asked her.

When she didn't answer right away, I noticed that this usually happy, bubbly woman was wiping her eyes and sniffling. She was collecting herself so she could answer my question, but it was clear she had been crying.

"Are you okay, Janice?" I asked.

"Sorry, Mandy. There's a problem with Paco. Let me get the list of apartments for you." She started moving papers around on her desk, clearly distracted by her motherly concern.

"That can wait. If Paco needs help, that's more important."

Janice looked at me as she wiped her nose. "Thanks. I've finished everything else, so if it's okay with you, I would like to leave early to see him."

"No problem. What's wrong, if I might ask?"

"He's having a bad asthma attack. My sister took him to the clinic earlier, but they said he was just trying to get attention and didn't need anything other than his usual inhaler. They sent him home, and my sister's very concerned."

I wondered if Janice's son had received the care he needed. As it is often difficult to fill jobs for physicians in the Indian Health Service, I'd heard rumors that their doctors are often not the sharpest. Even so, I figured asthma, a common condition, was likely to be appropriately handled even by a mediocre physician. Janice's sister was probably overly concerned.

I wanted to get close to as many people as possible at Umbroz, not knowing who might help me in the future, and I thought this would be a good opportunity. "I have some medical training," I said. "I worked in a pediatrician's office when I was younger and learned a lot about asthma. I'd be happy to examine your son and tell you if it looks serious if you'd like."

Janice smiled. "Even though you're not a doctor, you're probably better than most of them who work in the clinic. Several kids from my neighborhood have died of asthma in the past few years after being sent home from there. Please, I'd like you to see my boy."

I followed Janice out of the building, onto a waiting bus in the parking lot. She explained to the driver I worked at Umbroz and was going to her house. Looking around, I saw that the bus was almost full. "Don't worry," Janice said to me, "I'll drive you back here to your car later."

The engine started up several minutes after we were seated. The driver headed to a road exiting the parking lot on the side opposite the one I'd entered on. "I thought there was only one road in and out of Umbroz," I said.

"This road connects Umbroz to the rest of the reservation. It's not on most maps." We stopped at an automatic barrier gate, where the driver passed a card in front of a detector on the left side of the road. The gate's arm raised, and we passed through. "Only residents and their guests are allowed onto this part of the reservation. Umbroz is the only place on White Mountain anyone in the public can drive to."

The bus made several stops along the bumpy road, with people getting off at each one. The view out the window didn't vary much, the terrain flat and covered with a patchy growth of lawn and weeds. Old cars were parked along the side, and clusters of houses were scattered haphazardly between expanses of nothingness. An occasional collection of small rusty trailers with cars or tents attached to make extra rooms appeared especially pitiful. I noticed a few groupings of large, new houses, but for the most part, the homes looked beat down, in need of paint and repairs. Broken windows and torn-off shingles on roofs were common. Small children played outside, often under the watchful eye of adults sitting on chairs or sofas in the front yard, drinking beer or soda.

We arrived at Janice's stop after thirty-five minutes. Two people exited the bus with us but went in different directions. I followed Janice up a small side street, Golden Bear Road, reminding me of Golden Bears, the mascot of my alma mater, UC Berkeley. She led me to a modest house with a large porch, one of the few houses I'd seen that didn't need a fresh coat of paint.

Inside the house, I was greeted by the aroma of something savory cooking, the giggling of children, and the drone of the TV. I met Janice's sister, Denise, her son I estimated to be around fourteen years old, and two young daughters.

"Do you live nearby?" I asked Denise.

"Just down the hall," came the answer.

It didn't take me long to realize they all lived in this one small house.

"How is Paco doing?" Janice asked.

"I don't think he's any better," Denise said. "He said he wanted to lie down, so he's been in the bedroom for about an hour. I checked him a few minutes ago. I don't think the inhaler is helping him."

Janice took me into one of the three bedrooms to see Paco. He was lying in a fetal position on a queen-size bed, facing the door while hugging a pillow. His breathing was slow and labored, the sound of his wheezing reaching the doorway. My muscles tensed. This wasn't going to be easy.

"Hi, I'm Mandy. Your mom wanted me to come by to check on you because I know something about treating asthma." I watched as Janice's son struggled to breathe, the muscles in his neck straining with the effort. "Is it okay if I listen to your chest?"

The boy nodded. I wished I had my stethoscope with me but was prepared to improvise. I walked around the bed, lifted his shirt in the back, and put my ear to his chest, my actions largely ignored by Paco. I heard wheezes throughout.

"Paco is having a bad asthma attack. Can you bring me all the medications he's on?" I asked Janice.

"It's just the inhaler." Janice looked around the room, then under the pillow Paco was holding. "Here it is."

I took the red plastic boot-shaped inhaler from Janice and lifted out the medication canister, labeled Albuterol in large letters. It felt light, and on shaking, I discovered it nearly empty. I panicked, thinking Paco had taken close to a whole canister of this medication in a few hours, likely a lethal dose, especially for a child his age. Not only does albuterol relax airways, but it can cause heart problems and seizures. I felt Paco's pulse—sixty-five and regular. I had expected his heart rate to be much higher from the albuterol. Next, I looked more closely at the medication label. Once I saw that Umbroz was the manufacturer, I relaxed a notch. I doubted the inhaler contained anything close to the prescribed concentration of albuterol.

"It looks like he's getting fatigued from all the effort he's putting into breathing. He needs more than an inhaler. Is there a hospital nearby?"

Janice clasped her hands, a worried expression on her face. "The nearest hospital is miles away, outside of Raintree."

"What about the clinic? Is it open at night for emergencies?"

"No way." Janice collapsed into the single chair in the bedroom, hugging her shoulders as tears streamed down her face. "Do you think he might die?" she whispered.

"There's something else we can try. Does anyone in your household take steroids? Like prednisone, dexamethasone, or hydrocortisone?"

"I know what steroids are, but nobody here takes them." Janice looked at the floor and shook her head as if defeated.

"What about neighbors? Do you have any neighbors with arthritis or lupus?"

Janice looked up and wiped under her nose, the beginning of a smile on her face. "The lady two doors down takes steroids. She has arthritis." Janice stepped into the doorway and shouted for her sister. Denise ran to us down the short hallway, whereupon Janice told her to hurry to the neighbor and get some of her steroid pills, emphasizing that speed was of the essence.

Once her sister had left, Janice lay on her side next to Paco, her arms caressing him. She had barely settled in and started singing to him when Denise returned. She was out of breath and bent over, one arm on her knee supporting her torso, the other outstretched towards me, holding a pill bottle.

I took the bottle and inspected it. The first thing I checked was the manufacturer. I breathed a sigh of relief when I read "Merck," a reputable drug manufacturer. The bottle was from a hospital in another state and contained Decadron, a brand name for dexamethasone, 0.75 mg.

"Perfect," I said. "Can you get a glass of water?"

Denise ran to the bathroom across the hall and returned momentarily with a glass of water. I shook a pill into my hand and asked Janice to help Paco sit up and take the medication. I watched as the boy put the medicine in his mouth and washed it down with the water.

"This will start to help in a little while," I said. "It will buy us some time while we drive to the hospital. Meanwhile, Paco needs to hang in there and keep breathing. It will get easier once the medication kicks in."

"I'll drive," Denise said. "Tawa, my son, can take care of his sisters."

Denise helped Janice walk her son to the car parked in front of the house, a Ford Fiesta hatchback. The car looked to be twenty years old, with a rusted chassis. Janice and I sat in the back, Paco between us. I was pleasantly surprised when Denise started the car right up, and we were on our way.

We sat in silence, the sound of Paco's labored breathing filling the air as Denise drove over the potholed streets, avoiding parked cars and children playing. When the sun started to set, I noticed the wheezing sound begin to subside as Paco continued breathing steadily.

"I think the medicine's kicking in," I said. I waited a few more minutes and saw the muscles in Paco's neck relax, the wheezing sound becoming fainter yet. "I'm certain of it now. His airways are opening up."

Janice started crying as she held Paco tighter. "Oh, I'm so happy. My baby is going to be okay." She was smiling, even as the tears streamed down her face.

"Maybe you could loosen your hold on him a little," I said. Just brought back from the brink of death, I didn't want Paco to be suffocated by his mother's loving, yet overzealous, embrace.

"Sorry," she said, loosening her grip while wearing a broad smile.

By the time we reached the hospital, Paco's breathing had significantly improved. I accompanied Paco, his mother, and his aunt to the emergency room and explained the events to the triage nurse. We were quickly escorted to a patient cubicle, where a physician examined the boy. Although he was doing better, the doctor wanted to admit him for observation overnight. Denise arranged for her children to spend the night with a neighbor so she and Janice could stay with Paco. I called for a taxi to drive me to my car, still in the Umbroz parking lot. Before leaving the hospital, I requested Paco be given non-generic inhalers upon discharge.

By the time I reached my car, I was exhausted, yet energized. Bringing Paco back from the brink of respiratory failure and death was fulfilling, something I loved doing. In addition, I figured I had made a friend I could count on.

CHAPTER 23

I stopped off at the diner for something to eat and reached my hotel room at 9:30 p.m., shortly after the sun had set. As expected, someone had been in my room to make the bed, change the towels, and clean the bathroom. I checked the folder with information about sightseeing in the area I had purposefully placed under some clothes in the dresser. The tiny crumbs I had left between the second and third sheet of paper had been moved. Someone had gone through my things.

After showering and getting comfortable in the flannel pajamas I'd purchased for this trip, I confirmed the hairs I'd left inside my suitcase's false bottom hadn't been disturbed. I retrieved the external drive Lim had bought me and uploaded all my recordings from the day. Then I transferred the files to my phone and emailed them to Lim. I didn't want to use the hotel Wi-Fi which, as I had predicted, lacked security. I checked my phone for messages and saw that Daisy had arrived and was in a room on the floor above me. I felt more relaxed knowing she was around. I texted her to meet me at the soda machine on her floor in ten minutes. Not knowing if the actions of hotel guests were monitored in hallways, we had agreed ahead of time not to have anything other than bogus personal conversations with each other at the hotel. Feeling so alone, I wanted to see Daisy to boost my spirits.

Meanwhile, I started reading the journal article Petter had given me earlier. It was titled "Prevention of Rheumatoid Arthritis in Susceptible Population." The abstract described screening adults with rheumatoid arthritis for a particular gene variant associated with developing the disease. Young children of adults with the gene variant were then tested, and the children who had inherited the same variant were treated with RA23567. This is a proprietary medication that stimulates a cell surface protein called adenosine receptor 3. Stimulation of this protein inhibits the activity of neutrophils, a type of white blood cell that is part of our immune system. In rheumatoid arthritis, neutrophils are not controlled correctly, and they release joint-destroying chemicals. By stimulating adenosine receptor 3 in susceptible people, RA23567 might theoretically prevent the harm perpetrated by neutrophils before joints would otherwise be injured.

I read no further, as it was time to meet Daisy. I'd learned enough to conclude that the neutrophil suppression caused by RA23567 had been sufficient to render Skylar Reinhold incapable of mounting a proper response to the Nocardia bacteria she came in contact with while gardening.

I put my jacket on over my pajamas, grabbed my purse, and hurried to the first-floor vending machine. I fumbled around in my bag, pretending to look for change, then ascended the nearby stairs to the second floor. A few steps away, Daisy was checking out the drinks available for purchase. I relaxed upon seeing her.

"Excuse me," I said, unable to suppress a smile at seeing my best friend, "but I don't seem to have the correct amount of money, and I'm dying for a coke. Do you have change for a five-dollar bill?" Daisy always carried lots of dollar bills for tipping when she traveled.

Daisy smiled. “I can only spare two dollar bills. I’ll give them to you for your five.” Daisy was being a brat, and loving it.

I wondered if we were being watched or listened to. I saw a ceiling sprinkler above us, but it might have been a camera. As we conducted our financial transaction, I handed Daisy a note telling her to meet me in the hotel parking lot at 8:00 p.m. the following evening.

As she put the paper in her pocket, Daisy asked, “So how is this town? I just got here a few hours ago. I’m starting a new job tomorrow at Umbroz.”

“What a coincidence,” I exclaimed, proud of my Oscar-worthy performance. “I started there today. Seems like a great place to work. I’m in the QC department. How about you?”

“IT, so I’ll probably be seeing you there since IT is involved in every department.”

“Yes, and generally not too popular.”

“For some reason, we always get a bad rap.”

“I’m sure you’ll do your very best to make sure you provide excellent service.” I smiled, or more accurately, smirked. I stopped myself from suggesting she bring in three dozen donuts on her first day.

“All I can do is try.”

I put two dollar bills in the machine, completed my coke purchase, and collected my change of two quarters.

“Maybe I’ll see you tomorrow,” I said as I turned to walk away, all the time wanting to stay and chat. When I returned to my room, I called home. Even though it was an hour earlier in San Francisco, it was past Maya’s bedtime. I was glad Lim had allowed her to wait up for my call. I found out about her earlier visit with her aunt and cousins and learned that both Ting and Mingyu were out of bed most of the day. Lim told me he would organize all the information I’d sent him earlier after Maya was asleep.

Once the conversation was over, I dumped the contents of the coke can down the sink in the bathroom, then finished reading the journal article. I learned that, to my surprise, Umbroz had indeed followed FDA rules and submitted their research protocol to a commercial Institutional Review Board, although I doubted the consent forms the parents of the clinical trial participants had signed contained all the information they were bound by law to have. Umbroz had probably found a dishonest for-profit board willing to ignore gross transgressions of standard procedures and data collection.

According to the paper, none of the participants receiving the Umbroz medication had developed rheumatoid arthritis or suffered any side effects. In those who received only a placebo, five percent had developed early signs of rheumatoid arthritis, a finding I had a hard time believing, given the young age of the participants. I doubted the veracity of anything reported in the paper.

The authors were Haakon Rakvag, another Umbroz employee, and a University of California professor of medicine who hadn't published any other papers in the past seven years. Doing a Google search, I surmised that this professor remained on the faculty of the university because of tenure, but was no longer productive. Umbroz had likely found him by searching for someone with his unimpressive profile, then convinced him to lend his name to the study, thereby boosting his credibility and ego. I had to admit, the results looked impressive. If only they were real.

I slept well that night, knowing Daisy was close by. The next morning I dressed, got breakfast at the diner, and drove to Umbroz. I stopped by the HR department to see Janice. She smiled and thanked me again, telling me the doctor had said Paco would likely have died before reaching the hospital without the steroid pill. He'd slept well the previous night and would be discharged later that day. Her sister, currently unemployed, would drive him home.

On my way upstairs to the QC lab, I passed by Daisy, who was being escorted to HR. I smiled and nodded, as did she. After all, we had met briefly by the vending machines the night before.

In the QC lab, Petter and I analyzed more antibiotics, all specimens showing precisely the expected results.

"How often do you find one of your pharmaceuticals to be out of range?" I asked.

"I can't remember that ever happening," Petter responded. "But if it did, we would retest it. If there was still a problem, we would, of course, recall the batch of pills."

I knew that even in drug companies following Good Manufacturing Procedures, failures happen. There are so many steps, each with the possibility of a slight deviation, that chance alone leads to some lots being out of compliance.

I was invited to join Petter and two of the other QC techs, both women, in the cafeteria where I could choose from a nice assortment of sandwiches, salads, and soups, as well as sliced reindeer meat and three types of herring. One of the other women and I chose a salad while Petter had reindeer meat and the remaining tech ate a sandwich she'd brought from home. Over lunch, I learned that the woman who had chosen a salad was born and raised in South Dakota and had only worked at Umbroz for three weeks. The other woman, from a town outside of Stockholm, had been at Umbroz three months. I was surprised none of them had worked there for long.

After lunch, Petter showed me a printout of the QC procedure we had used for cephalexin analysis. Other than our lab receiving the pills after they'd already been dissolved, it appeared to be typical of those I'd studied before coming here. I noticed a small letter "A" in the upper right corner of the paper.

"What's the 'A' for in the upper right corner?"

Petter's face turned red, and he seemed to be searching for words before speaking. "That means it's the first procedure written, I think."

"It hasn't been updated since it was first written?" That would be highly unusual. Not only are mistakes often noted when written protocols are put into action, but rules regarding testing are changed by the FDA over time, and these changes need to be incorporated into procedures.

"Did you find anything wrong with it?"

"No, but—"

"Then you see, there was no need to rewrite any of it." As soon as he spoke, Petter gazed downward, avoiding eye contact.

I decided it would be best not to pursue the subject. I wondered if Petter had learned of some of the company's transgressions and felt uncomfortable with them. I imagined he felt conflicted, unsure what to do or how much to say.

Petter and I analyzed the remaining antibiotics that afternoon, and all the results were, as expected, perfect. At 6:00 p.m., most of the staff had already left. I was getting ready to leave, disappointed that so far, I had only observed small things pointing towards the unreliability of the company's QC data. I was wondering what I could do to collect more incriminating information, a smoking gun.

My thoughts were interrupted when I overheard the South Dakotan talking to another worker. "Dammit! I forgot to QC the storage area earlier today. I don't want to stay late tonight because it's my husband's birthday, and I have to get to the bakery before it closes."

"I could do it for you," I volunteered, eager to have an excuse to look around the facility.

"Thanks, Mandy. You're so sweet."

It took me a second to realize she was addressing me, as I still wasn't quite used to my name. She explained details about filling out the form, thanked me again, and left. I was almost giddy with excitement, having an excuse to nose around alone downstairs. I decided to do the required QC work, then explore nearby rooms to see what I could find. Meanwhile, I hoped Daisy would uncover something useful.

I grabbed my phone and took the stairs to the basement where the ingredients were stored. It didn't take me long to find the room with the chemicals needing documentation. I noticed all the room numbers had "A" next to them. This hadn't caught my attention before, but seeing them then, I wondered if this was related to the "A" in the procedure manual.

Clipboard in hand, I looked at each large container and verified the information on the labels, checking them off as I went along and captured images on my recording equipment. All was in order. To find everything on the list took thirty minutes and brought me into three separate storage rooms.

When I finished, I reflected on the fact that the Umbroz employees seemed to take quitting time seriously. All the workers in the lab had already gone home before I came downstairs, and I hadn't seen another person since I'd started my inspection. I had initially intended to return to the QC lab upstairs, collect my things, and leave for my hotel when I had completed my work in the storage area.

Instead, I made a spur-of-the-moment change of plans. I took three slow, deep breaths and proceeded down the tunnel I'd seen the day before, past a sign that read "Apartments. Residents Only." I realized I might be stopped, but the worst they could do was fire me.

After walking past the tunnel's curve, I saw that it led to a set of gray doors about a football field length away. On my left, I noted an alcove leading to a door labeled "Stability Testing B." I was in "B" country. I tried the door, but it was locked. Going farther down the tunnel, I saw about ten similar entries, each labeled with a lab function, followed by "B."

When I was close to the double doors at the end of the passageway, my chest tightened and, although it wasn't hot, sweat dripped down my forehead and my sides. My body was warning me to go no farther, but I overruled it, noting that this was the whole reason for my trip. If I didn't succeed, lives would be lost. I was sure of that.

I stopped for a moment to collect myself. The thud of automatic doors beginning to open startled me. My eyes were almost blinded by the bright lights exposed as the doors at the end of the tunnel slowly parted. I jumped sideways, into the last alcove before the tunnel ended. A group of three men in suits, two over six feet tall, walked out, speaking, or more accurately, arguing about something. They didn't see me standing in the shadow of the alcove as I strained to listen to their conversation. I held up my pen to record their words and, after a few moments, realized I couldn't understand them because they weren't speaking English. Most likely, they were conversing in Norwegian. The group passed under one of the overhead lights as they went by, so I got a good look at all of them. I gasped when I saw that one of them was the man I'd seen dining at Kokkari Estiatorio—I was standing a few feet from Johan Rakvag.

CHAPTER 24

I stopped breathing until the men passed me. Then I quietly stepped out from the dark recess to see what I could through the doors, which stayed open for several more seconds before starting to close. All I could make out was a large space filled with cardboard boxes leading to a series of hallways. I didn't see anyone aside from the trio that had just walked by and disappeared around the curve. I took a few pictures and considered running through the doorway before the doors slammed shut, then thought the better of it.

My body was tense as my heart beat rapidly. I was paralyzed with fear and stood frozen like a statue watching the doors. The instant they clanged shut, I regretted my inaction. I had to keep it together and get what I needed. I was about to lose my medical license and livelihood. They couldn't do much more to me. I decided to hide in the alcove until someone else left through the doors, then run inside while I had the opportunity. I'd wait for hours if need be.

Fifteen minutes later, a woman wearing a lab coat similar to mine exited the doors to the tunnel. I waited until she passed me, breathed in deeply, and took long, low steps as quietly as I could until I was through the doors. Once inside the empty room, I stood beside the doorway to catch my breath and assess my surroundings. Over the sound of my breathing, I heard the voices of people approaching from a hallway. *Shit. I need to hide.*

Seeing the door to a ladies' restroom nearby, I sprinted, pushed the door open, and entered. I found myself inside a foyer with comfortable-looking chairs lined up against two walls. A table and mirror like one might find in an upscale department store or restaurant were at the far end. *I might as well pee now that I'm here.* I went through a swinging door and entered an area with sinks and stalls. My heart raced upon seeing a young woman washing her hands at a sink.

She looked up and said something I didn't understand. Uncertain how to react, I stared, motionless.

"Sorry, I see you don't speak Norwegian," she said in English with a heavy Norwegian accent, laughing slightly. "Are you new here, to B? I haven't seen you before."

With adrenaline surging through my system, I felt tense and alert. I decided to fake being a member of the B team as long as I could get away with it.

"Yes, I'm new here. In fact, I'm really embarrassed, but I'm kind of lost."

"I found this complex confusing, too, when I first started here. The A building is much smaller and simpler. Sorry, I assumed you were Norwegian when I first saw you. As you know, most of us are. We try to remember to speak English when we know there's someone around who doesn't speak our language. Don't be offended when people forget."

"I'll try to remember that."

"Where do you want to go? I can send you in the right direction."

"The QC department."

"Lucky you, one of the easiest departments around. Seems like they hardly do any work. I'm sure they've all gone home by now."

"You're probably right, but since I'm so new, I'm slow and didn't finish everything today. I don't want to start off on the wrong foot, so I want to go back there and finish up."

"After two weeks here, you'll probably have a different attitude. I'll wait for you and show you where to go."

"Thanks." I went into one of the stalls, peed, then washed my hands. "I'm ready."

The woman escorted me down a hallway that led to another tunnel, then into yet another building. We passed by several other workers, who nodded and greeted my escort. I relaxed with her at my side, as her presence seemed to give me credibility.

We walked by a bank of elevators with a sign reading "Disease Prevention Project." At the next group of elevators, she pressed a button for me. "I don't know how you got so lost, but here's the closest elevator to QC. Do you remember what floor it's on?"

"Oh, gee. Now I'm not sure. I think it was two."

"You are pretty hopeless. It's three. Try to remember that tomorrow when you come back to work. Signs will direct you to the QC area. You'll see them as soon as you exit the elevator on your floor."

"Thank you."

The woman left as the elevator door opened. Thankfully, it was unoccupied. I stepped in and took several slow, measured breaths. As the doors closed, I felt tense and excited, anticipating what I might find on the third floor.

Upon exiting the elevator, I saw a sign directing me to the QC lab. Another pointed to the ingredient storage area. I followed the arrow to the QC lab and tried the main door. Locked. I peered through the windows opening into the hallway and saw that the dimly lit room was deserted. Thankfully, a smaller door at the far end of the lab was unlocked. As I entered, my pulse quickened with excitement.

I stood for a few minutes to let my eyes adjust, the only illumination coming from the hallway. There was no way I was going to turn on more lights and possibly bring attention to myself. The benchtops were neat, giving the impression that the workers there were either very fastidious or didn't do much. I looked around and saw four HPLC MS machines, similar to those in the QC lab I worked in. Each was uniquely identified by a large number, one through four, affixed to the front.

Ethernet cables, one from each machine, were clipped into what appeared to be a homemade metal device designed to keep the lines neat and separated. Each cable was labeled with the number of the instrument it was attached to. The ends hung in the air, precluding transfer of information to the main computer.

Nearby, four additional cables ran from a metal plate in the wall to a lidless box on the benchtop. Inside the box, the cables were labeled one through four. Each had a connector on the end. I surmised that each HPLC MS instrument was kept offline, but when a desired result was obtained, the cable from the machine would be connected to the corresponding numbered cable coming out of the wall so data could be transferred to the main computer for storage. Usually, however, data generated there likely stayed there. Failed tests records weren't saved. *What happens in Umbroz QC stays in Umbroz QC.*

On another bench, I noticed pill jars lined up next to test tubes containing crushed pills, ready to be dissolved. I tried to read the labels on the jars, but the lighting was too dark. I carried several bottles to a window for more light, where I saw that each contained pills from a brand-name pharmaceutical. I couldn't think of a good reason for brand-name pills to be anywhere near the QC department of an honest generic drug manufacturer.

Walking back and forth several times, I brought all the jars to the window so I could read them. Included were the medications we would be testing the next day. If it wasn't clear before, it was now. Technicians in this lab, QC B, were dissolving brand-name pills and sending them to QC A for analysis, where the results were recorded as being from the corresponding generic Umbroz drugs. I videoed as much as possible with my glasses, hoping the light wasn't too dim to capture what I saw.

I left the QC lab and followed signs to the reagent supply area. The quiet of the hallway was replaced by a low din that got louder as I walked. I was startled when a man in a white coat suddenly came into view as he turned a corner into the hallway I was in. He walked quickly and seemed to take no note of me when he brushed by, as if I were invisible.

I followed the signage and turned down the hallway the man had appeared from. Continuing, the ambient noise became louder, the illumination brighter. I was soon under intense lighting. Several workers were milling around, transporting large containers of chemicals on trolleys. They ignored me as I watched them disappear through automatic double doors. Each time the doors opened, the noise level increased dramatically. I looked through an adjacent window, into a vast space filled with workers tending to mixers, conveyor belts, and complex machinery. I was looking at an area of drug manufacture many times larger than the one I'd seen my first day on the job.

I turned down a hallway and found a nearby storage room. As I walked amongst the rows of chemicals, I took pictures of many of the labels. This area was much larger than the storage section in area A.

I thought about going through the double doors into the manufacturing site but decided not to press my luck. It was clear the smaller A site was for show only. That's where visiting FDA inspectors would be taken to inspect the facility and go through data to verify Umbroz complied with Good Manufacturing Practices. An expensive sham operation, obviously worthwhile.

I was due to meet Daisy in the hotel's parking lot in a little over thirty minutes. I stepped into the hallway to leave as two men, one in a suit, approached from a distance. I wanted to avoid men in suits, as they might be more suspicious of me than the workers who were merely concerned with getting through their shifts. I jumped back into the storage room and waited as the men's footsteps approached.

As they passed by the doorway to the storage area, I caught a glimpse of them. I recognized one of the men from photos I'd seen: Haakon Rakvag. The other was a large, muscular man dressed in sweatpants and a T-shirt. His dirty blond beard tinged with a small amount of gray matched his stringy shoulder-length hair. It was easy to imagine him wearing a metal Viking helmet, a spear in each hand. As they were speaking in Norwegian, I didn't understand what they were saying, but I did recognize one word: Martha.

CHAPTER 25

I wondered if the Martha they referred to was my Martha, and why they were mentioning her. *Were they looking for her? Worried she might disclose information to the authorities? Or was she still working with them after duping me into believing she was living with her mother and no longer wanted anything to do with Umbroz?*

When Haakon Rakvag and his associate were a safe distance away, I emerged from my hiding place, took the elevator down, and found the tunnel leading back to A. On the way, I walked by several workers but managed to stay calm on the outside, nodding ever so slightly as I passed them—intentionally not smiling, so I didn't appear to be unNorwegian, my stomach in knots. I couldn't wait to be back in my car.

I returned to the QC lab, left my lab coat, and picked up my purse and jacket. I didn't have time to stop for dinner at the diner and reached the hotel parking lot thirty seconds late. Daisy was standing outside her car, pretending to look for something. Lucky for me, there were empty parking spots all around her. I pulled into one of them, leaving space for one car between us.

"Lose something?" I asked as I exited my car, buttoning my jacket against the cold night air. The sun was still up, but a heavy cloud layer made it the coldest night yet.

"I had a small gold stud earring in my purse, and now it's gone. It's really small. My sister gave it to me just before she died, so it has great sentimental value."

I gave Daisy a look that I hoped conveyed the message, *don't be so melodramatic*, as I walked over. "I'm good at finding small things," I said. "I once found a contact lens on a football field a player lost during the game."

"Now look at who's being ridiculous," Daisy whispered when I reached her.

"Did you look under the seat?" I asked loudly, followed by a whisper, "I got a lot of info today. How about you?"

"I opened up a portal for Lim to access. I already sent him all the information he needs to hack into their system," she whispered back as she checked under her car seat.

"You should quit now. Leave tomorrow. It doesn't sound like there's anything more you need to do, not if Lim can access everything from the safety of our home."

"I was thinking the same thing. I found there are two separate systems, called A and B. They communicate only once every six hours. That's when B can be accessed. Otherwise, it's air-gapped."

"Great work. Reserve your flight for tomorrow. Text me with your flight information tonight."

"Will do. What about you? What have you found?"

"Maybe I should look around the back seat. It could have rolled back there," I said, probably louder than I should have. I opened the back door and started looking around the floor. "I got tons of stuff. Probably everything I need," I whispered. "Just need to send everything to Lim when I'm back in my room. I couldn't read every label I got pictures of, but if the evidence shows what I think it will, we'll have a tight case."

"Maybe you should leave tomorrow too."

"I thought of that, but there's one more thing I want to follow up on. I don't quite know how to go about it, though."

"What's that?"

"I heard the owner of the company mention Martha's name. I want to know if she's still really in cahoots with them or if they're trying to find her. I'd want to warn her."

"I thought you were sure these people weren't dangerous. Unless you're taking their medicine, that is."

"I saw a scary-looking guy walking with the owner of the company today. It got my imagination going. Maybe they're not quite as averse to violence as Martha thinks. I'll ask Janice if Martha's on the books there. I can say I worked with her years ago and heard through a mutual friend she worked for Umbroz."

"Martha made her bed. Whatever her involvement is now, I think you'd better get the hell out of here if you even think there's a chance these guys are dangerous."

"I want to know about Martha, one way or the other. If Janice can't help me, and if nothing else turns up, I'll say I'm not feeling well and leave. I'll drive to Great Falls tomorrow afternoon."

"Better yet, why don't you leave in the morning and call Janice on the way to the airport. Tell her you're sick and ask her about Martha. Don't go in at all."

"You're right. There's no need for me to go in. I'll reserve a seat on the same flight as you. Text me when you get in your car tomorrow morning. I don't want it to look like we're leaving together, so I'll check out fifteen minutes later and head to the airport. I'll see you there." Then I yelled, "I found your earring," and held up a speck of yellow lint.

"Thank you," Daisy said.

"Glad to help," I said as I headed back to my room.

Once inside, I took out two energy bars I'd packed for the trip and scarfed them down. I followed that with two glasses of tap water. Refreshed, I uploaded all the information I'd gathered that day to my portable drive, transferred it to my phone, and emailed everything to Lim.

Daisy texted me her flight itinerary. She'd be leaving the following evening, arriving in San Francisco late that night. I reserved seats on the same flights, then called Lim.

"I'm planning on leaving here tomorrow," I said. "I'll drive to the airport in the morning and call HR on my way to take care of a few loose ends. I'll be back in San Francisco late tomorrow."

"That's wonderful. I'm sure Ting will be excited to see you. She and Mingyu are doing great. My mother said they even walked outside earlier—Ting, Mingyu, Wang Shu, Kang, and my parents. I wish I could have been there."

"I'll bet. That's what you get for being a successful entrepreneur."

"But I was here when Maya recited the alphabet earlier."

"Damn. I wish I could have been there."

"That's what you get for being a successful spy." Suddenly, Lim was yelling in Chinese. I heard him drop the phone, take several running steps and open a window, yelling the whole time. Then I heard Kang's voice, sounding upset.

A few moments later, Lim was back on the phone. "Kang climbed the building again and was outside our living room window. I don't know what to do with that boy. The rock-climbing gym wasn't the answer. I'm going to march him downstairs."

"Okay, see you tomorrow. We can talk about what to do about Kang then," I said, feeling his rush to get off the phone. I didn't have time to tell him I'd heard Martha's name. No matter—for all I knew, it could have been a different Martha. Making the arrangements for my trip home made me more homesick than I was already. Before I went to bed, I texted Lim my flight information.

The next morning, I kept checking my phone for Daisy's text as I packed my bags. I was getting hungry and planned to stop by the diner on my way to the airport. Finally, about ten minutes after I should have left for work, Daisy's text came. She was going to her car, about to leave for the airport. I texted back my wishes for a safe drive.

I made one last sweep of the room as I always did when leaving a hotel. Needing to kill time, I scrolled through the emails on my phone and checked the weather forecast. I found a YouTube video about making Play-Doh animals. Ten minutes later, I grabbed my purse and luggage, checked out at the front desk, and headed to the parking lot.

As I approached my car, I mentally prepared for my call to Janice. I'd ask her how Paco was doing, then find out if Martha was listed as an employee. If she were, I'd inquire about her current address and phone number. Although against the rules, I was pretty confident Janice would oblige me, given how much I'd helped her son.

If Martha's old address and phone number were listed, that would lead me to believe she was probably no longer working for them. If the information had been changed to a place in Nebraska or elsewhere, I could be sure she was still helping them. If Martha wasn't in their system at all, I wouldn't know what to make of that.

I was looking down, fumbling in my purse for my car key, when I was abruptly sandwiched between two men who seemed to appear out of nowhere. I recognized the larger of the two men as the Viking-like man I'd seen with Haakon Rakvag the previous evening. The other man was shorter, less muscular, and well-dressed, with graying hair. He appeared to be about ten years older than his associate. Looking over the hood of my car, I saw a windowless van parked ten spaces away. I hadn't heard it pull in. It had probably been parked there, waiting for me when I walked out.

"Give me your purse," the smaller man said in a heavy Scandinavian accent. He said something in Norwegian to his companion. Seeing no choice, I complied. "We go to the van now. Don't cause trouble."

Still sandwiched between them, the men pushed me towards the van. I didn't see a good outcome to this turn of events, so I took off running toward the road in front of the hotel. I felt foolish when the Viking caught up to me before I was halfway to the street, grabbed me around the waist from behind, and lifted me up. I tried to wriggle from his grasp, my arms flailing and my legs kicking, but he didn't seem to notice. I felt like a chicken being held by a farmer on the way to the chopping block. Resisting was futile. I resisted anyway. I saw a maid pushing her cart on the second-floor walkway. I screamed, sure she could hear me, but my cries were ignored.

The Viking took slow, lumbering steps toward the van, where the man with my purse was waiting, the back doors to the vehicle open. The large man shoved me in, and the doors slammed behind me.

CHAPTER 26

It was nearly dark inside the van, with no windows and only a few small slit-like spaces around the partition separating the back of the vehicle from the front seats. The two men spoke in Norwegian and laughed as they walked to the front of the van, then got in. The door to my rental car remained open, my luggage still on the adjacent asphalt. That was the least of my problems.

The engine started, and we moved forward. Listening to their voices, it appeared that the Viking was sitting in the passenger seat while the other man drove. I couldn't hear much of their conversation over the drone of the engine, but that didn't matter. I wouldn't have understood them anyway.

My heart was pounding, and my body was tense. I tried breathing deeply but found no relief. With each bend in the road, I was glad my hands weren't tied and was able to prevent myself from rolling around uncontrollably. There was no question in my mind these men worked for Umbroz, and they were bringing me someplace where something unpleasant would happen. I wondered if I was being brought to the Umbroz facility or elsewhere. Either way, I dreaded discovering what awaited me.

After a half hour, the van stopped briefly. I listened intently and heard the driver lower his window. I perceived the sound of an electronic beep like the one I'd heard when the bus drove me to White Mountain two days earlier. The driver rolled the window up, and we were moving forward again. I wondered why we were going to the Indian reservation.

Around ten minutes later, we came to a stop. My heart pounded harder as footsteps approached the back of the van. The men had a short conversation, then the doors swung open. Trees overhead partially blocked the sun, although it was bright enough to hurt my eyes. As I blinked against the light, I saw the same two men, the older one holding my purse. He said, "We are here. If you behave, if you don't try to fight and run away, we won't tie you up. You try anything, we tie you. Very uncomfortable. Your choice. Understand?"

I nodded in the affirmative as I answered, "I understand."

"Get out."

I scrambled to the edge of the van, dangled my legs over, and pushed myself to a standing position. I looked around and saw a portion of a large building. The loud hum of a motor running filled the air. We were in what appeared to be a delivery dock. I tried turning and arching my back in an attempt to see more of the structure before me, but before I could see much, each man grabbed one of my arms and walked me upstairs to a landing outside the building. Just before being shoved through a doorway, I turned my head to see a large truck, the word "Nilsen's Dairy" on the side. I surmised that the sound I was hearing was from the truck's refrigeration system. No one was around the truck, and I saw no evidence a grocery store was nearby. I was left to ponder why a large dairy delivery truck was left sitting there, the refrigeration running.

As the men escorted me down a hall, past several rooms, I scoured the area for a knife, blunt object, even a gun I could grab to make a getaway, but saw nothing. I was taken into a dark room where one of the men switched the overhead light on. A heavy curtain covered the single window. The only furnishings were a rectangular wood table and several folding chairs.

"Sit," the smaller man said, pointing to one of the chairs. My heart was pounding, and my throat was dry as I sat without comment. I'd seen my share of spy movies, and this looked every bit as foreboding as the rooms where political prisoners were tortured and interrogated.

While the Viking stood guard, the other man left the room, returning with three glasses of water on a tray which he set on the table.

"Take. Drink," he said.

Not sure what to do, suspicious of a drug or poison in the water, I sat motionless.

"You take. We drink others."

I took one of the glasses, the one closest to the Viking, and held it. The others each took one of the remaining glasses and began drinking. While that allayed my suspicion, I began to wonder if they had done experiments and determined that, say, eighty-nine percent of the time, a prisoner would take the glass I had chosen. Feeling parched, I reasoned that if they wanted to kill me, they could do it another way. I drank.

The smaller man dumped the contents of my purse on the table, just beyond my reach, and sorted through the contents. He looked closely at my keys, then opened my tube of Red Passion lipstick and twisted the base, raising the stick of creamy, hydrating pigment as far as possible. After making several red streaks on the table, smashing the end of the lipstick in the process, he tossed the tube aside. Then he checked around the edges of a small mirror, dumped out a box of throat lozenges, and scrutinized the box and each lozenge. After an item was inspected, he placed it to the side. Each compartment in my wallet—those for credit cards, business cards, coins, and bills—

was explored, the contents placed with the other items he'd already examined.

The inspection was interrupted by a call on his cellphone. Feeling warm, I removed my jacket and placed it over the back of the chair as he spoke in a normal tone of voice, knowing I wouldn't understand a word. As he listened, his expression turned from neutral to angry. He disconnected the call and put the phone in his pocket. Then he looked at me as if to say *how dare you?* before speaking to the Viking, who looked at me similarly.

"Give me glasses," the smaller man said.

Damn. Someone was probably going through my suitcase and found the electronics hidden in the false bottom.

I inconspicuously activated the camera on my watch and handed the man my glasses. He shook his head from side to side, smirking, as he inspected the temple and opened the little door, removing the micro-SD card. Then he looked carefully at every pen on the table and found SD cards in three of them.

"You are a very foolish young lady," he said. "You get into our restricted area and walk around, take pictures and videos. Don't you think we have cameras, better than your little cameras in pens and glasses? Our security people saw you on video running into the restricted area last night. Then they reviewed all the film and saw you sneaking around all over the place. Tell me, what were you looking for?"

As the man spoke, the Viking stood nearby, staring at me. I wasn't sure how far these men would go to find out what I was doing. I was comforted a bit by noting there were no knives or firearms in sight. On the other hand, the big guy looked like he could easily kill someone with his bare hands. I wondered if he ever had.

I was tense, my heart pounding. I tried to speak, but my throat was so dry, the words didn't come out. I took a few more gulps of water. My only hope was to talk myself out of the situation.

"I'm so sorry I lied to get this job. I've never done anything like this before, but my company, Celgene, wanted to steal some of your secrets. That's a high compliment, really," I said, laughing nervously and looking at each of the men, buying myself a few seconds to plan what I was going to say next. They remained stone-faced. "To be honest, I wasn't sure what to look for, so I took pictures of what I could."

"You said, 'to be honest.' I know you're not being honest with us, Doctor Erica Rosen. We know who you are, so stop with the playing of games."

I sat frozen, realizing they knew who I was and that I was after evidence of fabricated data. *If I confessed to everything, would they let me go? What would be a satisfactory endpoint to them? Could I promise never to release the information I had gathered?* Doubtful. I remained silent as I weighed my options.

"We found the false bottom of your suitcase containing a portable drive capable of transferring all the information from the SD cards onto your cell phone. Tell me, Doctor, if I look at your phone here, will I find all the information you recorded?"

I grabbed the water glass again, trying to buy time while I thought of an answer. I'm sure they heard the noise my throat made while I swallowed.

"Here," the man said, thrusting my cell phone at me, "put in the password for your phone."

"I . . . I can't," I said.

"Can't, or won't?"

"I won't." *What were they going to do now, kill me?* I didn't think so. They wanted to know if I'd sent any information out, and if so, who I sent it to. If, worst-case scenario, they killed me, they wouldn't find out. They'd be vulnerable, not knowing where the information had landed. They needed me.

"We can do this the hard way or the easy way, Doctor. I would suggest the easy way."

"You can't get away with kidnapping me. People are looking for me right now. The police in San Francisco know if I don't check in with them every two hours, they need to send people to rescue me."

The man laughed. "You have a good imagination, Doctor. If Mr. Rakvag wasn't such good friends with the mayor in your beautiful city, I might believe you. Probably not, but I might. But since Mr. Rakvag is such good friends with him, and the mayor is so close to the police chief, he would know of any investigations that don't relate to the homeless demonstrations going on now. I know you're lying. Nobody is looking for you. Even if they were, it would be hard to find you here."

"Where are we exactly? Are we somewhere on the Indian reservation?"

"Very good, Dr. Rosen. Here on the reservation, they have their own police department, and the local police are very loyal to Mr. Rakvag. The local police of Raintree don't come here unless someone from inside asks them for help. It wouldn't matter, though, because they are also very loyal to Mr. Rakvag. Umbroz also has a very wonderful relationship with the tribal council here. In fact, the chairman is on the board of directors of Umbroz and is well-paid for all his valuable advice. In return, the company employs many people on the reservation. Before Umbroz, the unemployment rate here was forty-five percent. Now, it's eight percent. Did I mention the nice parks and schools Umbroz has generously donated?"

"Even if nobody's looking for me now, it's only a question of time before they do."

"As much as I've been enjoying our little chat, I'm starting to get bored. Let me show you what happens to people who try to cause us trouble." He looked at the Viking and nodded.

I became more terrified than I was before. What were they going to show me? A medieval torture rack? Dental equipment capable of causing terrible pain, like that featured in the 1970s movie *Marathon Man*?

The Viking grabbed my arm and pulled upwards until I was standing.

"Let's go for a little walk," the shorter man said. With the Viking still gripping my arm, he led us out of the building into the cold air, down the steps, and toward the rear of the refrigerated dairy truck. I doubted they got people to talk by forcing them to drink milk. Perhaps they intended to lock me in the cold, dark truck until I broke. I knew I wouldn't last long, so I concentrated, trying to think of something I could tell them. The last thing I wanted to do was divulge I'd sent all the information to Lim. I didn't want to put him in danger.

Once we were standing at the rear of the truck, the shorter man said a few words to the Viking in Norwegian. He needed to speak loudly to be heard over the noise from the refrigeration unit. As I stood shivering from a combination of cold and fear, I noticed a power cord running from the truck into a large shed.

The Viking said, "Ja, Sven," before picking up a portable set of five wooden steps nearby. It probably weighed over fifty pounds, but he seemed to lift it effortlessly. He placed the stairs behind the truck, climbed to the top, then rolled the door of the truck up and stepped inside. The man I now knew as Sven pushed me towards the steps. "Go," he said. I was leery but followed his instruction. When I stood on the top step, the Viking pulled on a string hanging from the truck ceiling. Lights inside the truck turned on, revealing the contents.

I'm sure they heard me gasp when I realized what I was looking at. Three oblong shapes, five to six feet long, each wrapped in a white plastic sheet. Ropes were tied around narrow areas near each end. I was looking at three dead people, neatly wrapped in plastic, secured with rope around the neck and ankles.

"The refrigeration keeps them from smelling. When it's time, my friend here will drive the truck way up north and bury them. Of course, in wintertime, the bodies stack up because the ground is frozen, and they can't be buried until it thaws."

"What did these people do? Why did you kill them?" I asked without thinking.

"One, sadly, is a local teenager who died at home, possibly from effects of a drug we were testing. The others were troublemakers."

"What do you mean by troublemakers?"

The man grinned diabolically, then said, "Let me show you." He nodded at the Viking and gave him an order.

"*Min glede,*" the large man replied. He obediently tore at the plastic sheet around the head of the smallest body. At first, all I saw was a mass of brown hair. As he peeled away more, I saw part of a face—a woman's face. He continued stripping away the plastic, revealing two eyes looking back at me. The woman looked at peace, a single bullet hole in her forehead. It was Martha.

CHAPTER 27

I felt numb, trying to process what I'd just seen. My legs felt weak, and I was nauseated but didn't sense I would collapse. I must have looked faint because the Viking grabbed me by one arm and practically lifted me off my feet. He led me down the steps, away from the truck, up the stairs to the building, and back to the room we'd been in before. Feeling gut-punched, I didn't have time to dwell on Martha and her demise at the hands of these horrible people. By the time I was sitting in the same chair I'd been in earlier, I knew I had to concentrate on getting out of there or I'd never see Maya, Lim, or Daisy again.

Sven entered the room and resumed the interrogation. I looked around once more, hoping to see an object to help me escape, as if someone might have dropped off something useful while I'd been out of the room. Other than the contents of my purse on the table, there were no loose items. No baseball bats or heavy paperweights to bash their heads in, no fireplace pokers to stab them with.

"Now you see what happens to people who don't cooperate," Sven said.

"How do I know you'll let me go even if I cooperate?"

"You have no choice but to trust me."

"Martha trusted you, and look what happened to her."

"Martha is someone we trusted. Then she betrayed us. So, you see, her situation was a little different. We never had a trusting relationship with you, but I'd like to establish one now. Of course, if we do come to an agreement with you, and you back out, well, I suppose you would wind up like Martha."

"What if I decide not to cooperate?"

"I think you will. It may take a little time, but I'm sure we can develop a mutual trust. In Scandinavian culture, mutual trust is very important."

"Mutual trust, yes, I understand that, but you're perverting it by requiring loyalty under penalty of death."

"I don't seem to be making much progress with you, Doctor. Perhaps I can show you something more persuasive."

I'd already seen Martha, dead. I couldn't think of anything more compelling than that.

The Viking pulled me up to a standing position and walked me down the hall towards the outside door. He stood me in front of the last door in the hallway and quietly nudged it open several inches. I looked inside, and my heart sank. There, seated facing sideways, was Daisy. Her arms were behind her back, her legs and hands tied together with a length of rope that held her to the chair. A wad of something was secured in her mouth, preventing her from talking or yelling. I took in a breath, planning to scream out her name, but before I could, the Viking shoved me away and closed the door. I yelled out her name anyway, not knowing if she heard me.

Seeming to lose his patience, the large man picked me up as he'd done before, my legs kicking, brought me back to the room we'd been in, and dumped me in my chair.

I started to speak, my throat so dry I hardly recognized my voice. "How did—"

"You want to know how we knew she was involved in your little scheme? Your idea was ingenious, I'll give you that. Fooling our system into thinking the two of you had sent in your applications over a month earlier so we'd rush them through. Donna Liang—or should I say Daisy Wong?—is very clever with computers. Our organization would welcome the two of you if you agree to join us. You're both smart and well-trained in your areas of expertise which, by the way, I know does not include quality control. And, Doctor, you could play an active role in recruiting more patients into our studies."

"No way would I help you and your sick organization." As soon as I spoke, I regretted coming on so strong, knowing Daisy's life might depend on what I said next. On the other hand, they knew who we were, so they had to be aware we had loved ones who would come looking for us if we didn't return home soon.

"You don't need to decide right now. Wait until I explain all the benefits of working with us. Financial as well as career-wise. Umbroz has lots of connections in high places, connections that could help both you and your friend, Daisy. I understand she is planning to get married soon. Every couple can use some extra cash when they are starting out."

"We don't need your money."

"You are one tough customer. There's one more thing I should tell you. If you don't cooperate with us, and by that, I mean tell me everything I want to know, Daisy will be on the truck with Martha by the end of the day."

I was speechless, feeling more defenseless and vulnerable than I'd ever felt. There was no way I would cooperate with them. Or would I? They were threatening the life of my best friend. I couldn't let anything happen to her. If it weren't for me, she'd be safe at home with Arvid. I thought about telling them everything they wanted to know, asking Lim to delete all the evidence I'd gathered, and allowing them to continue their illegal studies unchecked. They might ultimately make beneficial medical breakthroughs down the road.

Get real. What are you thinking? There's no way you could guarantee the evidence you'd collected would be deleted. They aren't idiots. They need to know who received the information. Once they know, they'll probably kill all of us. Me and my big mouth. I've insisted on taking the high road and telling them I would never work with them and can't be bought. Now they know they can never trust me. All I can do now is try to convince them otherwise. I need to buy time.

"Why don't you give me specifics? If I were to work for you—and I'm not saying I would—how much money would I make exactly, and what would I have to do to get it?"

"Now you're being smart. If you cooperate fully, you and Daisy can leave and continue with your normal lives. The work you would need to do wouldn't take much of your time."

"You'll let Daisy go if I cooperate?"

"We would need to be assured she wouldn't cause trouble down the road."

"How much money are we talking about, exactly?"

"I can't give you an exact figure right now, but it will be in the range of an extra twenty grand a month."

I tried to look thoughtful, like I was considering their offer, making calculations of my own. I needed to appear credible, if only for a while, until I could think of a way to escape. "After listening to all you had to say, I was hoping we were talking about a lot more. Say, two million a year."

"Now we're getting somewhere. You can't be bought unless the price is high enough."

"You're making me feel like a hypocrite."

"My apologies. I have nothing but admiration for you, making a realistic assessment of your predicament. How did you come up with two million?"

"I've always wanted to have an art collection with pieces by famous artists. I'm a big fan of the impressionists. My favorite is Degas, although I also love Monet, Manet, and Renoir." *And I thought that art history class I'd taken, where I learned the impressionists' names, would never be useful.*

"That would definitely cost quite a bit."

He seemed to be thinking. I wasn't sure if he was buying it, but I thought he was at least considering I might be telling the truth, that maybe my loyalty was, in fact, for sale.

He walked to a corner of the room and took out his cell phone. All I could hear were occasional Norwegian words. I thought about telling him not to bother being so secretive—I wouldn't understand a word of what he was saying even if he spoke loudly in front of me—but I restrained myself.

After several minutes, the conversation was over. Sven pulled up a chair and sat next to me. "What, exactly, would you be willing to do for our organization?" he asked.

"Before we talk any more, you need to let Daisy go. She's only here because of me."

"Whatever the reason, she's here now and knows too much to just let her go."

"What if you pay her, too, and convince her never to speak of this?"

"If I understand you correctly, you are suggesting we pay both of you and trust both of you to remain silent. Is that right?"

"Exactly."

"My boss would never go for that, not if you each want two million a year."

"You wouldn't have to pay her. She'd be overjoyed just to get out of here."

"There's still the trust issue."

"She doesn't know anything that could hurt you. She's not a doctor. Doesn't even know much about science. She only cares about computer code. I told her we were doing corporate spying to get manufacturing secrets for Celgene."

"Why would she risk getting caught for breaking the law just because she's your friend?"

"We're not such good friends." I was winging it, saying whatever I thought would be helpful at the moment.

"That's not what she told us."

"I'm not surprised. She'd like us to be good friends, but to tell you the truth, I find her rather dull."

"You expect me to believe she did this so you would like her?"

"That, and two thousand dollars."

"She didn't tell us you paid her."

"Of course not. Daisy doesn't want anyone to know how desperate she is for money. Her job pays okay, but it's expensive living in San Francisco."

"If it's so expensive, why do you have enough money—enough to pay her?"

"I make more than her, and my husband draws a modest salary, so we've been pretty comfortable."

"But not comfortable enough to satisfy your appetite for expensive art."

"Exactly."

"Why do you care so much about what happens to Daisy?"

"I'm a doctor. I'm all about saving lives. I know Daisy is planning on being married soon. Even though I'm not fond of her, I don't want her or her fiancé to suffer. I don't in any way approve of what you did to Martha. What's done is done, but I don't want any more killing."

"I need to talk to my boss again."

As he retreated to a corner to speak softly on the phone in Norwegian again, I checked my watch. It was already 2:00 p.m. Although the watch camera was no longer recording, I was sure it had collected enough to bring kidnapping charges, should I survive. The call ended, and Sven walked back towards me. "He's going to think about it. Meanwhile, give me the passcode to your phone as a sign of good faith."

"No way. I want to have a solid agreement about my payment and some assurances—in writing—before I divulge anything more. I'm getting awfully hungry. I'll bet Daisy is too. Can you get us something to eat?" I was hoping to get some food served with cutlery. A knife, maybe even a fork, would be helpful.

"I'll see if I can find something in the kitchen." He spoke briefly to the Viking and left.

Under the watchful eye of the large man, I sat quietly, my arms folded in my lap. My guard appeared bored, took a small pair of scissors from a pocket, and began cutting his dirty fingernails. I thought about jumping up, grabbing the scissors, and stabbing him in the neck with them, but saw the futility. If I was going to try to escape, I would need to be successful. I figured the chance of me getting the scissors from him was less than ten percent, and my chance of successfully escaping went down from there. While I waited, I kept my eyes on the scissors anyway, hoping he might drop them.

Sven returned with two plates, a sandwich on each, as the Viking was still giving himself a manicure. "I got two bologna sandwiches," he announced, placing one in front of me. "Hope you like mustard and mayo."

"That'll be fine," I said. I was hungry and willing to eat almost anything, even a bologna sandwich. To my disappointment, he hadn't brought any cutlery. The paper plate would not serve me well in trying to escape. Neither would the bologna sandwich.

"I'll bring this to Daisy now," he said, heading for the door with the other sandwich.

"You'd better untie her hands so she can eat."

"I'll remove the gag, but not the ropes. She's pretty—what's the word—feisty. Put up quite a fight. Not agreeable like you." His comment caught me off guard. I felt pathetically weak, ashamed even. All the more reason I had to figure out how to escape. "She'll have to eat without her hands. Don't worry—if she's hungry enough, she'll figure it out." He left the room, returning shortly without the sandwich. By then, I was taking my last bite of lunch.

"I need to go to the restroom," I said.

"Hold it."

"I can't. I drank the water you gave me, and I haven't gone since you brought me here." I hoped there'd be a window to crawl out of, or something I could use as a weapon, in the bathroom.

Sven said something to the Viking, who nodded and left.

Shit. They're going to bring me a bucket to pee in. I refuse to pee with these two men looking at me.

The Viking returned shortly with a middle-aged Native American woman.

Sven ordered her, "Take her to the bathroom. Watch her the whole time. She must not be allowed to escape."

The woman nodded. "Come," she said to me.

I followed her down the hall to a small, windowless restroom. "Here," she said. I walked in, and she followed. I wasn't loving the situation, but it was tolerable. The woman stood in front of me as I peed while looking around for something I might pick up to use as a weapon later. Washing my hands with a large bar of soap, I couldn't think of a way to sneak it out or use it to escape. After I dried my hands using paper towels from the stack next to the sink, the woman walked me back to the interrogation room and departed.

I sat in my chair and waited as the two men stood in the opposite corner talking, each holding a can of Mountain Dew they'd gotten while I was in the restroom. With Daisy just down the hall, it was vexing not being able to communicate with her. I wondered if she was planning an escape, too, and if she realized how close we were to meeting the same fate as Martha, if Daisy even knew what had happened to my former assistant.

That's when I decided I needed to escape if the Viking left. There was no way I'd stand a chance trying to decommission him, but with Sven, I figured I had a chance. Maybe only a slim chance, but a chance, nevertheless. I had to try. Otherwise, Daisy and I would surely die. Unless the Viking was wearing astronaut diapers, I figured he'd need to take a bathroom break soon. Although I'm usually in a hurry to get things done, I knew what I had to do. I'd wait patiently.

CHAPTER 28

We negotiated for the next hour, requiring Sven to run back and forth between me and a printer in another part of the complex. Each time, he left me alone with the Viking for about five minutes. Upon returning, he either verbally offered me more money or showed me abstracts of papers written by the University of California scientist associated with Umbroz. He was trying to appeal to my greed with money and my interest in medicine by convincing me the studies Umbroz was doing were worthwhile. While he was failing on both accounts, I kept up the ruse of pretending to strongly consider working with them. Meanwhile, the information in these abstracts provided me with the rationale for Umbroz's shady clinical trials.

One abstract described their approach to preventing type I diabetes. The Umbroz drug decreased a certain class of lymphocytes, a type of immune system cell that, in type I diabetics, attacks the cells that make insulin in the pancreas. The preliminary results reported that after two years, significantly fewer children receiving the Umbroz drug RC7249 developed type I diabetes than the controls. The only adverse reactions reported were mild headaches and gastrointestinal upset, both of which were short-lived. I had no way to know whether the favorable findings described were accurate or fabricated, but I suspected the latter. I had to agree, however, that prevention of type I diabetes is undoubtedly a worthwhile goal.

It appeared the medication did significantly reduce the number of the targeted cells as planned. Unfortunately, depletion of this type of lymphocyte led to deregulation of Epstein Barr Virus in two of my patients, with potentially deadly consequences. Cassandra had suffered from an overwhelming EBV infection, and Ryan developed Burkitt's lymphoma, also related to EBV infections. I wondered how many children in the Umbroz study suffered from unreported potentially lethal side effects of the drug.

Another abstract dealt with emphysema prevention. Emphysema can be inherited by way of a mutation that results in the lack of a protein, alpha-1 antitrypsin. This protein normally protects the lungs from another protein, elastase. Elastase is produced by inflammatory cells and breaks down lung tissue in the absence of alpha-1 antitrypsin. When unchecked, elastase damages or destroys the walls of alveoli, the microscopic sacs in the lungs where oxygen enters the blood. This leads to abnormal enlargement of alveoli, decreased blood oxygenation, and difficulty breathing.

In the Umbroz study, children who inherited the mutation leading to emphysema were given a medication, RM85244, to inhibit elastase. While the study showed no side effects of the drug other than mild, temporary nausea, my patient Lucas had suffered significant liver damage. I imagined Umbroz had other patients in the study who also suffered liver damage, but they suppressed that information.

I was already familiar with the data presented in the third abstract Sven gave me, describing the success of RA23567 in preventing rheumatoid arthritis.

"These reports are very impressive," I said, attempting to conceal my disgust.

"I was told you believe you had some patients who reacted badly to our medication," Sven countered, obviously trying to discern if I was attempting to hide the fact that I still wanted to put an end to their research.

"I did think that at first, but since your papers show that so many have been treated without negative effects, I'd say the illnesses I saw with my patients were probably unrelated to the Umbroz drugs. I certainly couldn't prove the medications caused their conditions, even if I wanted to."

"What if, over time, you saw a pattern—successful treatment of many, but with a few patients having dangerous side effects? Could you overlook the people who don't do well in order to prevent thousands from coming down with these horrible diseases?"

What do you mean by "a few patients," exactly? One percent, ten percent, fifty percent? "By overlook, do you mean not report the bad outcomes?"

"We all know that given enough people, something bad will happen to some even without any medication. Drug trials can be longer and more expensive than they need to be when every little side effect, including those obviously not related to the medication, are reported."

Yeah, little side effects like cancer, liver failure, and death. "I suppose I'd be willing to overlook such things if I could be sure, or pretty sure, the medication didn't directly cause them." I wondered if I sounded convincing. The idea of not reporting patients having potentially lethal side effects in a clinical trial report ran against every principle I held dear.

"You seem very reasonable, Dr. Rosen, and I sincerely apologize if we have caused you or Daisy any distress. I hope you understand that sometimes we need to be a bit forceful to get people to hear our side of things. If a child joins a cult, the parents may need to kidnap that child to show them they have made a mistake. Likewise, some people, especially doctors, need to be shown that rules of the medical establishment have become so onerous, progress is hindered."

I suppose we shouldn't have safety regulations for automobiles because most people wouldn't be killed if we didn't have any at all, and they add slightly to a car's price tag. "I appreciate that now, now that I've seen the fantastic progress you've made in preventing these dreaded diseases. I'm all for decreasing overall suffering. On the other hand, I can't overlook what you did to Martha."

"I'm afraid it was necessary. We tried to reason with her but couldn't convince her of all the good Umbroz is doing. With the lives of millions of children at stake, we had to part ways. As long as you and Daisy cooperate with us, you will find your relationship with Umbroz very rewarding in terms of personal fulfillment and financial goals. As you can see, however, we will not put up with anyone who stands in our way. Again, I apologize for our initial encounter."

"If we can come to an acceptable agreement, apology accepted," I said.

"My boss will fax over some documents he wants you to sign indicating you have joined our studies as a principal investigator. Then, you will need to give me the passcode to your phone and sign forms to add your name as a co-author on papers soon to be published. He thinks that will boost the stature of our studies."

"You already had my name listed as principal investigator on your studies without my permission."

"That's what your patients were told, but your name wasn't on the documents we filed. This will make it official."

I didn't want to give him my passcode or sign any papers that could be used later to show my cooperation, but I would if given no other option. I convinced myself they already knew who my husband was, so I wasn't protecting Lim from them. They wanted to get my name on their papers and studies to provide them with credibility. I could always claim coercion subsequently if I managed to survive. Sven was probably only pretending to believe me when I agreed to go along with them. I imagined he might even take a picture of me signing to prove the signature's legitimacy.

After that, they would have what they wanted. Daisy and I could mysteriously disappear. Lim would never believe I'd signed such papers willingly, but there would be no way to prove I'd been forced to do it. I was running out of time.

Sven was leaving the room to check the fax machine when the Viking stopped him. They spoke back and forth several times before Sven nodded, and the Viking left.

"Where's he going?" I asked.

"It's—how do you say it—nature calls. Don't worry, he'll be back soon. He'll pick up the papers I want you to sign on the way back."

My muscles tensed, and my heart thumped so loudly I wondered if Sven could hear it. *This is my chance. Probably my only chance. I hope it works.*

CHAPTER 29

I looked around the room quickly, knowing I had to move fast. I stood, then leaped onto the seat of my chair before Sven could react. "Look," I shrieked, doing my best imitation of a helpless woman in fear. Pointing to a corner opposite me, I yelled, "There's a mouse. Go get it."

After looking around and not seeing anything, Sven stepped closer to the corner. As he did so, I jumped down from the chair, grabbed one of my pens from the table with my left hand, and ripped a hair extension from my head with my right, probably pulling out some of my own hairs in the process. My scalp hurt, but I didn't care. The adrenaline was flowing, my heart pumping.

I held the pen in my mouth as I gripped each end of the hair extension and reached high, looping it over Sven's head. As I pulled the hair tight around his neck, Sven let out a scream. He struggled, reaching his hands behind his shoulders, trying to grab me. I was determined to succeed as if my life depended on it, because it did. I concentrated on the task at hand, managing to wrap the ends of the extension around the pen. If his neck had been any thicker, the extension wouldn't have been long enough.

I twisted the pen, tightening the hair garotte, as he alternated between trying to loosen the pressure around his neck by trying to pull the extension away from his skin, and attempting to grab me as I stood behind him. He bucked, but I maintained my grip. It was minutes before he slowed down, the back of his neck swelled a bit and turned blue, and he fell to his knees. He tried to speak but produced only grunting noises. I wondered if Daisy heard the scuffle and had figured out what was going on.

I held on tight. My fingers were tiring out, but I couldn't afford to ease off—my target was still moving. When he collapsed to all fours, I repositioned myself, straddling his back while being careful to keep my feet as far from his hands as possible. I didn't know if he had the strength to grab me, but I wasn't taking any chances.

He was still bucking. Not as forceful as the mechanical bull I'd seen throw people off in a bar years earlier, but I still had difficulty holding on. *Can't let go. Can't let go.* I wondered how much time it would take for him to lose consciousness. If the Viking returned before I made my escape, there'd be no hope for Daisy or me. I continued holding, pulling on the hair extension as forcefully as I could. Finally, Sven collapsed to the floor, face down, unconscious. I turned his head sideways. His face was blue and bloated. He was out cold, but not dead, and might regain consciousness in a matter of seconds. I removed the cartridge from my pen and used the point to stab him multiple times as quickly as I could over his right carotid until blood oozed out, then did the same over the left. If that didn't kill him, it would impair him for longer.

I scraped what I could from the table into my purse and ran to Daisy's room. She had been gagged again after eating her lunch, so I pulled the cotton from her mouth while telling her the large man was in the bathroom, and I had incapacitated—possibly killed—the other.

She didn't waste time by asking me for details about what I had just accomplished but began directing me. "There are two black barrettes in my hair. Take one and use it to cut me free."

Before I had time to ask any questions, Daisy said, "Months ago, Arvid sharpened an edge on each in case I needed them. He's obsessed with self-defense."

The barrettes weren't easy to see against her black hair, but I found one. The sharp edge wasn't very long, but it was good enough to saw through the rope holding her hands together.

Daisy shook the ropes off her wrists, then ran her fingers through her hair and found the other barrette. Together we worked on sawing through the rope around her legs. Once done, Daisy jumped up.

"We need to run like hell," I said as I handed Daisy the barrette I was holding.

Daisy grabbed her purse from a nearby table, then stood still and gasped as she grabbed my arm. *Why are you stopping now? This is no time to stop and discuss things.* I was in no mood for Daisy to question me. Then I noticed her eyes focused on something behind me. I turned slowly and saw the Viking, calmly standing in the doorway. I imagined him going through the different ways he might kill us.

I looked around the room quickly for a knife or sharp object, something more substantial than one of the barrettes, but saw nothing. Looking down, I noticed a can of ant spray on the floor against the wall, near my feet. With no time to think it through, I grabbed the can and ran at the man, forcing the end of it as hard as I could into his chest, above his left ventricle. I had read about commotio cordis, when a sudden forceful chest impact causes the heart to go into ventricular fibrillation, often followed by cardiac death. I was hoping that if it didn't kill him, the impact would at least incapacitate him, if even for only a few seconds, giving us time to escape. Unfortunately, he seemed to barely notice my attack and took a swipe at me, knocking me on my butt.

While his attention was on me, Daisy yelled like I'd never heard her yell before and kneed the Viking in the groin or, to be more accurate, in the testicles. The giant bent over, groaning. Daisy grabbed my arm as I sprung up, and we sprinted out of the building, but not before I bashed the Viking in the temple with the bottom edge of the ant spray can, hoping to give him a life-threatening basilar fracture. I regretted not spraying him in the face with insecticide as we ran outside onto the empty street. We raced down the road, then around the side of the first house we came to, through the backyard, around another house, and onto another street. A cluster of tall juniper bushes provided cover as we caught our breath between the greenery and the fence behind.

I was the first to speak. "Are you okay?" I asked.

"You just saw me decommission a Bond villain, and you ask me if I'm okay?"

"So you're okay physically. At least okay enough to kick someone in the balls."

"I've been waiting for the opportunity ever since Arvid showed me how. Didn't want to waste all that knowledge. Maybe now you'll let him teach you some self-defense skills."

"Now's not a great time to talk about it, but I'll certainly consider it."

"What do you think we should do now? It won't be long until they're looking for us. They've probably started already."

"I know. I think our best chance is getting someplace where we can get help."

"Good idea, Watson. Now, where do you think we can find such a place? The way I see it, everyone on this Indian reservation loves these guys. They've got the chairman in their pocket. The building we escaped from, where we were so hospitably received, is the community center. Guess who built it."

"Umbroz?"

"Exactly. Before you showed up there, the tribal chairman himself came in to explain to me how important the company is."

"As I understand it, Umbroz pays for all sorts of stuff in the community. They have a lot of influence over all the residents, so it's not going to be easy to find someone to help us." I checked my watch. It was 4:55 p.m. That's when a thought gave me a glimmer of hope. "I know someone who lives here who might help us. She should be getting home in about twenty minutes or so. Remember Janice from HR?"

"She seemed nice, but why would she want to help us?"

"I helped her son when he had an asthma attack. I'm sure she's loyal to Umbroz and the tribe, but there's a chance she'll side with us once I explain everything. She'll remember the bad medical care her son received, almost costing him his life."

"Does she live far from here?"

"Good question. Luckily, I remember her street—Golden Bear Road." As we spoke, I rifled through my purse, found my phone, and entered the street into Google maps. It was my lucky day—well, maybe not day, but afternoon, hopefully—the road popped up, and we were only a little over a mile away. Glancing up, I saw a car with two men inside drive slowly down the street, both men scanning the surroundings carefully. I ducked down as far as possible. "I'll bet they're looking for us," I whispered.

"There's probably a lot more people in cars like that trying to find us," Daisy whispered back.

I looked at Google maps again. "I think we should take a circuitous route. The most direct way takes us down a main street for almost a mile. I would expect heavy surveillance there. We should stay on smaller streets. It's a little farther, but I think we'll be safer that way."

"Say no more. We'll take the smaller streets."

We waited until the slow-moving car was out of sight, then, following the Google maps directions, ran past two houses and around the next corner. We caught our breaths while lying on the floor of a doorless rusted junker in front of a house.

"There aren't a lot of places to hide. Not much in the way of trees and shrubs," Daisy said.

"We'll have to try to spot something to run to each time we move. We'll be exposed for a bit. No way around it."

"Do something to look different," Daisy said. "I'm going to braid my hair. Maybe I'll fit in more."

"Good idea. There's nothing I can do to change my hair color to black, but I can take out the rest of these hair extensions. That'll change my appearance." I pulled out the remaining extensions, careful not to yank out much of my natural hair. "I wish I had a hat or a scarf," I said.

"Pull your hair back on the sides and fasten it with these barrettes. At least your hair color won't be as obvious from the front."

"What will you tie your braid with?"

"I cut off a bit of my shoelace with one of the barrettes. The shoelace is still long enough to tie."

"Brilliant," I said as I fastened my hair with Daisy's barrettes. I slowly rose halfway up to look out the front of the car we were in. Two houses away, I spotted another clump of bushes. "Let's run to those. It looks like there's room between the plants and the house where we can hide."

We waited for a car carrying a woman and two kids to pass by, then made a break for the bushes. Sprinting as fast as I could, Daisy beat me by a second or two.

As we stood bent over, catching our breath behind the shrubs, I said, "This is going to take forever."

"Maybe we should hide out until dark," Daisy suggested.

"Where? Do you see a place where we can comfortably stay for several hours?"

"I didn't say comfortably. We could stay right here."

Before I could respond, a door slammed close by. A stocky man and a broad-shouldered woman exited the house we were hiding in front of. They couldn't have been more than five feet away. Daisy and I crouched, then froze. I felt like I had to sneeze. A noise like that would lead to us being discovered, and we'd probably wind up back with our friends from Umbroz. I struggled to suppress the sneeze, and the feeling dissipated. Next time I might not be so fortunate, and I wouldn't be able to prevent a sneeze that would reveal our presence.

"Remember to be careful. Those Karens are dangerous," the woman said.

"Don't worry, I've got my Glock right here," the man said, patting his jacket pocket as the couple walked toward a car parked in front of the house. They were so close to us, their voices were crystal clear.

"I know, but I'll still worry."

"Just think of all we could do with the reward money if I find them."

"I know, I know," the woman said.

"They're vicious. They deserve whatever happens to them."

The couple kissed, and the man got into the car. The woman waited until he drove away, then turned and walked back to the house. A bug crawling on a nearby leaf caused me to thoughtlessly move my right arm a smidgeon just as she opened the door. She must have heard the slight rustling of leaves because she paused and looked around. I held my breath, my chest so tense I didn't know how much longer I could hold still. Finally, the woman entered the house and shut the door. I exhaled and heard Daisy exhale right afterward.

"Looks like they're offering a reward for us," I whispered. "I don't feel comfortable staying here."

"I'm with you. Did you see the size of that woman? She'd be hard to take down."

"Right. No balls."

"How far from Janice's house are we now?"

I checked my phone. "Less than a mile. Let's head for those woodpiles down the street. We could hide between the stacks."

After confirming there were no cars or people in sight, we ran past four more houses to stacks of firewood on the front lawn of a small house. We crouched between the stacks, each about three feet high. Although we were hidden on all sides from passersby on the street, anyone walking up to the woodpiles would see us, so we didn't feel safe staying for long.

Daisy and I peeked over the firewood, looking for our next hiding spot in the barren landscape. The closest opportunity for cover was a group of juniper bushes seven houses away. I was uncomfortable being exposed for such a long distance.

"We can't stay here 'til dark," Daisy said. "We're bound to be discovered if someone walks by. We're not very far from the front door of this house, so if someone goes in or out and walks in this direction, they'll see us."

"We need to get to Janice's house as fast as possible."

"Agree. See if you can run a little faster."

"We can't all be superwomen like you. It's these damn shoes. Can't run worth crap in them. You're wearing running shoes."

"Can't stand the fact I'm running faster than you, can you?"

"If you remember, I beat you in the fifty-yard dash once."

"Yeah, but I wouldn't be too proud of that. We both sucked."

"Okay. I'll count to three, and we'll head over to those junipers." I looked around and confirmed there was no one in sight. "One, two, three."

We took off running toward the safety of the shrubs. As we passed the third house, a child's voice yelled out, "There they are. Those are the bad women they're looking for. Let's get them."

I glanced over my shoulder towards the voices, and saw two children around six years old on the opposite side of the street, running after us.

Lucky they're so small. I should be able to outrun them. I followed Daisy towards a waist-high wooden fence adjacent to the closest house. We both managed to muddle over it by placing our hands on top, jumping to a straight-arm position, then clumsily swinging our legs over before dropping to the ground.

As Daisy and I ran around the side of the house, a woman yelled, "Get back here right now and finish your chores. I don't see anyone. If those women are out there, I don't want you going near them. They're dangerous."

The voice grew fainter as we ran farther into the backyard. Toys, old furniture, and a clothesline with sheets and clothing flapping in the breeze were visible ahead. I looked forward to stopping so I could catch my breath when I was startled by a low growl, then loud barking. I looked to my left in time to see a large dog baring its teeth and running towards us at full speed.

Daisy and I halted in our tracks. This was not the way I expected our escape to end. Knowing I couldn't outrun the beast, every muscle in my body tensed. I held my purse in front of me, despite it offering little protection. A split second later, the dog leaped towards me, roaring ferociously. I shut my eyes, held my breath, turned my head to the side, and braced for the assault. Hearing a dull thud close to my face, I opened my eyes a sliver and glanced toward the sound. The dog hung in midair for a moment, its front legs stretched out, then fell to the dirt below. On the ground, the dog backed up a few feet, ran, and jumped at me again, only to be stopped midair again by the metal chain holding it to a post in the middle of the yard.

Daisy and I backed away, keeping our eyes on the dog who kept trying to attack, each time stopped by the chain. With each attempt, I relaxed a little more, although I tensed up somewhat every time the dog leaped. As we slowly walked towards the back fence, past the clothesline, I noticed several items we could use.

"We can disguise ourselves with these clothes," I said. "They're looking for two women wearing exactly what we have on. If we change into something else, we could openly walk to Janice's."

"You mean hide in plain sight?"

"Exactly."

That's the first time I remembered being cold. We each put on several layers of T-shirts from the clothesline over our clothes to keep warm. My outermost shirt showed a picture of a dreamcatcher, Daisy's a colorful native American geometric design. I found a shawl and wrapped it around my head and shoulders, hiding my brown hair.

"Got any cash we can leave them?" I asked Daisy.

We each left two twenty dollar bills under a rock to pay for the clothes. After finding two shopping bags to hide our purses in, we put our sunglasses on and lumbered over the low back fence. Once we walked around the side of the house facing the next street, Daisy and I casually made our way down the road carrying our shopping bags. I hoped nobody would notice the sweat pouring down my face.

Fighting the urge to run, we maintained a leisurely pace, even as several cars cruised by, the people inside appearing to scour the neighborhood for dangerous women who didn't belong there. One passenger in a car rolled down her window and asked if we'd seen the outlaws, describing what we had been wearing. We told her we hadn't but were watching out for them, and were prepared to fight if we saw them. "Don't do that. They're armed and dangerous. If you see them, run away," she warned us.

Close to Janice's house, I became aware of a car following us. I heard the engine but didn't turn around.

"There's a car following us," I said to Daisy in a hushed voice. "Just act natural. We make a right here at the corner. Be sure to smile and laugh as we turn onto the next street. Starting now." We turned the corner and laughed. My heart was thumping, and I could hardly breathe. "I see Janice's place. Just two more houses to go."

I heard the car stop, then two car doors open.

"I think they're coming after us," I said while looking straight ahead. The sound of two sets of feet walking toward us convinced me they were in pursuit. "There's her house, with the blue door. Let's cut across this lawn to make it clear we're going there." It wasn't much of a lawn—more like dirt with rocks and scattered clumps of grass.

"I feel like making a break for it," Daisy said.

"Don't. Keep walking and laughing, like we're having the time of our life."

"Maybe the last time of our life."

CHAPTER 30

The footsteps continued behind us, even as we cut across the yard next to Janice's house and traversed the imaginary property line of Janice's yard. I dared not turn to see who was there. I stopped breathing as we stepped onto the walkway leading to the front door.

"What are you going to say? What if she wants to turn us in for the reward money?" Daisy asked in a whisper.

I'd been wondering the same thing but hadn't expressed my worries to Daisy. I felt like collapsing, the tension having extracted every bit of energy from my body, as we stepped up to the front door Janice had led me through two days earlier. I knocked loudly. The footsteps in the street stopped, just as I heard softer footsteps from inside the house approach the door. I noticed a peephole I hadn't observed before and imagined someone looking through it. The sound of more footsteps came from inside, and a discussion ensued, too quiet for me to understand. The sound of shoes hitting asphalt started up again in the street behind me and approached the house. My heart thudded in my chest as I resisted the urge to run. The front door opened slowly, and Janice stuck her head out.

"Can we come in? Please? Someone's following us." I spoke quietly, so the people behind us couldn't hear. Janice's expression was flat. I could tell she was thinking, trying to decide what to do. "I don't know what you've heard, but my friend and I aren't dangerous. You know us. You know that's not true. Please, let us inside so we can explain. We have nowhere to go but here. You can still call the police after you've heard us. Just give us a chance."

Janice looked beyond me, towards the street in front of her house. "Roy, Sandy, did you want to see me?" she yelled.

"You okay, Janice?" one of them shouted back.

She opened the door wide. "I'm fine. These are my second cousins visiting from Red Lake. They wanted to see the neighborhood."

"Tell them to be careful. There's some dangerous people on the reservation."

Daisy and I rushed inside. A moment before our hostess closed the door behind us, I turned my head and saw a man and a woman, both with guns drawn. The guns were aimed in our direction.

Once safely inside the house, I turned my attention to Janice and the others. Janice, her son Paco, her sister Denise, and Denise's children stood close together in the living room, staring at us.

"Thank you for letting us in," I said. "Let me explain."

"Come in and sit down," Janice said. "I hope your explanation is good. We'll be in a lot of trouble if it isn't. Denise didn't want to let you in, but I want to hear your side of things because you saved Paco. I trust you. Please don't make me regret my decision."

Janice gestured for us to sit on the couch while she sat in one of the two armchairs. Denise took a seat in the other armchair, a stern expression on her face, while the children stood silently behind her and observed.

Not sure where to start, I dove in. “I don’t know what you’ve heard about us. We’re not who we said we were when we took jobs at Umbroz. That part is true,” I began.

“No kidding,” Denise said.

“My friend here is Daisy Wong. She’s a computer programmer. My real name is Erica Rosen. I’m a doctor. A pediatrician.”

“Erica Rosen? Really?” Janice asked, a surprised expression on her face.

“Had we met before I came to Umbroz?” I asked.

“Well, no, but I recognize the name. Why did you lie—you’re already an Umbroz employee. You’re on the payroll.”

“I never worked at Umbroz or applied for a job there under my real name.”

“You’re one of our part-time workers. You work for us in San Francisco.”

“I do work in San Francisco, although not for Umbroz. I work at the University of California, San Francisco, mainly in the pediatrics clinic.”

“You help us enroll patients in our clinical trials. Unless there’s another Erica Rosen who is a pediatrician in San Francisco.”

“I’m the only one. I know because I check my name on Google now and then. People at Umbroz obviously got information about me and set things up to look like I work for them, but I never did. Not as a pediatrician. Only as Mandy Winston, a QC expert.”

“I’m not sure what’s going on here,” Janice said. “I believe you’re a pediatrician, whoever you work for. The way you took care of Paco—you knew what you were doing.”

“Who sent you here?” Denise asked tersely. She was going to be hard to win over.

"No one. I came on my own accord to investigate Umbroz. They're involved in fraudulent and, to be honest, dangerous activities."

"That's total bullshit," Denise said. The children giggled.

"Denise can be pretty hard on outsiders," Janice said, looking at me apologetically. "She doesn't usually trust them. Thinks I'm an apple because I do."

"Apple?"

"You know, red on the outside, white on the inside. She doesn't think I stand up for Native American rights as much as I should. That's not true. It's just that I'm willing to listen to the other side."

"To me, Erica or Mandy or whatever your name is, what you're saying sounds like the usual deceptions we hear from white people," Denise said. "But out of respect for my sister, I'll listen. Go on."

"I found out they were using my name without my knowledge to enroll patients in dangerous clinical trials. Before that, I was looking into problems Umbroz has with their pharmaceuticals."

"What sort of problems?" Janice asked.

"While working in my San Francisco clinic, I found that some of my patients didn't respond to their medication the way they should have," I said.

"Doesn't prove a thing," Denise said. "Maybe you're just a bad doctor."

As one who takes great pride in her work, I was deeply offended but didn't want to appear defensive. Ignoring her remark, I continued. "I sent some Umbroz pills to an independent lab and found them to have only a fraction of the medication they were supposed to have. They were basically useless."

Denise's posture and expression softened a bit. At least she was listening. I described the mysterious illnesses of my patients, finding out about the secret clinical trials, and the confession of my assistant, Martha, who was helping them out. With tears in my eyes, I told about finding Martha and two others, dead in the back of a refrigerator truck parked behind the community center.

Daisy gasped. That was the first she had heard about Martha's fate. "I'm so sorry, Erica. I had no idea. I know how fond you were of her, despite the recent difficulties."

Sitting there, the first time I hadn't been literally fighting for my life since discovering Martha's death, it finally hit me, and hit me hard. *Martha, my long-time trusted assistant is dead. Murdered.* Sure, Martha had done some horrible things after being manipulated by these people, taken in by the attention of a handsome, rich, seemingly thoughtful man. At first, she probably believed she was helping humanity even as she participated in the criminal operation to include patients in illegal drug testing. Ultimately, however, she saw the error of her ways and wanted to do what she could to stop Umbroz. She was a good person at heart. She didn't deserve this. I started crying uncontrollably. Daisy put her arm around my shoulder and tried to comfort me, but to no avail. There was no way around it. I needed a good cry. Janice brought me a box of Kleenex as my tears and snot started flowing. Finally, I pulled myself together and dabbed my eyes.

Looking up, I noticed the sisters staring, eyes wide. "Was there any writing on the side of the truck?" Janice asked.

"Yes. Nilsen's Dairy."

"I told you," Janice yelled at her sister. "I told you there was something fishy about that truck being parked there almost every time we were there."

"When were you there?" I asked.

"We go there a lot. It's where our council meets," Denise said. "All the reservation offices and meeting rooms are there. Janice and I often go there to clean, sometimes cook. Many of us in the community volunteer our time, and I'm very active in the government. I go to almost all the council meetings."

"There have been a few people from the reservation who have disappeared in the last few years," Janice said. "I wonder if—no, I can't believe Chairman Stewart had anything to do with that."

"What about employees at Umbroz?" I asked. "Have any of them disappeared? And what about the A and B? What do they stand for?"

Janice looked down, appearing to think, as all eyes fixed on her. She looked up at me and began to speak. "Now that you mention it, we've had a number of people leave suddenly. They all worked in A, and many of them came from different places across the country. They stayed a few months, then got fired or left suddenly. I was told it didn't work out."

"Did you ever get requests for their employment record from other companies after they left?" I asked.

"Hmm. I can't remember that ever happening. You don't suppose—"

"Yes, I do suppose. I think the company got rid of them because they found out something and threatened to expose what was going on."

"That might explain the A and B. Everyone always starts in A. Except for close relatives of the Rakvag brothers. People stay in A about six months, then go to B. Or leave. I was told new employees are oriented in A, and if they work out, they go to B."

"I don't think that's quite accurate," I said. "I think employees start in A, which is run pretty much like a normal pharmaceutical company. They are slowly introduced to the company's philosophy of using shortcuts and cheaper ingredients. Those who go along are sent to B. Those who don't are eliminated."

"By eliminated, do you mean killed?" Janice leaned forward as she spoke.

"I'm sorry," I said, "but yes. I believe the company has been murdering people, and your chairman, along with at least some of the council members, have been cooperating because they're getting money—probably quite a bit—from Umbroz in return for their support of the company."

"Everyone supports Umbroz anyway," Janice said. "They don't need to bribe anyone."

"I understand your community gets a lot of financial help from the company, with employment opportunities and money for schools, parks, and the health center," I said, treading carefully. I didn't want to risk alienating Janice or her sister by suggesting their community should do the right thing and forego all that Umbroz contributes. I knew better than to stand in judgment. It can be easy to justify things when a lot of money is involved, especially if someone has been severely economically deprived. When that deprivation is the result of generations of exploitation and everyday survival is a struggle, the lines between right and wrong can be easily blurred.

"Health center, my ass," Janice said. "Sure, it looks great, but it's pretty useless. Almost killed Paco."

"That's true," Denise said, nodding in agreement. "Still, we do get a lot of other benefits from Umbroz. Some of their medications may suck, but from where I'm sitting, that's a small price to pay for all their help."

While Janice seemed close to being on the same page as me, her sister was another story.

"I had access to their computer system," Daisy said. "They kept two sets of data for all their studies—their QC, their clinical trials, everything. While they only reported successes in their official clinical trial results, I saw the records of patients who had serious side effects, ranging from pain and debilitation to death. Some of those deaths occurred right here, in your community, on this reservation."

"That's the first I'd learned of this," I said, "as Daisy and I hadn't had a chance to compare notes from our separate investigations."

We sat in silence for a moment before Denise became animated. "Naomi, the lady with arthritis who gave us the pills for Paco the other day, her daughter was in a clinical trial before she died, wasn't she, Janice?"

Janice leaned towards her sister. "You're right. I remember her telling us how excited she was her daughter would never have to suffer the way she did because of a new drug made by Umbroz. She said she'd signed a bunch of papers brought over by Chairman Stewart. She trusted him so much, she didn't bother to read them."

"Do you remember when her daughter died?" Denise asked.

"She was sick for a while. I think she died about eight months after she started taking the new medicine. She kept going to the clinic with infections—skin infections, eye infections, pneumonia. They gave her medication each time, but she never completely recovered, in my opinion."

"Right. She finally died from a blood infection, I was told. Really smart, sweet kid. We were all sad when she passed."

"Now that I think of it," Janice added, "there's Paula on the next block. I know she has type I diabetes. Her son has been sick for weeks. Too weak to get out of bed. She said they've run tests on him but haven't figured anything out. He keeps getting worse. I wonder if he's in one of those studies."

"The drug they're giving to prevent type I diabetes causes a decreased number of a certain type of lymphocyte," I said. "That can lead to activation of a virus and subsequent development of a deadly lymphoma or a rare condition where the virus takes over, and the patient dies."

"Do you have Paula's phone number?" Janice asked Denise, who nodded in the affirmative. "Call her now. Find out if her son is taking some of the experimental medicine to prevent type I diabetes. If he is, tell her to stop it immediately."

Denise's sister scrolled through the address book on her phone. "I've got her number here." She pressed the call icon, and we all waited, staring at her, hoping Paula would pick up. "Hi, Paula . . . Yes, it's me . . . Yeah, I heard about that. I know. They're offering a lot of money for their capture . . . On the other side of the reservation? Really? Well, I hope they get them. As long as they don't come over here. We don't want any dangerous Pilgrims walking around in our area." She glanced at me and shrugged when she said "Pilgrim," a derogatory term for whites, I gathered. "Sure, but there's something else I wanted to ask you about. Your son, the one who's ill, is he by any chance taking medicine for a clinical trial aimed at preventing diabetes?"

I watched intently as she listened to her friend's answer.

"I see. Well, I was thinking. Janice told me she heard some people talking at Umbroz. They said there might be a connection between those pills and some illnesses similar to your boy's. They're just finding out about it now."

I watched as she listened again.

"You did? You already told them about his illness? Well, maybe they didn't have enough information at the time to connect the pills to his illness. If I were you, though, I'd stop giving them to him."

She looked at me as I nodded up and down enthusiastically.

"Yeah, from what Janice told me, I would definitely stop the medicine right away . . . You're welcome . . . Bye now."

As soon as she disconnected, I was full of questions. Did someone say they saw us on the other side of the reservation? Yes. Was Paula's son enrolled in a clinical trial to prevent type I diabetes? Yes. Was she going to stop giving the drug to her child? Yes. Was Denise finally convinced she should help us escape and try to prevent Umbroz from harming others? Again, the answer was yes.

We were all in agreement. The conversation was lively as we ate fish sticks and reheated Indian fry bread for dinner. Now, all we needed was a plan to get out of there alive. I turned to Daisy, who was still sitting next to me. “Were you really able to get records of specific patients who were sickened and died from the Umbroz clinical trials?”

“No. I figured we’d find it later.”

CHAPTER 31

I called Lim, while Daisy called Arvid. I imagined Daisy's conversation with Arvid was similar to the one I had with Lim. Expecting me to be well on my way home, Lim was speechless for a moment while I explained our predicament.

"This is where I say, 'Told you so,'" Lim said, "but I'll have plenty of time to do that after you're back here. Right now, we need to concentrate on getting both of you back home safely."

"I look forward to hearing you berate me in person."

"Before that can happen, we all need to brainstorm."

"I'll put you on speakerphone and connect with Arvid."

I asked Daisy to have Arvid dial into our call. Once he had joined, I introduced Janice and Denise to Lim and Arvid over the phone. Before we proceeded, I took a moment to apologize profusely to Arvid. After all, I was responsible for luring Daisy into this dangerous situation.

"I understand," Arvid said, his indecipherable Scandinavian impassiveness making an appearance. With no time to reflect deeply on Arvid's state of mind, I dove into the planning.

"I see two options," I said. "Car or plane."

"Even if we fly, we have to get to the airport," Daisy said.

"How connected are these people to law enforcement outside the reservation?" Lim asked.

"Pretty connected, I'd say," said Janice. Denise agreed. "Umbroz gives a lot of money to sheriffs and police organizations in all the nearby counties."

"I hear they also bribe all of the police chiefs," Denise added. "I have a friend who works in the office of Chairman Stewart. She told me lots of money goes to bribes. I always looked favorably upon that, thinking it was protecting us. Now I see it was also used to allow for some pretty bad stuff to happen."

"With the local police in their pocket, we need to be especially careful. We won't be safe if we're seen in a car anywhere in the area," I said.

"Could one of you drive them to the airport tonight?" Arvid asked.

"Which airport?" Janice asked.

"Great Falls, where they flew into."

"Not a good idea," Denise said. "Our Chief probably has people there looking for them right now. The Bozeman airport, which is much farther away, would probably be okay. Anything closer is too risky."

"How would we drive them?" Janice asked. "I heard on the radio there are roadblocks at every exit from the reservation and on all major roads in the area."

"I don't suppose you have a truck or a van with a false bottom, do you?" Lim asked.

"No," the sisters answered simultaneously.

"We share a car, but it's pretty small," Janice said.

"It's a hatchback," I added. "Not good for smuggling people past a roadblock."

"Maybe Arvid and I should drive there," Lim said. "One of us could sleep while the other drives. We could be there in twenty-four hours."

"I don't think it would be safe for us to stay here that long," Daisy said. "The longer we're here, the more likely someone will find out Janice and Denise are hiding us. The last thing I want to do is put them in danger."

"Also, you'd have a hard time getting onto the reservation," Janice said. "There's only one way in without an entry card, and it's a much longer drive to get there. You'd be stopped at the gate and questioned. You need the chairman's permission to enter without a card."

"Even if you got in, you'd never be able to drive out with Daisy and Erica," Denise said. "I'm sure they'd thoroughly search your car."

"I could buy a truck and rig it up with a false bottom, but it would probably take me a few days," Lim said.

"I could help," Arvid volunteered. "But we still wouldn't get there fast enough."

"I have an idea," Denise said, looking at Daisy and me. "There are a few trails that lead out of the reservation. They aren't used much and are in bad shape, but if you're willing to rough it a bit and be exposed to poison ivy, you could hike out. Janice could meet you outside the reservation. That way, you'd avoid the roadblock problem."

"How long is the trail?" I asked, hoping it was short.

"I'd say the shortest route out is about a mile," Denise said.

"That doesn't sound too bad," Daisy said. "Not that we have much of a choice."

"Is it easy to get lost?" I asked.

"Paco can take you," Janice said. "I'll let the three of you off where the trail starts. Paco knows how to follow the trail because he used to do a lot of hiking with his great-grandfather before he died a few years ago. My sister can pick all of you up on the other side in our car. I can't do it because I'd have to miss work which would raise suspicion."

"I know of an old, abandoned shack not too far away from where I'll pick you up," Denise said. "It will be a safe place for you to hide. I'll drop you at the shack and take Paco back home."

"Then what?" I asked. "Would one of you take us to the airport?"

"We'll have to think about how to do that," Janice said. "It wouldn't be safe to try to drive you all the way to Bozeman in our car. We'd have to rent a larger car or a van."

"That could be a problem," Denise said. "We've never rented a car. It would raise suspicion, and Chairman Stewart would find out. He's got lots of eyes and ears all over to help him, especially now that word is out about you two."

"I have an idea," Lim said. "Arvid, can you fly to Bozeman early tomorrow?"

"Sure."

"I'm looking at flights right now on Expedia. You can leave from SFO tomorrow at six in the morning. Sorry, it's so early—"

"I'll do whatever it takes."

"Good. You can be in Bozeman around noon, rent a van at the airport, and get to the shack where Daisy and Erica are waiting in six or seven hours. You can drive back to Bozeman, and the three of you can catch the 7:00 a.m. flight to San Francisco the next day."

"They might have people looking for us at the Bozeman airport," Daisy said.

"There are only a few airlines that have just one stop to San Francisco," I said. "Delta and United. Maybe we could take a less direct route."

"Good idea," Lim said. "I see a flight from Bozeman to Dallas leaving at seven-thirty in the morning. It's an American Airlines flight, so they wouldn't be looking for you at that terminal. You can fly from Dallas to San Francisco and be back around five-fifteen that evening."

"I'll make the reservations now," Arvid said.

"Meanwhile, I'll get busy organizing all the information I've received from the two of you," Lim said. "It's only a question of time before they figure out where both of you live, so the faster we can get the head of Umbroz and the people helping him arrested, the better. By the way, Erica, you've gotten a bunch of phone calls on your cell. I didn't answer any of them, but several callers have left messages. Could be important."

"Probably people from the medical board about yanking my license. And the peds department wanting to fire me."

"We'll handle all that once your back. Don't worry. We'll figure it out. After I forgive you for getting me and Arvid so worried."

"Thanks, Lim," I said, knowing there wasn't much he could do about my hopeless job and medical license situation. It was nice having his support, though.

"I hate to bring this up now," Arvid said, "but the florist for the wedding has called several times to let us know she can't get the white tulips you want for the flower arrangements, Daisy. She can substitute calla lilies or alstroemeria."

Daisy raised her voice. "I don't have time to think about that now."

"The woman keeps calling. I need to know what to tell her before she calls again."

"Okay. I really don't give a crap, but tell her alstroemeria. Anything else?"

"No, my beautiful blushing bride, everything else can wait."

Denise gave Arvid detailed instructions about how to drive to the shack. We had our plan. Now, all we needed was for nothing to go wrong.

Janice and her sister spent the evening getting things ready for our hike and long wait in the shack the next day. They filled two bags with crackers, granola bars, sandwiches, and bottled water. In case Arvid didn't find us before dark, they included a flashlight. Daisy and I offered them all the money we had in our wallets, but they refused payment.

"We have enough," Denise said. "When anyone comes to our house, we make sure they have enough to eat. That's our way. If we can't use our money to help good people, it's pretty useless."

I slept on the couch cushions that night, Daisy on the couch frame. I think I got the better deal, although I didn't sleep well. I know I fell asleep at some point because Janice woke me the following morning while she was getting ready to leave for work. She made extra coffee so Daisy and I could each have a cup. We hugged her and thanked her profusely. After wishing us luck, she left the house to catch the bus to work, as was her usual practice.

Daisy and I were still dressed from the day before. Paco handed me socks and a pair of his tennis shoes which, to my surprise, fit me. I was glad to have comfortable walking shoes for the upcoming hike.

Denise gave me a cloth hat to hide my hair, thinking it would be easier to maneuver through the forest in a hat than in the shawl I wore the day before. She put water bottles and snacks for the hike in a backpack, and we were ready to go.

Denise backed the Ford Fiesta up the gravel driveway, as close to the house as possible. We loaded the car with the backpack, our purses, my uncomfortable shoes, and the two bags of provisions to use in the shack.

"As expected, they're still looking for you," Denise said, scanning messages on her phone. "Let's get in the car now." Once we were seated in the vehicle, Paco in the passenger seat, Denise looked at Daisy and me in the rearview mirror. "Ready?"

I put on sunglasses, as did Daisy. "Yes," we answered in unison.

Denise started the engine and took us past mostly dreary, small, run-down houses. She drove slowly, smiling and waving to acquaintances she saw walking outside. Worried about being found out, I began taking in slow, deep breaths to ease my anxiety. When one woman waved Denise over to talk, my heart pounded. Denise whispered, "I have to talk to my friend. Act like you're asleep."

A moment later, Denise stopped the car and rolled down her window. Pretending to sleep, with my head bent uncomfortably toward my shoulder, I opened my eyes slightly and saw Denise wave as her friend walked up to speak to her. After they greeted each other, the woman said hello to Paco, and Denise asked how her husband was doing after his recent heart attack.

"He's doing better and will probably be home from the hospital tomorrow," she said. "I thought his cholesterol-lowering medication would have protected him, but the hospital tests showed his cholesterol was higher than ever. He must have forgotten to take his medicine."

I had a different take. *He was probably taking an inactive Umbroz medication.*

"Did you hear about those two dangerous women running around loose in our community?" Denise asked.

"Sure did. I was going to warn you to be careful. Those women are nasty. I don't think any of us will feel safe until they're caught. By the way, what are you doing driving around here, and who are your friends in the back? Aren't you going to introduce us?"

I felt like sinking in my seat as low as possible, as my heart pounded faster.

"These are second cousins visiting from Red Lake." She lowered her voice somewhat. "They were up late last night. I think they drank too much and need to sleep it off. Otherwise, I'd introduce you."

"I get it. I have an aunt who does that every time she visits."

"They wanted a tour of the reservation before leaving later today, so I'm driving them around and wake them up when there's something interesting to see."

"Well, be careful."

"What about you? You're walking around without protection."

Denise's friend lifted a small firearm from her purse. "I have my little friend with me. If I see any suspicious women walking around, I'll blow their heads off."

Her words sent a shiver down my spine, imagining there were others like her who, upon seeing Daisy and me on the street, would shoot us and ask questions later.

"I'm glad you're making sure you're safe. Who knows? Maybe you'll get the reward money. If you do, don't forget your old friends. I could sure use a new car."

"You're not the only one. Enjoy the rest of your tour. Frankly, there's not much to see in this area. I hope you showed them our beautiful medical building and the community center."

"I'm planning to, so I'd better get going."

We drove off, and I began to breathe easier. Daisy took in a deep breath and released it slowly. "Well done," I said. In retrospect, Denise had given a convincing performance, giving her friend no reason to suspect us of being the women they were searching for.

We reached the beginning of the trail ten minutes later. An isolated, wooded area, we looked around to be sure we were alone before leaving the car. After Paco put on the backpack with our hiking supplies, Daisy and I followed him into the thick growth of brush and fir trees. I turned when I heard the car pull away, although I couldn't see it through the vegetation. I felt vulnerable, knowing I was in an unfamiliar wilderness, and this boy, Paco, was all that was keeping Daisy and me from the vigilantes looking for us.

CHAPTER 32

Paco took a knife from his pocket and cut three tree branches, one for each of us to use as a walking stick.

"This will help when it's muddy and rocky. I'll lead, but let me know if I go too fast. My mom always says I go too fast for old ladies."

I didn't think his comment was meant to be an insult, but it encouraged me to walk as fast as possible.

"Thank you for helping us, Paco," I said.

"You saved my life. Now it's my turn to try to save yours."

I'd never expected to be helped by Paco when I treated him the other night and rushed him to the hospital. Although we were still far from safe, I shuddered, wondering if we'd have a chance of escaping if I hadn't happened to stop by Janice's desk to inquire about apartment rentals on the day her son had a severe asthma attack.

We walked in silence, Paco leading the way, followed by me, Daisy at the rear. Initially, the trail was easy to follow, but that changed quickly. It became narrow, hard to see, and often disappeared altogether. Paco seemed to know where he was going and never slowed down. He pointed out petroglyphs carved into stones along the way which, he said, confirmed we were on the trail. I stubbornly refused to ask him to slow down. Turning to Daisy, I asked, "Is he going too fast for you? I'll tell him to slow down if you want."

Daisy smiled. "I'm doing fine, Grasshopper. However, if you're having trouble, I'll be happy to accommodate."

She knew me too well. I'd have to get in better shape if I managed to escape, having let my regular regimen of exercise lapse on account of an adorable three-year-old girl. I swallowed my pride and asked Paco to slow down.

"No problem," he said. "Would you like to stop for a minute and have a drink of water?"

"Excellent idea," I said, feeling winded and welcoming the chance to catch my breath before we started up again at a slower pace.

We drank water from the bottles Paco distributed and feasted on generic crackers. "Shouldn't you be in school?" I asked, thinking for the first time about where Paco would normally be right now.

"It's okay if I miss it. My teacher knows I have asthma and have to stay home a lot."

"Well, I can't disapprove of you missing school today, of course," I said, "but I hope you take your education seriously and attend school as much as possible."

"My mom's very strict about that. She always makes me do my homework. She wants me to go to college, but I hear it costs a lot."

"Glad your mom has high goals for you. I can tell she loves you very much. I'm sure that if you set your mind to it, you'll graduate from college and make her very proud."

Daisy and I handed our water bottles back to Paco, and we started walking again. The trail, if you could even call it that, soon became very rocky and muddy. Although I was wearing athletic shoes, my feet started slipping, so I put my walking stick to use.

"There's a trail marker tree," Paco said, pointing to an oddly-shaped bent tree, one of the few oaks in the area. "There's not too many around here, but it tells me we're still on the trail."

"Why does it look so crooked?" Daisy asked before I got the words out. I was wondering the same thing.

"Some people don't believe they're real, but I do. My ancestors trained these trees to bend when they were saplings. It's one of the ways they marked trails."

"That's incredible," I said, walking over to the tree to inspect it. I wished I hadn't left my phone with my other things in the car with Denise. I would have liked to take a picture. The trunk was bent almost at a right angle a few feet off the ground, then ran parallel to the earth a few feet before growing straight up towards the heavens. "Ingenious."

We marched on over more rocks and through mud, then jumped over a narrow stream and pushed our way through thick vegetation. Several times, Paco warned us to stay away from poison ivy near our path. The plants were similar to poison oak, which is common in California, although the leaves were smoother around the edges. As we walked, my hands became covered with small cuts. I was thankful that clothing protected my arms, legs, and torso.

Tired and thirsty, we finally reached a clearing that led to a gravel road. Ahead I saw the front of a car. My muscles tensed, and my heart pounded until I recognized the Ford Fiesta with Denise behind the wheel.

"Let's run," Paco said. The three of us sprinted towards the car and piled in—Paco in front next to his aunt, Daisy and I in the back. I dared not look around until I was seated, and the doors were closed. Then I let the delicious sensation of relief wash over me.

Paco handed our water bottles back to us, and we all drank. Denise started the engine and pulled onto the road.

"Thank you so much, Paco," I said. "You were an excellent guide. I admit I was a little worried we might get lost, but you were confident, and for good reason."

Paco turned around and smiled. "Yes, I was confident I could follow the trail the way my ancestors did," he said. "But just to be certain, I brought this." He held up a compass, and we all had a good laugh.

Taking narrow, winding, gravel roads, we arrived at a dilapidated wooden shack obscured by trees. "Let me make sure there's nobody in there," Denise said. She disappeared around the back of the structure, then came back to the car a few minutes later. "It's safe. I can tell from all the spider webs nobody's been there for a while. That's the good news."

"And the bad news?" Daisy asked.

"There are some bats living in there, so it's not very clean. Lots of guano on the floor."

We couldn't afford to be choosy, but I found the idea of hiding out in a room full of bat shit unappealing.

We were quiet for a moment, considering our options, when the silence was interrupted by Daisy's phone ringing. She pulled the phone from her purse, then answered as we all watched. Daisy smiled and looked more relaxed than I'd seen her in a while. "Great news . . . yes, we'll be waiting here, the same place Janice told you about yesterday . . . will do . . . drive safely. Remember, don't speed. You don't want to be stopped for a ticket . . . love you too." Daisy disconnected the call and turned to us, still smiling. "Arvid is already in the rental van, on his way here. He should arrive in less than seven hours, so it won't be quite dark yet."

"Let me show you the shack," Denise said. She led us around to the back, through layers of dead leaves, needles, and twigs several inches thick, and over several large branches that had fallen. A squirrel skittered away and up a tree nearby. We reached the doorway, which had only hinges where the door should have been, and led us inside.

We all stood near the entrance and gazed around the small room. Built of partially rotted-out planks, the structure was about twenty feet in length. Rays of filtered sunlight coming through the open door and adjacent broken window were the only source of illumination. At the opposite end of the room were six brown bats, hanging upside down from the ceiling, their wings folded around their bodies, asleep. The floor was littered with black bat droppings, mainly under the area where the bats were hanging. A wooden bench, big enough for two, stood against the wall farthest from the bats. Fortunately, it was free of guano.

"I would suggest you stay inside here," Denise said. "I doubt if anyone will come by, but you never know." She and Paco went back to the car and returned with the bags of supplies Denise and Janice had prepared. "In case your ride doesn't show up before it's dark, remember that your flashlight is visible from a distance."

We thanked Paco and Denise with hugs all around, and they left. Hearing the car pull away, I felt unprotected once again. Daisy got close to the wall facing the street. "I can see through the wall here," she said. "There are gaps in the wood. We'll be able to see Arvid when he drives up."

"Can't be soon enough," I said.

We occupied the next hours sitting on the bench, talking about our discoveries at Umbroz, our conversation repeatedly interrupted by the sounds of animals—squirrels, foxes, deer, even a moose. Each new noise brought panic as we first cowered, then, one at a time, approached the window to look out. Those interruptions made the afternoon and evening more tolerable. We occasionally ran in place to keep warm and ventured outside only to pee. Sometime in the midafternoon, we ate our sandwiches.

Around eight in the evening, when Daisy was describing her kidnapping from the hotel parking lot the previous morning, she suddenly fell silent and poked my arm with her elbow. I noticed her pointing to the other side of the room, where the bats were starting to stir.

"What's going on?" she whispered.

"Bats are more active as the sun starts to set. We don't want them to bite us, that's for sure," I answered, my heart pounding as I prepared to flee. "They could have rabies."

"Let's move slowly to the door."

No sooner had Daisy stood than the bats flew single file through a small hole I hadn't seen before in the wall, near the ceiling where they had been sleeping. We both laughed with relief. Daisy finished the story about her abduction, describing how she was taken to the building where they held us and futilely tried to escape by using some of the techniques Arvid had taught her. She chuckled at her ineptitude, realizing Arvid had allowed her to throw him down using some of the karate maneuvers he'd shown her, boosting her confidence to a height she couldn't back up in a real situation.

"You may not be very good at karate," I said, "but if I ever need someone kicked in the balls, you'll be the first one I ask."

We were stifling our laughter, trying to keep the noise down, when Daisy's phone rang. "It's Arvid," she said, looking at her phone, smiling. "Hello . . . you are?" She ran over to the wall facing the street and peered through the rotted wood. "Be right out!" She disconnected the call, grabbed her purse and the bag Denise had given us, and shouted, "Arvid's waiting out front."

I ran outside after Daisy and was greeted by something that brought me an instant of relief—Arvid at the wheel of a white van. Daisy flung the passenger door open, jumped in, and hugged

Arvid as I awkwardly stood nearby holding the remaining supplies.

"Hey, lovebirds, we've got to get going," I said after waiting for what I thought was too long. We still weren't safe, and I was uncomfortable waiting in the open for Daisy and Arvid to finish their amorous reunion. "This isn't your honeymoon."

"Sorry," Daisy said.

I followed her as she went between the front bucket seats to the back of the van, avoiding a stack of blankets and a myriad of empty boxes.

"Now I have to arrange all the boxes in the back," Arvid said.

He opened his door and walked to the rear of the van, stretched, and opened the rear door. As he moved the boxes around, he instructed us to sit between them in such a way we could lie down and cover ourselves with blankets if we needed to hide. This wasn't going to be a comfortable trip, but at least we had room to straighten our legs out, and it was warm.

"I'm really sorry about all this, Arvid," I said when there was a moment of quiet. "It never occurred to me we'd be in any real danger."

"I believe you. Assuming we get back, Daisy and I will think of a way for you to repay us."

He didn't sound mad, which was reassuring. However Arvid and Daisy wanted me to repay them would be fine with me.

"I need to stop for some coffee. I passed a place along the way," Arvid said. "But first, I've got to pee." He walked into the woods for a few minutes and returned, looking relaxed. He started the engine, and we were off.

Due to our prior experiences with the difficulty of peeing on the road, Daisy and I declined Arvid's offer to buy us drinks as we pulled into the parking lot of a generic coffee brewery. Arvid left Daisy and me in the van hidden under blankets and returned with a large cup of dark roast. We wended our way toward the highway as Arvid sipped on his coffee and helped himself to the contents of a jar of licorice he had in one of the cup holders. He seemed to want to relax us by talking about where his relatives from Denmark would be staying for the wedding. We hadn't gone more than fifteen minutes before we came to a roadblock.

CHAPTER 33

It was almost dark outside. We were behind ten cars in line at the roadblock. The police were questioning each driver, looking in trunks with their flashlights.

"Damn," said Arvid. "Looks like they're going to search the car. I could probably floor this thing and get around the roadblock. What do you think?"

"They'll chase us for sure and probably shoot all of us. Remember, this isn't Denmark," Daisy said. "Why don't you tell them you're Norwegian, on your way to the airport to go to Oslo. With your Danish accent, they're sure to believe you."

"Good idea. I'll tell them I'm in a rush because my mother suddenly became very sick."

"If they ask," I added, "you could tell them your name is Petter Gustavson, my boss in the QC department—that's quality control."

"They might ask for identification."

"Tell them you put your wallet and a few other things in the back, and it will take a while to find everything."

"Got it. I'll say that on a long drive, my wallet is uncomfortable in my back pocket. Leave it to me," Arvid said. "Now hide under the blankets and be quiet."

I concealed myself under several blankets, moving around until my nose and mouth were near the edge of the covers so I could breathe. My internal organs were uncomfortably jostled each time the van moved forward incrementally. My whole body was tense, my anxiety amplified by not being able to see what was happening. I heard footsteps approach the car, and Arvid's window roll down.

"Can I help you?" Arvid asked in a heavy Danish accent, heavier than I remembered.

"Please step out of the car, sir. Who are you, and where are you going?"

I heard the car door open and Arvid step out. "I'm Petter Gustavson, and I'm going to the airport. I need to hurry to make my connection to Oslo. My mother is very ill."

"Oslo. That's in Norway, isn't it?"

"Yes, officer."

"You work at Umbroz?"

"Yes. Quality control. They are very nice to let me go on short notice to see my mother."

"What's all the stuff in the back?" I saw flashes of light through the blankets as I imagined the officer shining his light over the rear cargo.

"I, um, had to borrow this van from one of my colleagues. Just some old boxes and blankets he didn't have time to clean out."

"Okay, well, I hope your mom is okay. Have a safe trip."

I was expecting to hear Arvid step into the van and close the door when instead, my cell phone started ringing. *Damn. Damn. Damn.* I gritted my teeth.

"What's that?" the officer asked, anger in his voice.

"Oh, thank goodness," Arvid said. "I misplaced my phone. Thought I lost it, but now I see it must have fallen into the back when I was arranging things in there."

I imagined Arvid sweating as he concocted what I thought was a pretty good story on the spot.

"Let's go find your phone."

I was focused on every sound as I heard footsteps proceed from the front of the van, around the side, toward the back. With little time to think, I found my cell phone and gently pushed it out from under the blanket. I didn't breathe as the rear door opened.

"There it is," Arvid said after a long fifteen seconds. "My driving seems to have messed up everything back here and shook my phone out from where it was hiding. Here, I'll get it."

I felt the blankets shift as he put one hand down, narrowly missing my leg, and reached into the van to retrieve the phone.

"Let me see it," the officer said. "Missed call from Lim. You Norwegians sure have some strange names. Better hurry, so you don't miss your flight."

Heavy footsteps headed away from the van, and I took a deep breath. The rear door closed, and I heard Arvid get back in the driver's seat and start the engine. We were all quiet for at least five minutes as Arvid drove. Finally, he broke the silence. "You two still back there?"

Daisy and I threw the blankets back. "Sorry," I said. "Should have turned off my phone. That was quick thinking on your part, Arvid. Thanks."

"I hate to admit it, but I also forgot to turn my phone off," Daisy said.

"Mine was on, too," Arvid said. "I was hoping it wouldn't go off while we were looking for the one I said I'd dropped. I was working on an explanation in case that happened. Glad I didn't need it because I didn't have a good one. Here." Arvid tossed my phone over his shoulder so I could reach it. It was dark outside, so Daisy and I felt safe sitting upright on the floor of the van, using the blankets as cushions. Not very comfortable, but tolerable for the remainder of the trip.

I picked up my phone and called Lim. "Your phone has been ringing like crazy," he said. "I thought it would be a good idea to start answering it. You've got more friends than you think."

"What's happened?"

"I hardly know where to begin. Let me look at my notes. It's not easy being your secretary. Now I know how Martha must have felt."

The mention of Martha caused me to break down in tears. I hadn't told Lim about her yet—I know he wouldn't have mentioned her if he'd known.

"You okay?" he asked.

"Sorry, it's just that, well, they killed Martha." I broke down in tears again. I imagined the shocked look that must have been on Lim's face.

"Damn," he said. "I didn't know."

"You couldn't have."

"That must have been horrible for you. It's a good thing I didn't know. I would have been beside myself. I've been worried enough as it is."

"I'm a bit frazzled now, but I'll fill you in when I get home. Now tell me what's been happening on your end."

"First, there's Mrs. Reinhold. She's one tough lady. I think she spent a whole day on the phone with people from the FDA, getting information and chewing them out. She has a nephew who works in the White House and was able to get his boss to pressure people at the FDA to talk to her."

"What did she find out?"

"It appears they never actually ignored your letters, but the wheels turn very slowly there, and they don't typically share what they're doing with outsiders. There has been an ongoing investigation of Umbroz drugs, as others have complained. They haven't been able to gather data on any breach of protocol, though. They've had many surprise inspections but never turned up anything inappropriate."

"Sure, because they can't really be surprised. Since inspectors have to stay at their hotel, the Umbroz people know they're coming ahead of time and can prepare. Overnight they can print up whatever data they need to show and only allow inspectors into their smaller operation, where they follow strict guidelines. All that pretty much guarantees they'll never fail an inspection."

"That fits in with what you suspected before your trip."

"Remind me to thank Mrs. Reinhold when I get back."

"Will do. Also, you have a friend in the Pediatric ICU who followed up on your warning. She investigated the nurse you were worried about and found out he'd been in attendance shortly before Cassandra Roberts died, and before Skylar Reinhold needed to be resuscitated. There's no direct evidence against him yet, but he's been placed on leave."

"At least he won't be killing any more children. That's a relief."

"That's not all. The prosecutor has gotten involved, and I've spoken to her a few times. I feel I've learned more about medicine in the past two days than in all my previous years. I have to admit, it does seem interesting."

"Told you so."

"I've organized all the information you and Daisy sent me. I don't understand all of it, but the FDA has requested it, and if it's okay with you, I'd like to send it. They'll probably have questions I can't answer. You can take care of that when you return."

"Send it," I shouted. I felt my heart racing, but in a good way. I'd just ascended from feelings of hopelessness to a sense of immense optimism. The pieces were falling into place.

"They want you to testify before a closed committee next week in DC, so I went ahead and changed your appointment to the end of the week."

"I almost forgot about it."

"Good thing I didn't. I want you to know I'm going to have you protected by bodyguards as soon as you land."

"But—"

"No buts about it. They'll pick you up at the airport and bring you home safely."

"What about Daisy and Arvid?"

"I don't think they're in danger. You're the one these creeps are going to be focused on because you'll be testifying. To be safe, though, I'll ask the security company to cover them too."

After our conversation ended, I explained everything to Daisy and Arvid. I told them Lim was hiring bodyguards for them too. Arvid resisted at first, but Daisy and I convinced him of the necessity of protection.

The rest of the drive was unremarkable. Tired and hungry, we arrived at a hotel near the Bozeman airport. It was luxurious compared to the place Daisy and I stayed in Raintree. Confident we weren't being followed, Arvid got two rooms. We had dinner in the downstairs coffee shop, after which I went to my room for some much-needed sleep. Feeling I should keep my guard up, I slept fitfully, aware each time water ran through pipes, a door opened, or there were footsteps in the hall outside my door.

We had breakfast early the next day, returned the van, and took a shuttle to the airport. Vigilant until we had boarded the plane, none of us saw anything worrisome. Once we were buckled in on the plane and taxiing to the runway, I felt more relaxed than I'd been in days. I slept most of the way to Dallas, the first leg of the trip. During our layover, I phoned Lim to tell him we were on track to land at SFO in the early evening. He let me know that, unfortunately, he and Maya wouldn't be at the airport to meet me, as there wouldn't be enough room in the security vehicle.

The trip to San Francisco was uneventful. When the plane door opened, it seemed to take forever to deplane. Since we had no luggage, the three of us walked single file, darting around groups of slow-moving travelers, to the baggage area. There we were greeted by a man dressed in black holding a sign for "Mr. and Mrs. Summers" as Lim had instructed. I was already familiar with the man who had been stationed outside our condominium to guard Ting and her children. After checking Daisy's and Arvid's identifications, the bodyguard led us to the curb, where we waited for a black SUV circling outside. We all got in and headed for the freeway. Daisy and I recognized the driver, as he had guarded us after our return from China four years earlier.

The security team dropped off Arvid and Daisy first. One of the men exited the vehicle with them to make sure they reached their unit safely, and speak to a guard who was waiting there. He returned to the van, and we drove to my building. A guard walked me to the door of my unit but left as soon as Lim and Maya appeared. Unable to control my emotions, my tears started flowing.

We hugged for a long time, Lim's embrace tighter than usual, Maya's arms around Lim's and my legs. It was good to be home, and I wished that moment could last forever.

The first one to speak was Lim. "You're lucky I'm less mad at you than I am glad you're back."

CHAPTER 34

I still had tears in my eyes when I composed myself enough to speak. "I know, I really messed up. I had no idea how brutal the pharmaceutical industry is."

"I'm glad that's all behind you," Lim said, "but right now, there's a lot to do. We still have to nail those fuckers. We have a busy night ahead of us, so I'll make some coffee. You have ten minutes to relax before we begin."

Lim made a pot of coffee and produced a bag of Morning Buns he'd bought earlier at a local bakery.

"You're a bad influence on me," I chided him. "It's not even morning anymore."

"Do I get one too?" Maya asked.

"Certainly, dear." I'd really missed her. It seemed she had grown in the few days I'd been gone.

"I missed you so much, Mommy."

"I missed you a lot, too, dear."

"Show Mommy what you made for her," Lim said.

Maya went to her room and brought out a sheet of eight by eleven white paper. There, drawn in eight crayon colors, was

Maya's rendition of our family standing, holding hands, and smiling—Lim and I with Maya in the middle.

"This is temporary," she said. "I left room for a baby."

When did she learn the word "temporary?" I looked at Lim. He threw up his hands. "I didn't say a thing, honest."

I can attest that Morning Buns eaten in the evening are still delicious. I scrolled through text messages and listened to the voicemail on my phone, mostly friends and colleagues wondering what exactly was going on. Apparently, the rumor mill had been operating at full force, yet I still had people on my side.

The doctor who had been taking care of Cassandra Roberts the night she died left a message informing me that because of my suspicion and the later near-death of Skylar, she sent a sample of Cassandra's blood drawn just before she died during CPR to the lab for analysis. Her tryptase was sky high, indicating she had suffered from anaphylaxis, a severe immune reaction, before her death. The diagnosis was borne out by the medical examiner's findings at autopsy: laryngeal swelling and excess fluid in the lungs. Toxicological studies were pending the identification of unknown substances. The coroner had thus far determined the manner of death to be indeterminate. That meant homicide had not been ruled out. I took a moment to reflect on the enormity of that evidence, and the evidence that would likely surface soon.

Lim interrupted my train of thought, and we got down to business. He showed me how he had organized all the data Daisy and I had sent him, with each photo and video numbered. "They want to talk to you tonight," he said after he'd presented me with an overview.

"Who?"

"People from the FDA. The Center for Drug Evaluation and Research."

"Well, I'll be damned. I still can't believe they were taking me seriously. They must really want to talk to me—it's after nine o'clock there."

Lim checked the time on his cell phone. "They're going to call you in about five minutes. You can charge your phone while you talk. When you finish speaking to them, we'll go downstairs to visit Ting and Mingyu. They've been wanting to see you ever since they got back from the hospital."

"I can't wait to see them either. How are they doing?"

"Surprisingly well. They're able to go for walks outside every day now."

"I'd love to walk with them this evening. It won't be dark for a while."

Moments later, my cell rang, and I was connected to three doctors from the FDA. After introductions were made, they methodically asked about each of my videos and photos. I walked them through everything and learned that they had used my images of the chemical labels to determine that while the A building had the appropriate ingredients, the B facility had only inferior, much less costly components.

Using the evidence Daisy supplied, they obtained a warrant to access the Umbroz system with Lim's help, to see for themselves how much of the information they generated never saw the light of the FDA's day.

They were prepared to shut down the facility and had spoken to federal prosecutors in the Montana U.S. Attorney's Office who were about to issue warrants for the arrest of the Rakvag brothers and others who had signed falsified documents. FBI agents would be contacting me soon for details regarding the dead bodies in the back of the dairy truck Lim had told them about hours earlier.

The conversation was tedious, lasting almost an hour. At the end, they requested I fly to DC, present my findings to all interested parties behind closed doors, and sign documents attesting to the validity of the information I had sent. I agreed, surprised by how quickly things were moving.

I was finishing the last of the coffee before my much-anticipated visit with Ting and Mingyu when my phone rang again. An FBI Special Agent introduced himself and asked me detailed questions about my captivity in the hands of Sven and the Viking. I described my experience, the location of the community center on Google maps, and the injuries I inflicted on our captors. Much of my time was spent describing Martha's involvement and the bodies I'd seen in the back of the dairy truck. I implored them to be sure Janice and her family were safe. He assured me agents from the area would be on their way to investigate soon. There would be a wide-ranging investigation of the police department there, as well as in San Francisco, looking for payoffs from Umbroz. When I told him what I had learned about Cassandra Roberts, he promised to follow up with the nurse I suspected was directly responsible for her death.

Moments after my conversation with the FBI Special Agent ended, I received a call from Dr. Pressley, the esteemed member of the Internal Medicine department Martha claimed to have called regarding the quality of Umbroz medications. I figured Martha had probably lied about contacting him, but on the off chance he actually had suggested I review my clinical acumen rather than investigate a medication defect, I let the call go to voicemail. I waited quite a while before my phone signaled I had a voicemail message. Then I listened.

"Hello, Dr. Rosen. This is Roland Pressley from Internal Medicine. I know we haven't formally met, but I'd appreciate a bit of your time to discuss your recent discoveries about Umbroz Pharmaceuticals. I've had my own suspicions about their medications ever since our pharmacy began using their generics. I'd complained to the head of the pharmacy, but he couldn't be budged. Rumor has it he recently bought a pretty nice thirty-foot sailboat. The DA will be looking into how he afforded it on his salary. I had also written a letter of complaint to the FDA but never received a satisfactory response.

"Unlike you, I let it ride and didn't follow up. I'm mighty impressed at what you've done, and what I hear you've uncovered. Too bad we didn't have a chance to talk about this earlier, before you went to investigate the company yourself. Perhaps together we might have gotten the investigation escalated more quickly, and you wouldn't have gone through all the recent unpleasantness.

"There was an ad hoc meeting this morning with the dean of the medical school and some of us other doctors and administrators. I'm pleased to inform you the vote was unanimous to lift your suspension. You are probably not too happy with us right now, but I hope you accept our offer to come back. I look forward to speaking with you at your convenience so we can compare notes about our experience with Umbroz medications. Should you agree to remain on our medical staff, I would like you to head up a new committee aimed at fast-tracking any clinician concerns about medications in the future."

I listened to the message twice, making sure I didn't miss any details. In retrospect, it made sense. Martha had never phoned Dr. Pressley. If I'd called him myself, things would have been quite different.

Maya and I were ready to go downstairs to see Ting and Mingyu when my phone rang again. I answered to speak to the new acting director of the pediatrics clinic, who had just replaced Jeremy. He sounded nervous when he asked if I'd be returning to work.

"Sure," I said. "I'll never give up on my patients."

"I'm glad to hear it. The rest of the staff will be glad too. Everyone was upset about the way they treated you. We all knew you weren't taking drugs. In fact, we had started an investigation of our own, and many of us had become suspicious of Jeremy

Nilsen. He was the only one who demanded you be fired. He was very vocal about it."

"I don't want to work with him or his assistant."

"No worries. Neither of them works here now. You can visit them if you want to give them a piece of your mind. They're both in the county jail. Speaking of Nilsen, now that he's gone, we are very short-staffed. When would you like to come back?"

"Good question. I'll be gone at least two days at the beginning of next week." I turned away from the phone and yelled out to Lim, who was at his desk in the study. "When's my appointment?"

"Monday, week after next."

Speaking into the phone again, I asked, "How about a week from Tuesday?"

"Whatever you want. I'll put you on the schedule starting then. I'll be sure your first day is light so you can spend some time catching up on paperwork."

After the call ended, I closed my eyes for a moment, fully appreciating the feeling of having my life back.

"Are you okay, Mommy?" Maya asked, tapping my shoulder.

"Sure, darling. I'm very okay. Now let's go visit Auntie Ting and Mingyu."

Maya and I went to Ting's unit, where Ting and Mingyu greeted us at the door. It felt terrific seeing them outside the hospital setting.

"Kang and Wang Shu are visiting friends," Mingyu said, "so each of us can eat more of the sesame fritters Grandma made this afternoon."

"You both look so wonderful," I said. "Can I hug you?"

"No hug. Not yet. We both still hurt very much," Ting said.

I sat on Ting's couch, and Mingyu came over and kissed my hand. "I can't hug, but I can kiss," he said. "I'm glad you're back from your trip."

My heart melted, and it took great restraint to refrain from picking him up and squeezing him tight.

"Would you like to go for a walk, Mingyu?" I asked. "The sun will still be up for over an hour."

"Can I bring my ball?"

I looked at Ting. "Yes, you can bring your ball." She turned to me to explain, "Lim bought him a small soccer ball, made for children. He loves it. So does Maya. The homeless demonstrations are over, so there will be a lot of room for them to play on the sidewalk."

Mingyu got his soccer ball, and the four of us—me, Ting, Maya, and Mingyu—went downstairs and out of the building. No sooner were we outside than I felt closed in by the four security men who surrounded us. I'd forgotten about them until that moment.

"Sorry about the security," I said to Ting, "but Lim insisted on having them until I testify, sign documents, and the Umbroz dirtbags are behind bars."

"I understand. Security is very important. Those bad men might try to kill you."

She wasn't making me feel any better. "How is your new friend from the hospital? The anesthesiologist?" I asked, changing the subject.

For the first time I remembered, I saw Ting blush. "He is very nice, but I do not know what to think. It is hard for me to trust a man."

"You trust Lim, don't you?"

"He is different. He is my brother."

"Maybe your friend has a sister. You should meet his family and see how they treat each other. That can tell you a lot." I felt inhibited by the security men walking so close, unable to say everything on my mind.

Maya and Mingyu walked slightly ahead of us, taking turns kicking the soccer ball gently. I was impressed at the degree of control Mingyu had at his young age.

"You should give him a chance," I said. "Your kids love Lim, and he loves them, but he's their uncle. They'd love to have a dad, and you should have a full-time partner. You deserve to have a real family."

Ting started to answer, when Mingyu kicked the ball hard, sending it down the street, past numerous pedestrians.

Mingyu and Maya started after the ball, and Ting shrieked, "My boy! They want to kill Mingyu!" She became hysterical, as I'd seen her before. I momentarily wondered if she was imagining things or had indeed seen or heard something unusual. From that instant, the scene unfolded quickly. Ting tried to chase after Mingyu but was prevented when our security detail quickly surrounded the two of us.

Maya sped ahead of Mingyu, whose speed was limited by post-surgical pain. As one of the security agents left us and started after him, I heard someone running, approach quickly from behind, then pass us on the side. I looked to my right and glimpsed a light-haired man in shorts and a T-shirt dash by, my view of him partially blocked by the security contingent. *Was Ting right? Was an assassin gaining on Mingyu?* The runner ignored Mingyu, passing by him without slowing. I started to relax when, to my horror, he scooped up Maya and continued running for several yards, my daughter kicking and screaming. Seconds later, the man disappeared into a car, still holding Maya. The last thing I remembered before the vehicle took off, tires squealing, was the most heart-wrenching sound a mother could hear: "Mommy, help me!"

CHAPTER 35

I screamed and fell to my knees. Two of my security guards ran after the car, then returned. Mingyu lay on the ground, crying, not bothering to retrieve his soccer ball. The security guards and Ting gathered around and tried to comfort me, but there was no comforting a mother who had just seen her precious three-year-old daughter abducted.

I don't know how long I remained there, paralyzed with grief, but it was enough time for a crowd of onlookers to gather around. When I eventually regained my composure, Ting, Mingyu, and the bodyguards walked me back to my building. One of them accompanied me to my unit. I wondered whether this was a random kidnapping, or if it had something to do with Umbroz. The latter possibility was impossible to ignore.

Lim, my rock, broke down in tears when I told him what had happened. We cried together as the bodyguard stood patiently in the background, talking quietly on his two-way radio. When our tears subsided, he approached us and said they'd traced the getaway car's license and determined it was a rental. The vehicle hadn't been returned yet, and his colleague had asked a connection on the police force to send out word to be on the lookout for it.

"Who rented the car?" I asked.

"The name they gave was fake. Not helpful."

"Can you be sure? What was the name?" Lim asked.

"They chose a name to intimidate you. I'm sure they made it up and got a fake driver's license to rent the car."

Lim looked impatient. "Just tell us the name. Fake or not, it can't hurt."

"I didn't want to tell you, but they used the name of Anders Breivik."

"I'll bet he's Norwegian," Lim shouted. "This is your fault, Erica. This is some sort of payback for what you've done."

His words devastated me. I didn't know I could feel worse than the moment I saw Maya yelling for me, but I did. I sobbed uncontrollably.

A few minutes later, Lim put his arm around me as my body quivered. "I'm sorry, Erica. I know you wouldn't have knowingly put Maya in danger. Neither of us realized how ruthless these people are. We need to stay focused and work on this together."

Despite the horror of the situation, Lim's words were comforting, and my tears dried.

"First, I want to know who this Anders Breivik is." I opened my laptop and did a Google search after one of the guards reluctantly spelled the name for me. I understood his hesitancy to enlighten me about Breivik after I read about him. Breivik is perhaps the most notorious Norwegian, now serving a twenty-one-year sentence of preventive detention, the maximum in that country, for detonating a bomb in the capital city, killing eight, then murdering sixty-nine more people, mostly children, at a youth summer camp. His name had been chosen to frighten me, knowing I would chase down the name of the person who rented the car. One thing was clear. There was no doubt in my mind that Maya's abduction was related to Umbroz. It was all my fault.

"I doubt hurting Maya is their primary goal," the security agent told me. "Keep your phone handy. They're bound to call you with demands. I imagine they'll want you to cancel your agreement to testify and deny the veracity of all the information and videos you and Daisy supplied. Only then will they let Maya go."

"What should I say if they call?"

"Ask them what they want, and agree. Delay, delay, delay. That's the best option. Meanwhile, we're going to try to find your daughter."

"What if you don't?" I asked.

"Remember, they have no reason to want to harm her. She represents leverage over you. If they harm her, they won't have any control over you. They're likely keeping her in a comfortable place right now. She's probably frightened but well cared for."

"Do you have a plan to find out where she is?" Lim asked.

"First, I think we should notify the FBI."

"I can do that," Lim said. "I've been working with some of their agents. What do you think they'll do? Do you think they might put Maya in more danger than she is in already?"

"I doubt it. We'll have to confer with them."

Lim pulled out his phone, speed-dialed an agent he had been working with, and walked to the bedroom as he began talking.

As his voice faded, one of the guards asked me, "Do you have any ideas about where to look?"

"No. Chances are she is staying in the home of someone they trust, or in a rental. One way or the other, we need to find her." My voice was shaky, but my mind was pulling a blank about the best way to proceed.

"If we find the car soon, she might be nearby. Transferring Maya to another car would be risky, so they'll most likely drop her off, then ditch the car somewhere else. I doubt they'll return it to the rental agency."

Our conversation was interrupted by my phone ringing. Caller ID showed a number I didn't recognize. It was either a telemarketer or the kidnappers. I answered.

The first words I heard were, "Mommy, I want to come home." They were trying to pull on my heartstrings, and it was working. A man's voice replaced my daughter's. "You heard her. She wants to come home." The Norwegian accent was unmistakable. "You can make it possible. I suggest you don't search for her or call the police or any other law enforcement agency. You will need to cancel your meeting with the FDA and retract all the information you've provided them. You'll need to sign an affidavit stating all your photos and videos are not as they appear but were prepared to smear Umbroz so you could get your job back. Daisy helped by fabricating phony data files. You must promise to destroy all the copies you made of your recordings. Even if you don't, your affidavit will serve to discredit them. If you do not do as you are told, you will never see Maya."

"How can you do this? How can you hurt a child?"

"I have no intention of hurting your daughter. She's quite adorable. That's why we plan to sell her. I predict she will go for a very high price at auction. We're not in the business of selling children, but I've recently learned it's quite easy. There's a big market, couples who can't have children, and others with what I would say are more unusual needs."

I was sick to my stomach. "Let me talk to her again, please," I begged.

"We'll be getting back to you soon with specific instructions. Remember, no police if you want to see Maya again." The call was disconnected. I cried.

Lim, done with his phone call with the FBI agent, walked back into the room and held me until I stopped crying. I relayed what the caller had told me, including the warning against involving the police. The security agent said, "The first thing you've gotta do is get a call recorder app on your phone, so you can record the next call."

No sooner had he said that than Lim took my phone and downloaded the Rev Call Recorder app. "Done," he said when complete.

"Did you recognize your caller's voice?" the agent asked.

"No, but he had a Norwegian accent and sounded very scary. I'm sure he's connected to Umbroz."

"Are there any Umbroz people who live in town?" Lim asked.

"I believe the owner's brother, Johan Rakvag, lives locally," I said. "He must at least have a place in the area, although I saw him at the company in Montana the day before I was kidnapped."

"Two FBI agents will be coming over soon," Lim said.

"Tell them not to come," I screamed. "I told you, they said 'no police.'"

"They deal with this sort of thing regularly," one of the guards said. "Kidnappers always warn about calling the police."

"I don't care," I yelled. "Lim, don't let them come here. They could be watching."

"Okay," Lim said. "I'll have them stay away. We can set up a conference call." Lim walked to the bedroom again as he made a phone call.

"Before the FBI gets involved, we can start looking for Johan Rakvag's San Francisco residence," the guard said. He walked away from the couch where I was sitting to the kitchen table and spoke quietly into his phone.

A moment later, Lim returned.

"What can we do if we find out where Johan Rakvag lives locally?" I asked. "Do you think Maya's there?"

"I doubt it. But I'm sure he knows where Maya is."

"How can we get him to tell us?"

"I'll bet the location where they're keeping her is on his cell phone. We need to get his phone."

"Sure, but there's one problem. He's not going to give it to us. Even if we manage to get it, it will be locked," I said.

The agent put his phone in his pocket and walked toward us. "I got Johan Rakvag's address. He lives in a pricey condo on Nob Hill. Doubtful he'd bring your daughter there. It'd be too difficult to bring her inside without being noticed."

"Before we do anything, let's coordinate with the FBI. They're waiting for me to call so we can all talk."

Lim dialed a number and set his phone on the coffee table, the speaker on. Two FBI agents introduced themselves, and we filled them in on the information we had.

"This may be easy," one of the agents said. "We'll go to Rakvag's place and demand he tell us where Maya is."

"If you do that, we might never see her again," I shouted.

"People like that almost always talk once they're threatened with arrest. After we find out where she is, we'll have agents get her out—probably storm the premises."

"I don't like your idea," I said. "What if he doesn't tell you where she is? What if he has company when the FBI arrives, and they notify the people holding Maya? What if you storm the place where Maya is, but they are able to get Maya out to another hideaway anyway?"

"I have another idea," the other agent said. "We can have Dr. Rosen go through the motions. She can do everything they say, but we'll secretly document all the steps along the way, including signing documents under duress. Once Maya is free, we can move in and arrest them. We'll have proof the doctor didn't sign anything voluntarily."

Lim cut them off. "Thanks for your great ideas. We need to discuss them amongst ourselves. I'll get back to you."

"Why did you end our call so suddenly?" I asked as Lim disconnected the call.

"I don't like their plans. Even if they get the address where Maya is, I'm not confident they could get her out safely. The other plan where you go along with their demands will take too long. I can see many places where it might backfire, and people will never believe you when you try to retract your retractions. If you go back on the deal you make with them, they could kidnap Maya again."

"So now what do we do?" I felt hopeless.

"Now we come up with our own plan." Lim sat motionless, posed like Rodin's *The Thinker*. Finally, he came back to life. "I like my first idea best. I want his phone." He turned to the guard. "Can someone in your organization help me get it?"

"We have to follow all the laws to keep our license," the agent said, "but I have a friend who's a private eye of sorts. He's not as concerned about the letter of the law as we are. He could visit Rakvag's condo building and see if his car is parked in its assigned space."

"It could be parked there if he's still out of town and got a ride to the airport," I said.

"True, but if it's gone, we'll know he's not home," the bodyguard said. "If it's there, we can proceed as if he were home. It would help to know what kind of car he drives."

"As a matter of fact, I happen to know that," I said, remembering the day I saw him leaving Kokkari. "I don't know exactly what kind it is, but it's a pretty unmistakable expensive sports car. Yellow. Maybe a Lamborghini."

Lim showed me pictures of sports cars on his iPad. "It's that one," I said, pointing to a sleek, low-lying car with a hardtop, distinctive molding over the door, and five thick tire spokes.

"It's a Ferrari," Lim said.

"I suggest you hire my friend to check if Rakvag's car is there. If it is, he can mess with the door handles or rock the car until the alarm goes off. With a car like that, Rakvag likely has an alarm app on his phone. If he's home, he'll be down shortly. Once he's in the parking lot, my friend can get his cellphone. If Rakvag isn't home, my talented friend can gain access to his apartment and look for clues there."

"What if the parking lot is secured? How will he get in? I doubt it's open to the public."

"That won't be a problem. He's very good at following people into secured buildings unnoticed."

"What if Rakvag just deactivates his alarm from his phone?"

"Believe me, people with Ferraris always check things out when their alarm goes off."

"Once he's down there, then what? Is your guy going to mug him?"

"Why don't you talk to him yourself? I'll get him on the line."

The guard made a call, spoke briefly, then put his phone on speaker and placed it on the coffee table in front of us. "John Doe, meet your clients, Bill and Hillary."

CHAPTER 36

"Nice to meet you, John," I said. "You think you can help us?"

"This sounds easy." I detected an accent I found hard to place—probably Middle Eastern. "You want me to get the phone of this fellow Johan Rakvag. Like my friend already told you, if his car is in the garage, I'll set off the alarm. Chances are, he'll come to the garage with his phone out to deactivate it."

"What if he deactivates the alarm with the phone in his pocket?" I asked.

"No problem. I have a portable transmitter that can mimic a cell tower and reach nearby phones. It's capable of sending fake Wireless Emergency Alerts, such as Amber alerts. I'll use it if necessary, to get him to take his phone out."

"I have a feeling your device is illegal," Lim said. "Like a Stingray device."

"I see you're familiar with the technology. I'll neither confirm nor deny the legality of what I use."

"I don't think grabbing his phone and running is the best idea," Lim said. "He might be armed. I don't think he'll hesitate to shoot you."

"I'm not a street thug. I won't simply grab it. By the way, did my friend mention that you'll need to buy a few cell phones? It's going to cost you some serious coin."

"No, he didn't mention that, but we'll spend whatever it takes. We've got to get our daughter back."

"Understood. You'll need to buy an iPhone, a Galaxy, a Google Pixel, Motorola—ask what the ten most popular phones are, and buy one of each. Then buy black cases for them."

"I'm not sure I know where this is going," I said. "Buying so many phones will take a while, especially starting service for all of them."

"No need to get service. All you have to do is get the phones. I'll pick them up later. Once I get a look at his phone, I'll find a match and make a switch."

"I think I know where this is going now," I said.

"Right. So while Rakvag is dealing with his car alarm, I'll appear in my business suit and ask him if I can borrow his phone for an important call because I'm a bit late for a meeting. I'll show him my phone, which I'll say is out of juice. He'll hand me his, I'll make a call to a random number, pretend to tell someone I'm running fifteen minutes late, hand him back the matching phone you just bought, and leave. By the time he realizes I didn't go back to my car and returned a lookalike phone to him, I'll be long gone."

"Brilliant," I said. Then I thought for a moment. "Won't that endanger Maya, though? I'm sure he'll suspect it was someone working with us who stole his phone."

"He won't be sure. He probably knows others who want to get their hands on it too. At any rate, he'll feel confident no one can break into the phone, assuming he has it programmed such that if the correct password isn't entered in ten tries, all is deleted. Which begs the question—you do have his passcode, don't you? Without it, this is a waste of time. You won't be able to access his information."

"Don't worry about that," Lim said. "Just get me his phone."

"Have you done this before?" I asked.

"Once. But I knew ahead of time what kind of cell phone she had. And my client knew her passcode. It was a divorce situation."

"What if he's not home?" I asked.

"I'll get into his apartment. He most likely has the address written on a piece of paper or in an email on his computer or tablet. That'll cost you extra, though. I'll have to hire someone to be my lookout. If he has everything password protected, there's a good chance I won't be successful. Then we'll have to reconsider our options. One option would be to wait and hope he's in town and comes home soon."

"We need to do this tonight," Lim said. "We don't have much time."

"Understood. Do you have a picture of him? I don't want to risk taking the phone of someone else."

"I can give you a general description, but I don't have a picture."

"That'll have to do."

After I gave him a description, our bodyguard briefly spoke to his friend over the phone, then disconnected. "Let's get going to Best Buy. We can all go in the van."

We piled into the van—me, Lim, and the four security guards. Although they were in plain clothes, I'm sure we looked odd walking into Best Buy in a tight cluster as we headed to the cell phone section. One of the guards commandeered a sales associate, a skinny young person with short, wispy hair named Pat. Pat gathered the ten most popular phones, including three iPhones, three Galaxies, a Motorola, a Google Pixel, and a Nokia, which I didn't know was still being made. The sales associate began reciting an overview of the features of the various phones when one of the bodyguards interrupted. "We'll take one of each."

"Excuse me, which one did you want?"

"All of them. We'll take everything you've got here."

"Are you sure?" I felt sorry for the salesperson who appeared confused, trying to make sense of the situation. After a moment, Pat asked, "Would you like to get these insured?" I was no longer sympathetic. I always hate having to listen to the insurance pitch that accompanies the purchase of electronic devices.

"Just get us a black case for each of them." The request was curt, more of an order than a request.

"Sure." The sales associate disappeared for a few minutes, then returned with the requested cases. "Everything you wanted was in stock."

"Can we pay for this here?" Lim asked, removing a credit card from his wallet.

"I'll take you to checkout," the associate said.

Pat gathered everything up and carried it all to a cashier in the front of the store. We waited our turn in line, my stomach in knots at the delay. By the time Lim completed the purchase and we left the store, the sun had set. We all rushed back to the van, one of the guards carrying a bag containing everything we'd bought. Everyone but the driver shared in the effort to unwrap the packaging. We put cases on all the phones as we headed towards the rendezvous with John Doe.

One of the agents took the bag with the phones and exited the van in front of Macy's at Union Square. He disappeared into the store as we drove off. Fifteen minutes later, now empty-handed, he met us in front of the San Francisco Museum of Modern Art on Third Street and got in.

"Everything go okay?" the driver asked.

"As planned."

Lim and I returned to our condominium to wait with the bodyguard who had originally phoned the private investigator. I was queasy, and my chest felt so tight, each breath was an effort. We sat in almost complete silence for two hours.

The bodyguard's phone rang, and I hoped for good news as he walked away from Lim and me before answering. After a hushed conversation, he returned, smiling. I breathed a little easier.

"Did he get the phone?" Lim asked.

"Yes."

We were far from through with our mission to rescue Maya, but the first hurdle had been cleared. I closed my eyes and took some easy breaths, enjoying the moment.

"What kind is it?"

"iPhone."

"Let's get it. Then I need to get to Cyber Dash.

"What's that"? the bodyguard asked.

"That's my company," Lim said. "I'm going to hack the phone." He turned to me. "You want to come?"

"How could I not? I'd go mad sitting here alone."

We headed out to the van. This was going to be a long night.

CHAPTER 37

We all piled into the van and headed to our destination, which turned out to be the passenger loading/unloading zone in front of the Westin St. Francis Hotel. One of our bodyguards popped out and disappeared inside. After several minutes, he returned to the van, put on his seat belt, and handed Lim an iPhone. "Where is our next stop?" the driver asked.

Lim gave directions, and a half hour later, we were in the parking lot of his company Cyber Dash, located in Oyster Point, an area south of San Francisco dotted with tech companies. We entered the three-story concrete building, and Lim nodded to the night guard. Three of our security men remained with the guard in the lobby while one of the bodyguards and I followed Lim upstairs. The bodyguard and I both needed to run frequently to keep up, as Lim bounded up the stairs and turned down a hallway. The dark halls lit up as we made our way to the room outside Lim's office, where four tables were set up, each with several pieces of electronic equipment ranging from the size of a thumb drive to a microwave oven.

Lim looked around and located the device he wanted, a bread loaf-size contraption with a keypad, and plugged the attached

Apple lightning cable into Johan Rakvag's iPhone. "Wish me luck," he said, wiping his hands on his pants, leaving a streak of sweat. He took in a deep breath and let it out slowly, the same technique I used to calm myself. I hadn't seen him this nervous for quite some time. He began pressing keys on the device's keypad, and the machine sprung to life, making beeping sounds as lights flashed. Lim watched in silence, sweat trickling down his forehead, as the LED screen lit up with an ever-changing display. His gaze remained fixated on the readout while the bodyguard and I stood motionless, watching. What seemed an eternity later, the screen froze. Displayed was a single word in typical liquid crystal display lettering: SUCCESS.

Lim closed his eyes, wiped his brow, and allowed himself to smile. My muscles relaxed with relief.

"Step number one is complete. I have killed the kill switch. The data will no longer be erased after ten passcode attempts. Now I need to attach it to my passcode generator."

"What's that?"

"It will systematically enter all possible passcodes, including numbers and letters, until the phone is unlocked. It's the brute force approach."

"How long will that take?"

"Anywhere from a few seconds to twelve hours, depending on how soon it reaches the right combination. I've been working on making it faster, but this is as fast as it can be done now." He detached the iPhone from the kill switch deactivating device and took it to another piece of equipment, a black box about the size of a DVD player. Lim secured the phone in a metal holder attached to the top of the apparatus. Next to the holder was a black and white display screen and rows of buttons. He plugged the phone into the lightning cable exiting the box below. The screen lit up, and Lim pressed several buttons before placing a strange-looking black toothpick-size gadget on the iPhone screen. A thick cord connected the device to the equipment below. He pressed one more button, and the display screen began flashing rows of numbers at lightning speed. The way everything was hooked up, with lights flickering on and off, it looked like the cell phone was in the ICU.

"Now we sit back and try to relax," Lim said.

"Let's hope this doesn't take very long," I said.

We each brought over a chair from another area of the room and sat, staring at the flashing numbers. After a time, I heard the guard gently snoring as Lim and I remained awake, our eyes glued to the damn black and white screen.

The next thing I remember was waking up to a pinging sound. Lim jumped out of his chair and got busy unhooking the cell phone. The display screen was flashing "73c9Yx."

"Is that the passcode?" I asked, pointing.

"Sure is. I'm in," Lim said, a big smile on his face.

I glanced at my cell phone. It was 4:37 a.m. I looked up again to see Lim holding Johan Rakvag's phone in his hand, furiously scrolling through messages and emails.

Our bodyguard stirred. "What's going on?" he asked, looking around, then stood and scoured the room. "Everything okay?"

"Everything's fine," I said. "Lim's machine broke into the phone."

"Phenomenal. I didn't think you could do it," said the guard.

"Learning anything important?" I asked Lim.

"Not yet. There are lots of messages. Here," he said, handing me the phone. "I have to pee. Why don't you look while I'm gone? Maybe you'll have better luck."

I grabbed the phone and began scrolling through Johan's emails. My hands were shaking, making the task more difficult. An email from Karl Kanestrom caught my eye. I recognized the name of the man who recruited people in San Francisco into the Umbroz clinical trials. The message was short but in Norwegian. I'd run it by Google translate later, but first, I clicked on the attached link.

This must be it. I saw an ad for an Airbnb rental in San Francisco, near Golden Gate Park. A two-bedroom restored Victorian house, it would be perfect for hiding Maya. I showed the ad to Lim when he returned from the restroom.

"Let's translate the message in the email to be sure," I said.

Lim went to a nearby computer and brought up Google translate, choosing Norwegian for the left box, English for the right. As he entered the email message from Karl on the left, I watched the English translation take form on the right. "I found this rental on Airbnb. Very good find, considering the short notice. I have rented it for a week."

"This is it," I shouted.

"We need to check it out before we do anything else," Lim said, "but this is a great start." He entered the link into the browser on the desktop computer so we could look over the ad on a larger screen. "We're lucky. They have a floor plan here. As usual, the exact address isn't listed in the ad. Only the general location."

"Karl probably sent the address later. Look for more emails or texts from him."

Lim studied the phone for a few moments. "Found it. It's on Page Street. Let's take a look at it right now. Before the sun comes up."

Although I'd had very little sleep, the sudden infusion of optimism energized me. "Let's go."

We went downstairs, collected the three other bodyguards, two of whom were sleeping on the floor as the other stood watch, and buckled up in the van. After a twenty-minute drive, we were parked across the street from a charming pastel-colored Victorian house. Counting the bottom floor, mostly taken up by the garage, it was three stories high. The only outside lighting came from the regularly spaced streetlights and the half moon. Lim told me to wait in the car as he went to investigate. I was glad he happened to be wearing dark clothing, so he'd be difficult to see.

Lim walked down the street, past several houses, then crossed to the other side and approached the rental house, staying close to the neighboring homes. He jumped over a low fence on the side of the rental and disappeared into the darkness. I listened for the slightest sound that might indicate he'd run into trouble, my heart pounding until several minutes later, he appeared under a streetlamp on the other side of the house. He continued walking, past several residences opposite the direction he initially approached from, crossed the street, and returned to the van.

"I think I know the room Maya's staying in," he said. "There were two people, probably the night security, on the second floor watching TV. The upstairs was dark, except for one room with a dim light, like the night light we have in Maya's room because she's afraid of the dark. According to the floorplan, there's only a small bedroom, bathroom, and hallway on the top floor. That has to be where they're keeping Maya. Most of these old houses don't have air conditioning. The bedroom windows are open."

"That could be a way in," I said.

"Right. One more thing, though. Fortunately, the moon is out, so I saw they have tripwires set up all around. They're about five feet off the ground, so I had to duck a lot."

"Why do you suppose they're so high?" I asked.

"They don't want to be alerted by every dog or cat running around. Five feet is low enough to catch almost any adult.

"What do you think would happen if I ran over there right now and banged on the door?" I asked.

"You might never see your daughter again," one of the bodyguards said. "Don't do it."

"We'll get her," Lim said confidently. "But we need a plan. Let's not rush into anything without being fully prepared."

He was right. We needed a plan. I was excited yet frustrated, being so near yet unable to rescue Maya. I missed her and was terrified I might lose her forever.

We returned to our condo so we could prepare for the rescue. According to the bodyguards, the surest way to secure Maya would be to involve the FBI or the police. They had the officers, the guns, and the law on their side. We didn't like the FBI's plan and doubted they would agree to abide by any proposal we came up with. Given the connections Umbroz had with the police chief, I didn't want to involve them. At least not officially.

I was advised I would likely be called by the kidnappers again. I should tell them I was ready to cooperate, to buy time while we developed a strategy. I hoped we were making the right decision.

My cell phone rang at 9:00 a.m. I answered, this time recording the conversation. I spoke to the same man who called me previously.

"Have you decided to meet our demands?" he asked.

"I'll do anything you ask, as long as I'm sure you'll return Maya to me safely and will never bother us again."

"As long as you cooperate, we'll have no reason to contact you ever again."

"Tell me what to do, but first, let me speak to her."

I heard a scuffle, some steps, a door squeak, then "Mommy, Mommy, come get me. I don't like it here—"

This was followed by the man's voice, dripping with venom, "We will send a notary by your condominium tomorrow afternoon with legal papers for you to sign. In the papers, you will admit that all the information you have released to the FDA or any other agency is false."

"I would prefer we meet in a public place."

I heard muffled voices, then the man spoke into the phone. "How about Peet's coffee, Third and Mission? Don't try anything funny, or you'll be sorry. If you try to find her, you won't see her again."

"I'll do exactly as you say. I just want Maya back. When will I get her?"

"Signing the papers is just the first step. Be sure to bring all the recordings you have from your illegal visit to Umbroz. Instead of testifying before the FDA Monday morning, you need to meet with the San Francisco Chief of Police to retract everything you've claimed to know about Umbroz. I've already made you an appointment with him for ten o'clock Monday. One of our lawyers will accompany you, and you must claim him as your own attorney.

"After that, you have an interview with a reporter from the San Francisco Chronicle. At that time, I expect you to again retract everything you've said or submitted about Umbroz. Our attorney will be there, too. Sometime later on Monday, we will listen while you phone your contact at the FDA and convincingly retract everything. You will admit to substituting footage of labels from a local chemical company for video taken at Umbroz to discredit the quality of our ingredients. Once everything is done to our satisfaction, we will return your daughter."

As the man spoke, I heard Lim engage in an animated conversation with our bodyguard. I looked forward to hearing about their discussion.

"Do I have your word that once it's all done, you will return Maya?" I was sickened, thinking of complying with his request. I had already decided to submit to their terms, no matter how distasteful, should we fail in our rescue mission.

"Yes, as early as Monday evening. Be at Peet's tomorrow, 2:00 p.m." He disconnected the call before I could respond.

I turned to Lim and the bodyguard. "They want to meet with me at Peet's tomorrow to sign documents retracting everything I've said and turn over all my recordings. I sure hope we can rescue Maya before then, even if it means we'll all need protection until arrests are made."

"I have a plan I think will work," Lim said.

"I don't know, Mr. Chen. I think we should bring the FBI in."

"My wife knows a local police officer. We can ask her to come with some colleagues she trusts to be on standby, ready to step in if my idea fails. Whether or not she decides to help, we do it tonight."

CHAPTER 38

Lim explained his plan to bring an extension ladder to the house on Page Street and climb to Maya's window to rescue her.

"What about the trip wires?"

"That will make it more difficult, but not impossible."

"How will you get her out?" I asked. "You might not even be able to get through the window. I saw it—it's pretty small."

"If I can't fit, I'll get her to come to the window."

"I don't like the idea." I thought of many ways this plan could fail. "She could be asleep. You'll probably have to make a lot of noise to wake her up. The ladder might fall. They could hear you. We might be looking at a disaster."

"We have no choice. Worst case, we'll need the police. Now would be a good time to call April. Ask her to stand by, ready to storm the front door. She can bring some trusted friends on the force to help."

As I didn't have anything better to offer, I called April. After I brought her up to date on my situation, I explained our plan.

"I'm worried," I said. "What do you think?"

April was silent a moment before she spoke. "Of course you're worried. I'm a mom, too, and I'd be worried if I were in your situation. When it comes to our kids, sometimes it's hard to be rational. From my point of view, looking at this from the outside, I'd say it's doubtful they'd intentionally harm Maya. She's the one incentive they have to get you to cooperate. They need her."

"Maybe I should go ahead and do what they want."

"I would advise against that. You and your family will never be safe. These people won't ever trust you. As far as Lim's rescue plan using a ladder is concerned, I'd say there's a good chance it might work. From the information Lim collected, it appears all the people guarding her will be downstairs from Maya. If they hear Lim, it will take some time for them to get to her. I can be ready to enter the premises and control the situation."

I knew April fully appreciated my motherly concerns and would be strongly motivated to make Maya's safe rescue a priority. "Will that get you in trouble?" I asked.

"I'll talk to my sergeant."

"Can you trust him?"

"Absolutely. I've known that brother for years, and I helped him a lot during the homeless demonstrations. He owes me big time, and I expect him to approve. I know two officers I can depend on in any situation. Worst case scenario, we go without my sergeant's permission. Either way, I'm in."

With April on speaker, the rest of us sat in the living room to discuss the details. If all went well, Lim, Maya, two security guards, and I would leave directly from the rescue to catch a flight to Washington, D.C.

"I better tell Ting and my parents what's going on since we won't be coming back here," Lim said after we disconnected the call with April.

"I want to come too since I won't be seeing them for several days."

We went downstairs, where Lim explained his plan to Ting and his parents, speaking in English for my benefit. He drew a schematic of the house and pointed out the room where he thought Maya was being kept. Kang and Wang Shu listened intently as Mingyu rested on a floor pillow nearby.

"Let me do it! I want to save Maya," Kang said.

"I understand you want to help, but you're just a child," Lim said. "It won't be as easy as it sounds."

"You never let me do anything." Kang folded his arms and pouted, angrily staring back at his uncle.

"That's not true," Ting said. "We let you do a lot, but you can't do this. That's final."

Still pouting, Kang stomped off to the bedroom he shared with Mingyu and slammed the door. I was glad Ting had put her foot down, but I wasn't happy Kang was taking it so hard. A few minutes later, Kang returned wearing a Superman cape I'd bought him for his last birthday. He sat, listening to us, and glared. I wondered if he thought that by dressing like Superman, we would realize he had special powers and decide he could perform the rescue after all.

Lim finished explaining our plan, and Ting asked, "How will you see? It will be dark."

"I'll carry a small flashlight in my mouth. I won't have to see very far." Lim turned to Kang. "You want to go to Home Depot with me to pick up an extension ladder?"

"Can I wear my cape?"

"No. Only little kids wear costumes like that unless it's Halloween."

"Then forget it."

Lim left to buy the ladder, leaving Kang wearing his cape, sulking.

I returned to our condominium, where I booked flights on a red eye to Dulles International Airport in Washington DC that evening. Next, I reserved a large van equipped with a child's car seat from Alamo, and two hotel rooms with adjoining doors at the Silver Springs DoubleTree.

Lim returned from Home Depot, leaving the longest extension ladder they had in stock outside on top of the van. We packed small suitcases, and I gathered my notes and a thumb drive where Lim had stored all the information Daisy and I had collected from Umbroz. Then it was time to wait.

As Lim checked the batteries on the flashlight he planned to take, I brought up Kang's obsession with his Superman cape.

"Try to be more understanding of your nephew. Don't forget, Kang learned a lot of English by watching Superman videos when we were hiding at your investor's estate in the South Bay. The shows clearly made a big impression on him. He wants to be a hero. You should be glad he looks up to Superman instead of El Chapo."

"True, but that boy needs more discipline."

I couldn't disagree.

Anxious and restless, the afternoon was one of the longest I remembered. An hour after speaking to April, she texted me that her sergeant had approved, and she would be at the scene with her two trusted officers at the agreed-upon time. I ordered sandwiches to be delivered from a nearby deli which our bodyguard picked up downstairs. I wasn't hungry but forced myself to eat, unsure when our next meal would be.

When 8:00 p.m. rolled around, we sprang into action. Lim changed into a pair of black pants and a black T-shirt so he wouldn't stand out against the darkened sky an hour later. We took turns using the two bathrooms in our condo, and I made a last-minute anal-compulsive check to be sure no water was running, the lights were off, we'd packed everything we needed, including all the evidence I would present, and Lim and I had our driver's licenses handy.

Lim, our four bodyguards, and I piled into the van. My chest was tight, my stomach was in knots, and my deep breathing exercise was failing me. Lim took my hand to provide comfort, but there was no stopping my runaway anxiety.

We drove through traffic and arrived on Page Street as the sun was setting. Still too light to perform the extraction, we parked a block away, across the street. I noticed a black van parked fifty feet behind us. I recognized April in the passenger seat. One of our bodyguards exited our vehicle to speak to the police officers and supply them with communication devices using the same frequency our guards were using.

The light went on in Maya's room, then turned off fifteen minutes later. We waited another ten minutes until it was dark.

"You ready?" One of the guards said into a shoulder microphone.

I heard April through the guard's speaker. "Set your watch for ten minutes. Then we position ourselves on either side of the front door. Ten minutes later, Mr. Chen takes the ladder, and we begin."

As one of the guards set his watch, Lim exited the van on the side facing away from the house and loosened the ropes holding the ladder. He was starting to lift it off the vehicle roof when the rear door of the van opened, a small figure in a red cape exited and dashed across the street.

CHAPTER 39

As Lim scrambled to put the ladder in his hands onto the ground, the guard in the driver's seat opened his door and whispered, "Don't go after him. Get back in the van right away."

Lim complied, and we all sat in silence, watching Kang.

A guard spoke softly into his microphone. "Did you see that? Their nephew is running to the house."

Static filled the van for a few moments, followed by April's voice. "Keep your positions. We can't try to intercept him while he's running. He would likely resist and make a lot of noise. Once he's standing still, one of us will approach him quietly, get him to cooperate, and return him. Then Mr. Chen can carry on with the mission."

I had to squint to see Kang in the near darkness. He skirted around the illumination from the closest streetlight and headed for the house next to the one holding Maya. He cut left, then stood in front of the fence surrounding the target Victorian. In one smooth motion, he placed his hands on one of the posts and vaulted over. Puts his aunt to shame, I thought, imagining what I must have looked like when I was escaping from the Indian Community Center. As Kang walked toward the backyard, he came to an abrupt stop as his cape, caught in the fence, prevented his progress.

I barely made out the shape of a police officer who started to approach Kang. The boy quickly untangled the cape and took off running again. By the time the officer cleared the fence, Kang was far ahead of him.

"This could be a disaster," one of the guards said. "He's going to set off one of the tripwires."

"Don't worry about that," Lim said. "Kang is barely over four feet tall. He's almost a foot under the wires."

Soon Kang became an indistinct form as the night absorbed him. In a few moments, only his cape was visible, then nothing. I don't think anyone breathed—I know I didn't—until the light from Kang's flashlight broke through the darkness.

"Damn," Lim said. "He's at the base of the house. The officer wasn't able to stop him."

I remained tense as the dot of light from Kang's flashlight ascended, stopped, then ascended again. Every time the light moved upward, I felt an infinitesimal lessening of anxiety.

"He's going to do it," Lim exclaimed. "He's going to get to Maya!"

"You really think he can pull it off?" I asked. "Do you think he could carry Maya down on his back without falling?"

"After seeing what he did in the rock-climbing gym carrying a heavy backpack, I have no doubt."

With the glow from the flashlight still rising, I made out Kang's form near the top floor of the house, where the moonlight was no longer blocked by trees. He stopped his ascent, and the light wiggled around in the darkness.

"He's at the window," Lim said. "He's shining the light into the room so he can see where everything is."

The beam of light moved around for what seemed an eternity, then disappeared. The tension was unbearable. I closed my eyes.

Lim grabbed my hand. "I think he's inside. Now he has to wake Maya and get her on his back quietly."

I opened my eyes just before the whole room lit up.

"Damn it. Kang turned on the lights." I said.

"Maybe," Lim said. "I don't know why he would do that. Someone else may have heard something and is checking the room."

"What do we do now? If one of their guards is in there, they have Kang and Maya now." Tears began to stream down my cheeks.

"I'm going to investigate," Lim said.

"What will you do? They could kill you!" I became so overwhelmed with fear and anxiety, I started shaking as I cried uncontrollably. One of the bodyguards put his arm around my shoulder to soothe me.

"Two of us will go with you," another bodyguard said to Lim. "We have guns. I don't know where the police officers are at this point."

Maya's room went dark.

"The light's off. Maybe it's okay," the bodyguard comforting me said. "How about we wait a little?"

"Wait for what?" Lim asked. He got out of the van, joined by two guards. They were halfway across the street when the light from Kang's flashlight again became visible. It hung for several of my heartbeats, then started descending.

The tension in my neck and shoulders, the knot in my stomach, and the tightness in my chest washed away. I stopped crying and took in several deep breaths as the light continued to descend. I estimated Kang was about a third of the way down the side of the building when the light plunged to the ground.

The feelings of anxiety that had disappeared returned with a vengeance. *They fell. How could we have let this happen? Why didn't I check the back of the van before we left? I should have known Kang would try to come with us.* Despite being stronger than any other kid his age, he wasn't Superman, despite wanting to be. He'd met his kryptonite—gravity—and I hadn't prevented it.

To my surprise, no lights flicked on in the house. *Was it possible they hadn't made any noise when they fell, and the people guarding Maya were still unaware of Kang's rescue attempt?* Lim and the two security agents ran towards the house, jumped the fence, then disappeared into the darkness.

I stared in their direction, waiting for a sign to tell me what was happening. *Did they dodge the wires, and were they tending to Kang and Maya? Were they calling an ambulance? Were the police breaking into the house?* No lights turned on. I opened the van door and started to get out.

"Don't go," one of the remaining bodyguards said. "You'll only get in the way. My buddies will notify me if they're in trouble."

Sure, if they can.

I imagined Lim and the bodyguards being captured by whoever was guarding Maya and being executed right there on the front lawn, their actions hidden by the blanket of darkness, as Kang and Maya lay dying from their injuries. I wondered if my life, as I knew it, was coming to an end. I hadn't seen any flashes of light. Would I see one if a gun had been fired? I wasn't sure. If they'd used knives or garottes to do their dirty work, there would be no telltale sparks.

What could I possibly tell Ting about the involvement of her elder son?

These thoughts were swirling around in my head when, like a vision from a dream, I saw a splotch of red at the edge of the light streaming from one of the streetlamps.

As I stared, the splotch grew into the bottom of a red cape, blowing in the breeze. Then the entire figure of Kang appeared, a broad smile on his face. Before I had a chance to wonder where Maya, Lim, and the bodyguards were, they, too, appeared out of the darkness, Lim holding Maya in his arms, the bodyguards trailing.

My heart rose from a bottomless pit of despair to elation in the stratosphere. I ran out of the van, grabbed Maya, and hugged her tightly. When I came to my senses, I realized I was holding her so tight she couldn't breathe and loosened my hold. With her arms around my neck, I looked down at her sweet face staring up at me, and smothered her with kisses. I didn't want to let go of her so we could all leave. My rational mind took over, as Lim repeatedly told me to get back in the van.

Standing by the side of the van, I buckled Maya in, thanked Kang, told him never to do anything like that again, and gave him a big hug. Kang took a seat in the back of the van, and I got in next to Maya. After noticing everyone else in the car was ready to go, I put my seatbelt on. We drove in the direction of our condominium before heading to SFO.

On the way, one of the bodyguards said, "I wonder if there will be a story about this in the paper tomorrow. You can be sure the police officers are making arrests in that house right now."

Lim called Ting and explained that the rescue went well, and Kang was with us. We'd drop him off before going to the airport. Details would follow.

In the van, Kang excitedly gave his rendition of the rescue. "Climbing the building was even easier than I thought. When I got to Maya's window, I looked around her room. She was sleeping so I went inside. Then I woke her up."

"Yes, Mommy," Maya said. "I was so sad in my dream. Then Kang woke me. I thought I was still dreaming, but I wasn't. It was better than a dream. It was Kang and Superman there to rescue me." I was happy Maya seemed more excited from the rescue than traumatized by the whole ordeal. "Then there were footsteps. They come in to check on me at night. They turn on the light and look around the room. I always pretend I'm asleep.

I hear them go in the closet, so I told Kang to hide under the bed, quick. They never look there."

"That's what I did. I went under the bed until I heard them leave. There wasn't much room there, not enough for a grown-up. Good thing I'm just a kid."

Lim interrupted. "You're a kid, but I wouldn't say *just* a kid. You're a pretty fantastic kid."

"Thanks, Uncle Lim."

"What happened after the big people left?"

"Maya stood on her bed so she could get on my back. When I climbed out the window with her, she got scared. I had to talk to her, but I couldn't because I had the flashlight in my mouth. I dropped it to the ground so I could tell her not to be afraid."

"I wasn't afraid after that. Kang made me brave."

"That's quite a story," I said. "We're all so proud of you. Proud of both of you. And Kang, your mom's going to be very proud of you, too."

"Uh, there's one thing. Hope you're not too mad at me," Kang said.

"What's that?" Lim asked.

"Sorry, I forgot to pick up your flashlight. It's still there, on the ground. Do you want to go back? I could run out and get it."

"No," came the reply from me, Lim, and all the bodyguards, in unison.

CHAPTER 40

We drove back to our condominium building, where Lim and one of the bodyguards escorted Kang back to his unit.

"Why are we staying in the car?" Maya asked. "We live here too." She looked like she was going to cry. I realized that in all the excitement, I hadn't explained our plans.

"Daddy will come back as soon as Kang is with Auntie Ting. Then we're all going on a trip!" I tried to make it sound fun. "You, me, Daddy, and two of these nice men are going on an airplane to Washington, D.C."

"I want to go home. I miss my room." Maya looked so sad, it broke my heart. She was three years old and had been held in captivity for several days. Of course, she wanted to go home and sleep in her own bed. She looked healthy, without bruises or evidence of physical abuse. Any damage done to her was probably psychological. We'd deal with that once I was sure we were safe. I knew a child psychologist to call after we landed in DC.

"We'll come home in a few days, Sweetie. This will be a short vacation."

Lim was smiling when he returned to the van alone.

"I'll bet Ting was happy to see Kang back home safely," I said. "Were Mingyu and Wang Shu there?"

"Yes, but I didn't go into much detail about what happened because someone else was there, too."

"Who?"

"Remember Dr. Ron Yee?"

"The anesthesiologist?"

"Right. Ron and Ting were sitting on the couch together, looking pretty comfortable, if you know what I mean. I could tell the kids like him, including Kang. They were climbing all over him when I left, laughing and having a great time. He must have visited several times before, but Ting never mentioned it."

"I'm glad to hear that. Your sister could use some happiness. I don't want to assume too much, but I'd love to see her with a partner she can trust. Kang could sure use a father figure right now."

"Ron seems like a nice guy, so I hope it works out. He and Ting have some things in common. Like hatred for the Chinese government."

"Good start," I said.

"What time is our flight?"

"Leaves at ten fifty." I looked at my phone. "They'll be boarding in a little over a half hour." I looked at Maya. Her head was resting on my arm. She was asleep, and I hoped she was dreaming of something wonderful.

Our driver let me, Lim, Maya, and two of the bodyguards out in front of the United departure area, and we said our goodbyes to the driver. Lim carried Maya and pulled a small suitcase behind him. I towed our other suitcase, with one of our bodyguards walking in front, the other behind.

"We have to check our luggage," one of them said.

I saw the small suitcase the two were sharing and wondered why they wanted to waste time doing that rather than carry the bag on, when he said, "Checked luggage is the only way we can legally bring our guns."

"You think you need to bring them?"

"You never know."

One of the bodyguards checked their suitcase in at the nearby luggage check-in. We got our boarding passes ready on our phones as we walked through the terminal to the security line. The wait was the shortest I remembered, this being a red-eye flight.

After fifteen minutes at the gate, we boarded the plane and got settled. Maya, still asleep, sat between Lim and me. Soon after takeoff, I fell asleep, not waking until we landed. We deplaned, then waited longer than I would have liked for the small suitcase the bodyguards had checked. Lim held Maya, who was now fully alert. After we collected all the luggage, we picked up our rental van. As I buckled Maya into her car seat, the bodyguards retrieved their guns and loaded them. I didn't like guns, but had to admit to myself I felt better knowing they had them, and they were on my side.

It was after 9:00 a.m. by the time we got to our hotel. While we were checking in, the young woman at the front desk said to me, "There's a message here for you, Dr. Rosen. I'll get it."

"Funny," I said, turning to Lim, "the reservations are in your name. Did you tell anyone where we were staying?"

"Not even Ting or my parents. They have my phone number, so I didn't see the need."

The clerk disappeared for a short time, then returned and handed me an envelope addressed to Dr. Erica Rosen. My heart skipped a beat when I noticed the spelling of my name: the "o" in Rosen had a slash through it, as seen in Norwegian. Although not the proper way to spell my last name, it served as a warning. I opened the envelope and read the short message written on the single sheet of paper inside: "Go home." A chill ran down my back. "Did someone drop this off, or was it phoned in?" I asked the clerk.

"Someone dropped it off early this morning."

I excused myself and took a seat in the lobby, where I phoned several large hotels in the area and inquired as to whether they had received a note for me. All of them had. Each envelope had been dropped off early that morning in an apparent attempt to spook me by making me think the Umbroz people knew exactly what my plans were.

"We need to get out of here," I said to Lim and the bodyguards. After apologizing to the clerk and paying for one night's stay, we returned to the van, where I phoned some of the smaller hotels in the area. The first three didn't have adjoining rooms, but the fourth did, and they hadn't received a note for me. I gave the address to our driver.

It was almost 11:00 a.m. by the time we were checked in and settled in our rooms. Lim went next door to talk to our bodyguards so I could spend time alone with Maya. I looked through my suitcase and was glad I had packed one of her favorite books. I began reading to her while having second thoughts about my meeting with the FDA the following morning.

I was halfway through the book when Maya interrupted me. "What's wrong, Mommy?"

It was then I became aware of tears running down my cheek. "Sorry, Maya. I'm just overtired. Like sometimes you get overtired and feel upset."

"Everything's okay, Mommy. I can take care of you, just like you take care of me."

I hugged her tightly, so glad she had been rescued and I had her with me again. *I need to meet with the FDA to prevent other people's kids from dying.*

Lim returned, interrupting my thoughts and my hug. "We figure Umbroz has people stationed here in DC," he said. "That's the only way they could have delivered all those messages early this morning. Even if they discovered Maya was missing right after we got her, they couldn't have gotten someone here ahead of us."

"They probably have people here in DC who lobby congress or try to weasel their way into the FDA."

One of the guards added, "I don't know if they were counting on the message scaring you off, or if they plan to follow through on their not-so-subtle threat."

"They don't seem to make empty threats," I said.

"That's what I was thinking," Lim said. "We all need to be on high alert. No leaving our room. I'm not leaving your side until this is all over. Remember, you don't have to testify if you don't want to."

"I've gone too far to back out now. The Umbroz people will never trust me even if I sign whatever papers they put in front of me. They know I could turn on them at any time. I'll always be in danger, which means you and Maya will be in danger. We'll never be safe as long as they're walking around, free."

"You're right," one of the bodyguards said.

Our conversation was interrupted by a call from Daisy. "Let me get this. She may have something important to tell me."

Maya was on the bed, quietly singing a lullaby to the doll I'd brought for her. Everyone else in the room was quiet as I answered the call.

"Are you watching the news?" Daisy asked. She sounded excited, almost out of breath.

"No, we're trying to decide what to do next."

"Turn it on. It's on all the major channels. Promise me you'll turn the TV on right now. Then I'll hang up."

"I promise." I found the remote and turned on the TV.

"What's going on?" Lim asked.

"I don't know, but Daisy told me to watch the news right now." All I could see was an annoying screen showing all the movies I could rent while I tried to figure out how to find the news on the hotel TV with an unfamiliar channel lineup. I finally found CNN, and we all watched in silence.

I recognized a video of the community center at the reservation, the house of horrors where Daisy and I had been held. A large man I recognized as the Viking, handcuffed with his arms behind him, was being escorted into a black car by two men with "FBI" stenciled on the backs of their jackets. Seeing a large gauze taped to the side of his head, the area where I'd whacked him with the can of ant spray, filled me with pride. "I did that," I yelled, pointing to the gauze. "I hit him with a can right there."

"I guess I'm going to have to behave myself around you," Lim said. "I didn't know you had that in you."

Our attention turned back to the newsreader, who informed us over twenty people had been arrested so far, and more arrests related to a probe into the pharmaceutical manufacturer Umbroz were expected. The company was being investigated for involvement in crimes ranging from bribery to murder. The individuals arrested so far were named, and I was glad to hear Karl Kanestrom included.

Another inquiry exploring Umbroz's misrepresentation of manufacturing practices to the FDA was expected to wrap up soon. Before announcing that more would be forthcoming on this breaking story, a video of Haakon Rakvag being escorted in cuffs into another waiting car flashed on the screen.

"You did it," Lim yelled. "You shut the whole thing down."

"You think we're safe now?" I asked, hesitant to let my guard down just yet.

"Probably," one of the guards said. "The cat's out of the bag. No getting it back in."

"See, we're safe," I said, grabbing Maya and lifting her towards the ceiling. My sense of relief was exhilarating.

Lim and I relaxed in our room and talked to Maya about her experiences between the time she was grabbed off the street to

Kang's rescue of her. We learned that while Maya was kidnapped, she had been instructed to stay in her room and keep quiet. There were toys for her to play with, and she had enough to eat. My biggest fear, that she had been physically abused in some way, was put to rest. She described mainly being ignored. Although she was scared when the man grabbed her, one of the men in the getaway car told her no one would hurt her, and she'd be able to go home soon if she behaved. The relief I felt when she described this, my worst fears quashed, was overwhelming. After more hugs and kisses, Maya wanted to collect the lotions and shampoos in the hotel to take home.

"Let's wait until your testimony is over before we let our guard down completely," Lim said. "There still may be someone out there who doesn't quite understand how hopeless the situation is and may try something desperate."

"Unlikely, but possible," one of the guards said.

"Okay, so we'll keep you around until we return to San Francisco," I said.

"I suggest one of us escort you to the FDA meeting, and the other stay with your husband and daughter," one of the guards said.

"I want to testify without security," I said. "I don't want anyone to think I'm still afraid and might be coerced into recanting. You can both stay here with Lim and Maya until I return."

"How about we compromise?" one of the guards said. "One of us will take you there and wait outside the building until you're done, then drive you back. At least that way, you won't be at risk in a cab or Uber."

"Okay. I can live with that."

Daisy called back to talk about what we had seen on TV. She also spoke of being elated her cousin, Lan, would be attending her wedding. Lan had helped us on our mission in China and had been granted asylum in the United States two years earlier, along with Chang Wen, a woman who had provided me with valuable information and now worked at the United Nations as a translator.

I hadn't had an opportunity to spend much time with Lan after she arrived in San Francisco. It didn't take her long to land a lucrative job in Seattle with Microsoft, where she was helping the company manage Chinese phone apps. "I look forward to getting to know her better," I said. "Is she bringing Hunter, the boyfriend you told me about last month?"

"She dumped him a few weeks ago. She's got a new one but doesn't want to bring him, so she'll come by herself." I reflected on the similarities between Lan and Daisy. Both fiercely independent, hard to tie down. I was happy for Daisy, figuring Arvid had to be pretty much perfect for her to agree to marry him.

Lim and I spent the rest of the day trying to entertain ourselves by watching TV and playing Fish with Maya. The guards brought in dinner from a nearby Chinese restaurant. "My mother cooks much better than this," Lim complained.

"I know. I should have told them to avoid Chinese food. You're never satisfied with what they make in restaurants." I opened Maya's fortune cookie and read it. "'A lifetime of happiness awaits you.' That's the best fortune in the world," I said, hugging her. "What's yours, Lim?"

"'A soft voice may be persuasive.' I think it's referring to you, dear," Lim said, laughing. "What about yours?"

"'A new person will enter your life soon.'" I looked at Lim. "I didn't believe in fortunes before," I said, "but now I'm not so sure. Maybe there's something to this." We both laughed.

I spent the rest of the evening going over my notes for the next day and slept well that night. By the time the guards brought us breakfast the following morning, I was up and dressed. One of them drove me to the building where I would be testifying, a boxlike brick building five stories high. He escorted me to the door, looked around, and gave me his okay. I opened the door and walked in, on my own for the first time in days.

CHAPTER 41

Wearing my professional-looking, no-nonsense black skirt, a white blouse, and black flats, I checked in at the front desk, where the receptionist gave me a lanyard holding a temporary badge with my name on it. I draped it around my neck and proceeded to the room on the third floor where I would present my information and answer questions. I had butterflies in my stomach, not from fear, but from excitement. I wanted to ensure no Umbroz products would ever be given to patients again, and those bastards would be put away for a long time.

Entering the room, I was greeted by about twenty people sitting around four long tables in a square configuration. I was directed to a seat in the middle of the table at the front of the room. Behind me was a large wall-mounted monitor where the audience could view the material being presented. The man and woman sitting on either side of me were friendly and engaged me in small talk. More people strolled in and filled the seats around the tables until all were occupied. Additional attendees were left to sit in chairs against the walls. Finally, the woman to my right stood and called the meeting to order.

"I'm happy to announce that, as you all know, we have Doctor Erica Rosen from the University of California, San Francisco, here to walk us through the infractions she and her associate discovered while visiting the Umbroz Pharmaceutical plant in Montana. I'm sure you'll have lots of questions, but please hold them until she is through."

I remained seated and spoke into the microphone in front of me. The room was large, and I was glad my voice was amplified so I didn't need to shout.

"It all started when I was in the ER at our hospital and witnessed a girl having a seizure." I recounted my experiences with Rosa and Ethan, prompting me to send Umbroz carbamazepine and cephalexin to an independent laboratory. "Analysis there showed both medications to be deficient. At that point, I wrote to people here at the FDA but got no meaningful response."

I scanned the room and noticed many people averting their eyes, taking notes, or doodling rather than looking at me.

"I understand you're all busy here, so I didn't give up. Little did I know then that my clash with Umbroz was just beginning."

I went on to describe my patients who developed unusual, life-threatening illnesses, the strange goings-on in the clinic, and the secretive behavior of my long-time assistant, Martha. I choked a bit when I mentioned her name but pushed on with my narrative. I described my subsequent meeting with Martha, who explained how she helped arrange the illegal testing of my patients' samples to screen for genetic susceptibility to certain diseases, and how they were enrolled in fraudulent clinical trials. I told of her vow to help me set the record straight and prevent Umbroz from harming more people.

I believe everyone was shocked upon hearing about the drugs planted on me and felt compassion as I described the humiliation I suffered when my clinic and hospital privileges were revoked. Feeling alone, with no apparent help from law enforcement, the

FDA, or my peers, I believed my only option was to visit Umbroz myself to get evidence of their subterfuge. For that, I brought along my good friend Daisy Wong, a computer expert. I glossed over the specifics of how we got ourselves hired, omitting details about obtaining false identifications and letters of recommendation.

"I showed up to my first day of work in the QC department armed with recording devices." I put my thumb drive in the USB port of the computer in front of me and started my video presentation, which was shown on the monitor behind me. I walked the audience through the areas of the lab at Umbroz where I worked, showing pictures of the already dissolved pills to falsely validate the composition of the Umbroz medications I analyzed. While I showed the video, I recapped what Janice had said to me—most workers were from Norway, and new workers, especially if not Norwegian, didn't last long. I described the A and B divisions, with the chemicals in the B of low grade. I didn't have with me the papers Petter and Sven gave me regarding clinical trials the company performed on their medications to prevent rheumatoid arthritis, type I diabetes, and emphysema in genetically susceptible children, but I remembered enough to summarize them. Anyone interested could find copies of the papers despite being published in obscure journals.

I moved on to present the evidence Lim had accessed through the portal to Umbroz's computer system Daisy had opened for him. Document after document clearly showed the presence of separate data for A and B, as well as hidden information regarding the ill-effects of their experimental medications, never included in their published reports. Like the Nazis in WWII, the Umbroz officials maintained excellent records of all their misdeeds.

After describing my kidnapping, I related my shock upon discovering Martha and others had been murdered. Cold-blooded execution was the best way they found to get rid of employees who disagreed with their business plan.

I gave kudos to Janice and her family, without whom I doubt Daisy and I would have survived. I ended with Maya's kidnapping and her daring rescue, and a photo of Kang smiling proudly in his Superman cape.

The presentation took five hours, not including an hour break for lunch. A flurry of questions followed, and I was asked to sign a statement. By the time we were finished, it was after 6:00 p.m. I was tired, and my throat was dry from talking for such a prolonged time. Mostly, however, I felt relieved. It was over, save possibly more questioning, which could be done by phone.

I left the room and stopped by the restroom down the hall. When I entered, a woman smiled at me on her way out, and I found I was alone. I enjoyed the quiet while I took care of nature's calling, then refreshed myself by splashing water on my face. Walking down the near-empty hallway, I was looking forward to flying home with Lim and Maya that evening. As I got into an empty elevator to go down two floors, a man rushed in as the door was closing. He looked at me and my name tag.

"Ya, Dr. Rosen," he said. "I've been looking for you."

The Norwegian accent was heavy. My chest tightened, and my heart pounded. *What a fool I was. Just when I thought it was over, they caught me. Is he going to kill me right here, in this elevator? I'm not going anywhere with him without a struggle.* I was speechless.

"Sorry," the man continued. "I hope I didn't alarm you. I'm from the Norwegian consulate. I want to talk to you about one of our citizens who showed up there earlier today. He wants safe transport back to Norway, but I was told your government plans to extradite him. I heard you might be able to shed some light on the situation and advise us on whether we should refuse extradition. He works for a company called Umbroz, which I believe you've heard about."

He showed me his credentials, and I began to relax.

"I have a car waiting for me outside," I said. "Perhaps you could come to the car with me. We can talk there."

"Whatever makes you more comfortable."

We exited the building together, and I phoned the security agent who was parked nearby. He pulled up, and I sat in the passenger seat while my bodyguard called the Norwegian consulate and confirmed the man's identity. I moved into the car's back seat and invited the diplomat to join me. I answered all his questions, and he left, assuring me the man would be returned to our government once all the proper paperwork was completed. I was glad to know that not all Norwegians were evil—probably the vast majority were good people. Even if, as Arvid said, they aren't very friendly.

The guard drove me back to the hotel, where Lim and Maya were waiting. We checked out and caught a flight back to San Francisco. Gaining three hours, we were in our condo before 10:00 p.m. Maya was excited to see her room again. It was good to be home again, with no life-and-death decisions to make.

CHAPTER 42

My first day waking up at home, Lim brought me coffee in bed. We spent the morning watching the news, flipping between cable channels showing the arrest of Umbroz executives, and interviews with prosecutors and the FBI special agent who spearheaded the arrests in Montana. My name was mentioned several times, but, thankfully, not many. Daisy's name was mentioned twice.

I received calls from reporters around the country and answered most of their questions but refused to meet them in person. The last thing I wanted to do was leave the safety of my building. Fung made a fabulous early dinner. I realized too much time had passed since all of us—Lim, Maya, Fung, Enlai, Ting, Wang Shu, Kang, Mingyu, and I—had crowded around the table in my in-laws' condominium. I sat back and closed my eyes, appreciating the sounds—chopsticks clicking, children laughing, and conversations in English and Mandarin. I felt like I was in a cocoon, surrounded by warmth, love, and joy.

"Are you okay?" My thoughts were interrupted by Lim grabbing my arm gently.

"Never better," I said.

"Did you try the long beans? Mom did something different with them. They're delicious, better than usual."

I dug in, long beans being one of my favorite vegetables. Lim was right. They were super good. After dinner, Daisy and Arvid came by, invited by Ting to surprise us. We had a four-way hug—me, Lim, Daisy, and Arvid. It was good to see them again under such happy circumstances. Arvid said he had decided on my punishment. He would take my place to name the next restaurant we would go to. I happily agreed. A half hour later, Ron, the anesthesiologist, joined us. Quiet and dignified, he appeared stiff and formal at first but later loosened up as he played with the children.

Kang stood on the coffee table and shouted, "I have an announcement to make. Your attention, please." All were quiet as Kang continued. "Maya and I will now re-enact her daring rescue."

Kang put on his superman cape and jumped up onto a portion of the kitchen counter visible from the living room. The top shelf of the cabinet behind him had been emptied of most of its dishes, and in their place sat Maya, her legs dangling. Kang turned towards us, and Maya wrapped her little arms around his neck.

Before I could object, he reached back and grabbed Maya from behind with one of his arms, yelled, "Truth, justice, and the American way," and with Maya hanging on, jumped to the floor, clearing the counter by several feet.

Maya ran towards Lim and me, yelling, "Mommy, Daddy, did you see that?"

We grabbed her and laid her over our laps, tickling her as she laughed and wriggled. "Can we do it again?" she asked.

"I think once was enough."

I noticed Ting and Ron talking quietly in a corner as Daisy told me about a disagreement between her mother and the musicians for her wedding. The string quartet was supposed to arrive a half hour before the guests started coming, but there had been a mix-up, and they wouldn't be able to arrive until ten minutes before the arrival time. We both had a good laugh about that. It was nice to be concerned about a string quartet rather than murderers on a Native American reservation. Around 9:00 p.m. Lim and I headed upstairs to put Maya to bed.

I returned to the clinic Wednesday to a standing ovation. It was nice to be back. I wasn't scheduled to work until the following week but wanted to catch up on paperwork and hire much-needed staff before seeing patients the following Tuesday. Two physicians were coming later that day to interview for vacant positions, and four applicants were finalists vying to be my assistant. I missed Martha. There would be no replacing her and the communication we had without speaking a word.

Both doctors I met with were qualified and personable, with previous experience in pediatric clinics. I still had more to interview later in the week but was comforted knowing that these candidates would suffice even if the others were disasters.

I was unimpressed with the first two applicants for my assistant. While they looked good on paper, in person they left a lot to be desired. The third candidate, a young, dark haired woman wearing a large gold cross on a chain around her neck, had an unspectacular resume. When I met her, though, it was obvious her resume didn't do her justice. Personal and friendly, I could tell she was a doer. Most importantly, she passed my test. I had purposefully dirtied the front of my white coat with chlorhexidine, leaving a rust-colored stain.

Before sitting down in my office for the interview, she said, "Excuse me, Doctor. It looks like you spilled chlorhexidine on the front of your coat. Can I get you a clean one? I saw the room where they keep them on my way to your office."

"That would be wonderful," I said. "I take a medium." I waited for her to return, wondering if she would come back with the right size and do it quickly.

Before I had a chance to complete my thought, she was back with a clean white coat. I emptied my pockets, took off my dirty garment, and tossed it to her. Without hesitation, she placed the dirty coat over her arm and held the clean one open with both hands. I slipped it on, noticing it was size medium. It seemed she was almost reading my mind, like we'd done that maneuver a hundred times before. She wasn't Martha, but she was probably the closest to her I would find. I hired her on the spot. Later that week, I hired two pediatricians to staff the clinic, one of whom I had interviewed on my first day back.

Friday afternoon, an FBI special agent called to tell me the information we had supplied them was more than enough to put the Umbroz conspirators away for a long time. Some of the information retrieved was in code, but their cryptographers found it easy to decipher. They now had the names of over thirty children who had been sickened or died as a result of Umbroz medication.

By the weekend, news coverage of Umbroz had died down. Lim agreed not to go into the office all weekend. We spent two days lazily walking around the city, enjoying the sights a tourist might visit. For the first time, Maya was able to walk the whole length of the Golden Gate Bridge and back. No small feat for a child her age. I wondered if she was athletically gifted, despite having only the genes she'd inherited naturally. Any athleticism, I figured, was inherited from Lim.

Sunday afternoon, I called Janice. She told me the tribal chairman, several board members, and many local police had been arrested. Denise was working with the elders to appoint a new chairman to serve until they could hold an election. Unemployment had sky-rocketed at the reservation, as many people had worked at Umbroz. She was optimistic another company would come to town, probably a food processing plant. I offered to help her relocate to the San Francisco Bay area and find her a job, but she wanted to stay on the reservation she loved, the only life she'd known. Also, she didn't think she'd like the hot weather she'd heard about in California. Lastly, I told her I'd be setting up a savings account to pay for Paco's college fund. She promised to stay in touch.

Early Sunday evening, while Maya played with her dolls, Lim and I had wine on the terrace as we enjoyed our spectacular view of the Bay Bridge.

"Let's drink it in," Lim said. "We won't be doing this for a while. The wine, that is. Want another glass?"

"Sure."

"I'll go to the appointment with you tomorrow."

"I'll be fine on my own. I've been through this before, remember?"

"I know you'll be fine, but I'm going."

I smiled and took his hand. "We can go to lunch afterward."

The next morning I was on the exam table under a paper blanket, bare from the waist down. Lim was seated nearby.

My doctor walked in. "First, we'll do an ultrasound to make sure everything's okay." She poured goop on my belly and studied the nearby screen as she moved the transducer around. "Everything looks good," she said. "You ready?"

"Absolutely."

She left, and a few minutes later her assistant came in and gave me two pills which I washed down with water. Then she guided my feet into the stirrups.

My doctor returned, wheeling a tray on a stand containing everything she would need. She disappeared behind the paper blanket covering my bent legs and began. "All done," she said shortly. "Piece of cake. You can get dressed now."

"How are you?" Lim asked me. "Do you feel different?"

I laughed. "No, I don't feel different. It'll be a few days before it's implanted."

"You ready for lunch?"

"You bet."

"Now we have to agree on a boy's name."

"No hurry. We have about thirty-eight weeks to decide."

Lim and I returned to our usual erratic work schedules, enjoying the return to normal. A week later, Ting came to our unit in tears. She had just learned that Mei's son had died of liver failure in China. Despite her best efforts, she was unable to arrange a liver transplant for him, the government having offered no help. "I am so very glad I came here," she said. "If not, Mingyu would be dead. Instead, he is a healthy boy. I look at him now and see no sickness."

I couldn't disagree. He had returned to preschool, enjoyed spending time with his friends, and did the things other kids his age enjoyed. Only if you saw his abdominal scar would you have a hint of what he'd been through.

Ting and I decided right then to work with our government and Mei to help other Chinese boys with failing livers, the victims of the same genetic engineering that led to liver failure in Mei's son and Mingyu. Mei knew of at least two such boys. They'd have to come to the US with their mothers, and we'd need to arrange for their surgery.

"You think we can do all that?" Ting asked. "I know Lim and Ron will help."

"Small potatoes compared to what we've accomplished," I said.

"Yes, potatoes here are very good. We don't eat them in China. I'm not sure how they will help save the children."

I laughed. "Small potatoes. It's just an expression. Means it's not a big problem."

Ting smiled.

*

By the time I was matron of honor at Daisy's wedding, my old friend morning sickness was visiting me every day. I hadn't put on much weight yet and still looked pretty fetching in my teal mist gown. The flower girl, Maya, wore a short dress with petticoats in a matching color. Daisy looked beautiful in the white wedding dress she'd found discounted at Nordstrom several weeks earlier. We hadn't had as much time as we had planned to pick out our clothes for the wedding, but we'd managed to get close to what we wanted.

The ceremony was short and simple, Daisy's mother sobbing with joy the whole time. There were no more than fifty guests, which included Ting, her children, her new beau, Ron, and Daisy's cousin, Lan. After the ceremony, Kang started running around the room, jumping on chairs. Ron took him aside and spoke to him gently. After that, Kang calmed down for the remainder of the event.

When it was time for Daisy to toss her bouquet, we all gathered around. She threw it high over her head, perfectly aimed at a group of six single women, which didn't include Lan. All jumped to catch the prize, but one jumped noticeably higher than the rest. When it was over, Ron walked over to congratulate Ting on her accomplishment.

*

Three months after Daisy and Arvid tied the knot, they joined Lim and me for dinner at Le Colonial, a French-Vietnamese restaurant not far from Union Square in San Francisco. As we approached, I said, "Arvid, why don't you take the first fifteen? Anyone object?"

"Not me," Lim and Daisy said, almost simultaneously.

With its white tablecloths and old-world atmosphere, I always felt transported to another time when we ate at Le Colonial. I was disinterested in the wine choice as I was in my second trimester of pregnancy. I let Lim, Daisy, and Arvid make that important decision. When the wine arrived, I informed our waiter I wouldn't be drinking any. Since I was noticeably pregnant, I'm sure he wasn't surprised. As he removed my glass, he congratulated Arvid on the bundle of joy in the making.

"He had nothing to do with it," I said, then pointed to Lim, who was sitting next to me. "He's the daddy."

Our server's face turned red as he blustered his way through congratulatory remarks aimed a Lim. When he had finished pouring the wine and was out of earshot, we all busted out laughing.

"That didn't take long," Arvid said. "Looks like I win."

I wondered if we'd ever get tired of watching people get flustered when they found out I was with Lim and Daisy was with Arvid. Or, better yet, if, over time, people stopped assuming I was with someone who looked like me. It wouldn't happen overnight, but I expected it would happen.

I lifted my water glass, and we all made a toast to the future.

When we'd finished the toast, Lim said, "Arvid and I have been talking."

I looked at Daisy, who said, "Uh, oh."

"Now, ladies," Arvid said. "No more trying to save the world. Considering the danger you've been in, you're both lucky to still be alive and unharmed. You have people who love you and depend on you."

"Exactly," Lim said. "We need you to agree not to get involved in any more of these escapades, no matter how important they seem."

"Agreed," I said. Daisy followed suit.

"Great," Arvid and Lim responded, Lim's voice slightly louder.

I can't speak for Daisy, but at the time, I really did agree.

UNFORESEEN ACKNOWLEDGMENTS

Feedback from others is indispensable, and I appreciate everyone who helped me with this project.

A big thank you goes to my brother, Seth Greenberg, who has, again, offered valuable suggestions otherwise known as criticisms. Years ago, I never would have thought my pesty little brother would someday be so helpful. I am also thankful for the input of my critique group members George Cramer, Jim Hasse, and John Schembra. Once again, I am indebted to Rosalyn Jamison, who offered considerable helpful feedback.

I am extremely grateful to my developmental editor, Nicole Ayers, for her invaluable suggestions and advice. I am also tremendously appreciative of Violet Moore, my copy editor, for being so picky, making corrections on almost every page.

This book owes its life to Reagan Rothe and the staff at Black Rose Writing, who published *Unforeseen*.

I am indebted to Bob Roth, MD, PhD (aka Dr Dr Bob), who generously shared his knowledge of pharmaceutical data collection with me.

My biggest thanks again goes to my Amazing Husband, Glen Petersen, who not only offered suggestions on my work, but has given me encouragement and support at every turn. He still brings me coffee in bed every morning.

ABOUT THE AUTHOR

Fiction writer Deven Greene lives in the San Francisco Bay area. Ever since childhood, Deven has been interested in science. After receiving a PhD in biochemistry, she went to medical school, obtained her MD degree, and trained as a pathologist. She worked for several decades in that field before starting to write fiction. Deven incorporates elements of medicine or science in most of her writing. She has published several short stories. Her first novel, *Unnatural,* was released in January 2021. *Unnatural* is the first book of the *Erica Rosen MD Trilogy*. *Unwitting*, released in October 2021, is the second *Erica Rosen MD* novel. *Unforeseen* is the final book in the trilogy.

NOTE FROM THE AUTHOR

Word-of-mouth is crucial for any author to succeed. If you enjoyed *Unforeseen*, please leave a review online—anywhere you are able. Even if it's just a sentence or two. It would make all the difference and would be very much appreciated.

Thanks!
Deven Greene

Made in the USA
Las Vegas, NV
26 October 2022

58207071R00194